McSWEENEY'S
SAN FRANCISCO

McSweeney's and colophon are registered trademarks of McSweeney's, an independent publisher based in San Francisco.

ISBN: 978-1-95211-985-9

Hack Barlow cover painting by Brent Engstrom

Hack Barlow action figure illustration by Jordan Speer

Kayfabe cover lettering by Kyle Letendre

10 9 8 7 6 5 4 3 2 1

www.mcsweeneys.net

Printed in China

KAYFABE

CHRIS KOSLOWSKI

McSWEENEY'S
SAN FRANCISCO

For Jean

"The men watched as the players jogged to the line of scrimmage. Theismann's right leg was intact, as straight and strong as an Ionic column."

—Chris Bachelder, *The Throwback Special*

"I am the man."

—WWE Superstar Becky Lynch, October 18, 2018

ONE

Man is meat. So said one of the broken wrestlers who taught Dom to bump and run the ropes in a drop-ceiling gym spitting distance from the Mason-Dixon. As a kid in a business that ate its young, Dom was used to shit advice. That line stood apart.

There were nights, especially after Dom had taken Pilar from their mother, when he tried to parse why it stuck with him—why he spit it through his teeth on the bench, toasted no one with it before downing a shot, mouthed it while he lay on the floor and watched his kid sister flop herself to sleep on their trash-day futon. He wanted to make it smart, to make it more profound than where it came from. Man is meat. He can be cut. He can be cooked, chewed, and swallowed.

On the East Coast's independent wrestling circuit, a loose network of promotions busting chops for pocket change, Dom was a heel. His job was to stay big and act mean. And lose. Heels did the heavy lifting. They blocked the matches. They tuned the marks. The more heat Dom could spark, the brighter the spotlight on the baby faces.

Though his bouts were theater, the risks were real. Dom's day-to-day was managing that risk, calculating when a dangerous maneuver was necessary to get the pop he wanted. Even in a routine match, spines could snap. A pound of pressure could collapse a windpipe. It had happened to better wrestlers. It happened to guys with necks as thick as tree trunks. Every wrestler had only so many rolls of the dice.

From the entry gates, the Sumter County Freedom Festival was tents, flags, trailer pop-ups fringed with neon, and all things sugar and grease. A whiff of fry oil reminded Dom of how hungry he was. The place was aggressively pastel. Some festivalgoers had parked themselves under shade, closing their eyes to rest them. Even the ground, a once-turfed lot flattened to hay, reflected the sun with a vengeance.

Aside from a few permanent show buildings and restrooms, the fairgrounds were wide open to the blazing Midlands sky. The place was packed. Braised skin pulled as taut as the tents. Tattoos of every shape on every possible surface, with no offense neglected. Dom didn't take ten steps into the crowd before seeing people in all stages of consciousness—some comatose and cooking in the sunlight, others grinding away to the bass thumping from a music stage.

"I'm gonna get a sno-cone," Pilar said.

"Why?" Dom asked.

"Because I'm melting. And sno-cones are delicious."

Dom gave her a look. She was punching at her phone.

"So much for rare and appropriate cheats," he said.

Her thumbs tapped with a pianist's flourish. "This is rare. Can you even imagine a ball of ice on a day like this? Miracle of science."

"You can't out-train a bad diet."

"Jeez, coach. Ease up. You nervous or something? You're sweating buckets."

"You'd listen to a real coach," Dom said.

"You know me so well, bro. I love taking orders."

Pilar elbowed Dom and skipped ahead, eyeing the endless line of food trailers. Dom's career had brought them to the South. He was working with Mid-Coast Championship Wrestling, an indie outside Charlotte with a respectable draw, usually a couple of hundred per show. Main stage was the Hangar, a repurposed maintenance building on an old airstrip outside the 485 beltway. When Dom wrestled the Hangar, he'd loiter until curtain to scrounge leftovers from the food trucks parked outside. Pilar had sworn off heavy meats as she ramped up her training. Any money Dom saved on free meals meant his sister could get more creative at the grocery. Fresh out of high school, she had a sharper look and a straighter shot at the top than Dom ever had.

Several bookers had already inquired about the young Contreras sister. But Dom was determined not to feed Pilar to these salivating men. He hoped Bonnie Blue would give her a look. After the death of her longtime partner, Bonnie was now in control of MCCW. The sleazy showmen of the Southeast would have sold Pilar's ring time with implicit demands for certain private performances. Bonnie was different—the rare woman in a sea of bullies and louts. She was cold and hard and hungry. She could boost Pilar to stardom.

Pilar rode shotgun to Dom's summer gigs. It was worth cutting into her training time. The gym, much as it could build muscle, could never prepare Pilar for the lifestyle. The road was hard. No breaks, no offseason. To make a real living, to be able to afford the basics—and build a nest egg for the inevitable injury—a wrestler had to be on the road three hundred days a year. This meant long nights down dark stretches, joints aching from the pain of a half-dozen weekly matches. At least Pilar could fit into Dom's Civic, still going strong after two hundred thousand miles and modifications that transformed it into the world's most pitiful RV. Dom's head had worn a bald patch into the driver's-side canopy. Every pothole posed a serious threat.

MCCW ran satellite shows in partnership with smaller promotions across the Carolinas. Dom leaned hard on these for extra cash and to keep sharp in case an opportunity rambled down the I-95 corridor. At the Freedom Fest, Dom was booked to wrestle a satellite show as, once again, Hack Barlow. His lumberjack gimmick had drawn decently in the Ohio Valley before fizzling and forcing him to move south. In indie wres-tling, if you weren't climbing, someone else was bound to use your neck as a stepping stool. Dom had dropped forty pounds and was planning on distancing himself from the burly Barlow in favor of a sleeker and more maintenance-friendly frame. Who he would become was an unanswered question. His old jeans and flannel hung off him as if he were a kid who'd made a Halloween costume from his dad's clothes.

When a community celebrated "freedom" in the Carolinas, it was typically code for "firearms." But this festival wasn't like the mash-ups of fair and trade show and Second Amendment circle-jerk that Dom was used to. The first sign was the leather, any trace of it much too much as the temperature climbed. Armbands, spiked collars, chaps, leashes, hoods, corsets, and, unbelievably, full-body suits. All this amid Stars-and-Bars types browsing cases of assault weapons, slurping from tall boys as they meandered from tent to tent. Outside a doughnut truck, a middle-aged woman fingered the trigger of an Airsoft replica Glock. Nearby, a fuzzy-lipped teenager read the fine print on a roll of flavored condoms. At a booth crammed with obscene trinkets, a man in a striped polo and salmon-colored shorts squeezed a dab of clear liquid onto his index finger, thoughtfully rubbed it with his thumb, and sniffed.

"Doesn't matter how long you've been on the road," Dom said. "You've never seen everything."

Pilar wedged her phone into a front pocket of her jean shorts. Half the screen stuck out over her waist and the hem of her bright green tank top. She wagged a finger at her brother. "You love this, don't you? Maybe we've found your kink. El fetiche de Domingo. Wait. It is *fetiche*, right? *Fetiz? Fetrices?*"

"I have no idea," Dom said.

Pilar scrunched her face. "Well, we should do some shopping. You'd look good in this stuff. Are you a leather or spandex man?"

"You don't know? I thought we were close, Pilar."

"Shut up. I'm serious. We could build a new character for you right here on the cheap—cowboy, sergeant, gun nut."

A man wearing a beret and a bandolier walked by sucking a camo-colored pacifier. "I'll think about it," Dom said.

"You have to seize the opportunity. Trust your gut."

"Right. Why would I *think* about the most important decision of my career?"

"Just saying—both of us should be making moves. In fact, why don't you talk to the booker and get me on the card? Preview of coming attractions. They can pay me in sno-cones."

She was so eager, Dom thought. He never snickered. Plenty of the old boys would have—men whose hulking bodies were like muscle cars with moldy leather interiors. Every greenhorn in the business fought with a chip on their shoulder. Few made it far. There was no way to tell where Pilar's enthusiasm would lead. Wrestling was changing. More women were climbing into stardom. The business was filthy with men waiting to pounce on those who would stop at nothing to get there.

"You only get one debut," Dom said. It was a line he'd used before.

Pilar drew her eyes to the sun and let them bake for a second before she pried out her phone and started tapping. "Service is so bad here," she said. "When you booked?"

"Five."

"Heat of the day. Super. I'm gonna browse around for you."

"I'll save you a seat," Dom said as the cool blue of an ice cream trailer drew her away. A man wearing black and purple vinyl crossed with hot-pink zippers shouldered past her.

"Dom the Dominatrix!" she called out.

"No!" Dom replied.

TWO

The ring stood at the rear of the festival, squeezed between food tents, music stages, and a live bear show. Dom walked through the game barkers and vendors selling guns and sex toys and gun-shaped sex toys. Three sets of bleachers surrounded the ring. Stage right was the entrance and ramp with black privacy curtains separating front and back of house. Nothing was covered.

Two amateur-looking boxers were fighting before a crowd of about sixty people, many of them filling plastic beer bottles with dip spit. Even at events cosponsored by MCCW, it wasn't unheard of to discover the local booker was either stupid or greedy enough to cram boxing, wrestling, and MMA into a ring not meant for any of them. A boxing ring could kill a wrestler, and the give of a wrestling canvas could snap untrained ligaments.

The boxers danced around each other, their knees wobbling. The mat was some kind of plastic. The men's boots left shallow imprints in it that a thin layer of foam slowly filled in. There were three ropes instead of the typical four. They looked chintzy, their quiver the telltale sign of bungee wrapped in rubber. They'd be much harder to climb than padded cable or actual rope.

Dom found the opening to the backstage area. An older guy guarding the entrance—his staff shirt baggy and worn—didn't raise an eyebrow when Dom strode past. The back of house was barren, even by festival standards. No signs, no managers, no catering table with expired deli platters. Dom stepped over a line anchoring the adjacent tent. It smelled of wet dirt and barnyard waste—animal auctions. He rapped his business knock on what might have been the booker's trailer. No answer.

He passed electrical cords snaking through matted grass. Beer cans and water bottles littered the ground. He didn't call out. He figured he'd run into someone or he'd pop onto the stage—a grand and unexpected entrance—and they'd have to swerve the boxing match into a triple threat.

A man appeared like a troll from under a folding table topped with a sound and light board. A battery pack on his belt powered a ridiculously showy headset. On his black, sweat-soaked T-shirt were bold letters spelling "SUCK IT."

"Who the fuck are you?" the troll asked.

"Hack Barlow," Dom said. "Where's the locker room?"

"You're late," the troll said, wiping his nose.

"I'm not," Dom said. "If anything, I'm obnoxiously early."

"You being smart with me, asshole?" The man straightened and puffed out his neck.

Dom sighed. "Just tell me where the locker room is."

"There is no locker room. And even if there was, no way in fuck I'd tell an asshole like you where it is."

Dom set his duffel on the table, then hopped up to sit beside it. The table sagged under his weight.

"What the blue fuck are you doing?" the troll said, his eyes widening.

"What's it look like?" Dom said. He tossed off his shoes and tugged down his pants. Dom's pubic hair was shaved into an H. Months ago, he'd lost a gym bet in Greensboro and decided to keep it going.

The troll tore off his headset. "Get the hell off of there or I'll—"

"Or you'll what?" There was no trace of anger in Dom's voice. He removed a bottle of baby powder from his duffel.

The troll stuttered. "There's an Airstream," he said. "Walk that way and you'll see it. Door's open. It's a piece of shit and there's no AC, but it's what we got."

Dom dumped half the bottle on his crotch and slapped it around. A cloud billowed out, and the troll scooted away to avoid breathing it in. A dusting settled onto the table's electronics.

Not bothering to put his pants on, Dom snaked his way through the labyrinth and found the Airstream. Outside, Gorilla Trotsky was waiting for him.

"Holy shit! If it ain't the son-of-a-bitch torino! Dommy, what the fuck? It looks like you got a blow job from a snowman!"

Gorilla was a veteran of the indie circuit whom Dom had known since he was Pilar's age. He creaked out of a chair and laughed himself into a coughing fit. Once he hacked out the phlegm, he put up his dukes.

"We're working tag tonight, Dommy. Been a while, huh?"

"No kidding," Dom said, shadowboxing his friend. "You look like you got caught in a Mack truck's wheel well."

Gorilla smiled and took a pull from a two-liter bottle. Lumps of who knows what floated in the brown liquid. "Good!" Gorilla said, holding up his brew. "Adds to my character."

Gorilla was built like a boulder. Coarse hair peppered with gray covered his shoulders like a charred forest. His beard rode up to his cheekbones. He was half into his red and gold singlet, the straps bunched at his hips. He'd been working the same Eastern European monster angle since the eighties. Dom guessed Gorilla was in his late forties, old for any wrestler, ancient for an indie scrub who worked match to match. They'd mostly tagged and shared a few battles royal. Gorilla was slow and safe. Guys liked him because he never made a fuss. Dom thought he called too loud in the ring and talked too much after, but Hack Barlow paired well with him. Gorilla looked like he'd been taken captive in the Caucasus and shipped to America as a sideshow. Selling the team of the crazed lumberjack and Marxist mountain man was a short order.

"You ready for our first match of the post-Clout Crawczak era?" Gorilla asked.

"You say that as if Bonnie hasn't had MCCW by the balls since the start," Dom replied.

"Oh, her grip's been strong," Gorilla said. "But you watch. Now that Clout's six feet under, she'll be looking to mix things up. It's a good time to show off our stuff."

"Who we putting over tonight?" Dom asked. He pulled up a chair and dusted some excess powder into the grass.

"Local greenhorns," Gorilla said. "Couple of tykes. Saw one here for a hot minute with two girls, both ripe on the vine."

Dom checked his wrestling trousers, a pair of jeans he'd weathered with sandpaper, wine, and chocolate, holes over the knees. He debated staying bottomless until the last minute. He'd need sunscreen, and the cream would cake the powder.

"You were always good with kids," Dom said.

"Like a fuzzy teddy bear," Gorilla said, scratching his belly. "How's your sister? I hope you've smartened up and told her to flee before you turn her into one of us."

"She's looking strong. Wants in on a show."

"Damn. How old is she?"

"She'll be eighteen in a few months."

"Eighteen? No shit. We're getting old, Dommy. I'll tell you what. If she needs a sparring partner, someone to break her in before you throw her to the wolves, you call me. I can teach her a few things."

Gorilla's laugh sounded like a plucked bass. They threw jabs while the boxing wrapped up. Dom not so politely refused a snort of Gorilla's beverage.

"C'mon," Gorilla said. "This is the good shit. I promise."

"I've got my own," Dom said. He flashed Gorilla the small sport bottle in his bag.

"What's in it?" Gorilla asked.

"Trade secret."

"You make it?"

"Yes and no," Dom said.

Gorilla huffed and took another gulp. "Fine, Mr. Mysterious. All I'll say is that I hope it's your secret. Food, drink, helpers, even your grandma's goddamned hot cocoa—if they're not saying what's in the sauce, then you're the mark."

Dom shrugged. "If it helps, what does it matter? Placebos work even if you know they're placebos."

"Is that what you got? A placebo? How sure are you?"

Dom had a lot of practice letting older wrestlers think he'd heard their advice. He fetched his boots and laced them paratrooper-style. The laces looked like a series of folded arms, a ladder of limbs climbing to his knees. He pumped with resistance bands—biceps, triceps, chest, neck, quads.

"Not bad," Gorilla said. "Cut that mop and take a brush mower to that Duck Dynasty bullshit on your chin, and I'd mistake you for the Brawny Man."

"Ain't he shaved now?" Dom said.

"Horseshit."

Gorilla curled his lip and took out his phone. "Goddamnit," he said. "They gotta fuck with everything, don't they? Famous woodsman gimmick, and they turn him babyface."

"Gotta stay fresh," Dom said. "Especially when you're in the cleaning business."

"Freshness doesn't matter," Gorilla said. "You give people what they want. No one outside some slick marketing asshole is going to want to make over the Brawny Man. Who is he without that moustache?"

Dom rolled his neck. It cracked like popcorn. "Nobody knows what they want. You have to dictate. You've gotta sell."

"Oh yeah? What are you selling?"

Dom stretched an arm behind his head, taking his elbow past twelve o'clock. His fingers brushed a zit starting to form on his shoulder blade. He set his jaw and squeezed it to the surface. Pus flowed and he took off his shirt to let the sun at it, practically hot enough to cauterize.

"What if I mix it up tonight?" Dom said. "Give ole Hack a rest?"

"You got a bench? Who's on it? Bayou Cult Leader? Knockoff ZZ Top?"

One knee at a time, Gorilla got himself into push-up mode. The transition was creaky. Once he started, his triceps bulged. He smoothed into the exercise like an old pickup slipping into gear.

"That's the thing," Dom said. "Nothing feels right."

Gorilla slowed his push until he was barely moving, his arms train pistons steaming to a halt. With his final rep, he blew through his teeth and locked his elbows.

"I've got an idea," Gorilla said, getting to his feet. He rifled through his travel case and fished out a pair of black wrestling trunks.

"One size fits all, brother."

Dom held up the trunks at a distance. Skeptically, he took a whiff.

"Who am I supposed to be in these? Generic Man?"

"Don't you know your history? Pick a superstar. Buddy Rogers to The Rock—black trunks were all they needed."

"It's kind of boring, isn't it?"

Gorilla peered around as if he expected to find a hidden camera. "Listen, torino. Was Steve Austin boring? What about Flair? Everyone remembers his peacocking, but what did he wear when he got to work? It's all attitude. Like you said, it's the sale. Good salesman can push water to a drowning man."

The trunks were seamless. No marks. No tags. No washing instructions. They had a satisfying stretch. They were custom-made, likely by someone familiar with the business. Dom dusted off and tugged them on.

"They suit you," Gorilla said. "You're gonna feel like a new man out there. I can't believe you've wrestled all these years with your nuts flopping around in those goddamned Wranglers."

"So no character at all," Dom said. "A blank slate. That's a tough angle to work."

Gorilla scoffed. "Angles! As someone who's worked the same angle since the Gipper was in office, trust me. You've got the talent to be yourself. Just crank it up."

The trunks were snug. Gorilla asked him to stand tall and snapped a pic. Dom scrutinized this new wrestler on Gorilla's phone. The trunks showed off his legs. They were always the core of Dom's strength. For years he was a delivery van with a racing engine. Now, the trunks accentuated his quads and hamstrings. They had the vasculature of a casual jock's forearms. His once-bulging gut was flat against the waistline. He looked younger, closer to his actual twenty-six years than he'd appeared since he was a teen.

"I look okay," Dom said.

"Better than okay. You get no points for modesty. You look like you crack skulls for a living. Make them believe it. Maybe make the boss take notice. And if you need some help getting mad, I've got just the thing."

Gorilla pushed his bottle into Dom's hand.

"Something's curdled in this," Dom said.

"Puts hair on your chest," Gorilla said.

"So I see," Dom said, his fingers curling around the bottle. "What should I toast to?"

"No toasts! Bad luck before a match."

"Okay," Dom said. "No toasts."

Gorilla smiled as Dom tilted the two-liter to his lips. He plugged the bottle with his tongue to prevent the sour liquid from entering his mouth.

THREE

The tag team Dom and Gorilla were wrestling called themselves the Federal Titty Inspectors, FTI for short. Gorilla asked why not FBI, and the two stared as if they didn't understand the question. Their names were Maxwell and Cee-Saw. They were doughy, thick necked, and rosy cheeked. Their ring gear included poorly dyed FTI T-shirts with a pair of chest-high cupped hands. Cee-Saw was the huskier of the two. Sweat was already blooming on his shirt between and beneath his flabby pectorals.

The Inspectors shook the heels' hands and asked what they'd planned for the match. Their only request was a hero spot with their managers, two unsurprisingly chesty ladies named Mackenzie and Bria. Gorilla would give chase outside the ring and get his bell rung by the ring bell, a blindside from Mackenzie. Gorilla was more than happy to oblige.

A dark cloud blocking the sun gave everyone's eyes a break. Dom dawdled through his warm-up. He could smell the fried Oreos and funnel cake on the midway. Users on his fitness board had crowed that after starting a diet, once they began to notice results, they didn't even think about the foods they could no longer eat. There was rarely a moment when Dom's cravings didn't hound him. He couldn't believe that the gym rats, addictive personalities pretty much by definition, never thought about cheating. The fair made him salivate. More than the smell, the consumptive attitude of the place was a warm sea feeding a hurricane. Dom wanted to smash a yard-long corn dog dipped in drawn butter. He wanted to seduce a woman in leather lingerie and lick strawberry elephant-ear topping off her fingers.

The minutes before curtain were the most ritualized part of Dom's prematch routine. First, he swallowed a few squeezes from a sport bottle. In it was Yucca Mountain Sludge, his concentrated espresso brewed from the trash grounds of the cult coffee place close to where he and Pilar lived in Charlotte. Though Dom always drank it at ambient temperature, its burned-tire taste centered his focus. When Dom's strength started to fade at the end of a match, the drink would kick on the afterburners and let him overclock his muscles for a good finish. Dom was otherwise monk-like in his coffee abstention. The satisfying, jitter-free jolt would hit him like an atom bomb, gamma rays seeding a persistent jones, even if Dom went a week between matches.

Sludge consumed, Dom cracked every knuckle one by one and followed with five big-toe pops. They reminded him of those gunpowder snappers kids threw at each other on July Fourth. Under his breath, he said his sister's name: Pilar Contreras. He traced the scars on his left hand. Then ten high knees, ten cross-body punches.

"I've been thinking," Gorilla said. He finished his own sequence of crosses and grunts. "You want it now or later?"

"Whatever," Dom said.

"When you get a free day, you and Pilar should stop by my place. Let me treat you. I can do up some fried chicken. We could tell some tales."

"I'd kill a man for a drumstick," Dom said. "I'm still cutting."

Gorilla laughed. "Then rabbit food, whatever. Hell, we could all puke into the same bucket."

"Super. It's a date." Dom paused and made a show of looking off into the distance. "Somewhere out there, a cold shiver is running down Pilar's spine."

"She loves me," Gorilla said. "Unlike you, I never tap out of a good time."

"You're lucky. She's developed this bad phobia of shoulder skin. So your hairy ass is right up her alley."

"Magic carpet ride, torino. Want a turn? Wait in line."

Dom tightened his wrist tape. He was accustomed to checking buttons on his flannel, but he wasn't Hack Barlow tonight. He adjusted his trunks and tried to feel less constricted.

"One more thing, Dommy," Gorilla said.

"Listening."

"No matter how this goes, promise me you won't clear-cut that beard. You'd be an ugly son of a bitch without it."

When it was showtime, the wrestlers got into position behind the black curtain. Headset guy appeared and yelled instructions. He swallowed his bark after Dom fired him a wink. Rain started to fall, but there was never a question—the show would go on unless lightning struck a ring post. Behind the entry curtain, they could hear the MC hyping the draw. The cheers were louder than Dom had anticipated. When the music hit, they'd walk in, scowl, antagonize, wait for the tykes and their women. Dom's entry song when he worked solo was an edit of Jimi Hendrix's "Voodoo Child." He loved the guitar riffs. They revved like a rusty buzz saw, wild and mean.

But since Dom and Gorilla were entering the match together, they opted for Gorilla's music. The speakers squealed and horns boomed what sounded like a Soviet march. Dom and Gorilla bumped heads and went out. They cursed the marks and beat their chests.

About three hundred people had gathered close to the ring. The alluring Freedom Fest funk tweaked Dom's palate. A woman in a spiderweb onesie scarfed a pork chop on a stick. A child shrieked in French. Two figures in gas masks gaped into Dom with rat-skull eyes.

The rain picked up, bringing relief and excitement. The sky was dryer-lint gray and darkening. The swampy air fed the clouds. No one had their phones out. Dom could see every face. Some smiled. Some were dripping with lust—catcalls, writhing tongues. Were they hungry for him or the action? It was tough to tell. Everyone leaned forward as if trying to hear a whisper. Dom found a kid on the rail trying too hard to look tough and screamed maniacally in his face. The kid cowered back to his seat. The adults around him shot Dom stink eyes and booed. So far, so good.

Gorilla shouted Russian at a shirtless man whose chest was tattooed with an M16. The hulking bear adjusted his singlet straps, reached underneath the ring apron, and pulled out a Soviet flag. He climbed to the center of the ring and waved the red and gold with pride. Dom scaled a turnbuckle to the second rope and gestured to the banner, damning all American scum in attendance.

Jeers rang out. They welcomed the heels, held them close and dear. The roar was whitewater surging through a canyon. Feet pounding on bleachers blended with the approaching thunder. Even though the ring, the seats, and the rigging were all meant to be folded up and shipped down the highway, even though the cheap rubber ropes were drooping under Dom's weight, the place sparked with the electricity of Madison Square Garden.

Dom scanned the first row for Pilar. She could always find her way to the front. Sure enough, she was hanging on the rail next to the timekeeper's table. Her eyes met Dom's, and she laughed and shook her head. She wanted in so bad. This was no high school gymnasium sprinkled with jaded diehards. This wasn't Ballroom C at the airport Days Inn. This wasn't even a Mid-Coast pay-per-view. Each mark in attendance had the moxie of ten regular fans. Dom knew what it was like to pull heat. This was scorching.

When their music ended, Dom and Gorilla stood in their corner. Police chatter splintered through the amplifiers. The Inspectors came out, and the sky opened.

The house went berserk.

Pouring rain. Dance music blazed at max volume. Bria and Mackenzie had changed into white T-shirts knotted at the back with plunging V-cuts. In seconds, the shirts soaked and clung transparent. Maxwell flipped a magnifying glass from his trunks and Cee-Saw produced brass opera specs. True to their name, they examined and evaluated. Grade: thumbs-up, fist pump, and after a synchronized crotch chop from the ladies, the Inspectors were blown off their feet. With unexpected dexterity, they tucked into rolls and sprang out, bounding to the ring, tugging the ropes, raising their arms to the feral crowd.

Sheets of water. Thumping bass. Shaking, flexing, gyrating. Lured by the spectacle, festivalgoers on the midway crammed the openings between the bleachers. A few hopped over the guardrail and, with no one to stop it, a flood rushed in.

The music cut and the ref stepped between the ropes and sloshed into a puddle forming in the ring. His comb-over had slipped to the wrong side. A cross of black duct tape obscured the WWE logo on his zebra stripes' breast pocket.

"This is fucked," said the ref, kicking water. He bent over the ropes and yelled at the men sitting with the timekeepers, trying to wave one over. A group of women in tactical gear caught wind of his attitude and demanded they ring the bell.

The ref flicked his hair and threw up his hands. He splashed over to Dom, the first comrade to fight. Gorilla stood behind on the apron, stretching the ropes and growling. The ref grabbed Dom's wrists and pretended to check for illegal items.

"I'll count. Otherwise you're on your own," the ref said. "Make it quick."

Dom's boots on the mat were like old gym shoes on a wood floor. Watch the knees, he thought. Keep your feet underneath.

"We're in no hurry," Gorilla said. He punched the turnbuckle padding and laughed.

The ref blew water off his lip and skulked to the opposite corner. Dom embraced Gorilla.

"Don't catch a cold," Dom said.

"Don't tire yourself out," Gorilla said. "You've got a pin to eat."

Gorilla snarled and clapped Dom's head between his palms. Dom broke free and paced his corner like a caged animal. He glanced to Pilar once more. She grinned and flipped him off.

The ref spun away from the Inspectors' corner and called for the bell. Three quick strikes, and the crowd erupted.

Hack Barlow had close to a decade's experience between the ropes. Whoever Dom was now was as green as a spring twig.

How would he perform as this sleek, snarling, nearly naked heel? He channeled Gorilla's advice. Dom Contreras loved this crowd. He was skeptical of his opponent's abilities. He was feeling more and more confident as the rain dripped from his beard down his chest and abs—he had abs! When Cee-Saw charged him, Dom dodged to his right. The Inspector's momentum carried him to the corner, where Gorilla snuck a cheap shot. Dazed, Cee-Saw took another run. Dom again slipped away, smacking Cee-Saw on his ass as the runaway train careened into the ropes. On his rebound, Dom tripped him up and dropped an elbow into his diaphragm. Cee-Saw sold it well. Dom popped up and flexed to the audience. They booed him wonderfully.

Hack Barlow was a monster. He growled. He lumbered. He chopped his opponent's legs and felled them like timber. The wrestler Dom was becoming was a cocky son of a bitch. He eluded his opponent's grasp. He struck fast and hard and gloated every step of the way. After he tagged Gorilla, he worked the crowd. He antagonized, waggling his hips. Gorilla planted Maxwell with a solid forearm. The Inspector splashed onto the drenched surface of the ring. Dom yelled, "Yeah, babay!" drawing out his vowels, mocking Mackenzie and Bria with an over-the-top crotch chop.

A few fans called it back to him. Even as a heel, Dom was winning them over. He received Gorilla's tag and climbed the turnbuckle, taking a moment to soak in the glory.

More people joined in the cheer. It was spreading fast, too fast. Dom strained to hear over the pounding rain. He didn't make sense of it until Mackenzie and Bria joined in, spitting it at Dom like a curse. They weren't shouting "Babay!" They were chanting "Olé!"

"Olé! Olé-olé-olé!"

The audience sensed Dom's realization and chanted louder. He froze. There were so many ways he could react—conduct the chanters like a symphony, clutch his head as if it were melting his brain, lean in, push back. Instead, he straddled the turnbuckle and steeped in the sound, doing nothing until Maxwell seized his trunks and heaved him from his perch.

Maxwell lunged for the tag, and Cee-Saw sprang to action. Dom sold his offense with peak theatrics, hoping the drama would stun the draw and squelch the chant. Cee-Saw's elbow crunched Dom's jaw. He wrapped Dom's neck in the crook of his arm, bending him. He dropped Dom headfirst—a devastating DDT. The crowd continued its chant.

"Olé! Olé-olé-olé! Olé. Olé!"

Cee-Saw popped to vertical, raising his arms in triumph. He couldn't hide his scowl. He tried to spark an F-T-I chant. The draw had none of it. He tangled Dom into a submission, leaned close to his ear.

"Snap them out of this. We're going over, remember?"

"It's a taunt," Dom replied.

"I don't give a shit. They need to cheer us."

"Let's wrap this up, ladies!" the ref shouted.

Tag Gorilla, Dom thought. If he screamed enough Russian, maybe the crowd would shift gears.

"Reverse," Dom called.

"It's *our* comeback," Cee-Saw said.

"Do it," Dom said. Cee-Saw complied. Dom overturned the hold and slammed his opponent. He spun to their corner for the tag. Gorilla wasn't there. Outside the ring, he gave chase to the women, who were setting him up for the spot with the ring bell.

Unsure of his next move, Dom took Cee-Saw into a standing headlock.

"You're out of order!" the Inspector cried. He was starting to resist for real.

"Trust me," Dom said. He kneed Cee-Saw in the gut, doubling him over. Dom threw Cee-Saw's arm over his shoulder and took hold of his waistband.

"Suplex," Dom called.

"Fuck you," Cee-Saw said.

Dom compressed his core and set to lift Cee-Saw high, but the maneuver was foiled from the start. Cee-Saw stalled at the top of the arc. He was too much for Dom to hold. He plunged like a stone, striking the canvas with the crown of his skull.

Cee-Saw was a heap on the mat. Dom writhed next to him, his tailbone selling itself. Needles pricked his spine. He sprawled out, gasping for breath. So much water. The chanting blurred into the rainfall's white noise.

The ref was counting. "Three... four... five..." Very slowly, a whisper. Had the crowd finally stopped? How bad had it been? The glare of the lights refracted through millions of drops. He couldn't see.

The ref leaned forward and announced a count of seven. He was counting with both arms, throwing each into the air as if unfurling a blanket. Dom waited for the quick smack of Cee-Saw slapping the mat in pain or the soft bass of a rise to a knee. Nothing came.

Cee-Saw was motionless—forehead kissing the mat, left arm chicken-winged under his body. Dom masked a grab to Cee-Saw's free hand. He didn't squeeze back.

Dom had called for a vertical suplex. The maneuver required the men to work together. Dom was the base on which Cee-Saw would perform an assisted handstand. He hadn't put enough into the jump—a sure sign of hesitation, or worse, sabotage. Had Cee-Saw been less bloated, Dom might've been able to take him up the rest of the way, but his legs had buckled.

"He's hurt," Dom said through his fingers to the ref. The count hit eight.

"Stop the match," Dom said.

The ref faked interest in the kerfuffle outside the ring. He knew Cee-Saw was booked to go over. Maxwell held Gorilla in a triangle choke as Bria went ham with chops across his chest. They looked confused, not having seen Cee-Saw's spine-cracking fall. Mackenzie slammed her fists on the apron. She screamed and tried to coax the slumped wrestler to his feet.

"Hey, he needs help!" Dom said, not hiding it this time. The ref looked right through him. He meekly threw up a nine count.

Dom pulled to his knees and crossed his wrists above his head, the trouble sign. No medics came running. Dom didn't see anyone beyond the rail. Rain continued to pour.

Dom felt constriction around his ankle, as if someone had tugged his bootlaces. It was a hand. Cee-Saw's.

"What're you doing?" the fallen Inspector said.

Dom dropped to straddle Cee-Saw and put him in a noodle-loose leg lock. The ref stopped counting.

"You okay?" Dom said. "Neck?"

"I'm good," Cee-Saw said. "Cinch up."

Dom flexed but didn't tighten. "You got KO'd."

Cee-Saw didn't hear. Dom spun on top of him and spoke to the bones behind his ear.

"I'm good," Cee-Saw said. "Elbow, whip, hip toss." Cee-Saw labored to a knee, forcing Dom to take his ankle tighter.

"Cool it," Dom said. "We need to finish."

"Bullshit," Cee-Saw said, rising to his feet. Dom appeared to struggle mightily against him. The draw's chants swelled, unmistakable. It was likely they'd never stopped, only blended into the storm's roar. Cee-Saw ripped at Dom's bicep and flailed behind him. "Never out. Selling."

"I checked you," Dom said. On a sunny day, marks in the bleachers would've heard it.

"Scary, yeah?" Cee-Saw said. "Don't drop me next time."

Cee-Saw wedged a shoulder between Dom and the hold and broke it. After an uppercut, Cee-Saw whipped Dom into the ropes and flung him over his hip on the rebound.

Dom stewed until his toes curled and cramped. He'd danced with guys who'd worked stiff and fought dirty. Sickos who got off on pain. No one had ever faked a real KO.

Cee-Saw brought another elbow down and wrapped Dom into a sleeper hold. The pressure on Dom's throat was a tight collar, just right. Despite the car-wash conditions, he could smell whatever high-school-locker-room body spray Cee-Saw had bathed in. Dom hadn't dropped this sandbagging motherfucker. It was a miracle he got as high as he did with his pip-squeak assist.

"What's the call?" Cee-Saw asked.

Dom wanted to tap and get out. It would've been the smart thing. Return to Charlotte with the Inspectors in his rearview. Stop by Yucca Mountain for a refill. He locked onto the chant, still rolling through the crowd. The drone cycled into one round after another. It showed no signs of stopping. If anything, it was gaining strength, spooling up to cross the gap into Dom's next match.

Cee-Saw jerked Dom's neck. "What's the call, asshole?"

Dom slid his lips into the crook of Cee-Saw's elbow and bit down.

Cee-Saw shouted and threw Dom out of the hold. He was staring at the teeth marks in disbelief when Dom swung his boot to Cee-Saw's nose. The wrestler didn't topple stiffly as he would with a sell. He crumpled, leg muscles slacking like snapped rubber bands.

Reflex brought his hands to his face, so Dom heaved himself onto the middle rope and springboarded above Cee-Saw, dropping a heel on his solar plexus. Cee-Saw deflated and choked, paddling his arms in want of air. Dom pivoted to his left and seized Cee-Saw's wrist, anchored his legs around the Inspector's face and chest, and yanked the arm over his hip.

Crack.

FOUR

In Connecticut high society in the late 1960s, Bruce and Helen Blue hadn't considered how a name like Bonnie might affect their daughter. If they'd heard about the nickname for the Confederacy's flag or had watched Rhett Butler's blue-eyed girl fall from her pony, it had been long forgotten in the whirlwind of country-club politics and manic corporate evolution. BluCon Industries was riding the crest of the postwar manufacturing wave. The company Bruce inherited from his father had grown from a regional candle maker to a major player in plastics. By the early 1980s, BluCon was one of the country's top toy producers, hitting line drive after line drive with the fad-crazy public and rounding the bases with their home video game console, a rip-off of the Atari 2600.

At a glance, Bonnie was a millionaire's dream child. She took advantage of every privilege. She outpaced her tutors. She was fluent in French and Spanish, conversational in German and Japanese. Her giraffe-like sleep schedule allotted her a dozen naps dispersed throughout the day—during rides to school, in between courses at dinner, and, if the rumors swirling through the Blues' staff were to be believed, even while standing for her dress fittings.

Remarkably, Bonnie's superlatives appeared to come at little cost. She told good jokes. She could kick a ball. She knew the starting lineup for the Hartford Whalers. Bonnie loved her parents, and they loved her back. When calendars permitted, their family dinners filled their cavernous dining room with conversation.

One particularly stressful tax season, Bruce gave Bonnie a look at his books. He thought he'd show her the basics, give himself a minute for his eyes to uncross and his heart rate to slow. Instead, she focused all her mental firepower on Bruce's troubles. Within a few days, Bonnie had researched a strategy that exploited a charity loophole previously unknown to the company's senior accountants. She saved the firm a substantial sum. More importantly, she found lawful, if somewhat morally questionable, channels for BluCon's money to flow.

Bruce was awestruck. He knew Bonnie was smart, but he couldn't explain her nearly overnight transformation into a financial wunderkind. It scared him, but only briefly. Bruce wasn't a man who questioned when the universe broke his way. He diverted his take of the windfall into an investment fund and gave Bonnie free rein to play. She invested in a Vermont candy company, Raytheon, and Big Apple Wrestling, a small New York City promotion headed by Karl "Clout" Crawczak, a retired jobber to legends like Killer Kowalski and Bruno Sammartino.

Clout was among the first professional wrestlers to understand that his mouth was his meal ticket. Love him or hate him, when he spooled out the microphone cable and flapped his gums on BAW's regional television program, everybody had an opinion. Everyone listened, especially Bonnie. She wrote to him. Clout, smelling a sucker, wrote back, and so began an unlikely correspondence that would last a lifetime. Clout quickly found that Bonnie was no mark. Her investment helped BAW withstand competition and claw into a protected hollow with the fight-crazed degenerates of the five boroughs. From Clout's letters, Bonnie learned the business, its artistry, and most importantly, its potential.

One might expect a gifted child sharing a name with the banner of secessionist states to rebel. There are, of course, many shades and degrees of rebellion. By measure of her swelling dividends, her spotless report cards, and the number of cheek kisses exchanged between Bonnie and her parents, the girl was perfect. Her parents simply failed to predict where her perfection would lead.

There were no secrets with Bonnie. If her mother criticized a family friend's choice in a second wife, Bonnie would not filter those barbs from conversation if, say, the friend stopped by to talk biz and cigars with Bruce. Bonnie's glass-edge memory

meant she could preserve every detail, every clumsy portman-
teau her mother patched together describing the new wife—the
ladder rat, the pecker piper, the diseased New Jersey sand crab.

Punishing their daughter in the wake of incidents like these
was nearly impossible. Grounding Bonnie would only clear her
schedule for catch-up on her reading. She'd do such a good job
cleaning the kitchen or polishing the silver, Bruce would have
to manage housekeepers anxious about their job security. In
their last effort, her parents locked Bonnie in a closet. Thirty
minutes later, they opened the door and found her in blissful
meditation.

For most kids under a certain age, it's very dangerous to learn
authority figures have little power to enforce rules. Bonnie was
fully aware of how easily she could frustrate her parents. Helen
and Bruce couldn't bring themselves to anger. Whatever they'd
done—genetically, environmentally, subliminally—had produced this child. Bonnie would one day inherit their business,
and with her potential, she'd take over Silicon Valley or Wash-
ington or maybe the country. They should have understood that
prodigies need directing. With the world open to her, Bonnie's
perspective solidified. With no one to offer a challenge, her
confidence grew.

In the early nineties, after a video game market crash and
the rise of competitors seizing the industry from the old giants,
both Atari and BluCon were struggling to tread water. Atari's
flailing hit the Blues hard in the form of a lawsuit—$500 mil-
lion for a grocery list of patent infringements on the Atari 2600.

BluCon took it to court, hoping a protracted battle would sink Atari first.

It was national news the day Bonnie Blue, the youngest senior manager in the company's history, testified against BluCon, unleashing reams of evidence proving the theft of the 2600's design. For days, Bonnie held the stand. Her words were efficient and sober, like a surgeon delivering bad news.

The media devoured Bonnie's story. She was, for a news cycle or two, a household name. But she granted no interviews. She signed no book deals. Most knew her from a shot by a young photographer from the *Hartford Courant*. Bonnie was shouldering through a mob outside the Norwalk Superior Court. Her attorney, a severe woman with a helmet of ink-black hair, scowled at a photographer beyond the frame's edge, her arm carving a path through the crowd. Behind her was Bonnie. A gust of wind flared her raincoat open, revealing her tall, gaunt frame. Her eyes were lunar craters on her face, darkened and creased and burned to ash from a month of bankrupting her family and a lifetime of sleepless nights. She stared straight ahead, ignoring the microphones brushing her cheeks.

Near the courthouse doors, at the end of the trench Bonnie and her entourage had cut through the swarm, stood her parents. Their bodies folded into each other, curling with grief and confusion. Minutes earlier, there'd been a scuffle in the court. Bruce had tried to force his way to Bonnie, and it took both legal teams and several court officers to stop him. He demanded to speak with his little girl. He called out to her over and over, her name becoming a whimper.

She didn't acknowledge him. Giving anything would make his pain worse. She'd known since the suit went to trial that her parents wouldn't wriggle free from the law. Her father had tripped over himself opening every drawer, pulling up every rug, showing her how to manage a global company. He'd assembled the bomb that would destroy BluCon right in front of her, betting she wouldn't detonate it. When he'd exposed her to the company's secrets, Bonnie could only think he'd wanted her to tear it all down.

Bonnie marched from the courtroom, and Bruce pressed after her. Helen pleaded him to stop. When the *Courant* photographer raised his camera, Bruce's tie was loose, his shirt untucked. He stretched toward Bonnie, and it was difficult to tell if it was his last, desperate reach for her, or if he was trying to block the sight of his only child walking away. He looked small and broken.

The lawsuit vaporized the family fortune and turned BluCon under the dirt. Bonnie's name flashed in the papers once more when she liquefied her personal assets to charity. She cut all contact, bought a secondhand Jeep from a no-showroom dealership in rural Connecticut, and left.

Decades later, Bonnie received Clout's final letter, hand delivered by one of the wrestlers in vigil at his bedside. She was an expert at deciphering Clout's concussed scrawl, but his jagged lines on a leaf of hospital notepad were illegible. Still, she wondered what the letter could tell her.

She was sitting in a quiet spot on the vast expanse of the old tarmac outside the wrestling venue Bonnie and Clout had built together. Fifteen years after that *Courant* photograph, Bonnie had ended her long exile and partnered with Clout to buy the defunct Queen City Skyport. They renovated the largest building on the airport's property into a 1,200-seat venue they'd christened the Hangar, home base for their newly founded Mid-Coast Championship Wrestling. Underneath its starry tract of sky, the runaway was immense. The breeze tumbled over the concrete, rustling the weeds and scraggly elm shoots poking through cracks in the tarmac. Its sound was the soft hum of a distant highway.

When the docs broke the bad news, Clout had welcomed the fight. He hadn't faced a worthy opponent in years. But the knockout punch came quickly. When the cancer took his voice and Clout understood he'd be finishing his run speaking in whispers, he tapped out of the fight. Bonnie had ensured everything was prepared. MCCW was profitable—its bottom line bolstered by satellite shows, internet pay-per-views, and a loyal core of crowdfunders. The promotion was among the first to take advantage of twenty-first-century revenue streams, providing an immediate advantage over its competitors struggling for relevance in the shadow of Vince McMahon's sprawling WWE empire.

Clout, his edge blunted by an extended stay on Rikers Island for a drug charge, had followed her lead. She'd made him a rich man. His family estranged, his peers long passed, Clout had lived and breathed MCCW. Now that he was gone, Bonnie could guarantee his wealth would not go to waste.

A tattered wind sock caught the breeze and squeaked on its axis. Bonnie pictured the once-mighty Clout struggling to write his last letter, mucus crackling in his throat like fried bacon, knobbed fingers barely strong enough to lift the pen. She folded the letter neatly and slid it into her tote.

The side-access door to the Hangar flew open and two wrestlers stormed out. The more mountainous of the two led the charge. He was in street clothes. The T-shirt draped awkwardly from his broad shoulders read "Big Frog." Following was another man, smaller, tightly coiled. His wet hair hung like tentacles. It made the first man's regulation cut look fake, the coiffure of a Ken doll.

"We've got a problem here, Bonnie," the bigger man said, each step registering on the Richter scale.

"No," the other said. "Duke's got a problem. His brain's smaller than his balls."

The bigger man spun to him. "I'll whoop your ass, you piece of shit."

"Try it, mate. I'll rip out your shoulder blades."

The two pressed their noses together and made tough-guy sounds.

That night, Duke Natterjack, the bigger man, had pinned the newcomer, Ruckus Brody, in the first of a series of bouts to determine the number one contender for the MCCW World Heavyweight Championship. The newly acquainted wrestlers had put on a passable show. Duke had pinned Ruckus with his finisher, a top-rope Flying Crucifix. Ruckus, not wanting to appear weak, broke from the script and kicked out right after the three count.

"It's a fucking insult," Duke said. "To me and Bonnie's booking."

"You've got the smarts of a tadpole," Ruckus said. "I'm impressed you can speak in sentences."

"This guy is already going into business for himself," Duke said. "What's going to happen a month from now? Asshole's going to be no-selling chair shots."

"You'll be on the streets by then," Ruckus said. "Your boss is finally going to realize you're not half as good in the ring as you are crying about me."

They pressed noses once more. Duke bellowed like an alligator, and Ruckus's neck stretched into a pumpkin stem. Ruckus saw an opening and threw a punch into Duke's solar plexus. The giant wrestler staggered forward. Before he'd gathered himself, Duke balled his fist and launched it like a shot put. Ruckus, too quick to follow his strike, took the swing on the jaw.

The dazed wrestlers squared off. Bonnie smirked at this display of efficiency: brainlessly male, full of posturing. This is what people would pay for—if only it could be reliably reproduced. The great lie of sports like boxing and mixed martial arts was that they were real, as if real fights happened under bright arena lights, within equiangular polygons. Professional wrestling's origins were rooted in kayfabe, the closely guarded secret that wrestling was theater. That artifice had suffered a million blows—slow-motion replay, the internet, tell-all autobiographies. In 1989, in a successful effort to dodge state athletic regulations, Vince McMahon had testified to the New Jersey Senate that pro wrestlers were, more or less, circus performers. Still, the show had winked hard and carried on, and that had earned Bonnie's respect. Wrestling wasn't staged so much as it exploited the stage. In its fictional world, feelings difficult to perceive in the muted routine of daily life were laid bare. The match was only the tip of the iceberg supported by weeks or even months of conflict. A good booker sensed the right time to apply pressure and tip the iceberg over. Wrestling could tell great stories. Bonnie knew she could do better.

Ruckus connected with a solid right, crumpling Duke to a knee. Ruckus grinned and counted teeth with his tongue.

"What do you think, Sugartits? You want a go? I promise I'll put you down faster than I did this thick-skulled horse's ass."

Ruckus approached Bonnie, who casually got up from the folding chair she'd brought from ringside. Even in the dark, Ruckus was close enough for her to see the cut on his bottom lip. He caught her looking and lapped at it, sucking the juices.

"Whaddaya say, love? I promise I'll keep it nice and clean." He blew on his fingers and brushed Bonnie's straight, gray hair off her shirt collar.

"Feels good to throw a real punch," Bonnie said. "Doesn't it?"

"Careful now. You'll tempt another out of me."

Bonnie twirled one of Ruckus's moist tentacles around her knuckle. "It's a pity these scuffles end quickly. We're such fragile beings—so little time for drama."

Ruckus popped his tongue over his cut and curled it across his teeth. "I'll show you a scuffle. It'll last all night."

Bonnie smiled. "You're a talker. Reminds me of Clout."

Ruckus snorted. He blew out air too forcefully, and the snort cracked into a high-pitched whistle.

"Enough jaw for one night," Bonnie said. "You and Duke have a rematch in the main event next weekend. You call it. You go over. We'll see how you do. Good?"

Ruckus's scowl melted. "Peachy," he said.

"Splendid. Now shake and get your coworker to his feet."

Duke was wheezing and holding his side, knees glued to the tarmac. Ruckus hooked the crook of his arm and pulled him up.

"My ribs!" Duke squealed. "I think my lung is punctured."

"Let's hope you heal up quick," Ruckus said. He seized Duke's hand and tried to crush it.

"Please, no!" Duke yelped. "Uncle! Uncle!"

Ruckus tossed Duke away, wagged his tongue at Bonnie, and left.

"A rematch?" Duke said. He sputtered as Ruckus climbed into his pickup. Smoke belched from the tailpipe, and the heel tore off.

Duke continued yelping. "Bonnie, you couldn't! Please!"

"You're laying it on a little thick, don't you think?"

"Fooled him, didn't I?" Duke said. He straightened up and cracked his neck. All traces of distress were gone.

"Next week's a shoot," Bonnie said. "Play along until it gets boring, then do whatever it takes to pin him. Not every experiment can succeed, but at least we'll get two decent matches out of him."

"Gladly," Duke said, sly as a cat.

"You did well," Bonnie said. "Followed my instructions precisely. It's not often you find someone in this business you can trust to plan a shoot and remain discreet."

Duke bowed. "You hear him say I had a brain like a tadpole's? Tadpoles are actually smarter than virtually all fish of similar size. Amphibians are excellent role models. To thrive in this pond, you need to be a master of adaptation."

"Seems to me adaptation has nothing to do with it. They just grow up," Bonnie said.

Duke paused. "Are you getting smart with me?"

"Wouldn't dream of it. Here, I need your help with this."

Bonnie reached in her tote and tossed Duke a length of rope. It was ten feet long and wrapped in MCCW ring tape. With Duke holding one end, she stepped away until the rope was taut and popped the lid on a can of white spray paint.

"Did you always like wrestling?" Bonnie asked.

"What's it to you?" Duke replied.

"If we're to collaborate further, it would be useful to know what brought you into the job."

"If we're collaborating, it should be a conversation, not an interview."

"Fair enough."

Duke tightened his mitts around the rope.

"My old man was a fan. Didn't give a lick about sports, but he loved wrestling. We watched it all the time."

"Me too," Bonnie said. "It was my secret vice. I'd sneak on the TV at night, turn the sound way down."

"Your parents should've cut you off. Would've saved you trouble."

"My father tried. He found me one night. I surprised him. I was a no-nonsense kid. He watched with me. It became our little tradition. Once a week, late at night, popcorn, whispering—it was fun."

"Then you sold him out."

A puff of white escaped the can of paint's nozzle, and the breeze took it away. Bonnie held the end of the rope, crouched down, and began to spray an arc with Duke at its center.

"I didn't sell anything," Bonnie said.

"So what happened? He quit on you? Did he postpone daddy-daughter night for a PYT at the office?"

"He told me it wasn't real."

"And?" Duke slacked the line. Bonnie shook it until he held it taut again.

"I couldn't watch anymore. I saw the strings—pulled punches, razor blades, the teamwork. It was right in front of me. I wasn't paying attention."

Duke laughed. "Yeah. It's called suspension of disbelief."

"It was embarrassing. The show was never as good."

Duke shuffled to his right, keeping the rope straight between him and his boss. Somehow, the spray didn't touch her black sneakers.

"Clout was asking about you," Duke said. "Right until the end."

"I'm glad you were with him," Bonnie said.

"It was terrible. He looked like snot on a sick mule. Wheezing something terrible, like he was breathing through a straw. And his face—twisted like a tragedy mask."

Bonnie paused, checked her work, and kept painting. "You know Clout did time in Rikers?"

"I thought they shuttered that place in the sixties."

"That's Alcatraz. Rikers is in the East River—New York City. Clout was there for twelve years. Not once did he have a visitor."

Duke shook his head. "It's your company now. You gotta learn how debts get paid, what talks when nobody has any real fucking money."

Bonnie finished her circumnavigation, leaving Duke at the center of a white circle twenty feet in diameter.

"Clout took you under his wing," he said. "He saw a lot of us through hard times. You were his partner, for Christ's sake. You owed him at least one lousy afternoon."

Bonnie popped the cap back on the can. "Thanks for your help."

Duke peered at the white line encircling him. "What is it?"

"It's exactly what it looks like," she said.

"Looks like a waste of my fucking time."

Duke took a step in what was to be a long, loud stomp to the Hangar when he realized he was the same distance from the curved line as he would be from the ropes if he were in the center of a wrestling ring.

"There's the instinct," Bonnie said. "Under twenty feet, I'd trust you dogs more than a tape measure."

"Your grand plan is a ring gimmick? That's Mickey Mouse shit. We'd go belly-up in two months."

"No gimmicks. A new promotion. You'll want to hear about it."

"Whatever you say next, you better say straight up," Duke said.

Bonnie folded her arms and rubbed her chin, eyeing the wrestler from his boots to the sculpted mesa atop his dome. "You want it straight?"

"Damn straight I want it straight. I'm your top draw. Show me respect, or I'll walk." The force of Duke's words pushed him onto his heels, activating an old spur. A blast of pain shot to his skull, where his brain sponged it up.

Bonnie stepped into the circle and stopped in front of Duke. At her full height, she barely reached his chest. He leaned over her, casting a wide shadow.

"This is your last run," Bonnie said. "You'll shoot on Ruckus and work a program to the championship, then you're lying down. Retirement match."

"Who the fuck said I was retiring?"

"I did. You're forty-three. You're almost certain to suffer a career-threatening injury within the next six months. The numbers don't lie—and I'm not one to bet against them. I'm incredibly skilled at getting people to do what I want, and even I would have difficulty convincing you to throttle down. Your heart says you've got a lot left in the tank."

Duke looked as if he were about to clock Bonnie out of her cross-trainers.

"I see what you're trying to do," he said. "It's not going to work."

"Oh, you do?" she said. "How much money am I about to offer you?"

"I told you to be straight with me," he said.

"I am," Bonnie said. "As I mentioned, quite clearly, there's a new promotion in the works. We're going to retire you from the main roster, and you'll debut in its inaugural match. You'll do the job, one night only, and you'll be compensated."

"How much?"

"Five times what you make in a year with MCCW. All of it up front. Then 25 percent payments of that sum every year."

"Fuck off. That money could buy out half the boys."

"It's a very generous package. Necessary, I believe, to ensure you leave the ring for good. Your knees are shot. Your spine's bone on bone. If you continue with some other promotion, you *will* fall to injury. And then you'll bankrupt yourself trying to claw back."

"You think you can wave a bunch of Monopoly money in my face and get me to roll over? You think I'm in this goddamned business for the cash? When did you start giving two shits about my long-term well-being? I just took a sucker punch to the liver for you."

"There's of course one unusual stipulation to this offer," Bonnie said. "It's nothing contrary to your best interests, but I won't bore you. You know what I'm trying to do, right?"

Duke raised his fist. He caught himself and masked it by pointing a finger at Bonnie.

"No deal," Duke said. He willed his legs to carry him to edge of the circle. Once on the move, he found his swagger, the walk of a man who put asses in seats, who sold a ton of fucking T-shirts. Children slept beneath his posters. Women waited for him in the cold.

"I'm glad you were there for Clout!" Bonnie called out. "It was the right thing to do."

FIVE

On the road, the Civic was Dom's home. Parked in a Walmart's shadow or on the shoulder of a quiet back road, it looked no different than its thousands of clones. American-flag blue. Fogged headlights. Tires sagging, even after a fresh fill. To notice anything odd, a passerby would have to cup their eyes against the window.

Fuel and maintenance ruled out an RV. A lot of wrestlers traveling together would split motels, cramming five or six to a room. Dom was young on paper, but he had too many miles under his belt to sleep on floors. The Civic had a low enough profile to remain undisturbed while parked overnight.

With duct tape and superglue, he'd transformed the rear seat backs into a cushioned bed extending into the trunk. There was a clear dip in the threshold between the cab and trunk, and Dom didn't have much wiggle room around his waist. If he tucked his knees, there was just enough. He'd rigged a series of curtains on PVC rods that obscured the rear windows and enclosed his sleeping compartment. His climate-control options were opening windows or crawling inside his sleeping bag. If he was alone and the night was survivable, he bunkered in the Civic. He'd drift away quickly, fatigue overtaking the ripening ache from an evening's match.

When Pilar began riding with Dom to his summer events, the siblings doubled the Civic's maximum occupancy. In a pinch, Pilar could recline the passenger seat while Dom slid into his trunk bed. Mostly they drove, taking turns if needed while the rider dozed.

They packed light. A typical run started with a Friday-night show in South Carolina, then a daytime gig in metro Atlanta, and back to Charlotte for a Sunday-night MCCW pay-per-view. They both brought gear. Dom was friendly with a dozen wrestling-school owners throughout the Southeast who'd let him steal a few minutes of ring time, or even borrow a sparring partner for Pilar.

When Dom broke Cee-Saw's arm at the Freedom Fest, he forced the ref to stop the match and award victory to the Russian and his cocky sidekick, the bad guys. After the bell, Dom and Pilar booked it. Pilar drove. Dom was thankful to take traffic's stop-and-go from shotgun.

Dom woke up Pilar's phone and thumbed to her texts. "What'd you want to say?" he asked.

"Tell her, 'No. You'll smell like fry oil and Mac sauce,' " Pilar replied.

Dom typed the message as dictated and pressed send. The contact was labeled "B." Dom didn't pry. Pilar had agreed not to text while driving if Dom promised to play secretary without asking too many questions. The deal was the same when he was behind the wheel.

Pilar's phone buzzed, and Dom read. "B says, 'I really need the money,' frowny face."

"You'll never be able to eat there again," Pilar said.

"Decent perk," he said, transcribing.

"You wanna stop at Sol's?" Pilar asked. "It's on the way."

"I need to dry out before I think about the gym. But if you want to."

"Let's do it. You think he'll be around?"

"You kidding? Sol's a rat in there. I think he's built a nest."

A buzz. Dom read the message: "I'd die before giving up McNuggets. They're my crack." "And then," he said, "there's a diamond emoji, which I guess is supposed to be crack. When are you going to introduce me to this chick?"

"Tell her she's worth more than seven twenty-five an hour."

Dom sent it. He conjured an image of B in his mind, then a completely different one, enjoying the mystery of her. He flicked away the message window and stared at Pilar's wallpaper—a photorealistic drawing of some alien-looking flower with neon-green leaves and rose-pink petals.

"Is this thing real?" he asked, holding up the phone.

"I dunno," she said, huffing.

Dom scrolled right so most of the app buttons were hidden. "It's got little thorns in the center, like teeth. Where'd you find it?"

"Some website," Pilar said.

"Well, no shit. I mean where? This from one of those Japanimation shows?"

"Japanimation?"

"Yeah, like Pokémon or whatever."

"Oh my god. I don't know where it's from. Someone drew it, and I thought it looked cool."

The sun hovered above them. The road cut through sandy hills and swampland, tall pines choking off a view. Dom kept Pilar's phone on his thigh and took out his, an old model with beat-up edges. He punched in his unlock code and, after seeing no new texts, pulled up his dating app.

"So, black trunks, huh?" Pilar said.

"I know," Dom said.

"There were so many weird vendors. We could've made you into anyone."

"It was a mistake, okay? Let's leave it there."

They were silent for a while.

"How's your back?" Pilar asked, her voice softer than before.

"Hurts," Dom said, reaching for his tailbone. "The botch compressed it pretty good."

"Did you two slip or—"

"He sandbagged and faked injury. Dude shouldn't have been within a mile of a ring. We can talk about it later. I need to chill right now."

Pilar kept her eyes on the road and chewed the inside of her cheek.

Dom flicked to his dating app and checked his messages. Five new women in Sumter had matched and sent him notes. Three said, "Hi." One said, "Hola guapo," and another asked if he'd like to be "Dominated." A year ago, he was lucky to get five matches in a month, and it didn't matter how charming or assertive or complimentary he was. They all left him hanging. Dom learned early that the stories of wrestling legends fucking around the country were true enough, but those men were famous, and their playground was the 1980s. In the twenty-first century, ring rats were an endangered species. Plenty of guys turned a lot of tail using their bodies or charisma. Some played the numbers. Nobody led with wrestling.

At first, Dom hadn't understood this. He uploaded Hack Barlow pictures and pecked out a wall of text declaring wrestling as his life's mission, the cradle of his soul. He didn't think about how a potential hookup would read it. Dom Contreras, twenty-five, north of three hundred pounds, Queen City, but good luck finding him there. Photo number one: at the gym with gut-roll sweat stains. Photo number two: a portrait of a zombie logger. Photo number three: leaping off the top rope with murder in his eyes.

When his peers asked why he was dropping weight, Dom cited health and longevity, all those wrestlers with exploding hearts. After an eight-month cut, he didn't know what character to play in the ring, but his dating-app persona had never been more popular.

Another text popped up on Pilar's phone.

"Yeah? How much are you gonna pay me then?" Dom read. "Tongue-sticking-out face."

"Ugh, this girl," Pilar said. "Send her the same face."

In the spring, Dom had expunged every mention of wrestling from his profiles. He'd updated his pictures. The first showed him shirtless, next to the Catawba River, the only time he'd been there. Then there was a selfie of him laughing in a coffee shop. And a snap of him at an empty Hornets game, looking over his shoulder with his sleeves rolled up. He kept his description simple and let the photos talk. A month before Pilar's semester ended, he was 250 pounds and falling. He had more than thirty active conversations with women in a dozen cities. More than once he'd drop a line, forgetting he had already used it with the same person.

He'd slept with only a few of them—one in Charlotte, one in Macon. In Tuscaloosa he'd fooled around with a college student in the back of the Civic. The frame pinned them across the threshold between the cab and the trunk. Foreplay was sharp elbows and apologies. They fogged the windows as local used-car ads played on the radio. There wasn't a second date.

"You swiping?" Pilar asked. "Anything good?"

"Couple new ones," Dom said.

"A couple—are you collecting them? When's the last time you took someone out?"

Dom shrugged. "We've been too busy, and I like chatting."

"It's so fake, though. Everyone's hustling. You could spend less time texting and actually meet one of them and have a real conversation."

Dom had quit giving out his number. He could chat with women for weeks. In person, they were aliens. He'd squirm the entire date. After they left, the hangover would hit him like a stiff clothesline. He was self-sabotaging. His mind was betraying him after his body had busted ass to shape up.

"What's so good about real?" Dom asked. "This is fun."

"Seems like work to me."

"It's not work until they get to know you, and then they start noticing things you wish they didn't."

Pilar stuck her jaw forward and stared through a clearing cut for high-tension wires. Fifty yards from the road, at the base of a tower, a small memorial wilted in the sun.

A text from B read, "I heard what ur doing this summer. You could use an apprentice ;)" Dom didn't recite it. He blocked "Hola guapo" from his message list and wrote responses to the others—three said "Hey," and one said "You think you can Domesticate me?"

"Okay, sorry, I have to ask. What happens after a finish like that?" Pilar said.

"Like what?" Dom said.

"A shoot."

"Who said it was a shoot?"

"Uh, the crack of the dude's elbow? The part when he screamed, 'You broke my fucking arm?' "

"Accidents happen."

"Will they pay you?"

"I worked, didn't I? Fifteen minutes."

"So the promoter will let it go?"

"What does the fucking carny care? He got his match. And now he knows not to book those idiots. You don't work an injury without telling your partner."

Pilar popped open a tin of breath mints and crunched one. She looked to pass a slow-moving timber hauler in front of them. A line of cars was fast approaching in the opposite lane.

"From where I was sitting, it looked like a good sell," she said.

"What?"

"Cee-Saw. He wasn't hurt bad. Ref thought the same thing."

Pilar's phone buzzed. Dom let it drop between his legs. "Did you see me check him?"

"Yeah."

"Did you see him squeeze back?"

"Well, no, but—"

"But what? You were too far? It was too subtle? You had rain in your eyes?"

"Whatever." She blinked hard and gripped the wheel.

Dom leaned on the window and stared at the trees—rows upon rows of them repeating as if he were on an old Hollywood

set with the backdrop on loop. His neck, he realized, was puls-
ing with pain. Everything hurt. His body marinated in the
familiar ache, routine after years in the ring. A sharper tinge
hit his spine. His wrists crackled as if bone dust had fallen
into the joints. He opened his glove-compartment pharmacy
and sifted through the mess of a stash. He removed some over-
the-counter painkillers, washing them down with a warm diet
drink. It tasted like microwaved fudge popsicle drizzled with
vegetable oil.

"I'm a little pissed right now," Pilar said. "There's a good
chance you won't get another call from that promoter. It's upsetting how you can break a guy's arm and torch a contact without
thinking about what it does to me."

"You don't want those kinds of jobs. And you won't need
them."

"Oh? Are you the prophet of pro wrestling? You tote me
along on these trips and keep me in a glass jar. I should've
been meeting people. Instead I'm in the seats watching you
kill whatever hopes I had of working in Sumter—"

"I'm so sorry I've ruined your big break with the Titty Inspec-
tors," Dom said. "To think you could've been spending your
Saturdays on Cee-Saw's lap spraying another groupie with a
Super Soaker."

"Do you know what business we're in? What woman wrestler
hasn't had to do that shit?"

Dom pressed his palms flat against the canopy and tried to
stretch the ache from his vertebrae. Pilar was better than some

carnival sideshow. She had a direct line into MCCW, straight to Bonnie Blue. She'd impress at a tryout. She'd climb the ladder. She could stand atop their promotion, and if she caught wind, she could ride her youth and skill high enough to reach for the sun. Dom wouldn't allow Pilar to claw into mediocrity as he had. He'd witnessed too many women wrestlers clinging to the edge of the grinder, fighting the fall into its maw, not strong enough to pull themselves out.

"And Dom, we need the money," Pilar said. She was pitched forward in her seat, her head craning to see around the timber hauler. She inched out across the dotted yellow, swerving right as an SUV came barreling by.

The meds churned in Dom's gut, their familiar effects bubbling through him. Pressure increased in his skull. His eyelids were heavy.

"We do need the money," he said.

Pilar saw her chance and floored it. The Civic coasted, as if it were waiting for Pilar to change her mind, and then begrudgingly accelerated. They passed the trailer wheels, half the height of the Civic. The driver looked down and flashed a peace sign, or maybe a victory sign, Dom wasn't sure.

He reopened B's text window on Pilar's phone. Another message had arrived: "You could use an apprentice." Again, Dom elected not to read it. He stared straight ahead, and the tunnel of trees continued, breaking occasionally for a trailer home or a dirt road that led nowhere.

SIX

Sol's was a few minutes off the highway in a Rock Hill industrial park. The steel building housing the gym was tucked behind a silica processing plant and a Gothic soap factory that stood in a state between restoration and disrepair. The factory had always reminded Dom of a shrine—the brick towers like a pair of steeples looming over a crumbling cathedral, the skeletal gravel machines the remains of prehistoric beasts. Sol's gym was wedged between a craft distillery and a shop that cut tubes for Daimler and BMW. Like every other unit, he had a garage door for docking semitrailers. Sol's was wide open. Every bug in the South took notice of the fluorescent light inside. A dented aluminum sign, probably fashioned years ago by one of Sol's neighbors, hung next to the entry door. It read "Solomon Lung's Athletic Training."

The two rows of equipment stretched the length of the unit. Benches, cable machines, squat and bicep racks—black and gunmetal with visible welds and sharp angles. They were in good shape, with green vinyl covers free of wear and oil marks. The free weights were cast-iron. Two giant fans in steel cages buzzed out hot air and kept the moths fluttering in the front of the gym. Mirrors hung on each wall. Dom liked Sol's because it was empty. No one stepped foot on its Mars-colored floor without knowing exactly what he was doing.

Pilar threw the Civic into park at the garage door's threshold and zipped inside, heading straight for the business office. Dom lugged himself out and heaved their duffels from the trunk. He heard Pilar and Sol's shouts of greeting.

He let them have a moment, walked to the rear of the unit, and hopped on Sol's practice mat. A layman might've thought it was a trampoline or power-lifting stage. Dom knew better. Though it was rectangular and ropeless and flush with the wall, its bump was the truest of all mats Dom had wrestled. It was perfect for practicing the fundamentals—learning to fall, stringing a chain, stomping to enhance the pop of a strike. He took a moment to himself, stretching his back, enjoying the solitude.

The office door had an opaque window with Sol's name on it as in an old noir film. The walls were papered with yellowing posters from the NWA and AWA. One card, framed behind Sol's desk, was a GCW poster from the 1970s promoting their Christmas special. At the bottom, the poster read "GRUDGE

MATCH—KING SOLOMON VS. RANDY POFFO." At the time, Poffo was an unsung minor-league baseball player in his offseason. In later years, he'd debut in the WWF and hit megastardom as the Macho Man Randy Savage.

Sol leaned on his desk and showed Pilar a model spaceship. It was silver and boomerang shaped, with dark highlights and a shock of deep red.

"Dom, baby, how the hay are ya?" Sol hugged Dom with one long arm, careful not to bump him with the wet model. He was tall and looked as if he could squeeze in a marathon before bedtime. Decades ago, in his wrestling prime, King Solomon had been built like an NFL defensive lineman. He'd topped out over three hundred pounds, but he regularly beat men half his weight in sprints. For nearly fifteen years in the seventies and eighties, Sol never bought himself a drink. He was either buying rounds for the bar or guzzling down his winnings from various bets and feats of strength—arm wrestling, one-handed push-ups, balancing eggs, naming all the US presidents.

Now, Sol was the epitome of a retired athlete. He'd dropped the weight gradually, taking up yoga before most Westerners had heard of it. Hardest of all, he'd learned to moderate his lifestyle. Transitioning from the carnival world of wrestling had killed a lot of tough motherfuckers. Tougher than Dom. Smarter than Dom.

Dom winced at Sol's embrace. The old vet sensed it.

"Sore coccyx, huh? Bad leg drop?"

"Botched suplex," Pilar said.

Dom spit a glance at her, then steadied himself on a folding chair and said he was fine. Sol smiled. His arms were dark and veined. Aside from his eyebrows, there wasn't a hair on his head.

Sol angled his model so both Pilar and Dom could see it. "As I was saying, the Cylon Raider is my favorite starfighter, probably the most interesting weapon in all of science fiction. Have you seen *Battlestar Galactica*, Dom?"

"I don't see a lot of movies," Dom said.

Sol chuckled. "Best television series of the twenty-first century. You know *The Terminator*, right? Killer android with a metal endoskeleton covered in living tissue. A Cylon Raider is the opposite—metal armor protecting the viscera beneath. The Raider looks like a ship, but it's an organism. The Cylons' attack fleet isn't piloted or remote-controlled. It's unleashed like a pack of wolves."

"Have you seen this show?" Dom asked Pilar.

"A few episodes," she said. "Starbuck is a badass."

"Starbucks?" Dom said.

"Kara Thrace," Sol said. "Pilot for the Colonial Fleet, call sign Starbuck—one of the main characters. She figures out a way inside a downed Raider and pilots it to the *Galactica* to use on a later mission."

"I thought you said they were flying dogs," Dom said.

"Cybernetic dogs. Their systems can be hacked."

Pilar widened her eyes at Dom as if it was his fault for not following.

"When a Cylon gets killed, its consciousness is automatically uploaded into a new model. This also goes for the Raiders, provided a Resurrection Ship is within range. In its demise and rebirth, the Raider has gained valuable experience a human pilot can never have."

Dom interrupted to say he was hitting the john. The men's locker room was small, basic, and clean. Twelve high school lockers lined one wall, a wooden bench kneeling before them. Manila tile. Nickel drains. Shower tree with four nozzles. The toilet stalls were solid. Exhaust fans whirred. The noise added to the privacy—Don savored the isolation, especially since Pilar had moved in.

Dom latched the door, dropped his shorts. The seat was cool and flat. He tapped to his phone's camera and pulled off his shirt. In the screen he inspected his battle wounds. A Florida-shaped bruise started near his hip and curled under his pectoral. His sternum glowed sunset red from Maxwell's chops. The gash on his abdomen from a misjudged fall on the ring steps was healing nicely. No scab remained—only a pinkish, flaky ridge eroding into the surrounding skin.

He looked good. The cut had sloughed off the excess, revealing his powerful core. Dropping so much weight had taken tremendous effort. His center of gravity was higher. He wasn't Hack Barlow anymore. Every cent he'd earned since he quit his landscaping job junior year of high school had come through the lumberjack. He knew every inch of that old body—how it bumped, what parts could cushion a fall, how his knees and hips stressed under its weight. His new frame was safer. It would last. He'd done the right thing, but he'd become a stranger to himself. One of the gravest threats to a wrestler was a lack of confidence.

He flicked away his camera app and opened Omegle. In seconds he was live streaming video and sound to some dude with brown-orange hair and dark circles under his eyes. Dom angled his camera to show only his torso. He couldn't keep the point of his beard out of frame, nor could he ensure the tile locker room wall didn't peek around him. Dom straightened his shoulders until pain sparked from his lower back. The guy on the other end soured his face and disconnected, and the app lined up the next chat partner. The app's gimmick was its randomized, anonymous pairings. Anyone who hit its big blue Start a Chat button could see Dom's bruised six-pack. There were voyeurs and exhibitionists. The curious and the lonely. It wasn't a bad place to practice.

The next partner was someone in a horse mask. The figure turned in profile and shook its head like it was laughing. Garbled dance music drowned any greeting. The figure snapped its snout to center and disconnected.

The next partner was a man in a dark room. He nodded as if he were expecting Dom, then disconnected.

The next partner was a young man with a British accent and a flat-brimmed ball cap riding close to vertical. He asked Dom if he was having a wank, then disconnected.

The next partner wasn't a partner at all. An animated GIF of an attractive woman in a bikini danced above blue text urging Dom to visit her private chat room. This time Dom disconnected.

The next partner was a shirtless man, much less muscular than Dom, covering Jason Mraz's "I'm Yours" on acoustic guitar. Dom listened to the entire song. He congratulated the man for sticking it out and singing well. The man asked Dom if his voice turned him on. Dom said not particularly. The man asked if Dom was hard. Dom told him no. The man peered into the screen for a while, not saying anything, until Dom asked how the man learned to play. The man opened his mouth as if to answer, then disconnected.

The next four partners were men of various ages in dark rooms. Upon seeing Dom, they all disconnected.

The next partner was a woman masturbating. She was lying flat on a bed and holding her phone between her feet. The only sounds came from the jostling device and her fingers as they did their work. Dom waited to see where it would go or if she would look up to glimpse who was watching. Suddenly, the feed clipped. Her fingers stuttered and froze, and she disconnected. Dom laughed. He liked imagining the woman had the dexterity to hit the skip button with her toes.

The next partner was a young woman with her hair in a ponytail. She was sitting cross-legged in a bed with pillows fluffed around her. Her glasses didn't obscure the tired eyes behind them. A pair of expensive headphones covered an ear, and she wore a hoodie that said "Warrior Football" across the front.

Her eyes widened, and she started typing. The clacking keys were loud even in Dom's tinny speakers.

"Best bod I've seen tonight," she wrote.

"Thanks," he replied.

The woman leaned forward. "Hard to hear u."

"Sorry," Dom said. "I don't have a keyboard."

"Or ur hands are busy," she wrote.

Dom smiled and told her to wait. He froze his video with his chest and abs filling the frame and tapped open the text window, which covered the right half of the screen. The young woman's feed shrank and settled on the left. "There we go," he wrote. "Now I have two thumbs."

"Didn't know there was an app," she said.

"It's buggy, but it does the trick."

The woman pulled out a thin strand of hair from her ponytail and twirled it. Dom waited for her to respond. It was like working a match blind. He had to think on the fly.

"What brings you to Randomsville?" Dom asked.

"Practicing," she wrote.

"Practicing what?" Dom returned.

"If I told you, it wouldn't be practice. Where are you?"

"Gym."

"U an athlete?"

"Just staying healthy," he said.

She pushed for details. Dom's default answer was mixed martial arts, though sometimes he could get a read before the question came up and pick a less violent pursuit—stunt double, adventure racer, whatever strength-and-conditioning cult was popular at the moment. One night after a match against an opponent with dark body paint, Dom convinced a chat partner he worked on an oil rig. As a rounder man he'd never considered how many women had little interest in the stereotypical gym-rat sculpt until they learned it had been forged in the fires of necessity, built by manual labor. Dom had passed a lot of miles wondering if he could legitimately call himself a blue-collar worker. He'd earned his body the hard way and had the wear and tear to prove it, but the iron he'd lifted wasn't to lay rail or lift a jackhammer. He'd labored for years. He hadn't made anything.

"C'mon," she said. "Nobody looks like that just cause."

"I'm going to the NFL combine," Dom wrote.

The girl smiled and poked her tongue into her cheek.

"Oh really? Isn't it in February?"

"Early entry," Dom wrote. "I'm a special case."

"Ur full of shit," she said.

Dom bit his lip. "What makes you so sure?" he asked.

"I'm not a dumbass." She pinched her shirt and waved the Warrior Football logo into the cam.

Dom smirked. Maybe it wasn't a boyfriend's hoodie.

"You really think someone would go on the internet and tell lies?"

"I think whatever ur doing u don't want people to know."

The woman uncrossed her legs and split them out wide, her sweatpants riding up her ankles.

"If ur in a gym where are the weights?"

"Outside. I'm in the locker room."

"Creepy."

"I'm the only one in here."

"Honestly I think ur waiting to show your cock."

"Nah. Doesn't do it for me."

"No?"

"lol No."

"Then what does?"

Dom didn't have a quick answer. He could've told her about the time at a high school party where he'd retreated to the bathroom and someone had crammed a pair of panties under the door. He could have told her about the redhead at the Landing Strip outside Pittsburgh International. Many wrestlers were instinctually drawn to strippers, and Dom was no exception. He felt kinship with them, their bodies on display, navigating a kayfabe all their own. The redhead had danced on the T-shaped stage and afterwards strolled down the bar. She stopped in front of Dom, reached for his shirt collar, straightened it, and walked away. The gesture had been so intimate, so absolutely real. He recognized good work when he saw it.

He remembered when those memories would get him going. Now, the zip they'd once had had crusted over.

"I like talking to people," he typed. His thumb stalled over the send button. He whispered the sentence, frowned, and let his thumb drop.

The girl smiled. "Then why aren't u out there talking to people?"

"You're a person."

"I might be."

"If you're a robot, they've discovered AI and we're all doomed."

"Are u a bot?"

"Ha. There aren't any male bots."

"There sure are. And honestly I'm getting suspicious."

Dom had forgotten he'd switched off his camera. Even though he was watching the woman tap her chin with her index finger in real time, a still image of his torso was all she could see.

"How can I convince you?" he asked.

"Tell me what you're training for."

"Already did."

"Fine, liar. Show me ur cock."

"No can do."

"Holy shit. A first in internet history."

"I'm not like other boys," he wrote. After the sentence, he typed in a winky face and was immediately grossed out. He deleted it, hit send, and watched her read.

"Then show me ur face."

"No dice. Sorry."

"Why not?"

"Just don't do it."

She leaned forward, the closest to the camera she'd been. "I'm not letting it go. Are u ugly? Deformed?"

"No."

"Are u famous? actor?"

"I'm not famous."

"Then show me ur fucking face."

"Can we talk about something else?"

"NO. Why should I show my face when u won't?"

"You can stop your video if you want," Dom typed.

"That's not how this is going to work. Show me ur face."

"I'm not going to."

"Show me ur face and I'll flash my tits. We'll do it at the same time. It'll be fun."

"No."

"What are u afraid of?"

She raised her eyes from her screen and mouthed "do it" directly into her cam. Dom heard her tongue click on the inside of her teeth. One of her incisors was angled inward. It made her look even younger, like a teenager before braces. Dom wanted to reach through the screen and yank it into place. It would only hurt for a moment.

He moved his finger across her face and kept it going to the disconnect button. With a single tap, he cast himself into anonymity.

Her feed vanished, and in a few seconds, a new partner appeared on screen.

SEVEN

The garage door was open and the box fans hummed, but the lights were off in the front half of the gym. Only the training platform was illuminated. For such a low-rent facsimile with no ropes or apron, the stage glow was surprisingly good. Sol had rigged a few spots and Fresnel lenses in the support beams above. The wrestlers didn't cast shadows.

Pilar and Sol were circling each other, the mat clapping under their feet. They both wore ring gear, Sol in black trunks and boots, Pilar in blue trunks and a black sleeveless rash guard. Sweat droplets on Sol's head grew heavy and streamed down his neck. The skinny, raven-haired teenager and the chiseled veteran would never have fought in most promotions. Their pairing sparked electric.

The envelope of plausible wrestling bookings had been stretched in so many directions by thousands of promoters. Yet somehow there were stories that remained about competitors like the ones in front of Dom. Mixed matches between men and women were nothing new, but few had taken them seriously. When Dom imagined a draw clamoring to watch someone like Pilar work someone like Sol without gimmicks, without a male manager pulling her strings or coming to her rescue, the salesman inside him smelled cash. If it were possible anywhere, it was in a wrestling ring, where disparities in ability and stature could be and had always been part of the story.

Pilar charged full speed at Sol and leaped. Sol grasped her hips and boosted her launch. Pilar split her legs and landed the back of her knees on his shoulders. She whipped backward, throwing her head between his legs. With his hands on her hips, Sol sprang forward, completing a somersault in midair. He landed on his back with Pilar on top of him. Pilar hooked his legs for the pin.

"Textbook!" Sol said, catching his breath.

"You think?" Pilar said, panting hard.

"You gotta snap a little more," Dom said. "Looks like Sol's doing all the work."

Pilar rolled out of the pin. On the raised mat she and Dom stood eye to eye. "I'm like a foot shorter than him," she said. "He's gotta jump to clear."

Dom shook his head. "Should be easier with a bigger partner. More headroom."

"It's a fucking Hurricanrana. I'm tucking to the same place regardless."

"No one's gonna buy it. You gotta sell the snap."

"Sol, can you tell my brother he doesn't know how to wrestle?"

Sol kipped-up as if his legs were springs. "Dom," he said. "You don't know how to wrestle."

Sol hopped from the mat and shook his face into a towel hanging on a nearby pull-down machine. Pilar found a suitable spot on the mat and started her sets—push-ups, jump squats, handsprings.

"She's good," Sol said. "Can't keep a light under a basket. It's a sin."

"You're one to talk about sin," Dom said.

Sol snapped his towel onto the machine. "What about Mexico? She could get some real experience before a stateside debut. Plus, they'd love you."

Dom's neck tightened. "What's that supposed to mean?"

The veteran paused as if computing the answer Dom wanted to hear. "Pilar's been training *lucha*, and your newly tight ass better be planning on catching air. That lumberjack gimmick makes even less sense for you now. It clashed with your look from the start."

"That was on purpose. Had I gone your way, I would've been one of a thousand El Typicos playing the same damn stereotype my entire life."

"That's the business, amigo. You wanna guess how many times I've worked babyface?"

Pilar cartwheeled into a handstand and dipped into push-ups. She inched low and pushed her tightly woven hair bun against the mat. Sweat dripped from her nose.

"You wrestled in Mexico, right?" Dom asked.

"Dos años," Sol said. "Naulcapan y Ciudad de México."

"They like you down there?"

"Nah. In Japan you can earn their respect. Down south, you wear spit like a medal. One night someone's *abuelita* jumped the rail and took a swing at me with a tequila bottle. I swiped it and took a pull while they muscled her out of the arena. Nuclear heat."

"Can't play too close to the sun," Dom said. "Lots of sun in Mexico City."

Sol threw on a T-shirt with a sketch of a red-eyed Ninja Turtle. Wounds on his face and neck revealed a metallic endoskeleton. Aggressive lettering stamped beneath him read "Hasta La Pizza!"

"There's good work down there," Sol said. "Ask anyone."

Sol left for the locker room, and so ended the sell Dom had heard many times. Japan, Canada, England, Detroit—Sol had a pitch and a story for every market. For as much as he treasured Dom's visits, especially once Pilar had joined him, Sol never forgot to remind Dom to get out of Dodge. The advice may well have been wise. Dom had never considered his hovel in Charlotte anything more than a base camp—a place to refuel before the next run at the top. But Mexico was the moon. Japan was Jupiter. Both alien and inhospitable worlds. The States were tough enough to navigate. How was he supposed to negotiate a contract with a promoter in Tokyo who could fuck him over in three languages? How could he focus on performing when every part of his routine would have to change? Where would he sleep, what would he eat, what plug would he use to charge his phone?

Every Joe who'd told Dom about his lovely trip to Paris or his transformative years working some bullshit gig abroad had never really traveled. Dom had worked ten shows in eight cities in a week. He'd been stopped near the Texas-Louisiana border and threatened with deportation. Plenty of wrestlers worked internationally in the heyday of the business, when long-haired, juiced-up Americans were novelties. How many had sunk into drugs and alcohol to cope with the culture shock? How many hadn't lived to see fifty?

And there was Pilar. No one who'd told Dom to pick up and try his luck outside the States had considered her. They'd seen her, of course. They'd ogled her. They'd fantasized. They hadn't given a second's thought about what a move abroad might mean for her. None of them could name an American woman who'd got her foot in the door outside the country.

Dom wanted to hop up to the platform and correct Pilar's Hurricanrana. The postmatch ache in his knees and ankles stopped him. Pilar's rolls were smooth and precise. She'd advanced far from the clunk of her midteens. She easily masked the difficulty and strain of her contortions. Conventional wisdom insisted all young wrestlers be stretched. They were wild horses. No work could be done before they'd been broken. This hadn't been true for Pilar. She flowed like a river that had never run dry. Dom looked on with pride as her trainer, love as her brother, and a deep appreciation of her will to exceed the limits imposed on her. She'd never be the strongest. She'd never have the best teachers. She'd be lucky if she ever got the benefit of the doubt. Despite it all, she could reach the top.

"You're staring and it's creepy," Pilar said. She arched back, reaching her toes to her head. The bend would've snapped most men's spines.

"Marks aren't going to care about what offends you," Dom said.

"Yeah. I didn't think you'd be one of them." She uncoiled and rolled in the opposite direction, folding until her forehead was between her knees.

"Don't push too hard," Dom said. "That's how you get hurt."

"If I eased off, you'd say the same thing," Pilar said.

"Finish up. We're hitting the road," he said.

"Que te den, guiri," she said.

Dom dropped a foot on the mat. The boom echoed through the empty gym.

"Come again?" he said.

Pilar remained locked in her stretch and took her time replying. "Nothing," she said. "Go tell Sol we're done here."

EIGHT

After World War II, a dice-rolling developer flattened an old rail yard fifteen miles outside downtown Charlotte and built an airport ready-made to become the hub for the city's commercial carriers. With two runways, a luxuriously appointed passenger terminal, and a state-of-the-art baggage system, the airport was a monument to the mentality of postwar entrepreneurs who saw the country's triumph over foreign powers and domestic depression as proof that anything built with enough American grit could succeed. The Queen City Skyport opened with fanfare and circus elephants wearing cardboard airplane wings. The event was jolly and wholesome until one member of the herd bounded free and trounced through a patch of curing concrete near the outskirts of the complex. The elephant, chased by its handlers, hoofing it at full speed with a thirty-five-foot wingspan strapped across its back, became a sensation when a photo of the pursuit appeared on the front page of *The Charlotte Observer*.

The Queen City Skyport never took off. Its terminal often sheltered more squatters than passengers. Most of the airport was sold off a few years after opening due to various industrial concerns. Many of its buildings were razed. After losing all its commercial business to what would become Douglas International, Queen City limped along until the late nineties as a public-use airport—recreational props and flying instruction. It closed for good as Charlotte's sprawl crept outward, and the city's general aviation crowd moved to suburban airstrips in Concord, Monroe, and Rock Hill.

Bonnie's commute to her flat was precisely thirteen minutes on foot. She found the logic of the old airport grounds comforting. On her walk home, there was a story to read—evidence from a century of history and hints of what was to come. The big sky and level earth, acres upon acres scraped flat. Ornamental palms on the edge of their habitable zone lining an asphalt facility. Green fronds blazing like neon against the silver silos. Across the street, a pottery studio. Beyond, the rusting porticos of a machine-shop loading dock. A storage facility advertised by a hand-painted sign hanging from a barbed-wire fence. And then Bonnie's apartment, a hangar block for single-engine props subdivided into lofts.

Bonnie's apartment was simply furnished—a couch and a television, a dining room table, her study, where she spent most of her time. Three high-definition monitors made her work desk look like a command station. She enjoyed its contrast with her books, four stacks reaching from the floor like fingers. Wrestling biographies. Thick tomes on general medicine. Journal articles on the latest orthopedic surgery techniques. Histories of forgotten wars.

Everything was in its place, save her collection of letters from Clout Crawczak. On the night of his passing, she'd fanned them across her study's floor. They numbered 1, typed under Big Apple Wrestling letterhead, to 2,148—his final, incomprehensible note delivered from a bedside she hadn't visited.

She'd purchased banker's boxes with plastic dividers labeled by year to store the letters. She also had her shredder, which could devour the pages with the press of a button. As Bonnie's computer booted, she plucked a couple of Clout's letters at random.

November 9, 1985—*I lost a lot of respect for this country when blue jeans became everyday wear. How can a nation project exceptionalism when its kids are running around with frayed cuffs and holes in their knees? It's sloth, and we're going to pay for it. Looking like crap is disrespectful to the fallen.*

June 24, 2006—two weeks after Bonnie and Clout founded MCCW—*This business is a desert. You'd think only madmen would try their luck with it. When you've baked under those lights long enough, when you've shivered in all those cheap motels, you realize you gotta keep moving. When comfort sets in, this business will eat you. It will sweep you into a dust storm and bury you alive. If you're smart, you don't tie yourself down. You discover pockets of life, tiny oases which have withstood the droughts. You keep going, because one day the rain will come. When it does, the desert will bloom. The sand will explode in color, and you will be there, a survivor, a honeybee in paradise, ready to drink your fill.*

December 24, 2007—*Merry Christmas, Bonnie. You're sitting right over there. But it means more when it's on paper, doesn't it?*

The seven-year-old Christmas note was heavier than most. It was thick, as if Clout had used expensive stationery, a rarity for the old penny-pincher. She inspected the paper and found there was a second piece stuck to it. The edges had squared up so that she'd never noticed. She retrieved a knife from the kitchen and coaxed its point between the sheets.

Bonnie's computer dinged with a new email. Its subject line had obscenities in all caps. The sender was Gerard Clothier Sawyer, nickname Beef, owner-operator of a traveling firearms expo that hosted MCCW satellite shows when they looped through the Carolinas. Loaded with typographical errors, the note relayed the dire condition of Beef's son, Christian, ring name Cee-Saw. At the Sumter County Freedom Festival, he'd suffered a broken arm from Hack Barlow, an MCCW mid-carder. The email listed a series of outrageous and contradictory demands. Christian had likely sent the note under his father's account. Bonnie noticed the green light indicating Beef's availability for video chat. Though she was already annoyed with what promised to be a protracted exchange, she could settle the matter face-to-face and ensure Beef's support of the promotion.

The first attempt to hail him failed. A few seconds into the next, she got a connection. Though her screen remained dark, Beef's voice croaked through Bonnie's speakers.

"Chrissy! The fuck is happening? Get your ass over here and help Daddy!"

"Good evening, Beef. Bonnie Blue here."

"Bonnie Blue? Where you coming from?"

"What is it, Daddy?" a quieter voice said.

"Can you figure this fucking thing out? Bonnie Blue's on the line."

"She call you?" the voice said, louder now.

"My screen got all discombobulated, and now I hear her voice coming through it."

"She's probably got you on the video. Uh, hello, Ms. Blue."

"It's Bonnie, Christian. How's the arm?"

"Not very good at all, Ms. Blue. Your wetback son of a bitch snapped it in two."

"Satan's beard, Chrissy. What my son is trying to explain is that he's endured a grave injury perpetrated by one of your wrestlers. Three of Chrissy's ligaments are torn to pieces."

"Doc says I might never regain my motion, Ms. Blue. This is my right arm we're talking. Daddy, you know you got your camera taped over?"

"There's always this damned light shining in my eyes. All those California eggheads think everything needs to blink at you. Remember phones, Bonnie? You dial a number, you get a person."

The black video-chat window burst into color. Beef, in a choking tie and button-down, leaned toward the camera. His son hovered over his shoulder and rolled a piece of electrician's tape into a ball.

"I apologize to you and your son, Beef. We will of course cover Christian's medical expenses. But we need to discuss the requests you forwarded me."

Bonnie tried her best to keep her eyes off the letter.

"What requests?" Beef asked.

"We want him exported, Ms. Blue," Christian said. "We're willing to take this all the way to the IMF."

"Oh, Chrissy. Not again," Beef said.

"My damages go far beyond medical," Christian said. "Pain and suffering. Lost earnings. There's no Inspectors without Cee-Saw. We got a truckload of merch and three months of gigs to cancel. Freedom Fest was our biggest show yet. I've been cut down in my prime. My motion might never return."

Beef's cheeks puffed out like a bullfrog's. He held up a finger, asked for a minute, peeled off a sticky note and put it over the camera. Bonnie's screen went black, but the argument between father and son came through clear as day. After a minute, Beef was able to convince Christian to leave under the belief he was fetching some critical legal documents. When Beef reappeared, he was wiping his brow with a stack of fast-food napkins.

"It's the mystery of parenthood," Beef said. "Despite it all, I love that boy. I'd take a bullet for him. Hell, I'd intervene on his behalf with Bonnie Blue."

"Beef, I'm busy tonight, and I don't appreciate receiving Christian's poorly worded emails under your name."

"I apologize. And I offer my sincere condolences. I imagine times must be difficult given the passing of your partner."

"What's your ask?"

"Chrissy's no poet," Beef said. "Though he does have a legitimate grievance with your boy, not to mention a brand to maintain."

"You do realize Domingo Contreras is an American citizen. The best you could do is press an assault charge."

"We could sue MCCW."

Bonnie made a show of covering a smile. "Beef. C'mon."

"What?" Beef said, mirroring her grin. "Is something wrong? You're usually more sporting than this."

"Could you afford the lawyer you'd need to prove intent or even negligence in the context of a wrestling match? I'll make you an offer now that will be more than you'd get in a settlement."

"You are on edge. Did your shoe come untied today? Maybe some jam on your shirt during breakfast?"

"Beef."

"Or maybe there's a beau who's caught your eye. Is that it? Only the desires of the heart could shake someone as rock solid as Bonnie Blue. Is it one of your boys? I'd bet my lunch half of them are scheming to nab ya. Those poor louts. I have yet to meet a wrestler without an infatuation with authority."

"Full medical reimbursement and a year of rehabilitation," Bonnie said. "What else?"

"You're no fun. The money is fine with me. We also need to see discipline so I can stop Chrissy from bitching to the entire Carolina Bar."

"Fine. Contreras is gone."

"Gone?"

"Terminated from MCCW. Effective immediately."

"Damn, woman. I would've thought you'd step up for your boy."

"It's business, Beef."

"Point granted," Beef said, chuckling with his arms around his bulging abdomen. "You could probably come in here and run shop better than me."

"I could," Bonnie said. Her cursor hovered over the button that would end the call.

Christian's muffled shouts floated in. He couldn't find the right documents.

"What we do for love," Beef said, inflating his cheeks. "I used to wonder what a woman like you was doing in a mid-tier promotion. I'm beginning to piece it together. You can't help doting over what you bring into this world. All respect to Clout.

MCCW would've perished years ago if it weren't for you. It's your baby, ugly as it might be."

"Interesting assessment," Bonnie said. "A lot of my employees aren't convinced."

"Oh, Bonnie Blue, I know you better than any of your grapplers."

The call ended. Bonnie returned to Clout's letter and coaxed the pages loose.

It was dated December 29, 2007. Something had been spilled on it—a sticky substance, still faintly sweet smelling.

Dear Bonnie,

We need to write off Brooks. I went up to Mercy this morning. His goose is cooked.

I got the truth from Trotsky. Rumor's been going a while. Brooks was moonlighting for XCW. Working a deathmatch and took a light tube to the nose. Cracked his skull on a barricade.

We'll need to reach into the stable. Honestly I'm not smiling at the thought of inviting some kid up here to kill himself. Fucking Brooks. He's 22.

You said you wanted to start writing shit down. Here's a new policy. Anyone on MCCW contract caught working for those bastards is out. No exceptions. And they better believe I'll make sure no promotion east of the Mississippi hires them to clean the fucking toilets.

I'm sorry to be crass. This one's really got my goat. Kids aren't supposed to die. Every day it's faster, more intense, more risk, more aerial bullshit. These assholes don't understand. People don't watch wrestling to see real fucking danger. We're already on the edge. Anyone who goes beyond has blood on their hands.

I'm sorry. I'll get over it.
—*Clout*

Bonnie read the letter three times, committing its details to memory. She remembered Randall Brooks. Two years he'd wrestled for MCCW before the accident. His parents believed he'd wake up. They knew how strong he was. Eight months later, they'd let him go. His body had outlived Xtreme Championship Wrestling, shuttered by low attendance.

Bonnie set the letter on the desk and pulled up a roster with headshots of every wrestler in MCCW. She found Domingo Contreras, who was now fifty pounds lighter than he'd been in his photo. He didn't look like someone who would maliciously hurt another wrestler, but a look could be tweaked. Most importantly, she knew he could do it.

She scrolled down. Below the full- and part-time jobbers was a group of prospects, their candids snapped at wrestling events or copied from social media. There was a menacing ex–All American from Spartanburg, a kid from Durham with orange skin, a Miss Virginia Teen USA contestant squatting the back end of a Chevy Impala. Bonnie's cursor paused over a photo of a young woman stretching on a practice mat. Blue trunks, sleeveless black top. Black hair. She was thin, her core tight like a dancer's. Her legs were solid muscle. The label on the photo: "Pilar Contreras, 17, Charlotte."

Bonnie closed the roster window and read the letter again. When she finished, she placed it in order and dialed Domingo Contreras.

NINE

The three sodium streetlights above the sandlot near Pilar and Dom's apartment attracted swarms of insects. In the mornings, the cars were covered with gunk. On the worst days, birds arrived and ate themselves flightless. Feral cats came by the dozens to harvest the gluttons. Their territorial spats sounded like murder. When the cicadas emerged in late summer, their heavy wings struck the plastic covers around the lights. The noise could be mistaken for gunfire.

Pilar's drab corner of Charlotte was Vegas on fight night, the insect Times Square. She was at the spectacle's center. The tones emanating from the three shining sisters braided together in eerie harmony. Pilar imagined the sound slipping through the city. Though it quickly dropped below the threshold of the human ear, it was a siren song for anything with an exoskeleton—millions of ants, beetles, and moths. They would stretch their tiny bodies before the beauty and comfort of the lights. They'd slither up the poles and cover the bulbs in a squirming cocoon. Those blocked out would search for alternatives, scrambling for headlights, lifting off for the full moon. Eventually, they'd come for the hard fluorescents and the pale blue phone light in Pilar's apartment. She imagined their weight cracking the windows, the bugs spilling in like a mudslide. They'd envelop Pilar, pushing into her wherever they could. With maggots and leeches worming against her, inside and out, she'd find calm. No pain from a hard bump. No fears about what had passed or what was coming. Only pure sensation. Amniotic bliss.

Pilar left Dom in the Civic, which wasn't unusual. His fatigue often glued him to his seat. Other times he needed the space. So did she.

Their room was on the fifth floor. Pilar wasn't tired enough to trust the elevator. The stairwell lights were dead, save a few on the upper floors. With each step up, she thought, she was pulling herself from the muck. One day, she'd reach the roof, where she could fly or jump or be plucked away.

Inside the apartment, she tossed her bag on the floor, kicked through dirty clothes, and dropped onto the futon, her bed from day one in the apartment, when a brother she hardly knew took her from their mom. Pilar didn't remember that night. It was the last of those gaps in her memory. She'd quit her mom's habits cold. Not a drop of the hard stuff. Not a single pill, not even the ones Dom had begged her to take when a woman twice her size dislocated Pilar's shoulder in her first week of sparring.

The fridge looked like storage for road slush. An uncovered bowl of what might've been salad was fuzzy and blue and dripping with condensation. Pilar opened the freezer, found half a pack of spinach, set it to boil on the two-burner stove. With nothing edible in the cabinets, she twisted off the lid of the bucket-sized tub of protein powder. Beneath the stove hood's dim bulb, she peered inside the tub and sifted, looking for worms.

The blender pitcher was cracked, so she rinsed out a plastic cup, added water, and stirred in the powder with a spoon too short to reach the bottom. She glugged down the chalky mixture and stuck her mouth under the faucet. The water tasted slick, as if flavored with vegetable oil.

She drained the spinach and ate while flicking through her phone. Lengthy texts from B said she'd gone in for an interview at McDonald's. The manager was greasy and smelled like onions. He said B would only have to work a month without demerits, and he could bump her to assistant manager.

B wanted to meet Pilar to plan her next move. Pilar texted to say she was dead and had training in the morning. She added a frowny face, then deleted it.

She tapped through her Snaps, most of them photos of animals in cute poses from people she hadn't spoken to since graduation. She tapped the button for her forward-facing camera, and her face filled the screen. There was a raw spot on her left cheekbone where it'd scraped across Sol's mat. What was hopefully a pimple and not an ingrown hair announced itself with a pink splotch. Her crooked tooth had shifted. Her mouth was becoming a problem. She hoped whatever doc got the inevitable job of yanking an incisor cracked by a stiff elbow would throw in a wisdom-teeth extraction for free.

The spinach was gritty and tasted like the pot she'd boiled it in. The geriatric window AC sputtered out more noise than cold. Three mosquito bites, only seconds old, had swelled on her ankle. They always itched like mad down there. Bending over to scratch angered her spine.

Her feeds were brimming with bad jokes and sad sacks. She slurped her remaining spinach and balanced the bowl atop the mound of dirty dishes in the sink. She moved to the bathroom, stuffed a washcloth into the hole where the doorknob should've been, and flicked on the lights. The exhaust fan labored through the cobwebs and rust.

Pilar pulled down her sweats and kicked them beneath the door. She sat on the toilet and clicked open the in-private web browser on her phone.

She had a routine. She needed one, given how little time she had to herself. First were pictures she'd plucked from social media and hidden on an obscure hosting site. Mostly friends of friends who looked through her screen as if they saw what she was doing. Some were dressed for dances. A few older siblings wore tight jeans and club shirts. The wrestlers in the collection weren't wearing much at all—singlets, jean shorts, trunks. Candid shots from the gym.

A few dozen photos in, there was a picture of B. She was on the beach, the Cape Hatteras Lighthouse behind her. She was standing with her ex-boyfriend, each with finger pistols pointing skyward. The boyfriend was raising an eyebrow, and B was flashing a goofy smile.

The boyfriend was wearing board shorts and a baseball cap. B had on a green and blue bikini. Drying seawater curled her hair. Loose strands caught the wind and frizzed into the blue behind her. Pilar never understood why so many girls imitated the stupid *Charlie's Angels* pose until she saw B doing it. She was what every braces-wearing, slump-shouldered girl was going for. What every hot mess thought she was.

The photo reminded Pilar of how absolutely not like B she would've appeared to someone who could see her. Phone in her left hand. The right between her legs. Her elbow resting on the sink countertop. Ratty T-shirt wrinkled and damp.

Pilar closed her cache and streamed a video. She had a few go-tos on a free site, clips of actors who appeared to like each other, that showed everyone's faces. When she was close, she punched in the address to a site specializing in amateur art. She clicked through the browsing tree, through communities dedicated to movie posters, superheroes, and comics, and arrived at the NSFW section.

The drawings hastened and intensified what her imagination could do. Viewing them made sense of her bizarre fascinations, unshared obsessions from childhood. Her clamshell bath toys chomping her boats and plastic fish. The afternoon feeding ants to the creatures buried under the tiny, conical sandpits beneath the evergreen tree at the end of her block. Hours spent kneeling in front of her mom's television, adjusting the rabbit ears to get a clear picture of a nature show. The animals were always somewhere else, always looking for food.

She found a newly posted comic. In the first panel was a monstrous Venus flytrap, its neon-green and violet leaves fitting its alien surroundings. In the next was a human couple, beautiful and naked, immense insect wings sprouting from their backs. Lost in each other, they didn't notice their proximity to the trap's gaping leaves and sharp teeth. The panels depicted their unwitting approach. Closer. Closer.

Pilar heard the apartment door open. Before it crunched a delivery box preventing the knob from punching a hole in the drywall, she'd closed her browser. Labored footsteps shuffled to the kitchen sink. The tap running.

Pilar thrust her lower jaw forward and the guitar-string tension near her collarbone offered some release. She dressed and flushed and ran the sink water. Salmon-colored mildew ringed the drain and faucets.

Paying no mind to the noise, Dom was shoving dishes and pans aside, splashing water on his face. He was shirtless, bruised, and crooked.

"You up?" He uttered the words as if it hurt to open his mouth.

"I think you woke half the building," Pilar said.

"No one ever sleeps in this shithole."

"'Cause of neighbors like you." Pilar reached into the bathroom and tossed her brother one of the tattered towels hanging on the rack. He held it up in thanks and buried his face in it. Once dry, he opened the jug of protein powder.

"You take some of this?" he asked.

"Didn't have much choice."

Dom grabbed an old cottage cheese container off the dish stack, rinsed it, and scooped some powder. "Good. You need to get used to this shit."

The futon needed a bulldozer to clear everything off, so Pilar scouted the sharpest and hardest items and tossed them aside.

"So, what was your problem at Sol's?" she asked.

Dom mixed his drink and shrugged.

She tugged on the end of a weight belt burrowed beneath a cushion. Dom's weight belt. Most of the crap on her bed was his.

"I'm serious. You get moody. Then you ignore it, and I have to wait until it happens again."

Dom slurped and chuckled. "You think I'm bad? Wait."

Pilar emptied her lungs through her nose. "You know, with all your wise-elder bullshit, you're the one who's consistently the biggest pain in my ass."

"I'm the only one who treats you like a wrestler. You can guess what you are to everyone else."

Shut up, Pilar thought. She uncovered a bag of toy axes and threw them on Dom's bed.

"You do realize as good as you look, no one could give a shit, right?" Pilar said. "Drop you into a crowd, and you're one of a hundred muscled dude-bros."

Dom licked the protein accumulating above his lip. Pilar crumpled a stack of junk mail into a box of loose paper and pushed it toward Dom's bed, revealing an outlet. She plugged in her phone and untangled her power cord so it could reach the futon.

"Keep the noise down, or you'll be driving yourself tomorrow," she said.

"You're coming to the Hangar with me. You've got a tryout with Bonnie."

She sat straight up. "What?"

"Three hours before curtain."

Pilar stood, knocking her phone to the floor. "You tell me this the day before? Who am I working with?"

"Aren't you ready?"

"Drop this shit!" Pilar yelled as she shoved Dom's chest. A glop of protein drink splattered on the countertop. "Talk to me like you're my brother for thirty fucking seconds."

Three solid thwacks boomed through the kitchen wall. Muffled Spanish followed. The sounds tensed Dom before he took a breath and spoke, almost in a whisper.

"This was the best I could do. I just got word. It's how Bonnie works. You've got to be ready at a moment's notice."

"Bullshit," Pilar said.

"It's the way it is," Dom replied.

They argued through logistics and parted ways—Dom to the bathroom, Pilar to bed. She stared at the light under the door and her mind tussled between every word for *thank you* and *fuck you* she knew.

What she'd heard about Bonnie Blue spanned the spectrum between genius and crazy. Ceding so much control over her debut felt wrong. Riding the coattails of her middling, journeyman brother didn't scream badass, but a megastar was rarely plucked from obscurity. Most women wrestlers retired in their thirties. She had half the time to get up a steeper ladder than Dom or any man had to climb.

Dom emerged from the bathroom and fell into bed. After a second, he grunted and rolled out, wobbling to the kitchen to switch off the light. Wall to wall, the walk was about the distance between ring ropes.

He muttered good night. Pilar said nothing.

Dom was asleep in seconds. Pilar checked the time on her phone, the glow from the flower on her lock screen bathed her in blue.

She tapped open her browser and reloaded the comic. In one of the middle panels, the flytrap had closed over the man's torso. His body had slipped between the teeth. His wings were bent and punctured. Terrified, he grasped his partner, who tried to free him. In subsequent panels, the flytrap drew him deeper into its pod. The man gasped for air while the woman tore and slashed the trap without noticing the green tendril slowly wrapping around her ankle.

Without viewing the final panels, Pilar listened to the fridge kick on, the footsteps of their upstairs neighbor, and the swarm outside—its drone gifting her comfort in the sweltering night.

TEN

Dom was an early riser. He didn't need an alarm. In his wrestling youth, when his Ohio Valley money distracted from the future's uncertainty, he'd pin an hour of shut-eye before tossing awake, his joints complaining, his skull heavier than iron. Now, though Dom had never looked healthier, his shrunken waistline and newly defined muscles did not erase a decade of abuse. He was only in his mid-twenties, but in wrestling years, he was well into middle age. He'd been redlining his body his entire career.

Though it never stayed for long, sleep always came. At home, in the car, on the concrete in a hidden corner of a venue, fatigue dragged him under. Dom's final conscious thoughts would seep into his dream space. In his nightmares, the Civic's saggy tire turned molten, eating through the vehicle's rims. The bursitis in his elbow swelled and ruptured with worms pouring out like angel hair pasta.

Most mornings, Dom quit sleep before sunrise and ventured out. On mornings like the morning after the Sumter Freedom Fest—when Dom's back ached, when stepping outside was like breathing over a boiling saucepan—Dom folded himself into his gray sweats, limped out the door, and gradually increased his pace until his muscles yielded.

After a mile, the sweat from Dom's pits and chest had merged into a single blotch creeping down his hoodie. He felt so much heavier than when he'd started running, a completely different kind of heavy than he'd been the previous year. He could lose five pounds taking off his sweats, although it would be mostly water, a lie. Running like a high schooler trying to drop a weight class wasn't the healthiest way to log cardio. It was a treat, he told himself. He was allowed to enjoy his new body, to test its limits.

With each stride, the length of Dom's sciatic nerve pulsed as if it were trying to rip itself out of him. The jolts were comforting. They made sense. The botched suplex in Sumter had bruised his tailbone, compressed his spine, irritated discs he'd pushed far beyond their recommended service limits. He had an alchemist's regimen of stretches, icing, and salves to treat himself. He wasn't injured. He could run faster.

Early Sunday morning, Charlotte was silent. Too early for church. Too late for the drunks. Corporate types were high in their towers. Suburbanites were flung far past the beltway in labyrinthine neighborhoods connected by leafy boulevards. In Dom's part of town, he heard red-eyes landing at Douglas and air conditioners struggling in bedroom windows. Pounding pavement, Dom could see himself at the center of it all, even though the downtown lights were far in the distance. How many of the city's best had he beaten awake? The marathoners, the gym rats, even the pro football players—how many could he put down at their own game? For Dom, the city's morning sounds were far louder than the roar of a capacity crowd. He had more excuses than anyone to stay in bed, to take it easy. Yet he was working. Endorphins flushed out the pain. His second mile split was shorter than his first.

When Bonnie Blue had called the previous night, he'd been half asleep in the Civic. It wasn't a conversation. No small talk or negotiation. Bonnie dictated the terms of Pilar's tryout, and he agreed.

Bonnie wanted a match. She didn't buy someone without seeing them in action. When she'd recruited Dom, she was touring the Ohio Valley with a troupe of wrestlers to poach northern talent and make a few bucks along the way. She'd pitted him against a jobber called Tax Man during the bathroom-break slot on the night's card. Tax Man's gut was a beach ball. His arms were hypertensive pythons, muscles squeezing blood vessels through his rawhide. He tiptoed down the ramp wearing a casino visor and yards of ticker tape draped across his shoulders.

Dom had wondered whether Bonnie was playing him for yucks, ultimately deciding to keep his head and show his stuff.

After a few exchanges, it was clear Tax Man could go, and they put on a clinic for the few dozen spectators who weren't purging cheap beer from their bladders. Hack Barlow was a known quantity in the Ohio Valley, and most men with equal or even lesser repute would have thrown a fit over getting booked with this jabroni of the year. Dom swallowed this judgment, showing Bonnie he could be trusted. He could work a match with anyone.

If Bonnie had set a scheme for Pilar's tryout, she'd given no hints. She'd likely caught wind that Pilar had sparred with Blair Jackson, the semiretired former champion, while training with Sol. Dom guessed she'd want a fresh look at his sister with a new opponent. There was Savannah and Sarah Jade. The Lynx. Molly Maple—with whom Dom had shared a few regrettable nights early in his MCCW tenure. Tanya Flex, current MCCW Women's Champion, liked to test newbies. Johnnie May was a possibility. Dom had worked with her in a short run of mixed-tag matches, she the Babe to his Paul Bunyan.

Dom wasn't sure whether to prepare Pilar for a swerve. If Bonnie tried her out against some version of the Tax Man, Dom was confident she could negotiate it professionally. There was a chance she'd stretch Pilar against someone far better than her. Given the timing of her call, Dom was worried the tryout wasn't about Pilar at all. Bonnie would've gotten word of his match at the Freedom Fest. The numbers would dictate her response. What was worth more—the Contreras siblings' future earnings, or the message she could send by kneecapping Pilar's career?

Dom's best move was to wait, make sure Pilar was ready, and chew up the road beneath him. Morning was breaking over his run. Sunday Charlotte remained asleep. Today he was running sore. Tomorrow, he'd be tighter, quicker, his lungs more efficient. His body had miles and miles to go.

"On your left, buddy!"

The voice startled him. He shot right, caught his toe on the curb, and stumbled, narrowly avoiding a headless parking meter, its tip sharp and ready to impale.

"My bad!" the voice said. He was a kid. A high schooler or a college runt. He paused only long enough to make sure Dom hadn't become one with the sidewalk, then continued forward at a gazelle's pace. He was shirtless and stringy with neon-green shorts just long enough to keep him decent.

Once Dom swallowed a howl and overrode his instinct to crumple into the gutter, he stoked his boilers and cranked engines full ahead. After some ugly strides, he surged forward. His target was already fifty yards ahead, bounding efficiently over potholes and street trash. Dom locked on and gave chase.

The kid was built like a radio mast. His calves could be circled by a middle finger and thumb. His number-two buzz was brutally honest about the shape of his head. Dom wanted to feed him a porterhouse and ask him what he was doing with those meager biceps in this part of town. Running only got a man so far. Eventually, when his knees bowed and heels burst, the kid would wish he'd had the guts to turn and fight. He wanted to run this bony motherfucker down, give him a scalpel, and guide a cut across Dom's elbows and hips so the boy could see how much scar tissue looked like cancer. Then he'd take out his wallet to prove there would come a time in the near future when they'd be practically the same age.

First, Dom had to catch him.

The kid floated above the pavement, his rhythm easy and quick. Dom surged forward on his initial burst of energy. He sucked in heavy air and reached deep in his well. A frenzy of strides earned him ground. He lost it when he couldn't maintain the pace. When the kid took a corner generously wide, Dom seethed. He'd surely heard the wrestler's feet slapping the concrete. The back of his head said all he needed to say.

Dom ran until his lungs filled with phlegm. He ran until the kid disappeared into the distance. Then, as if his oil tank had burned dry, Dom's muscles seized, and he ground to a halt.

A regular cup of joe at Yucca Mountain Coffee tasted like Band-Aids. The help was lousy and turned over constantly. The building had once been a church for a group of Catholic charismatics no one could remember appearing or vanishing. The surviving pews were tacked together into creaky booths. The floor tile formed a mosaic of a figure in a nun's habit holding a rose and kneeling in a sunbeam. The tile above the nun's shoulders had been smashed and crudely filled with epoxy. A graffiti-scratched plaque on the wall identified the woman as Rita of Cascia.

As often as Dom heard the term *caffeine junkie* thrown around by people wearing branded workout clothes, Yucca Mountain was the rare joint where the clientele earned the title. There were no smiles among the men and women who'd filed in with the dim sunrise. Their focus could be read with a Geiger counter.

Dom tried to read the message behind these details. The time of day. The average distance between nose and screen. The ubiquity of fishbowl-sized mugs with no trace of a Yucca Mountain logo. The trim, tasteful outfits. No one inside the shop was older than fifty.

They came for the Yucca Mountain Sludge. Dom had discovered the drink right before Pilar moved in. Repairs on the Civic and a dry spell in MCCW had sucked away the last of Dom's Ohio Valley savings. His dire straits presented an opportunity. He'd been considering a cut since it became clear Hack Barlow had reached his peak. He knew cold cranking a diet would be like trying to get a bear to count calories before hibernation. He'd always eaten what he could as quickly as he could to keep his enormous frame moving at the pace the road demanded. His empty cupboards were his push off the starting blocks.

One morning, on a walk to escape the smells of his neighbor's frying sausage, he'd happened upon Yucca Mountain. It was on a corner he'd always assumed vacant. Dom had wedged his girth into a booth and stewed, pretending his glass of water was a milkshake. He'd nearly cracked a tooth when a man sitting next to him shot to his feet. The man flipped his laptop closed and stormed from the shop with the device cocked behind his head as if he wanted to heave it into orbit. When Dom had mustered the will to leave the shop, he'd picked up the mug the man had left to return it to the counter and caught a whiff. The brew smelled like scorched earth and was thicker than oil. The man had been sipping it like warm milk.

One taste was all it took. He thrust the cup under the patchy beard of the guy behind the counter and asked what it was.

"Beats me, man. I'm new."

"Didn't you make this?"

"Does anyone make anything anymore?"

Dom narrowed his eyes, and the barista's smile fell down his throat. The kid was a foot shorter than Dom and half as wide.

"Listen, hoss, I swear. There's a tub of it in back. I just ladle it out."

"What's it cost?"

"Seventy-five dollars."

"No, I mean for a cup."

"Seventy-five dollars."

"Nice rib. Seriously, I'm not in the mood."

"What's wrong with my ribs?" the barista asked, poking around his chest as if he'd sprung a leak.

"Fuck, nothing," Dom said. "Tell me what's in the god-damned coffee."

"Jesus, man. I'm sorry. I literally just started, and already I have to decide whether I'm going to piss you off or leak company secrets."

"Please?" Dom asked, cracking his knuckles.

The barista disappeared and returned with a grocery bag. He discreetly opened it and wafted out the smell—strong enough to wilt nerve endings.

"Some guy came by yesterday and hauled away like fifty pounds of this stuff," the barista whispered. "I think it's the spent grounds they make the drink from. I took a little off the top. I bet if you throw a scoop into ole Mr. Coffee at home, you might not be drinking what they're drinking, but you'll be feeling good, man."

The barista slipped the bag over the counter, and Dom balled it up to fit in his fist. There had been less than a cup of grounds inside.

"Level with me, brother," Dom said. "What kinda secret sauce you brewing here?"

"Bro. On my life. It could be unicorn shit. I have no clue."

MCCW had only tested Dom once, right before his interview with Clout and Bonnie Blue. He'd never heard his results. Tests were a formality for a promoter like Bonnie, who knew on sight what was and wasn't helping Dom. There was always the chance a suit up north would give him a call, someone who had to worry about public relations and stockholders and feds seeking a scandal to redirect the public eye.

Dom thanked the barista, who stuck out his hand. His fingers were like a child's in Dom's grip.

"You big guys are all right," the barista said. "Some of these skinny dudes act like the world has it out for them."

Dom's lip twitched. He flared his nostrils and squeezed the shit out of the barista. The kid squeaked and whimpered.

At home, Dom packed the grounds into a dusty moka pot lifted from his mother's place. The resulting sludge rushed straight to his brain stem, his spine sparking as if clamped between jumper cables. Though Dom was a few credits shy of his older colleagues' pharmacy degrees, he'd experienced the highs of most mainstream stimulants. The sludge was unique. He didn't get the jitters, nor did he feel invincible. He cared a lot less about anything past or future. One Sunday, a few casual slurps led to an afternoon of driving the Civic until it ran out of gas. Another time, he fell into a YouTube hole watching a guy from New Zealand taste test military rations. Dom realized the sludge demanded an experimental approach. Drinking before a workout rendered him acutely interested in a single exercise. He found himself losing track of time and executing set after set of skull crushers, reducing the weight until he could barely lift the bar. He tried drinking after he woke up. Within minutes he was completing the word puzzles and mazes on the box of his budget-brand cereal. He felt deep appreciation for the team of artists who dreamed up these diversions.

Dom determined the best time to drink the stuff was before a match. The jolt through his nervous system created a threshold between performance and the real world, and the enhanced satisfaction with the present helped him shrug off botches. The big moves still hurt, and Dom was thankful. In the long term, substances that dulled or blocked pain were always bad news.

With a squeeze bottle of sludge down his gullet, Dom could sense an added dimension to the pain, as if he were feeling the bass kick of a back bump or the sting of a chop across his chest, the fans just outside the rail. Each strike he absorbed fit neatly into a long history of scrapes, blows, stretches—a lifetime of injuries minor and life-threatening scarred into his tendons, etched into his bones.

Though Dom returned to the shop exactly one week after his first visit, there was a new and visibly green college-aged woman behind the counter. When he asked about the grounds, the barista disappeared through an Employees Only door and emerged with a sour cream container. Dom opened it and reeled as if a claw had yanked out his nose hairs. He asked the barista how much. "On the house," she said.

The ease of obtaining his second batch unnerved Dom. He tossed it into his fridge and considered trashing it. Within a day, opening the fridge was like setting off a stink bomb. He tried entombing the container in Ziploc and doming it in the butter compartment with a box of baking soda. The smell still soaked through.

Eventually, he broke down, brewed a cup, boiled the shit out of it, and let a few drips of the liquid sit on his tongue for a while. Reasonably convinced the drink wouldn't kill him, he downed it through clenched teeth. Soon after, the sludge's familiar effects rolled in.

Every few weeks, Dom's trip up the Mountain was punctuated by a new worker behind the counter. All of them followed the same procedure. Spent grounds. No charge. When Dom asked what was up, they became avoidant and nervous. The most he could extract was that they'd been told explicitly and as a condition of their employment to provide Dom with his ration of grounds, no questions asked. Early on, he was a fugitive—skulking into the shop, taking the goods, disappearing into the morning haze. After a few weeks, picking up his grounds became another errand among many needed to stay in wrestling shape.

So Dom ran, sweat, walked in, and nodded at poor, pixelated Rita lying headless on the floor. The weight started melting. His body felt more efficient, as if less flesh to fix after a rough match allowed what remained to heal faster. The positive feedback set his efforts, and he lost forty pounds over the spring and summer. He took to spending more time in the Yucca Mountain pews, trying to summon his next persona. He'd watch the congregation, all of them clacking keyboards, scrawling notes, and he wondered if this was how it started, if he was on track to becoming one of them.

They were all so alike. Rarely did he see one leave. A balding man with red shoes narrowed his eyes when Dom entered. A tall lady with a wrinkled blouse sat near the counter. Dom could find his way blindfolded to the empty table, his table, where he would smell his grounds, dry off from his run, and think. So rarely had routine been this peaceful—no traffic, no bruises, no slurs from the crowd. The Mountain was a nature preserve, sequestered from his life. He thought this had to be the place where a new character would come to him. The sludge spurred ideas he'd never invent on his own. A scientist in a biohazard suit fighting the contagion. A politician from Appalachian Kentucky. A ruthless mercenary addicted to jelly beans. The characters materialized and dissipated. Dom considered each carefully. In this space, he was content to work at the pace the sludge desired.

After months of tranquility, his calm was disturbed. It happened the morning after the Sumter County Freedom Festival, after he'd been burned by the human stick insect. He entered the shop. Sitting at his table was the Omegle Girl.

She faced the door to the right of Rita's rose. She'd ditched the hoodie for a suit fit for the high offices of the downtown bank towers. She was staring directly at Dom.

Had she not immediately lowered her gaze to her laptop screen, Dom might have fled. Recognizing someone from the internet in three-dimensional space was uncanny. Even planned dates had been unsettling—the oil of his digital life trying to mix with real-world vinegar. Running into a random chat partner, one of a thousand anonymous faces so quickly forgotten, frightened him. She was on his screen, and now she was here, in his seat.

Her averted eyes gave Dom permission to enter the shop. He toed in and remembered this was the first time she'd seen his face. She'd been so insistent in the chat. Dom hadn't given in. She knew him only by his torso.

Behind the counter was a new guy around Dom's age who was so maddeningly crisp, Dom imagined breaking him in two just to hear the snap.

"Good morning, sir," he said, setting down a drink he was making. "The usual?"

Dom grunted, and the barista took the well-worn trip to the back. The Omegle Girl was typing. Every few sentences she'd toss a hand in the air to let gravity pull the shirt cuff off her wrist. He couldn't see what was on her screen.

"Here you are, sir," the returning barista said with a slight bow. "Will you be enjoying anything else this morning?"

Dom shook his head and burrowed the container, a Greek yogurt cup this time, into his hoodie pouch. He scuttled to the accoutrements table and made himself look busy. He couldn't make sense of why she was here, why she was dressed the same as the other patrons. Had she always been a part of the congregation?

"Caitlin?" the barista called. "Your order is ready."

Dom stumbled over himself when the Omegle Girl popped up and rushed to the counter. She seized her drink from the barista.

"I didn't give you a name," she said, sneering.

"I remembered it from your card," the barista said, smiling.

She cracked her knuckles against the countertop before taking her drink to the accoutrements table, an arm's reach away from Dom, who felt every square inch of his frame. She picked through the glass shakers in the spice rack and looked annoyed by the offerings—pulverized eggshells, powdered peanut butter, cayenne pepper, cardamom, pink salt. Frowning, she inspected a thermos cryptically labeled "RAW."

"Any clue what this is?" she asked Dom.

His eyes scanned her top to bottom, searching for a feature to inflect his response. There was always something—a tic or insecurity, a secret poorly concealed. Dom's radar pinged on her clothes. In the suit, she looked older than in the football hoodie. She had a line on her wrist that could've been a scar or a crease worn in by a hair tie. She looked up and caught him staring. A "no" somehow bubbled from his mouth.

"This place is bizarre," she said. She poured a spot of RAW into her palm, stuck her nose in it.

"Woof. Do *not* try that." She took a whiff of peanut butter next and, after a more positive reaction, shook some on top of her drink. "You come here a lot?"

"Kinda," Dom said. "I usually don't hang around for long."

"Is the barista always an oblivious asshole?"

"He's new, I think."

She unwrapped a straw and sank it into her drink. "He read the name off my card. That's totally out-of-bounds, right? There's, like, a million reasons he shouldn't do that."

"Yeah. That's no good," Dom said, thinking of his full name on his ID.

"I'm Mary," she said, extending her hand.

Dom took it and almost said his name. Had he told her his name online? He couldn't remember.

"I'm Hack," he said.

"Hack. Awesome. Great to meet you, Hack."

The girl—Mary, Caitlin, whatever her name was—returned to her pew. Dom slinked into an empty booth at the rear of the shop. His hand slid to his hip, across his sweats' elastic waistband and down his thigh. He wanted his phone. It was instinct to reach for it in situations where there was no right place to look. His pockets were empty.

He cursed himself for not buying one of those armband things. He scratched the table and watched his thumbnail pale and redden with the pressure. He peered across the shop and determined he was the only one without a device. Even the barista was tapping away at a tablet docked on the counter.

She wasn't the first to ask Dom to show more. Her persistence, her youth, her openness—he'd seen it all before. Yet, as he cowered in the booth, he felt exposed, as if she could see every fucked-up thing he'd done.

She downed half her drink, then grew tired of it. She laughed at her laptop, likely the same machine she'd used to chat with him. He saw her attention stray from her screen and land lazily on the shop's front windows. He noticed a few regulars, men and women both, had levered their eyes from their devices to join him in scrutinizing her, as if they'd all read the Omegle chat log.

A man entered the shop, a skinny-fat guy with a V-neck and sculpted bed head. He spotted the Omegle Girl and greeted her professionally, as if arriving for a job interview. He removed a laptop and tablet from a leather carry bag. The girl took the devices and fit them into her own bag. With a tip of her drink, she invited him to sit.

The casualness of the exchange didn't make any sense to Dom. They didn't look like spies or mobsters. Nothing about her presence made sense. Rooted in his seat, Dom struggled to remember if he'd chosen some option to privilege chat partners by proximity. He watched, trying not to be conspicuous. There was little to distinguish them from any two people on a coffee date or business meeting, but Dom could not look away.

ELEVEN

The buzz of the floor's washing machine was a nuclear-attack siren in Pilar's dream. When the bomb detonated, she was under it, an ant before a giant sequoia engulfed in flames. She woke and inhaled sharply. The apartment was dark. Her throat was dry. She scratched her back against the corner of the countertop, squatting to get the blood pumping in her legs. Dom was gone.

How he started his motor on so little sleep mystified her. When she got up, she struggled to push the night off. If she wanted to squeeze in a gym session before her tryout, she had one shot to catch her bus. After two transfers and a hop across the state line, it would drop her close enough to reach Sol's on foot. She threw a bag together and left.

The driver was one of the less sociable ones, so she sat up front, hoping to dissuade riders from talking at her with a pair of conspicuous over-ear headphones she'd taped together from a Goodwill junk bin. She felt guilty for shutting herself off. Most people on the bus were friendly. She'd read Americans were especially guilty of small-talking to strangers as a reflex against boredom. In her experience, older men were the worst offenders. Guys her age snuck glances but rarely tried to engage.

She wished she could signal she meant business without communicating the nature of the business. Men had a tough time getting people to take a pro-wrestling career seriously, and Pilar would never have the credibility her brother's biceps could earn. Though the landscape was changing, and more women in the fighting world got press for their abilities instead of their figures, when Pilar confessed what she was training for, eyes would often drop to her body, looking for signs of what they expected—Trish Stratus's tits, Sable's ass. She hated people focusing on what she had or what she was rather than what she could do.

A wrestler was a storyteller. All of the best storytellers understood people. She wouldn't learn how to win a crowd by cocooning herself against the chatter. How could she ever be comfortable with a microphone in front of thousands if she couldn't deal with the fuckheads on a city bus?

Under her breath, she practiced. She cut promos on the bus driver, the dented pickup cutting them off, a bench with a realtor's face on it.

"You're pathetic," she whispered to the pizza-chain spokesperson grinning from a billboard. "Your pizza tastes like cardboard, and you've been making pizza your whole life. I'm having my first real match today, and I'm already the best wrestler in this company. Let's see how you smile with your teeth kicked down your throat."

The hour was too early for Sol, so Pilar let herself in with a key hidden behind the cap of a dry fire hydrant. The gym was tropical, so she flipped on the fans. After changing, she hopped onto the training platform and tested its bounce. With her tryout looming, she needed only to loosen up, take some easy bumps.

She stretched. Each move weaved balance with tension. Her limbs were most comfortable in motion. Her transitions between exercises were sharp.

Pilar was younger than most when she discovered professional wrestling wasn't quite as it seemed. Dom had smartened her up when he first got into the business, when Pilar was eight years old. He didn't want her to think he fought people for a living. He'd told her it was a game. No one got hurt. She'd sniffed his lie when he came home with black eyes and gashes on his forehead. One night, while they were watching VHS tapes of old matches, Pilar had forced Dom to explain how those injuries happened, why they weren't bad enough to make him quit. Dom had demonstrated how to pull a punch while slapping skin and stomping to mask it. He'd coiled a headlock around Pilar's chin. He could squeeze and squeeze without hurting her.

Dom had introduced Pilar to the squared circle. Its layers of canvas and plywood. Its suspension. He'd leapt high into the air from the ring post, dropping an elbow on a folded gymnastic mat. The crash landing had boomed through the gym like a gunshot. It hurt, he'd explained. Though the ring had some give, its padding was thin. He'd trained his body to absorb the impact. He'd let Pilar pound the mat with her fists and take a run at the ropes. A dark bruise had bloomed on her shoulder.

Pilar hated the F-word, but she hadn't found an alternative. *Entertainment* had been corporatized by the WWE. *Predetermined* better described a fixed boxing match than a pro-wrestling bout. She'd tried *kayfabe*. She hated how everyone pronounced it with two syllables instead of three.

She thought about who her first opponent would be. The promotion paid eight full-time girls. For special events, it hired a dozen semiregulars for extra eye candy. Pilar had sparred with a woman named Orchid who'd been friends with Sol for years. She'd danced a little with Blair Jackson, the former MCCW Women's Champion. She'd never shared the ring with any of MCCW's active wrestlers.

Johnnie May, one of Pilar's favorites, was once a ballet dancer. By her early twenties the tendons in her feet were wrecked. Surgery couldn't clear the scar tissue. Once signed to MCCW, she bulked while maintaining her flexibility. She had a spidery frame—black widow meets tarantula. Pilar dreamed of a body like that. Women wrestlers were always under pressure to emphasize some curves and flatten others. To a certain threshold, muscles meant maturity, mass meant badass. Women like Johnnie May were lusted after, but they were also respected. Until Pilar's metabolism evolved and she earned enough to keep a healthy diet, she'd lack the agency of stronger women. In the meantime, she could be quick. She could play the underdog.

Another wrestler Pilar admired was Tanya Flex, a former fitness model and current MCCW Women's Champion. Easily six feet tall, she dwarfed Pilar. She could make anyone look good, and Pilar longed to face her. If Bonnie wanted a squash, Pilar would sell her heart out. If they wanted more of a match, Pilar could fight clean or dirty, winning over the draw or pitting it against her. She'd wow them any way they wanted.

Pilar pushed out sets of fifty burpees and shoulder rolls. The contact with the mat kindled her skin. She slapped her triceps and soaked in the endorphin rush. She felt as if she could spear a ring post and break it in two.

She took a bump, kicking her legs out from the imaginary strike, landing with her shoulders square to the mat, extending her arms to maximize surface area. Her first bump, taken at a twiggy fifteen, had hit like death. This one energized her, reminded her how strong she'd become. She took another, whipping her neck as if receiving a stiff lariat. A third sent her flipping backward, careening chestfirst to the mat. There was pain, and she didn't care. She transformed it into adrenaline, focus, the drive to take on more.

There were no ropes on Sol's practice mat. The sides opposite and left of what would have been a camera in an MCCW ring were only two feet of padded carpet away from the gym's cinder-block walls. Pilar sprinted to the left-side wall, aiming to leap the carpeted gap and hit the wall feetfirst, flipping off it. She loved to screw around with the move during practice, testing how high she could run up the wall before gravity compelled her to kick away. It was a totally badass kung-fu thing most men were far too bulky to do.

When she left her feet, she knew she'd flubbed it. She was pushing too hard, too fast.

Her legs found the wall in time to keep her from smashing into it. They coiled and misfired, shooting Pilar on the diagonal across the mat's corner. She overrotated and couldn't tuck her head. She struck the seam between the mat and carpet with her neck and the top of her shoulders. Her head snapped and the momentum rolled her knees up and over, into the wall.

Again, there was pain. No more or less real than what she felt before. Though it locked her in place, though she wasn't sure if she'd been bruised or paralyzed, she could think beyond it, and those thoughts caved into a dense point of shame. How cocky. How careless. How fucking dumb.

A minute passed. She caught her breath. Her kneecaps were screaming. She set her jaw and flexed her toes. There was a wave of relief with this. Her spine had escaped damage.

Her neck hadn't. The weight of her head was too much to support. Electric sting shocked her muscles. If a vertebra had cracked, a bone shard could come loose and that would be it. The safest option was to wait for help.

"C'mon," she said.

She tried to sit up, grabbing her knees and wrenching herself vertical. Once her head found stability atop her shoulders, the downward pressure eased the sting. Carefully, she tested it. Only a half turn to the right, nothing to the left.

She slid to the edge of the mat and, as if balancing a stack of books on her head, rose to her feet. She shuffled to a cabinet near Sol's office and cracked a couple of cold packs. Raising her arms brought more pain. She rested her elbows on a dip bar and held the packs against her neck.

She was standing like that when the dock door activated, spilling the line of sunlight beneath it into the gym.

"Hijo de perra," Sol said. "You broke your neck."

"It's not broken," Pilar said.

"Oh! You mean I've had an X-ray machine in here this whole time?"

"Shut up. I'm fine."

"If you were fine, you would've removed yourself from that silly-ass stance before I waltzed in."

Sol clasped Pilar's wrists, set them down on the bar, and put the cold packs aside. Then, he placed a pair of fingertips behind each of Pilar's ears and felt his way down.

"What happened?" he asked.

"Took a bad fall."

Sol frowned and tested Pilar's range of motion. Some left rotation had returned. She could nod a little. When he tilted her head back, she had to swallow a yelp.

"Every wrestler has a punch card," Sol said. "All the bumps she'll ever take are on it. For some, there are a million teensy circles. For others, there's a big one smack in the center. You punch all your holes, you're done. You shouldn't be wasting them by yourself on a Sunday morning."

Pilar sniffed in a wad of mucus. Sol shook the blame from his face and smiled.

"It's probably a bruise. Maybe a strain," he said. "Three weeks' rest would do you good."

"Bonnie's trying me out today."

Pilar could only hold Sol's eyes for a moment. They were so heavy. Her confession seemed to remind Sol of every pitiable thing he'd seen.

"Today," he declared.

"Before the house show at the Hangar," she said. "I wanted to warm up for it."

Sol, washed in the light streaming through the dock, offered her the cold packs. Pilar reached for them. Too far for her neck.

"Fuck," she said, wincing.

Sol held the packs to Pilar's neck until she mustered the strength to raise her arms to rest again on the dip bar.

"Bonnie Blue," Sol said. He dried his hands on a towel hanging on a rack and folded it neatly into place. "When I met her, I remembered her face. The photo outside the courthouse was in all the papers. She buried her entire family. Sounded like a story someone in our biz would dream up."

"I don't know what I was thinking," Pilar said.

"Lotta pressure trying out for Bonnie Blue," Sol said. "Can be hard to convince your body to work how it should."

"What do you mean?" she asked.

Sol dug a flake of skin from the corner of his mouth. "How long were you standing like that?"

"Too long," she said.

"You want to sit? You can rest your arms on the preacher bench."

Pilar said yes, and Sol helped her cross the gym floor. Once she was situated, he unzipped the synthetic he was wearing and sat on an incline bench nearby. Underneath the jacket was a sleeveless compression shirt struck with white and black like Stormtrooper armor. Any other man his age, even those with similar physiques, would've looked ridiculous in it. But retirement-age Sol could've modeled the shirt in a commercial.

"A long time ago old Clout Crawczak brought me in to work muscle for one of his protégés. Easy gig. Look good for the cameras. Take a few bumps. Snarl at the rug rats. One day, the guy I'm valet for misses a taping. Clout gets a call. This guy's wife is in the hospital. She was attacked by bees. A goddamned swarm of bees. She wasn't even allergic. She got stung so many times her heart wasn't ticking right.

"It happened outside their place in Morningside. We all thought it was bullshit, but he had pictures, doctor's bills, police report, everything. This was a legitimate freak bee incident. Pretty good excuse for missing work. Only when he shows up the next week, there's been a change of plans. Me and this guy are going to tease a breakup, and at the next pay-per-view, I'm going over. His fifty-five-year-old, has-been, no-name valet is going to beat his ass.

"This guy is young. He's drawing. I'm entourage. It's clear they're burying him out of spite, and it isn't Clout. Clout's a sonofabitch. He's not a villain."

"It was Bonnie," Pilar said.

"Of course it was. Bonnie Blue had her tongue in Clout's ear from day one. So I tell her I'm not doing this. Find someone else to pull your heartless shit. And as sure as we're sitting here, Bonnie sits me down and tells me yes. Yes, I am. Then she pulls this file. It's got everything. My whole history. Every gold star I'd won in every pea-puddle promotion I'd worked. She's got all these projections and surveys and outlines, pages and pages of storylines. My chase for the title. Feuds with everybody. My reign as champion. I'd been pigeonholed as a heel my entire career, and I was posting highway speeds. Didn't matter. Bonnie was certain. I was the guy."

"You never won the title," Pilar said.

"Blew out my knee before the next taping," Sol said, swinging his left leg. "And MCCW blew right past me. Never wrestled for them again."

Pilar balanced a cold pack on the peak of the preacher bench and tried to squeeze blood into her pale fingers. "She didn't wait for you to heal? All the work she did to convince you to take the top spot—she threw it away?"

"A lot of work to us, maybe," Sol said.

"Did she bury the guy you were muscling for?"

"My knee bought him a few extra paychecks, then she canned him."

Pilar brought the other cold pack down. The exposed skin burned.

"Whelp. Nice pep talk, coach."

She clutched the sides of the bench and pulled herself up. She needed to get out of the gym. At home she could soak in the bath and maybe scald the hurt away. Or she could stay on the bus, riding until they forced her off. She'd let the bumps flop her head whichever way it wanted to go.

"Sit down," Sol said. He strode to her and squatted. His torso was so long, she still had to raise her eyes to him.

"I've watched you grow," he said. "I've watched you fight."

His face was like a sandstone cliff. His breath was sour.

"How bad do you want this?" he asked.

"Sol, I—"

"You want it or not?"

"Yes," she said. "It's all I've ever wanted."

The hard edges of Sol's cheeks and chin softened. He nodded like a waiter who'd been reamed for poor service. Pilar was worried she'd said the wrong thing. He retrieved a plastic bag from his office. Inside, two types of pills—one chalky and green, the other white and glossy. Eight in total.

"Don't ask what they are. Don't look them up. Take one of each now and then again about an hour before your tryout. Do not let anyone see you take them. Do not try to get more."

"I've taken shit before," Pilar said.

"Yep," Sol said. He gave her a water bottle.

Pilar waited for him to say more. They both knew there was no need.

Trying not to bend her neck, she fished out two pills, popped them in, and drank.

Sol closed the gym and took Pilar to Charlotte. His Volvo was clean. Like Dom, he drove with the seat slid back. The crown of his bald head brushed the canopy. The radio blared with the nasal voices of two guys arguing about *Star Wars*. It didn't annoy Pilar as much as it should have.

She tried to sense the drugs' effects. Her neck was better, though her full range of motion hadn't returned. She suspected a muscle relaxer, maybe a painkiller. She'd seen what pills could do to a wrestler. Half the MCCW roster was a cautionary tale. A small blessing from her childhood was that Pilar could never deny the monster that claimed her mom also lurked inside her. She understood Sol's caution, though she couldn't help imagining the difference in the exchange had she been one of his male students.

Her phone buzzed with a text from B. One word: "mcnuggets?"

Now there's a fucking addiction, Pilar thought. She checked the time. She hadn't planned on leaving the gym so soon and certainly wasn't counting on a door-to-door commute. B could help her avoid counting down the minutes alone in the apartment, drinking lumpy protein, and stressing about her neck.

Pilar typed, "Fine. Ur buying... And picking me up."

None of her frequently used emojis were right for the occasion, so she scrolled right, struck by how many tiny drawings flew past, how many were utterly useless. Two kinds of paper clips, black-and-white squares, a bunch of clocks.

When they rolled up to her apartment building, Sol gripped the wheel and swallowed. "Come down tomorrow. Take a cab if you want. I'll pay for it."

"I'll be fine," Pilar said.

"You will," he said. "And that means we're probably not going to see each other as often."

Pilar considered this, and a note from B buzzed in—"that u in that car?" Sol wore a strained smile and was blinking more than usual. He wasn't ready to leave. Pilar felt the tilt of their relationship. What had she ever given this man? He'd sweat with her, bled with her, never asked for anything. He opened his gym like a home.

She tried to smile. "What if I need a valet someday?"

"Find someone younger," Sol said. "And cheaper."

Pilar couldn't say goodbye. Her training had demanded collision after collision. The most entangled maneuvers between them were nothing like this. Pilar shrugged and held up a fist. Rather than bumping, Sol wrapped it in his giant mitts and held on.

TWELVE

B's old Geo Tracker was waiting curbside. On her way over, Pilar peeked into the apartment lot and saw the Civic. She thought about jetting upstairs to tell Dom her plans. B laid on the horn.

Pilar raised two middle fingers and kept them up until she opened the passenger door.

"Let's go!" B said, bouncing in her seat. "Nugs! Nugs! Nugs! Nugs!"

"You know what's in those? Grease and pink slime."

"Ugh, my name is Pilar Contreras," B screeched. "Can I have, uh, some apple slices, a parfait—just the granola—and, um, a salad, dressing on the side."

"More like a bottle of water and nose plugs."

B unbuckled and nearly jumped on Pilar to embrace her. "Where have you been all my life?"

The definition in B's shoulders was remarkable, noticeably more toned than the last time they were together. Pilar had no evidence her friend had ever stepped foot in a gym.

"I'm carny trash now," Pilar said. "I go from one sideshow to the next."

B cranked the air-conditioning and chunked the Tracker into gear. Her face was bronze, and her arms weren't far behind. Pilar's skin loved the sun. She could tan in minutes. B was several shades darker.

"So who was that?" B asked.

"My trainer," Pilar said. "I've got my first match tonight."

"No shit! Congrats, girl! I'm totally coming to watch."

"I don't think it's a public thing."

"It's good I'm not the public then," B said, her eyebrows leaping.

The McDonald's wasn't far, an exit down the freeway between a rusty Ford dealership and a dollar store. It had yet to get the facelift given to other joints in town. Inside, Pilar ordered a cheeseburger and water. They took a booth with the vines of a dusty plant licking the seat back. A few tables over, two guys wearing far too many layers for the weather were staring at Pilar in the way men only stared when they were in pairs. The one who would be facing away, chinstrap goatee and acne craters dotting his ruddy face, did a 180 in his chair to watch her sit.

"Is this where you interviewed?" Pilar asked, trying to ignore them.

Oblivious to the men, B opened five different dipping sauces. She dunked a nugget and poked at her phone. "Huh?" she said.

"You said you talked to a guy, and he was gonna bump you to assistant manager."

"Oh," B said without looking up. "No, he's closer to my side of town. This place is gross."

Pilar picked up her burger. A pickle slice stuck out like roadkill tongue. She took a bite, and as her teeth sank through the bun and meat, Pilar thought she heard the burger let out a squeak.

B swiped her phone screen with a flourish, raised her head with a smile, and stuffed the smile with another McNugget.

"I've got a live one," B said. "Good chin. Nice pecs. And he's got a screenplay."

"A screenplay?"

"Yeah! They film a lot of stuff in North Carolina. Like that new show with the dome, the whole town trapped under it? Anyway, he said he might have a part for me once it gets produced."

Pilar barely had to chew her burger. Slicked with oil, the bite slid down. Chinstrap, who kept staring, raised his brow and took a sip of soda.

"You gonna finish that?" B said, pointing to Pilar's burger. Her cheeks were packed with nugget meat.

"We just got here," Pilar said.

B snorted. "I'm joking. I thought you'd be packing it in. You know, for energy."

Pilar's skin got hot as if she were blushing.

"So you're actually fighting someone tonight," B said. "You nervous?"

"Not really," Pilar said, resisting the impulse to rub her neck.

"Awesome. You should totally go ham with a folding chair. Those have to be fake, right?"

"No. They're usually cheap, metal chairs. We'll probably keep to chain wrestling, maybe some low spots."

"English, please."

"Basic stuff. Nothing fancy." Pilar labored through another bite of burger.

"You gonna wear face paint?"

"Wasn't planning on it."

"Then what's your character gonna be?"

Pilar swallowed a burp. "They just want to see what I can do."

"You want to perform, yeah? Isn't that the point? Like, you're an insane postal worker and you're clobbering the girl who thinks she's a werewolf."

"It's not so cartoony anymore. Usually wrestlers are themselves, only more intense."

"Isn't your brother a killer lumberjack?"

"Can we not talk about this?"

"Sounds like you're nervous."

"Maybe you're making me nervous."

"This is going to help. All the best actors step into their characters. When you get out there, you can't be scared little P anymore. You gotta be somebody else."

Pilar's midsection tightened. A wave of fatigue rolled over her. It was getting hard to listen. B sounded like Sol was feeding her lines. For a second, Pilar's brain considered the possibility. She watched Chinstrap lick his lips and wink. It was so over-the-top, even for a creep in a McDonald's. He snickered to his friend and slapped his hand.

"I've got it," B said. "We do you up all pale and shit, straighten your hair, get a nightgown from Goodwill. You could be one of those scary Japanese girls."

"I'm not Japanese," Pilar said.

"You have the whole ethnic thing going. Imagine all the lights go out, then you appear in the center of the stage. Freaky!"

"That's not wrestling," Pilar said. Her eyes fluttered, and she had to rub them to clear her vision.

"Wrestling isn't wrestling," B said. "It's theater, or worse. They're gonna strut you out there like a piece of meat, and they're all gonna jerk it to ya. You're better than that, P."

Chinstrap knocked his friend on the shoulder and gestured to the women. The friend gobbled fries and stood, and the two headed over. Pilar's gut churned. Her hot skin flashed to cold. The gooseflesh on her arms was sharp enough to grate cheese. Her mouth filled with saliva.

The room pitched down, and Chinstrap followed its slope to them. He opened with a knock on the top of their booth. "You know," he said, "if you two ladies were vegetables—"

"I'm gonna be sick," Pilar said. She shot to her feet and hurried to the restroom.

The soul withering that usually accompanied the vomit wasn't there. In its absence, Pilar hovered over the bowl and considered its contents. Since the food had been so new in her stomach, she could identify the components—meat, onions, pickles. She realized her neck was bearing the full weight of her head with no pain. Her range of motion was limited only by a mild stiffness. Sol's cocktail was working.

"P, honey, oh my god!" B was behind her in the stall. She raised her hands and, finding her friend's hair already gathered in a ponytail, gave her head a pat.

A knock on the bathroom door. "You okay in there?" a male voice said.

"Yup, just puking my guts out," Pilar said.

She smiled. Not one complaint from her neck. B's face shrank into itself.

Pilar made a gulping noise the men were sure to hear. "Oh no," she said. "Round two!"

She tore a stretch of toilet paper to wipe her mouth, and without leaning into the bowl, feigned a tremendous retch, punctuated with coughs and sputtering.

Muffled obscenities preceded another knock. "Hey, should we call someone?"

"No, no, she's fine," B yelled as Pilar heaved.

"My intestines!" Pilar screamed. She hammered the stall and stifled laughter.

"The fuck are you doing?" B whispered.

Though it had started with something real, like a wrestling

bump, the discomfort was temporary. It was a release. In its wake, Pilar could show her friend the fun part—the reaction, the sell. It was less performance than a celebration.

Pilar bellowed, clutching her stomach, grinning like a child. B's face began to change, her confusion drowning in the absurdity. She let out an exaggerated choke.

"B! Help me!"

"There's—ugh—so much of it!" B said through hiccups. "I can't—I can't—"

"The manager's coming over," said the voice outside the bathroom.

B slammed herself against the trash can. "Oh god. It's the nuggets!"

"I told you! I told you!"

B convulsed, burped, and spat saliva on the tile. "It's like my stomach's been firebombed!"

"That's really bad!" Pilar screamed.

They burst from the restroom and hopped into B's Geo. They couldn't stop laughing. They got the horn from an F-150 when B failed to see the light change. They took the wrong on-ramp to the highway and had to loop around. Pilar wondered how bad it would be if they cranked the music, rolled down the windows, and kept driving.

"Did you see their faces?" B asked, bouncing in her seat.

"Fuckers were ready to stick their fists down their throats," Pilar said.

"Did you hear the line he was about to use? 'If you girls were vegetables, you'd be cute-cumbers.' "

Pilar stamped the foot well and struggled to breathe. "At least we're vegan!"

"I'm going to eat you," B said in a deep voice. "I'm going to dip you in my milky ranch, little cute-cumber."

"Excuse me, ladies?" Pilar followed. "I'd give anything to pickle you."

"I'm going to peel your skin and chop you into my salad, baby."

"We are delicious!" Pilar yelled.

B's hair was flying everywhere, catching the sun, shining a brilliant gold. "Seriously," Pilar said. "Look at us. I'd eat us. We're a goddamned delicacy."

B stuck her tongue out of a grin a mile wide. "You puke and rally like Rocky. Half your guts are in the toilet and you're like, time to clown these motherfuckers! I mean, what kicked in there?"

Pilar bit her lower lip. "You wanna know?"

B weaved through the postlunch traffic, cut off a merging semi. Pilar wasn't sure what highway they were on, and she didn't much care as she reached in the back seat for her duffel.

THIRTEEN

For a man with so much muscle, Dom was patient. The world didn't expect it. Mechanics spoke to him plainly. Doctors slipped into his exam room minutes after the nurses left. Children got quiet in his presence.

Late one night when Pilar was in middle school, he'd staked out his mother's house. It was winter, freakishly cold, the air damp, refusing to dry despite plunging temperatures. He couldn't afford to waste gas running his car, so he sat and shivered. Every quarter hour, he cracked a window to clear the fog.

When his mother arrived, he took a video with his cell phone, caught her struggling to parallel park. She staggered to her apartment. His sister followed, her gait similarly clumsy. She tripped on a crack in the sidewalk and reached out to their mother to catch herself. Her hand landed on their mother's shoulder, and she knocked it off as if she were swatting an insect.

Dom kept recording until the pair was out of sight. In a creased notebook he used to track his workouts, he wrote the date, time, how long he'd waited, his mother's condition. It wasn't easy to strip a child from a parent. A judge would sooner run from the courtroom than sign him custody rights. He kept the journal and saved the evidence. He thought the record would will him to action. If he couldn't bear speaking with his mother, he'd confront her in his notes. One day he'd turn too many pages.

Before leaving, Dom walked around the building to Pilar's bedroom window. The light was on, and she was asleep—no sheets, pillows, or blankets. She tugged her legs to her chest, the movement jostling the knit cap from her head. Her hair was greasy and knotted.

His mother came in the room then and rummaged through the nightstand drawer. Dom ducked, then quickly stood, angry his instinct was to hide. She had on a blue sweater with its sleeves rolled up, her bony wrists crossed with veins. Her hands looked splotched with purple and blue. She'd bitten her nails below her fingertips and the surrounding skin had cracked. She removed a lighter from the drawer and shook it next to her ear. She looked at the window Dom was peering through.

He stood his ground, unsure whether the light inside concealed him. As she lit her cigarette, her eyes looked hazy. They stared a hole into Dom.

Dom had trained for quickness in the ring. His persona was a lumbering monster. To achieve the effect, he needed only to move a step behind his opponents. Most casual fans didn't appreciate wrestlers' speed. When his patience wore thin, Dom was swift to strike.

Dom couldn't leave the café—not while she was there.

He ran the odds. What if his memory was failing him, and he'd mistaken this composed professional for a teenager trolling from her bedroom? What if she'd hacked the system, found out his info? What if she was after him?

The paranoia disturbed him, and the hypocrisy made him sick. He was the one who couldn't stop staring. He was the one lurking in the pews, watching her talk over her laptop screen with the man. They were speaking quietly. Dom caught a word here and there. She was writing. The man would receive his devices in two weeks. The Yucca Mountain hype was real. Her drink was delicious.

Dom reached for his phone and remembered again he didn't have it. Instead, he touched the yogurt container holding the grounds. He opened it and took a whiff. There was no way to brew it, so he pinched off a little and packed it between his lip and gums.

His taste buds sounded the alarm. His mouth flushed with saliva. He tried to keep a poker face. To his surprise, he was worried about the regulars seeing him squirm.

His jaw cramped. The moisture activated the grounds, and Dom imagined the plug burning through his incisors. Bitter, so bitter, it tasted sweet and then bitter again.

"Hey, you're Hack Barlow!" The shout made Dom jump. A hand flew at his nose.

"Oh, jeez. Sorry to scare you!" The hand was attached to a man wearing pressed khakis and a shirt with a wild-eyed lion on it. He was gangly and breathing too hard.

"I can't believe this. Hack Barlow, the Timber Terror! You're a legend, man. Your work rate has been off the charts. And got-damn, you look amazing in person. The cameras don't do you justice. Can I ask you a few questions?"

"Cup," Dom said.

"Excuse me, Mr. Barlow?"

"I need a cup," Dom said, inky spittle dripping down his beard.

"Oh, of course. What an honor!" The man downed his drink like a shot and handed Dom its paper cup.

"I got some napkins, too," the man said.

Dom spit into the cup. His salivary glands relaxed as his body remembered the substance. He touched the bulge in his lip and noticed how much liquid his beard had absorbed.

"My friends and I have a bet," the man continued. "Last year, at SlaughterFest, you and Doctor Graveyard worked a thirty-minute broadway. You got some serious color, like point eight oh Mutas, and they say you gigged after Doc walloped you with that golf club. I think you went hardway. I mean, crimson like that had to be a shoot, right?"

Dom blinked as if his eyelids were pulling weight. "What?"

"Or what about Forsaken IV—you ate the pin for The Carolinian Dragon Bruce Knuckles. Strong showing there, five stars for sure. One of the best *enzuigiri* ever. And that moonsault? From a competitor of your stature? I was marking out. I thought for sure they'd put you over. Anyway, I bet you've seen ole Brucey making waves in New Japan as B. K. Brown. How does it feel to have dropped a match to a possible champion of a major international promotion? Do you and Dragon correspond?"

"Look, brother," Dom said. He scratched the edge of the table, filled his lungs and let the air out slowly. When he opened his eyes, he first saw the fan, smiling expectantly. Then he saw the Omegle Girl's pew. It was empty.

Dom nearly tipped the table launching to his feet. His spit cup spilled. A dribble of black muck oozed out. Dom scrambled to the door, and the patrons paid him little mind save the man in the red shoes, who gave a harrumph as Dom sprinted from the café onto the street.

"Slow down, Speedy!" a man yelled from a sedan driving past. Dom scanned the cars. He looked for the Omegle Girl's long hair, her sharp suit. A figure caught his eye, and he cut hard to change course. The force slung the yogurt container from his pouch. It hit the pavement and burst open.

Dom collapsed, scraping his knees. He tried to salvage the grounds. He was drooling a river onto the pavement. His head swiveled up the street and down, to the coffee shop. She wasn't there.

The container was only half full when he took off. He ran south, where a few cars were stopped at a light. Maybe one of them was her. He could memorize the plates, look up her address, her last name.

He reached the stopped vehicles as the light turned green. The first burned rubber. All Dom saw was the back of the driver's head—possibly female, possibly hers. He gasped and pumped his legs. The car easily outpaced him. He scanned for a license plate. The rectangular indent where it would've hung was empty. In the rear window was a temporary plate angled so the characters were lost in the reflection of the sky.

The friction in Dom's hips and knees ground him to a stop. Cars pulled into the oncoming lane to pass him, creating as much cushion as possible. He cracked a smile. On two occasions he'd chosen to keep his distance, yet losing sight of her brought him shame. It was dense enough to burrow a fresh wormhole into the network connecting every disgraceful moment of his life. His grin fell as decades of humiliation burst into the present. He thought of the skinny runner, probably halfway across town. Dom would sooner catch the kid than he'd get the Omegle Girl or anyone to slow down and see him.

He kicked a parking meter hard and square with his middle toes. The pain registered solidly, so he did it again. It was good, he thought. He deserved it.

"What's wrong, Speedy?" a voice called. "Cheese too fast for you?"

The catcalling sedan pulled next to Dom. It was a Civic like his, and for a panicked second Dom thought it *was* his until he glimpsed its unmodified back seat. The passenger leaned on an unimpressive forearm as he barked through the window.

"We're foolin' you, buddy," the man said. "Everything okay? You were hauling ass."

The car was nicer than his—brighter paint, alloy wheels, phone mount plugged into the cigarette lighter.

"Nobody kicks it like that unless they're running from the cops or a woman," the driver said. "Can we call somebody for ya, holmes?"

The men were older than Dom, though not by much. The plug of grounds in his lip was dissolving into slurry thick enough to choke. He clutched the parking meter for leverage and spat a tar-black wad under the passenger's window.

The passenger gaped at him, then leaned out and saw the goop drip down the side panel.

"Fuckin' A," the passenger said.

"Did he spit on you?" the driver asked.

"He spit on the car," the passenger said, eyes darting between Dom and the slime.

The passenger opened the door. He was short, and he tried to ignore it as he anchored himself before the wrestler who now appeared much larger than he had from inside the car.

Dom recognized the men. He'd never seen them before, but he knew their type. The passenger flared his tough-guy face, a scowl that had likely won him a few showdowns against guys who'd never had their noses broken.

"What's your name?" Dom asked.

"You don't need to know my name," the passenger said. He got closer. If he'd been wearing a ball cap, he would've had to turn it around. His eyes were level with the roots of Dom's neck.

"You're a bully," the passenger said. "And like every bully, you're scared. You're an insignificant, unidentifiable speck in a vast and uncaring universe. You're pathetic."

The driver spun out of the car and tried to help the passenger retreat. He stood his ground.

"Well, you don't smell too good," Dom said.

The struggle between passenger and driver paused, and all was quiet for a moment.

"Excuse me?" the passenger said.

"You stink," Dom replied.

The passenger waited, then blinked. "That's it?"

The driver poked his nose behind his friend's ear.

"I think you smell okay," he said.

Dom struck so quickly that a crack shot down the street as if his fist had sparked a sonic boom. The blow's victim was neither the men nor the sound barrier, but the parking meter he'd kicked earlier. His knuckles burst through the dial's glass, the metal arc of the meter's crown crunching under the force. The men clutched their heads, cowering like a pair of spooked cobras. There was the gore of Dom's fist, speckled with glass, drops of blood draining between his fingers. What truly drove them to flee was seeing the bend in the meter's steel pole. Though it was only an inch or two off-center, they couldn't make sense of it. No one could be so strong without suspending the rules of reality. It was as close as either man had come to seeing a ghost.

FOURTEEN

The calluses on Dom's knuckles had protected him. The cuts from the glass were slight. He hit them with a double dose of peroxide and ointment. He slapped on a pre-snipped bandage designed to curl around joints. His medicine cabinet would've looked right at home behind pharmacy glass. More than once Dom had retrieved a designer cocktail from this well-stocked cache then balked into his empty, frostbitten refrigerator. It had been tough enough to keep it stocked before Pilar.

Dom started a scalding shower. The bathroom was instantly a cloud, the exhaust fan making a racket but moving little air. The water hit midway down his back. When his neck was sore, he had to kneel to rinse his hair.

The punch to the meter had been showy. He wondered if he would've been so brash without the sludge in his lip. A smarter

Dom would've walked away. Hand injuries were dangerous for wrestlers. The tiny bones and ligaments never healed well. Weakness led to accidents. Accidents birthed injuries. Dom had neither the charisma nor the fame to keep afloat if he earned a reputation as an unsafe worker.

The shower loosened him, so it wasn't too much of a struggle to dress. He put on a T-shirt and a pair of track pants, tying the drawstring so they'd stay up. He stretched out in bed and shot a text to Pilar. He wanted to call her, ask how she'd been preparing for the tryout. But he held off, recalling their exchange the previous night. Every time she blew up at him, Dom second-guessed himself. The hardest part was that he really had no idea who she was. Sister, student, traveling partner—she was all of these. She was none.

Without him, Pilar never would have heard of professional wrestling. Without him, she could've fallen prey to some far worse pursuit. He was her best shot at dodging exploitation, at protecting her body. Dom was no star, but he had honed a skill. If she wanted to learn, teaching her was the right thing.

Being reunited with his phone brought him comfort. He opened the web browser and realized where his fingers wanted to take him. He flicked the browser closed and brought up his dating profile. One "Hi" from Sumter hadn't responded. Another had spammed him with an ad for a dick pill. His last Sumter match said there was a surprise waiting for him on her Instagram account. Dom pulled her profile up and saw its latest post—a shot of her from the neck down. She was wearing a white tank top with a black bra underneath. A domino peeked out from under a strap.

"Jesus," Dom said, exiting the app without following her.

He had two new matches from the Charlotte area—a twenty-nine-year-old from Midtown with a Cam Newton jersey and Panthers-blue streaks in her hair, and a twenty-four-year-old from Lockwood in a pirate hat who was holding a toddler in a parrot onesie. He sent a "hello" to each of them.

One of his long-term conversations had replied—a woman from North Charleston. Dom could scroll up their chat window for a good minute without reaching the beginning. He never went into much detail about his past. He gave his honest opinion on movies, eateries, Carolina beaches, sex positions. He listened and offered support. Whenever the conversation grew too serious, she'd sense Dom's reticence and let off the gas. After a few weeks of this, Dom asked her what she'd thought about his failure to escalate. Her reply said she was willing to play the long game and enjoy his company in the meantime. This woman could've befriended an attractive, well-adjusted partner in real life with a quarter of the effort she'd spent on him. The image of her hunched over her phone, wondering if this would be the day Dom would consent to meet, made him consider unmatching out of mercy. But he kept on. Maybe this was the kind of relationship they were both looking for. Maybe this was the only way they could connect.

She'd asked if he'd ever been camping in the Appalachians. He said he'd been up and over. There'd never been enough people to keep him in the mountains. He didn't return a question.

He opened Omegle. He paired with an empty chair and energy-drink can.

"Bleak," Dom said to no one. He closed the app.

Unsure where to go next, he stared at his lock screen. His background image was an MCCW promo shot of Hack Barlow at his heaviest. His beard was knotted and wild. He held an axe the photographer had spurted with ketchup. The image was hideous, which was why Dom had put it on his screen. Each day, it was the first and last thing he saw.

He was going to do it eventually, so he decided to quit pretending. He pulled up his browser and started searching for Charlotte-area high schools with sport teams named the Warriors.

He found two—a Christian academy and Weddington High, a public school in Union County, south of the beltway. The blue on their "W" emblem was the same color as the "Warrior Football" on the Omegle Girl's sweatshirt.

It didn't take many clicks for Dom to feel like a predator. He tossed his phone on the bed and got up to stare at the dishes, stacked so high he had to partially dismantle the pile to fit a glass under the faucet. The water sloshed in his stomach. He mixed a double-thick protein shake. Its aftertaste was like soft serve that had sat in the machine too long.

On the edge of the bed, he retrieved his phone and pulled up Facebook, found the page for Weddington High School, liked it, and scrolled through its 2,200 followers.

Dom heard voices in the hallway outside the apartment, then a key turning in the lock. He flicked the list away before the door opened.

"Wait, is your brother home?" a woman's voice said.

"Hey, Dom!" Pilar said, leading with her hip through the doorway. She glanced behind her with a flat smile as the second woman entered. She was Pilar's age and looked strong, though not in the places a wrestler would be.

"Goddamnit, P," the woman said. "You should've let me change."

"Take a look." Pilar swept her arms around, stuck out her tongue in disgust. "We clearly don't give a shit."

"Hi. I'm B," the woman said, waving at Dom. "Sorry your sister picked today to introduce us. I swear it's barbecue sauce."

A dark red stain streaked down her white sleeveless shirt.

"Nice to meet you," Dom said.

"You're bleeding," B said, pointing to the oozing scabs on Dom's knuckles.

"You trip over a curb again?" Pilar asked. "I swear, B. The bigger they are, the harder they fall. He's living proof."

"I got angry and punched a parking meter," Dom said.

"Right," Pilar said. "Next time make sure you break it open and take some quarters."

"Three dollars will get you twenty McNuggets right now," B said.

Pilar cackled. B looked completely serious.

"Is your name actually B?" Dom said. "Like the letter?"

Pilar snapped her jaw shut and shot him a look.

"Oh my god. What's she told you about me?" B said.

"Not a lot, actually," Dom said, peeking over to Pilar. "She's been secretive. I thought 'B' was an alias."

B laughed. "Your sis wants me all to herself, doesn't she? B is short for the horror show of a name my parents gave me. And no, I'm not going to tell you."

Pilar reached for the top shelf and knocked off a shaker bottle. It bounced noisily and rolled behind the trash bin. "Shit. Where are they?" she said.

"You have any mysterious nicknames?" B said as Dom opened his mouth.

"No, just Dom."

"Domingo's his real name, and he hates it," Pilar said. "He hates all his names."

Now it was Dom's turn to fire off a look.

"Domingo!" B said. "It means Sunday, right? No es un mal nombre. Es el mejor día de la semana."

Dom nodded and squeezed out a smile. Brushing past B, he moved to his sister, now half under the bed. Items slid out beside her—a mildewed gym bag, a worn pair of cross-trainers, wrinkled copies of *Muscle & Fitness*.

"What are you doing?" Dom asked.

"It's a surprise—chill out," Pilar said.

B licked the corner of her mouth. "¿Qué quiere decir, nombres? ¿Eh, Domingo? ¿Cuántos nombres tienes?"

"Dejálo ya, que le vas a cabrear," Pilar said.

"¿Qué?" B said, raising an eye at Dom. "What did she say? I only got to Spanish III."

Dom chewed his tongue. He sensed the exact point it would bleed if he bit hard enough.

"He doesn't know Spanish," Pilar said.

B stared at him as if she'd missed the punch line. Dom didn't elaborate, and before B could ask a follow-up, Pilar had pulled herself from under the bed. She smacked the ground and kicked the bed's spindly frame.

"Four hundred fucking square feet, and I can't find a god-damned—*oh shit, yes!*"

Hidden under laundry was a plastic bag. Pilar ripped it open and a dozen plush axes sprang out. Cheering, she snatched one up and seized B by the neck.

"Dom, look at this!" she shouted, hacking at the stain on B's shirt. "This is exactly what you need!"

B sold the whacks, contorting her face and laughing.

"This is how you get out of your gimmick," Pilar said. "She's your prisoner. Kong and Fay Wray. You come out with her, say like you caught her and have been doing culty things at your cabin or whatever. The faces are all honorable and shit and try to free her. Then you beat 'em up, beat 'em up, until you've torn through the whole roster. Then you set up an altar in the middle of the ring for a sacrifice—like you're going to eat her heart and absorb her youth."

"So good!" B said. "If you find an old-school butcher, I'd bet he'd be so desperate for your business he'd give you a pig heart or whatever for free."

"No, bitch, he doesn't get your heart!" Pilar said, sliding her hand up to B's mouth and letting her friend toss it away. "You profess your love. You get down on your knees and say you want to serve him. You've been his prisoner for so long. He's your world now, or at least that's what he thinks."

Dom tugged on his beard until it hurt. One of the plush axes on the floor had already been kicked around enough to coat it with dust and crumbs. He wondered if Pilar had seen *King Kong* or only heard of it.

Pilar stood, orchestrating the scene with her axe, pointing to Dom, then to B. "You're about to cleave her, right? Then you're overcome with emotion. Think Savage-Elizabeth, Wres-tleMania VII, but, like, with a lumberjack. This expression of true, undying love worms into your empty soul. You let your guard down. You're rethinking your murderous ways. You wonder what life would be not as predator and prey, but as friends, partners."

"Lovers," B said, raising an eyebrow at Dom.

"Sure," Pilar said. "As this is going through your head, as the crowd sees you soften, at the perfect moment—"

"Axe to the neck!" B shouted.

"Yes!" Pilar cried. She jumped on the bed, clasped both of her friend's wrists and shook. "Dom, seriously. She's got eyes for this shit."

Pilar leapt up and swung the axe at Dom's neck. He stopped it and caught her gaze.

"What's up with you?" he asked.

Pilar ripped the axe into her chest. "Hear me out. Rubber axe slices your throat. You're rigged with blood packs, tubing under your flannel, the whole deal. You hit the deck, writhing in a pool of red, and she stands over you. Beauty killed the beast."

"Badass," B said.

"You kill your character in ring," Pilar said. "This gives you closure, a clean break. Then you cut the bird's nest off your face and re-debut as whoever you want. B becomes my manager, and I get the rub from her epic lumberjack slaughter."

"How about we concentrate on step one?" Dom said. "You remember? Tonight?"

"Do I remember?" Pilar said. "Did you remember to get my eye stuff?"

"You didn't ask me to get anything," Dom said.

"Shitballs, Dom! I need my eye stuff."

"I've got you covered," B said. She dug into her bag for a smaller bag with clear sides jammed with makeup.

"Score!" Pilar said. "Already earning your keep."

The girls shut themselves in the bathroom. Without a knob, the door stayed open a crack. Their talk faded into the exhaust fan's belabored whirring.

There was plenty to review with Pilar—her move set, what holds would cover a botch, how to work naturally to Bonnie's side of the ring. She and B were acting silly. That was the last thing she wanted to be in the ring. No one took giddiness seriously, especially not from a seventeen-year-old.

Wedging his head between the dishes and the kitchen faucet, Dom drank to flush the sludge from his system. The oily water reminded Dom of the juice collecting in a pack of old lunchmeat. To clear his mind, he tried to clean. There were so many places to start that he quickly gave up. He opened the browser on his phone, returning to the Weddington High School page.

He clicked around. Athletics, awards, faculty bios. He lingered on the French club page and smiled at the clip art—the Moulin Rouge, a bicyclist transporting a bag of baguettes, a cartoon Frenchman kissing the Eiffel Tower. The tower was bent as if trying to uproot itself and run away.

B emerged from the bathroom. After failing to seal the door shut, she shrugged at Dom and went rifling through her bag.

"Anything good?" she asked.

"We'll see," Dom said, summoning a fresh browser window.

"What model is it?"

"My phone?" Dom flipped it and saw only the back of his cheap case. "Not a good one."

B continued rummaging until it was conspicuous why she hadn't dumped out the bag's contents.

"Can I see it?" she asked.

Dom made a face, and B followed up. "Don't worry. I won't creep."

He gave it to her and saw her thumb was about as thick as his pinky finger. She twirled the phone, popped it out of its case, closed an eye and inspected the power jack.

"Wow," she said. "You weren't kidding. I have no idea what brand this is."

"It works, and it came with cheap data. Whatever keeps us in cat videos."

"Is that what you've been looking at?" She returned the phone, keeping her fingers around it longer than necessary.

Dom couldn't help rubbernecking to the stain running down her torso.

She asked for his number, and Dom provided it. After she punched in his info, she snapped a photo without asking. "For my records," she said.

"You said you wouldn't creep," Dom said.

"Candids work best. They're how people look in real life."

Dom shrugged and took a retaliatory picture with his phone. B crossed her eyes and twisted her face.

"Too slow," she said. "Tell me about this wrestling stadium we're going to."

"It's not a stadium."

"P said they steampunked an old airplane hangar."

"More like the set of a high school play."

B compared two sticks of mascara. Dom couldn't see a difference between them. She lowered her voice, quiet enough that Pilar wouldn't hear it.

"Lemme ask you something. I've got a little baby roll going right now, and I think it'd be super awesome if I could keep it alive while P thrashes some bitch. I peeked at your wares. You wouldn't miss a couple, would ya?"

She let her eyes fade up as if she expected Dom to play hard to get. For a moment he had no response. He'd let worries about Pilar's drug abuse diffuse over time. The problem had always been their mother. Removing her had bleached his sister's past and gifted a clean future. There'd been no evidence of backsliding, but with Dom's minimal guidance and imperfect example, what could he expect? And really, what could he do to prevent a teenager in his charge from getting whatever she wanted? Locking down his pharmacy or its satellite dispensary in the Civic would've signaled a lack of trust. Practically every wrestler in MCCW had a hookup, as did their girlfriends and trainers. One of his former tag partners got human growth hormone from his mail carrier. There was no avoiding it.

"What did you two take?" he asked.

"You two? Have you met Pilar? She's straight as a razor's edge. This is *our* secret."

B stretched her neck and squeezed her elbows together. Her closeness kindled a sense of uncomfortable nostalgia. As if to say please, she nudged him in the ribs.

"Little sore from the match yesterday," he said, holding his side.

"Sure," B replied. "My bad."

Dom scratched his chin. Flakes of skin fluttered from his beard. If he kept scratching, more would fall, and if he tore at his chin, he could make it snow. Tiny pieces of himself would collect on his shirt, in B's hair, on the floor between them. He'd never scratched for long enough to exhaust his supply. He had enough flakes to fill the room and bury them both.

"Well, you got it or not?" Pilar called, opening the bathroom door and bending her neck around it.

"Can't find it," B said. "We can use mascara instead. Little fakeup trick."

Before she closed the door, Pilar stared at Dom with her tongue pressed hard into her cheek. She'd evened her face. Her skin wasn't prone to breakouts so she hadn't needed much. She gulped her words and went back to work.

Dom watched the sliver of light escaping the bathroom. The girls laughed. Every so often one of them would cast a shadow across the doorframe, breaking the yellow beam. Pilar's bag was on the floor next to the bed. Dom rifled through it, not careful about what he disturbed. Wrestling gear. Water bottle. Pads. Gloves. Strips of fabric torn from old spandex pants. Wrestling boots. A battered copy of Chris Jericho's first book. Tape. Piece of cardboard covered with illegible scribbles. Shower stuff. An empty Ziploc bag.

It had no odor, crumbs, or residue. No evidence of anything. Still, Dom's mind filled it with the worst he could imagine.

"How does it work?" B asked.

"How does what work?" Pilar replied.

"Wrestling. Like, you're not really hurting each other. You've planned who wins. How do you know what to do? Do you memorize all the moves?"

Pilar had cleared a spot to stretch. She spread her legs and lowered her torso until her chest touched the apartment floor.

"No. They're not choreographed. It's hard to explain."

Dom's thumb was tiring from scouring Weddington's website. From the pep band's home page, he found a corner of the site devoted to the color guard—schedules, routines, history, and a ton of photos. Girls waved giant, green flags. There were close-ups, candids, shots taken from the football field bleachers.

"C'mon," B said. "If your brother can do it, it can't be rocket science."

Dom raised his eyes to her, and she mirrored his glance.

"It's more instinct than math," Pilar said.

"Are there canned matches?" B asked. "Like, if you meet the girl you're wrestling backstage, you'd ask her if she wants to do Match C, ending number four or whatever."

"Look, you know jazz, right?"

B frowned. "Do *you* know jazz?"

While the girls digressed into an argument about how hipster it was to appreciate lounge music, Dom found a series of Weddington color-guard group photos, one for each school year. Fifteen to twenty girls were sitting in rows on the school's front steps. They wore uniforms, brightly colored Lycra, better than most MCCW wrestlers' ring wear. In another photo they had airy, green dresses with sequined accents. In this picture, top row, second from the right, she was waiting. Dom zoomed in. The blurry image and artifacts didn't obscure her. She was younger, thinner in the face—the Omegle Girl.

The photo had no caption. None of the girls were named. Dom reverse searched the image—no results. Trying another angle, he identified the teacher coaching the color guard in the faculty directory and plugged her name into Facebook. He found her and entered her friend list. There were 1,122 people. He started scrolling.

"We talk before the match," Pilar continued. "Especially if there's a spot we need to hit. We also call stuff in the ring. Whenever you see a wrestler covering her mouth or leaning close to her opponent's ear, we're talking. We do a lot on the fly. There's rhythm to the match. You let your body move to the beat."

"So you can read each other's minds?" B said.

"You don't have to think about it," Pilar said. "It's putting one foot in front of the other."

Lots of the teacher's friends had private profiles. All Dom saw of those were names. Names of hypocrites, Dom thought. How many of them had done exactly what he was doing?

"You sound like an expert," B said. "I thought this was your first match."

"I've sparred a lot," Pilar said. "With Dom, coaches, a dozen others."

"Are you sure this won't be different?"

The words caught in Pilar's throat. She glanced at Dom, and her neck popped loud enough for everyone to hear. She winced and cried out.

"Are you okay?" Dom asked.

"Are you okay?" Pilar mimicked. "You look like you've been watching decapitation videos again."

"It's probably nothing," B said. "C'mere."

B reached for her friend's shoulders to give her a massage. Pilar dodged.

"I don't know where those hands have been," Pilar said, forcing a smile.

"Uh, like an inch from your face doing your makeup," B said.

Pilar shrugged and moved to the other side of the room, rotating her head without further popping. She flipped into a handstand next to the wall.

Dom put his phone on the counter and whispered to B.

"Go down to my car—blue Civic, mattress in the back seat— and look in the glove box for an ice pack."

B's eyes and mouth shrank. "A mattress?"

"It'll make sense when you see it," Dom said, winking.

The gesture bolted her in place, which made Dom wonder if people still winked at each other. He tried again to make sure she saw it.

"What's wrong with your eye?" Pilar called out.

"Fucking hell," Dom said. He seized B by the arm and led her to the door.

"I don't understand why you can't—"

"It's a red and blue pack in the glove box," Dom said, offering the key. He took her over the threshold into the hallway and whispered. "And a red bottle with a white cap. Best I can do."

The offer clicked and B puckered a silent "oh!" She returned an exaggerated wink. Dom waited until she reached the end of the hall before he closed the door.

"The fuck was that?" Pilar asked.

"You first," Dom said. "I got her out of here. Now be honest with me."

Pilar had arched her spine to form a capital-letter D with the wall.

"You've been on edge since you got here," he said. "And your neck."

"Just nerves. Nerves and tightness. I'm good."

"Were you two together all day?"

Pilar flattened into a plank against the wall. Her ability to contort into such straightness was more impressive than her most spectacular bend.

"I went to Sol's this morning."

"Get any advice?"

"Yeah. He said I might be fucked."

"What? Why?"

"He was joking. Trying to keep me loose."

She pirouetted so she was facing the wall, then walked her hands forward until her body became a hypotenuse. Dom noticed she held her head askance as if viewing the floor from her angle was puzzling.

"Is that why you're hanging with B?" Dom asked. "Staying loose?"

"The less I worry the better."

"She shouldn't come to the tryout," Dom said.

Pilar climbed out of her stretch.

"You want me to focus. Trust me. She'll help."

"I don't want you playing babysitter. This is your time."

"It is my time," she said. "And whether I nail this or fuck it up, I want to share it with who's been there for me. B's my best friend."

Dom waited for a punch line. When one didn't come, he nodded. He imagined siblings who'd grown up together getting to know each other over the years. He'd never have this with Pilar. It was easy to forget until moments like these snatched him by the chin and rubbed his face in the distance between them. What really turned the screw was the thought that if there was any person in Dom's life who could be called his best friend, it was Pilar.

"You're so good at what you do, I think you forget," Pilar said. "It's hard to enjoy stuff without people to share it with."

He reached for her shoulder, then hesitated, suspicious of her neck.

"I wish you could've seen me before you came here," he said. "You don't know how happy you've made me now that I get to share so much with you."

She smiled and stepped to the wall. She stretched high and brought her palms to the floor.

"You need a girlfriend, bro."

Dom sighed and picked up his phone. Pilar finished her warm-up. B returned, brushing by Dom closer than she needed to. She cracked the ice pack and pressed it onto her friend's shoulder. Pilar let it happen.

The girls took to the futon. B scrolled Pilar through a scandalous conversation with another fast-food worker. Dom reopened Facebook, where he was fed an ad.

It was drone footage of the early-morning desert. The camera tilted to reveal the sun breaking over a wide ridge. The motion was butter smooth until, suddenly, it wasn't. The picture tumbled and cut, as if the drone had been shot from the sky. Text faded in over black. "Discover the secrets. Sip the seepage. Yucca Mountain Coffee."

Dom had never seen an ad for the shop. It didn't seem like the kind of place that would advertise on social media. He clicked, but before the page loaded, he remembered what he was supposed to be doing. He flicked away from the Yucca Mountain website and got busy with the 1,122 faces on the teacher's friend list, searching one profile at a time.

After a few minutes he'd hardly put a dent in the As. Then he remembered the name the barista had called for the Omegle Girl's coffee drink—Kaitlin, or was it Mary? The barista had said two names as if she'd given him the wrong one at first. He flew down to the Ms but didn't find her. He picked through the Kaitlins, Katies, Kates—nothing. He scrolled to the Cs and saw one Caitlin and two Caties. Caitlin was an older woman in her fifties. One Catie had her profile hidden. Dom opened the third profile and saw an effigy, some thirty feet high, of a man with a black moustache. He was wearing a tan poncho with a colorful sash and a sombrero the size of a hot tub. Dom knew the statue well. In his time on the road, he'd driven by its cartoon smile and leering eyes countless times. It was one of the mascots for South of the Border, a tourist trap off I-95 on the state line between North and South Carolina. Below the man, minuscule in comparison, was a woman wearing sunglasses. Her arms were extended, gesturing to the carnival rides and Mexican-themed buildings as if she couldn't believe she was there.

Dom sucked a long breath. Pilar was laughing at B's phone. B held the ice pack on the slope of Pilar's neck. She poked her tongue between her teeth and winked at Dom.

Dom let it fly past him and concentrated on the photo. It was the only picture available in the profile. He zoomed in as far as possible, the edges of the figure crystallizing into pixels. He couldn't tell for sure if it was her.

Pilar had been fifteen when Dom took her. His run in the Ohio Valley had sputtered, and he'd scuttled south in search of a new flame. His income had stabilized. Guilt had held him by the neck.

In those first months in Charlotte, he'd internalized the vast expanse he'd put between him and his sister. Sometimes his road trips north would crest in the Virginias, and he'd drive through the night over the mountains, across the Mason-Dixon, only to sit on the curb outside his mother's house and stare for hours at the black windows, hoping someone would wake, give him a sign of life.

Those thousands of miles and painfully lonely nights had offered Dom a new perspective. He'd gathered his evidence. The longer Pilar lived under his mother's roof, the less time she would have. He hadn't been patient. He'd been a coward.

The night it'd happened, a light was on. His mother was sleeping on the couch. Dom put his nose to the glass. The TV was smashed, the floor a carpet of debris. A lit cigarette rested between his mother's fingers. The couch's arm had a mark—not a circular scorch from the tip of the cigarette, but a wide, black burn. She'd done this before. The couch had caught fire.

He'd broken through a window, found Pilar passed out on the mattress in her bedroom. He carried her from the house. Outside, she stirred in his arms, clinging to him as if starved for human contact. He coaxed her onto the bed in the Civic.

His mother staggered out. Her approach was reluctant, as if an invisible rope encircled her and was tugging her toward him.

"¿Qué estás haciendo?" she asked.

"Hey, Ma," Dom responded.

"Where are you taking her?"

"Charlotte."

"Did you ask her?"

"Ma, she's out. I had to carry her."

"And you're not waiting until she wakes up. You're stealing her."

"You think we haven't talked about this?" Dom said, his voice cracking. He tried to wedge past, and she held her ground. She smelled like a wrestler on her third match of the night. "What do you have?" she said. "I've seen your stunts, those brutes you fight. You think that's a better place for her?"

"She'll have a chance," Dom repeated. "I'm giving her a choice."

"Choice? This is kidnapping."

She wouldn't yield. Had Dom been patient, he would've talked. He would've moved home and gotten her help. He would've faced the childhood he'd tried so hard to forget. He would've tended his poisoned roots rather than cutting himself free.

Instead, he moved her. He grabbed his mother's shirt and pushed her away. It was easy. She weighed almost nothing.

FIFTEEN

Bonnie Blue stood in the ring. Beyond the glare of the lights were a thousand empty chairs, some on the floor, some stacked on risers. From its core, the Hangar looked like the remains of an ancient amphitheater—cannibalized, incomplete.

Bonnie appreciated the ring for how forthcoming it was with its lies. The mat bounced with every step. Underneath, a microphone amplified the bodies striking the canvas. Their slaps, stomps, and flat-back bumps boomed through the speakers like a bass drum and rattled the Hangar's old steel. The ring steps, diamond-plate aluminum, were hollow. Bonnie could lift two at a time.

The one secret the ring concealed was its simplicity. Metal. Plywood. Canvas. Twine. Hemp rope. Vinyl. There were no springs. No gadgets. No magic. A skilled crew could pack it down in fifteen minutes. It was a fine stage, though far from perfect. A ring could stand on an airstrip, on a carnival midway, or in the center of Boston Garden. Each place had limitations. As an icon of a business with a long history, it carried the weight of a million brilliant and atrocious performances. Not even Bonnie could change what people saw in a wrestling ring. But she could give them a different show.

The MCCW machine was revving up for the evening's production. Techs were stringing wires to the announce table. Vendors were setting up their booths. The Hangar had few native facilities—a small office and two-head restroom had been framed into a box hugging the arching wall near the middle of the building. The stage had been a Clout project. The wrestlers entered through a square proscenium rigged with smoke and lights, opening to a platform about forty feet long. Clout had ordered stagehands to weld scrap from the Queen City Skyport's remaining structures into decorative accents.

Pilar was due within the hour for her demonstration, and Bonnie had arranged for five-year MCCW veteran Johnnie May to be her opponent. Of MCCW's women wrestlers, Johnnie May was third in merchandise sales, barely enough to claim rack space at the T-shirt booth. She was as much an in-ring technician as MCCW's most proficient men. Her finisher, the Johnnie Driver, her homegrown spin on the brainbuster, was one of the most spectacular and dangerous signature moves in the company.

Wrestlers who worked with MCCW more than a few months eventually laid claim to an area in the Hangar they could make their own. Johnnie May had staked out a nook under the risers, stringing a hammock between two support columns. She had a few milk crates with weights and a station for assembling garments she sold online. A six-foot-long Rhode Island state flag provided privacy. A tarp, sticky from spilled nachos and beer, was bungeed taut above.

Bonnie announced her approach, and Johnnie May, already in makeup and her coral-green ring gear, toed a crate to her boss's feet and invited her to sit.

"How was Myrtle?" Bonnie asked, disregarding the offer.

"Too cold for this time of year," Johnnie May said. She kicked her leg up to a column and stretched until knee kissed collarbone.

"Loathsome city," Bonnie said. "In August it's worse than Death Valley."

"Sounds like you've never been to Death Valley."

"I've been everywhere."

"Then you know there's no way Myrtle Beach gets that hot. It's got an entire ocean evaporating next to it."

Bonnie frowned and noted a bowl of what might've been canned spaghetti molding under the hammock.

"There are different kinds of heat," she said. "Dry heat. Humid heat. Then there's Myrtle heat. It's discomfort you can only experience when the sun reflects off all those pastel beach shops and stacks of hotel windows. When the sea breeze carries tourist stink."

"You picked a hell of a job if you can't stand how people smell."

Bonnie bit her tongue into the pit of a molar and snapped out the vacuum.

"I have a favor to ask you," she said.

"Lotta favors recently," Johnnie May replied.

"The girl tonight? I need you to make sure you don't scare her off."

Johnnie May snorted.

"She's promising," Bonnie said. "If she has to be eased in, that's what we'll do."

Like a crane lowering its boom, Johnnie May brought her leg down, shook it out.

"Soft," she said.

"No," Bonnie said, her voice prickling. "You work her like you would anyone here. Nothing more. Understand?"

The wrestler sent up her other leg. As she put weight into the stretch, Bonnie could hear her hip crackling.

"Need pressure to make a diamond," Johnnie May said.

"I don't need a diamond," Bonnie said, her face reddening. She swung herself behind Johnnie May and thrust her nose in the wrestler's face.

"I've been exceedingly lenient with how you've treated new hires, and I know more about the motivations behind your behavior than your shrink would if you had the humility to visit one. You will take caution in ensuring Ms. Contreras can showcase her abilities, and you will do everything in your power to protect her from harm. Do you understand?"

Johnnie May rocked onto the tips of her toes like a ballerina and returned to earth. Bonnie noted how smoothly she lowered herself. It was remarkable a person could have that much strength in her feet.

"I think the cruelest thing someone could do to you is try to be your friend," Johnnie May said.

Bonnie took a breath, and her cheeks palled to their usual color.

"And the worst someone could do to you is let you languish in the midcard—too low to get noticed, too high to quit."

There was a trace of a smirk on Johnnie May's lips. "Your girl will be fine," she said.

Bonnie told Johnnie May to be sure of it and so ensured the wrestler would push Contreras harder than necessary. At best, the sister Contreras would falter, earning Bonnie a heavy bargaining chip. At worst, she would put on a spectacular show, opening a credible path to the top of the MCCW roster. As a fulcrum for negotiation with her brother, this was almost as good.

As Bonnie took her leave, Clout's warning from his recently discovered letter stuck in her mind. She imagined the young man Clout had mourned, the hubris of a professional wrestler moonlighting as a professional wrestler, the flash from his physical peak to perfect, terminal stillness.

She passed Gorilla Trotsky taping his ankles on a trainer's bench.

"I heard about Clout," Gorilla said. "I'm really sorry."

Bonnie paused, giving his condolences the space they demanded. She thanked him, and Gorilla bowed his head. For the first time, Bonnie felt the spark of soul beneath this well-practiced exchange. Clout's passing was remarkable in that he'd died in a conventional way. For a moment, Bonnie saw the chasm between her former partner, fading to black in old age, and the kid in his letter, knocked into oblivion before he was old enough to rent a car.

"Do you think we're pushing too hard?" Bonnie asked.

"What do you mean?" Gorilla said.

"I watched Clout when I was little," Bonnie said. "He was so fast. His strikes were lightning. You watch that old footage today, they're moving in slow motion. Do you ever think about that acceleration? About where it leads?"

"It's natural," Gorilla said. "Competitive business. Sink or swim. You gotta keep moving."

"That's what Clout said when we began our partnership," Bonnie said.

Gorilla stood from the bench and tested his ankles. The wraps were tight and symmetrical, not an inch of tape wasted.

"He knew," the wrestler said. "And you know, it's natural to get spooked, but let me tell ya, speed up or slow down, it all leads to the same place. The question is, how do you wanna get there?"

"That's wise," Bonnie said. "Thank you."

Gorilla bowed again and smiled with every one of his stained teeth.

"You're welcome. Please remember your sage veteran when booking the top of the card."

Many times Pilar had driven through the chain-link gate, over the pothole-laden drive to the Hangar's tarmac parking lot. Before, as a spectator, it had been easy to ignore the property's eccentricities. Of all the places to root for an indie wrestling show, someone had chosen this one, in the middle of a concrete desert. There must've been better options—old theaters, warehouses closer to downtown, spaces better connected to the city's infrastructure, designed to hold crowds, not aircraft.

"It's straight out of *Mad Max*," B said. She scrambled from the Civic. She was wearing one of Pilar's T-shirts, free of sauce stains. Even though Pilar had been training for months, and her friend had eaten two dozen McNuggets like a snack, the shirt fit B better.

The evening sun leaked through holes in the overcast. B stuck out her arms like wings and jogged down the runway, her voice mimicking the drone of a passing plane. She crashed into Pilar and wrapped her arms around her.

"You're gonna knock 'em dead!" she said, lifting Pilar and swinging her. When she returned to her feet, Pilar held on. Her neck did not complain. Did she even have a neck?

"Hey," B said. "You got this. Nice and loose, yeah?"

"Yeah," Pilar said.

Even with the threat of rain, the Hangar's giant doors were open to keep its temperature bearable. The three walked through, Dom taking the lead and nodding to the yellow-shirted security guy manning the entry gate.

Pilar saw the ring glowing under the lights as if God had cast it in a ray of sunshine. Men in black jeans and T-shirts fiddled with a control board. Wrestlers mulled about, stretching, chatting, sharing a smoke beyond the grooves in the floor upon which the Hangar's doors tracked open and shut.

Backstage, they ran into Gorilla Trotsky. He stood next to a trainer's table and was rocking on his heels, testing the tape job on his ankles.

"Dommy!" Gorilla said, and after a pause, "Ladies!"

"Where's the boss?" Dom asked. He leaned forward as if to keep walking, then stopped when Gorilla elbowed past him.

"Hello, my beautiful *devotchkas*. My name is Gorilla. Please tell me you're not biting the heels of this arm-breaking torino."

After a bow, Gorilla flipped a lewd salute to Dom and puffed out his chest. The women took his hand.

"Hang on. You're the sister, aren't you? Pilar Contreras, toast of the Iberian! Future MCCW Women's Champion. About time your brother pried his head out his ass and brought you backstage. You were in the seats yesterday, yeah?"

"I was," Pilar said. "I loved your sell with the ring bell. The sound really made it."

"My forehead makes that noise if you hit it hard enough," Gorilla said, his laugh becoming a cough that trumpeted like a goose honk. "Ugh. Apologies. I mean to say you have a good eye for theatrics, unlike your hot-headed brother. Between the ropes, he's money. Between the ears? Not so much."

"Have you seen Bonnie?" Dom asked again.

Pilar noticed B wince at the name. Gorilla's booming laugh centered her attention. The wrestler knocked his skull with his knuckles and pointed a sausage-sized thumb at Dom. "Check out Speedy over here. Yesterday you hit the road faster than a two-wheeled tricycle, and today you—"

Dom seized a fist full of Gorilla's shirt and pushed him back a step. Dom bared his teeth in a false smile.

"Bonnie?" Dom asked.

Gorilla shot a look at Pilar. "Yeah, sure," he said. "She was headed to her office last I saw."

"Good," Dom said, motioning for the ladies to follow his march.

B was quick to comply. Pilar stayed behind.

"Sorry about him," she told Gorilla.

He gave her a thin smile. "Piece of advice. Family is family, but business is business. Keep an eye on him."

When Pilar caught up, Dom was rapping on a door of what looked like the projection booth in her high school gymnasium. Instead of being on top of the bleachers, it was buried underneath its web of steel lattice.

"What a Creepy McCreeperson," B whispered.

"Gorilla?" Pilar said.

"Ugh, ladies," B said in a bad accent. "In old country, women love shoulder hair!"

"He doesn't talk like that," Pilar said.

"Communism not bad. Rohypnol subsidized!" B laughed like Santa Claus and bent it into a dramatic cough. "Apologies, ladies. In my youth, I toiled in the caviar mines."

A woman opened the door to the booth. She was taller than Pilar, with gray hair pulled tight in a ponytail. She looked like a mom of one of the kids in school, one who did intense yoga.

"The Contreras family," she said. "Come in."

"Hello," Dom replied with unsettling deference. "This is Pilar."

"Un placer conocerla, Pilar. Soy Bonnie."

"Hola," Pilar said. "¿Así que hablas español?"

"Un poco. Ojalá tuviera más oportunidades de practicarlo."

"Sí, a mí me pasa lo mismo," Pilar said, gesturing to her brother.

"Puede que un día él la sorprenda," Bonnie said.

Dom managed a pained grin. Bonnie's attention slid to B.

"And who are you?" Bonnie asked warmly.

"Pilar's friend," B said.

"She can wait outside," Dom said.

Bonnie ignored the interjection. "What's your name?"

"Same as yours," B responded.

"Your name is Bonnie?"

"You can call me B."

Bonnie paused. Dom looked as if he'd smelled smoke. Pilar was confused. B had never told anyone her real name. She'd somehow gotten their school to change it on all the class rosters.

And Bonnie wasn't a bad name at all. Pilar had always assumed it was some nineteenth-century mouthful—Bertha, Brunhilda. "If this is a super-secret wrestling meeting, I can wait outside," B said.

"Please, join us," Bonnie said, blinking away her silence. "It's nice you're here to support your friend."

Bonnie ushered B inside with a touch to her lower back. B widened her eyes and took shelter behind Pilar. Bonnie shut the door and offered the group a beverage from the room's minifridge. The girls waved her away. Dom asked for water.

"Awkward," B whispered.

Pilar shrugged. In her mind's eye, Bonnie Blue had been an unstoppable force. Everything Pilar had heard solidified her image as an icon, a person whose peers were meeting on the top floors of Charlotte's banking towers. This Bonnie wore sneakers and khakis. She worked in a dim, half-furnished office. A rectangular imprint on the drab carpet and the ghosts of picture frames on the wall told Pilar that Bonnie had been sharing the space.

"Thank you for coming on short notice," Bonnie said, taking a seat. "I hope you understand the pace of our industry necessitates a degree of improvisation. Two days ago, I would've told you our problem was an overloaded roster. Now we have a vacancy we're eager to fill with someone of your caliber."

Pilar noticed Bonnie was mostly looking at Dom.

"Pilar is thrilled for this opportunity," he said.

"Absolutely," B said. "So thrilled, she can scarcely speak for herself."

Dom shifted as if a cottonmouth was sleeping in his lap. Pilar questioned whether the cocktail of pills she'd taken was dulling her to a joke or test she had to pass.

"I've paired you with Johnnie May for your demonstration," Bonnie said. "I'm sure you're familiar with her work. Top-notch competitor. Student of the business. One of our best."

"She's a pro," Pilar said.

"Be sure to tell her," Bonnie said. "She loves flattery."

"Can't wait to meet her," Pilar said. Another silence followed. She waited for Bonnie to take the lead. The woman seemed content watching her.

"So why me?" Pilar asked. A flame sparked in her chest as she said it. "I'm sure you have plenty of prospects. What do you expect from me?"

Bonnie pressed her fingertips together and glanced at Dom, who was struggling not to choke on his water. "I've been following your progress. Your family has a reputation, and I don't have trouble getting those who've seen you to talk. I hear you have potential."

"Thank you," she said. "If that's true, why are you wedging in this tryout so close to tonight's event?"

"C'mon," Dom croaked. "The schedule is booked solid."

"Why not bring me here on a quiet day so you can give me your full attention? If I'm so great, why did you wait until last night to call Dom? Why didn't you call me? You could've gotten my number."

"She's right," B chimed in. "I got this McDonald's interview because my mom knew the manager. They called me directly. This same joint routinely misspells stuff on their sign."

"How many prospects do you treat this way?" Pilar asked. "You've never spoken to me. I had half a mind thinking you were the Wizard of Oz—that I'd be wrestling for some woman behind a curtain."

Pilar hadn't thought she'd shoot so hard. The satisfying tang of her words was all the assurance she needed.

"You've shown a strong hand, Ms. Contreras," Bonnie said, her voice the same as before. "I hope you'll forgive me for keeping mine close to the chest a little longer."

She stood and saw the sweat on Dom's forehead.

"I'll fetch Johnnie May. Don't worry, Domingo. So far, so good."

Bonnie smiled to the three of them and closed the door behind her.

"What a weirdo," B said.

"You don't know who the fuck you're talking to," Dom said. He cracked a second water bottle and gulped between shouts. "You think this hardball bullshit means anything to Bonnie Blue? She'll eat you alive."

"P's being real with her," B said.

Dom paced and wiped his brow. "She's always going to be five steps ahead of you."

"What is it with you and this lady?" B asked.

Dom threw up his arms, flinging water from the bottle across the floor, couch, and wall.

"Oh, great," Dom said. He fell to his knees and dabbed at the water with his shirt.

"I'm sure everyone says she's a bitch," B continued. "I bet all the knuckle draggers around here feel their balls shrink whenever she signs their paychecks."

Dom grunted and kept sopping, sweat dripping off his face as he went. Pilar lugged him up.

"It's okay," she said. "If she's the leader everyone says she is, she'll respect that I'm speaking truth to power."

"Good," Dom said. "Glad to hear you figured her out in all of five minutes. No need to be cautious with the woman holding the keys to your whole career."

Pilar bristled. "Don't pretend she's my only shot because this is as far as you've gotten."

"I forgot," Dom said. "You're hot shit. The prodigy. Can't even buy cigarettes, and already you've got the biggest head in the business."

"At least it's too big to fit up my boss's ass."

Dom drained the water bottle and threw it on the ground.

"Then handle this yourself. Pitch the idea you and your creative genius came up with and see how far you get. And when you start coming down from whatever shit you took to kill the pain in your neck, don't come crying to me."

Pilar clenched a fist and started toward him. B got an arm around her waist before she could build momentum.

"Don't," B said.

Such an intimate touch should've distracted her, but her hate was so pure, it had mass. She wanted to shoot it from her eyes.

Dom tore from the room and slammed the door. Pilar leaned against B and seethed.

"He can tell we're buzzing," Pilar said.

"Don't let his paranoia rub off on you," B said.

"I don't understand why he's still a million miles away."

"He's scared," B said, her breath on Pilar's ear.

"Coward," Pilar said.

"He's your brother. He's freaked out because he isn't sure how you'll get through a place like this. And be honest—you're figuring it out, too. If you stick around, you can teach him, and that's the best way to teach yourself."

Pilar let some of her anger escape in a long breath. "I guess that makes sense," she said.

"It does? Awesome! Maybe I *will* be your manager. I'll be in your corner crunching a cigar. 'Eat lightning, kid! Crap thunder! Go for the ribs!' "

"And I'll be like, 'Bonnie, ya gotta cut me!' "

"Ugh, don't say it!" B shuddered. "That was a spur-of-the-moment tactic and is not to be mentioned again."

"I think it worked," Pilar said. "She was rattled, and all I hear about this lady is what a mastermind she is."

"People like her plan too much. You need to be flexible. And P, lemme tell ya. I can be your wild card. Bonnie thinks she's got you figured out? In comes your secret weapon."

"Fuck Dom," Pilar said. "You're the one talking me through this. You're the one sticking around even though he has more at stake. I need you."

"You need as much help as you can get, honey." B took Pilar in her arms and held her. It was more than a hug. B enveloped her, consumed her like she'd imagined being swarmed by the insects outside her apartment—supported and safe within a million tiny bodies.

On her cheek, Pilar felt B's earlobe—soft and fleshy, with a fine covering of fuzz. Pilar turned her head and drew it into her mouth, pressing the lobe against her front teeth with her tongue. For a second, it was wonderful—this soft, perfect piece of her friend. Hers to taste.

B pushed away.

"What was that?"

B touched her ear and rubbed Pilar's saliva between her fingers.

"I don't know. I'm sorry," Pilar stammered. "That was gross. I'm sorry."

B stood blankly, processing. She felt her ear again and tentatively reached for Pilar's arm. "It's fine. You're stressed out. And it wasn't gross. It was fine—I think."

Pilar stared at her, unable to shrug off what she'd done.

"I'll go cool your brother off, bring him in," B said, offering a smile. "You hold it down, okay?"

"You need a minute," Pilar said. "It's fine. I'm sorry."

"I'm coming back. I promise."

After B left, Pilar's anxiety forced a sorting of the day's smart decisions from the brash, separating the latter into what could and could not be tied to the pills. Bonnie returned and reported Johnnie May wished to meet Pilar in private. Her sour tone told Pilar this arrangement was not part of her predetermined set of events.

"You certainly have the look," Bonnie Blue said as she led Pilar through the backstage area. "I'll be frank. Plenty of women do. There are promoters who would take one glance and write you a contract. I have far more respect for my employees."

Johnnie May's area reminded Pilar of a tree house. The tarpaulin roof. The hammock. The clothes strewn about on the gummy floor. Pilar recognized the same jug of budget protein powder they had at the apartment.

Johnnie May was doing pull-ups on one of the riser's horizontal bars. She clutched the beam's sharp angles without gloves or chalk. The veins in her forearms bulged. Pilar lost the rep count in the twenties after a yellow-spotted lizard skittered from under a pallet, diverting her attention. It balked at the giant mammals and vanished into the shadows.

Johnnie May dropped down and approached the women. She had a few inches on Pilar and was thicker all around, though her trunks fit her hips like cling wrap on a marble statue. Two black straps crossed her sternum like a challenge—hit me here, if you can.

"Pilar Contreras," Bonnie announced.

Johnnie May took Pilar in, starting with her feet. "That Spanish?" she asked.

"Yep," Pilar said.

"I've got family in Seville."

"I don't."

Bonnie excused herself, reminding the wrestlers they were due in ring in thirty minutes.

Johnnie May offered Pilar a seat—a milk crate she'd cleared of opened envelopes and spools of wire.

"I like your makeup," Johnnie May said.

"Thanks," Pilar said. "My friend did it."

Johnnie May snagged a juice box from a wholesale pallet she had stashed next to a pile of sweets and junk food.

"Drink?" Johnnie May asked.

Pilar wasn't thirsty.

"Makeup's going to smudge," Johnnie May said. "You'll need to buy the stage stuff. Holds better."

"I like when it smears," Pilar said. "Makes it look like I've been through a fight."

"You're not gonna look so tough when it sweats into your eyes."

Pilar expected Johnnie May to down her drink in a gulp. Instead, the wrestler took her time, sipping through the corner of her mouth.

"Your gear is pretty sick," Pilar said.

"I made it," Johnnie May said, gesturing to a table topped with a sewing machine and tools. "Pretty important to have a secondary source of income in this company."

"Wrestling's the only thing I'm good at."

"I doubt it. This place doesn't attract one-trick ponies."

Johnnie May asked whether Pilar was sure she didn't want a juice. Pilar was sure.

"What's your finisher?" Johnnie May asked.

"Shooting Star leg drop."

"That'll kill you five ways. I bet you've already got the hips of a forty-year-old."

"Maybe so," Pilar said. "Got any chondroitin hiding in your stack over there, or do you stick to Flintstones vitamins and gummy bears?"

Johnnie May sucked the juice, slurping air after it as if tasting wine. She kicked over the jug of protein powder, stood it on end, and sat next to Pilar.

"What do you think of Bonnie?" Johnnie May asked.

Pilar could smell the laboratory grape on the wrestler's breath.

"First impression? All these macho men can't deal with the fact that some gray-haired lady is their boss. They've built her into a monster."

"If you're smart, you'll learn Bonnie's a gigantic mark for herself. You can work her like any of them, even when she thinks she's working you."

Pilar remembered the last time Johnnie May wrestled for the title at an MCCW pay-per-view. She'd tapped in less than five minutes to Blair Jackson, the retaining champion.

"Here's the scoop," Johnnie May said. "Bonnie wants me to find out if you'll take a shine. Her opinion's not the only one that matters. If we go out there and put on a real match, people will talk. That's what the boss really wants."

"And what do you want?" Pilar asked.

"Hopefully you break out like everyone says, and down the road when you're facing someone younger, prettier, and poised to replace you before you hit thirty, you'll remember ole Johnnie May and make the right choice."

"I'm not prettier than you."

"I didn't say you were."

For a second, the pressure to calculate the best move weighed on Pilar. What did Bonnie want? What was Johnnie May plotting? How would Dom or Sol or even B advise her? In truth, she had a simple choice: wrestle or go home. The answer was always the same.

"My Shooting Star comes off the top rope," Pilar said. "Looks best if you don't tuck."

"Don't they all?" Johnnie May said. She slurped her juice to the last drop.

Dom searched the Civic's trunk for an extra shirt. The sun, dimmed by the overcast, teased the horizon. His shirt was cotton and would take all night to dry. He didn't find a second one, so he took his off and spread it best he could over the car's hood, pinning it down with the wiper blades. He felt a raindrop. He spread his arms and didn't detect another.

Catie's profile was waiting under his phone's lock screen. He opened a message window and started typing. His fingers mashed several buttons at a time, so he had to work slowly. A few sentences in, he'd written an introduction describing his run-ins with her and how he'd eventually found her page. He imagined the message pasted into a frantic email to the Charlotte-Mecklenburg police.

B emerged through the Hangar's doors. Duke Natterjack, wearing his wrestling trunks and a terry-cloth robe, moseyed across the door tracks and caught sight of Dom.

"Hey-o, HB!" he called. "This young lady's looking for you!"

Dom squinted at Duke and waved.

"Until next time, miss!" Duke said, snickering as he vanished into the bay.

B didn't acknowledge him. She stood next to Dom and sighed. "He gone?"

"For now," Dom said.

B leaned against the Civic's window. "How do you work here? Everyone is a goddamned cartoon character."

"That's what Bret Hart said."

"Bret who?"

"Famous wrestler. Wrote a book."

"Is he as insane as the rest of you people?"

"Never met him." Dom held backspace until the cursor ate every letter of his message.

B gathered her hair and twisted it into a bun. She took a breath, raised an eye to Dom.

"You look completely ridiculous right now," she said.

"Wait till you see the costume," he said.

"I'm done with all of you. As soon as Pilar's finished, I'm getting a ride outta here."

Dom didn't respond. His shirt was no drier. He wondered if he could catch Johnnie May for a second backstage and get a sneak peek at the angle she'd be running with Pilar. He'd worked a mixed-tag with her a few years prior. She was quiet, confident in the ring, always chewing sweets.

"Who is it?" B asked.

Dom let his phone drop to his side, separating B from the screen with his immense frame. "Who's who?"

"Whoever you're blowing up right now."

"Nobody," Dom said. He pocketed his phone and shook his shirt free from the wipers.

"Then why the secrecy?" B said.

Dom bit the inside of his cheek and gnawed on the fleck of mouth skin that snapped loose. "So there's this girl," he said.

"Chica bonita," B said.

Dom drew a breath and held it, letting B's public school Spanish dissipate.

"I had a chance to talk with her—a few chances, actually— and I didn't. I have this one last nuclear option."

"Take it," B said. "All missiles fire."

"Can't," Dom said.

"Press the button, Dom."

"How would you respond if someone like me popped into your life?"

"Pepper spray," B said. "But what's a little eye irritation against a chance at true love?"

"You've never been maced."

"Tell me about this girl. If I can't be Pilar's manager, I'll be your therapist. Though you gotta put some clothes on. No shirt, no service."

"You were so eager to join the biz. What happened? You letting Duke talk you out of a career?"

B cocked her head and pursed her lips.

"Shirt's wet," Dom said. "Deal with it."

"Then how about I take off my shirt and you see how awkward it is?"

"Knock yourself out."

"Whatever. Dude with the robe was a creeper. The world is full of those. I think Pilar is going through some heavy shit. Like, she's really nervous. She needs help."

"She say that?"

"No. I can tell."

"You mean you see how she's so scared and self-doubting, she started insulting the owner of the company within five minutes of meeting her?"

"She was asking legitimate questions. It's a good interview tactic. Boss can see you're independent."

"So she doesn't need help?"

"My point is maybe there's a middle ground between sticking your hand up her ass and moving her mouth and storming out here and pouting without a shirt as if you just got fired from Chippendales."

"What's Chippendales?"

"Really? It's the hottest all-male revue in Vegas. Maybe a good second career if you keep toning—no offense. I don't think they interview anyone whose abs weren't chiseled from Italian marble."

"Thanks for the tip."

"Can you, like, be there for her without getting pissed and trying to take over whenever she makes a move you don't like?"

"Can she trust me when I say she doesn't want to act like she runs the place on day one? This might seem like a room full of assholes play fighting, but the politics are real."

"Compromise! Yes! You two are a team. Today's the first day you've had to face this kind of stress together."

"She's not in there puking her guts out, is she?"

"She's fine," B said. "She puked at McDonald's earlier."

"Are you fucking serious?"

"It wasn't a bad thing! I've known P since sixth grade. I've never seen her so fierce. You had to be there. It was like an exorcism."

"Was she speaking in tongues? Head spinning all the way around?"

B's hand landed on Dom's and stuck.

"It was a good exorcism!" B said. "That girl has demons.

Nothing's worse than an old demon rotting in your gut. She's strong enough to get it out. I shouldn't be the only one holding her hair. You get me?"

Dom worked his fingers around hers and squeezed harder than he needed to.

"I get you."

"Good. You're going to cheer her on, right?"

"You're the one calling the car."

"After she's done. After. Clear your ears. Después."

Dom decided to put on his shirt.

"Better?" he asked.

"Yes. Thank you. I can only take so much exposure. When I get home, I'm going to sit in a dark closet and try to forget everything."

"You're welcome. Now the least you can do is tell me what Duke said to you."

"Christ. You're a gossip."

"This is opposition research. Never know when he might say something I could use."

"He complimented my top, and I was like, whatever, it's not even mine. He said he has a good eye for fashion because he's juiced himself to such ridiculous proportions he can't wear normal-people clothes anymore. Then he started flexing."

"Did he tear through his shirt?"

"No. Nobody wears a fucking shirt in this place. He flexed at me and asked if I'd seen his salamander."

"Duke loves his lizards."

"I thought he was gonna show me his cock. Turns out he's looking for a literal salamander, black with yellow spots."

"He calls it Damien. You help him find it?"

"He wanted me to."

"Did he tell you how big it was?"

B rolled her eyes. "Ew. No."

"I've seen it squiggling around. It looks malnourished."

"Fucking shush, dude. Forget what I said. Don't ever talk to that girl. You're a mental-health risk. You should come with a label."

"If I'm so hazardous, why you out here?"

"Palliative care," B said. She opened the car, fished the red pill bottle from her bag, and unscrewed its white cap. "I tried being sneaky. Discretion doesn't exist in this place. I doubt you could even spell it."

She tapped out two pills and chewed her tongue, working up the saliva to swallow her pills without water.

"You want some?" she asked, holding out the bottle. "They're yours, after all."

They were his, bought from Buddy Houston, an MCCW veteran and cage-match specialist. His supplier funneled helpers into most of the Carolina indie scene and even hooked up some of the big dogs when their national tours rolled through. Dom had heard the source was an old doc in Fayetteville who pumped out phony scripts to the military. It was too quaint to be true.

"Make it a double," he said.

"Way to go, Domingo," B said.

She poured out a few more than double with an expectant smile. Following her lead, he brought them to his mouth without water. When he gulped, he swallowed nothing. He palmed the pills, and when B wasn't looking, he dropped them under his heel and tamped them into a dusty fissure in the tarmac.

"Duke asked about you," B said.

"Oh yeah? What he want?"

"He asked if I knew anything about a match you had a few days ago. He'd heard you broke someone's arm."

"Would you believe me if I said the guy had it coming?"

The sun blasted through a gap in the overcast. Dom and B looked away. The abrupt switch from gray to a sunset palette was too intense to appreciate.

"He was curious how you did it," B said.

SIXTEEN

Bonnie determined there was no ideal spot to observe the action. The bleachers were too far. The ropes interrupted the view from the front row. On the mats between the ring and the gallery barricade, nothing prevented Domingo from roaming about and missing the match's critical moments. Bonnie decided to set the example and stand on the ring apron near one of the turnbuckles, the same spot Johnnie May's partner would have stood if the match were a tag-team contest. As expected, the brother Contreras positioned himself in the opposite corner. The girl who'd arrived nipping at their heels stood behind Domingo, on the floor and out of the way.

The women tested the ropes. The tension stressed their arms' definition, their veins and tendons. Though Contreras was secondary to her performance's effect on her brother, Bonnie realized she was rooting for her. She truly had the look of a star. Many would pay to watch her. As artless as the hustle could be, money was always necessary.

The girl on the floor, the friend, looked past the wrestlers. Her thousand-yard stare reminded Bonnie how lucky she'd been. Her family, for all its flaws, had ensured she never lacked for productive directions to exercise her skills. Her father did not drink or smoke or even pray. She found the lesson of his example quite profound. The real world was a beautiful place. To indulge in the shallow pleasure of viewing it reflected off a substance's fun-house mirror was a pitiable thing. To partake as a learned, wealthy person was tantamount to a crime.

Bonnie descended the ring steps and approached the friend.

"Do you want a job?" Bonnie asked.

"What?" the girl said.

"Here." Bonnie took hold of the girl's elbow and led her to the timekeeper's area. The ring bell, mounted to a square of plywood, rested on top of a table.

"Do you understand what this is?" Bonnie asked, picking up the claw hammer next to the bell.

"Is that a trick question?" the girl said.

"I don't ask trick questions," Bonnie replied.

"Okay. Yes, I understand."

"Good. When I say go, hit the bell three times."

"Three times."

"Correct. Do it quickly. Bing bing bing. This is an important part of the match. Can I count on you? Can Pilar count on you?"

"I guess."

Johnnie May and Contreras met in the center of the ring and shook hands. The ref looked to Bonnie, who, after climbing to the apron and savoring the energy special to those moments before the start of a match, pointed to the bell.

"Go," she said.

As instructed, the bell rang thrice.

They decided the open would have no calls. To let Pilar gather her feet, they chain wrestled. Johnnie May, the heel, led the dance. Wristlock, reversal, takedown, kip up, chinlock, reversal, armbreaker. They sensed the next steps. Their bodies in time. Smooth. Snappy. Their shouts echoed through the Hangar. Without the need to be heard over a noisy crowd, they sounded real.

Pilar whipped Johnnie May to the ropes, leaped her spear, and took her down on the rebound with a drop toehold, which she bent into a half crab. She tugged Johnnie May's leg, put her weight into it. "More," Johnnie May whispered, and Pilar pulled harder. "More," she said again. To shut her up, Pilar put force behind it until Johnnie May's heel touched the crown of her head.

Johnnie May was screaming her lungs out. Pilar didn't let up. She tugged, got the foot close to her opponent's shoulder. Johnnie May convulsed beneath her.

There was ugliness and beauty in that moment, a middle ground distinct from what Pilar had encountered in practice.

She thought of how they must've looked—two women in peak physical condition, their sharp lines cast in resistance. Under the lights, Johnnie May's vinyl ring gear smoldered like copper-green flame. It was so brilliant it didn't shadow Pilar—it elevated her, pushed her budget spandex beyond its potential. Pilar's confidence soared. She pulled her opponent so hard she was hurting herself, and her anguish was G-rated compared to Johnnie May's raw suffering. The contortion was as elegant as ballet, as repugnant as torture porn. At any moment, it seemed as if Pilar might've snapped Johnnie May's spine and ruptured her belly, spilling her across the canvas in a crimson bloom.

The veteran did not tap. She did not tell Pilar to quit the hold. She hadn't reversed it or thrown a disrupting elbow or used her superior strength to muscle free. Rather, she channeled her pain into her reaction. Cries shot to the rafters. Distress flooded her body with endorphins, allowing her ligaments another half inch of give. Her pain was real, and that was part of the show.

This didn't need to happen. Pilar could've pretended she was putting everything into the hold. Johnnie May could've comfortably bent well past the threshold where most onlookers would start squirming. Yet the moment that pain entered their act, what was a display of Pilar's ability transformed into something elusive. What was really happening? Could the audience sense Johnnie May's suffering? How could Pilar be sure her opponent wasn't far more flexible than she imagined?

How could she be sure Johnnie May wasn't enduring pain so immense she'd lost her ability to tap out?

Pilar's mind opened to the gift of this ambiguity. It felt artistic, and not like some sculpture collecting bird shit on a street corner. This was breathing. This was living.

Johnnie May got a finger on the bottom rope, and the ref broke the hold.

"Can't break me, Spaniard," Johnnie May shouted. Pilar stutter-stepped before remembering Johnnie May was acting the heel and was expected to antagonize.

"Just stretching you," Pilar said. "You can skip Pilates this week."

Johnnie May straightened and shook out the kinks, keeping ahead of the girl as they orbited the ring's center. Johnnie May slowed her rotation and raised an arm, fingers wiggling above her head. Pilar mirrored her. The two locked grips and thrusted themselves shoulder to shoulder. Pilar gained the advantage, bending her opponent. Then, to feign a burst of strength, Pilar pulled Johnnie May up, flipping their positions.

There were no cheers, no coaching from Dom's corner, no praise from Bonnie's. A few wrestlers watched from afar. They were mute, as if Bonnie would take their jobs at first holler. B's eyes were sleepily drawn to a group of male wrestlers in the corner tugging on elasti-bands. Bonnie was squared toward the in-ring action, but her focus centered beyond. The only plausible subject was Dom, and his body language confirmed it. He'd locked onto Bonnie as if she were the only person in the building.

Was it Pilar's fault? Was she boring them? Impossible. Her performance was sharp. If it hadn't been, Johnnie May would've told her—a hard chop, a yank of her ponytail.

They should've been watching her. She was a bird of prey soaring over a canyon. She was a living optical illusion. She was an opera made flesh, and they were missing her overture. These three people had rushed her, pushed her, raised hell to get her in the ring on half a day's notice, and they didn't give a shit.

Pilar kneed Johnnie May in the gut, flipped her overhead, and bridged into a pin. The ref counted one, two, and Johnnie May lifted a shoulder.

Where was Gorilla? He'd called her a future Women's Champion. Where was Sol? It might've been a closed-door tryout, but the Hangar bay was literally wide open. He could've paid an unexpected visit to one of his old ring buddies. He could've slinked under the bleachers. He could've stood a quarter mile down the runway and watched through a telescope.

Where were Pilar's friends? The boys who begged her to come to their prom-night parties? The "u up" texts? So curious about her at two a.m.?

Where were the teachers who'd offered to stay late to tutor her? Where were the counselors who'd begged her to apply to college? Where were all the people who'd claimed they'd loved her? Where the fuck was her mom?

Johnnie May struggled to her feet. Pilar kicked them from under her and dropped a leg across her stomach. Air popped from her opponent's mouth as if her lungs had burst. She gasped and heaved in such distress, every head should've turned. They didn't.

"Too much shine," Johnnie May whispered as Pilar hooked her leg. Pilar ignored her and bent her in half. Another two count.

Pilar wanted to scream. The injustice pained her more than her neck ever could. Bonnie, the fake. B, the flake. Her brother, the absolute worst.

Johnnie May was splayed out center ring. Pilar calculated the best turnbuckle and after a flurry of steps, she was standing atop the ropes. Her index finger and thumb formed an L. The gesture was priestly in its reverence. It had simply come to her as if the moment had decreed it, as if she had to ask Johnnie May's forgiveness for what she was about to do.

She leapt straight up, turning 180 degrees and landing feet-first on the ropes, her back to the ring. She absorbed the force, coiling her legs, her knees on her shoulders as she prepared to shoot herself skyward, reversing her typical Shooting Star drop, supercharging it with a double jump.

Her launch arc was the steepest she'd ever achieved. She reached more than double the height of the ropes. At the top of the parabola, the forces were too extreme. She panicked, planking her muscles. Her body was a piece of wood plummeting to the mat, her skull scheduled to strike first.

The impact was a lightning strike. Johnnie May had seen Pilar's underrotation and raised her knees to her chest. Pilar landed across her opponent's shins, saving her head from hitting the mat. Unprepared for the momentum swing, her neck snapped like a whip.

The veteran pounced and locked Pilar's arm into a loose vice.

"You okay?" Johnnie May whispered.

Pain radiated through Pilar's limbs, her arms and legs blistering on the inside as if her blood was boiling. It scooped out her brain and dropped it hours earlier when she'd been paralyzed on Sol's practice mat. Before he'd given her the pills, before she and B had taken them all at once.

She crunched her molars, squeezed Johnnie May's hand. She was too hurt to sell the vice. Screaming might've offered some relief, but shock stuffed her throat. Johnnie May barked, but it didn't register. She shuddered and flexed to keep a shoulder up so the ref wouldn't count. The half inch between her skin and the canvas stretched into infinity. Her body was an anvil forged from the heaviest, most toxic element.

Her back flush against the canvas, she felt the vibration long before she heard anything. It wasn't the smack of the ref hitting the mat. It could have been a truck on the tarmac or a stagehand rolling something heavy. It grew stronger and started to roar. Thunder, Pilar thought. An earthquake. No. The sound got too loud. Johnnie May released her hold and looked up. The ref dove as if he was going to count, but he ducked under the bottom rope and scuttled from the ring.

The Hangar shook. Lights swung and kicked off years of dust. A chunk of metal rattled free from the entrance stage. On the drum skin of the ring, Pilar was at the epicenter—the sound from above, the rumble from below. It was a plane, an airliner. Jet engines revving, whining. Pilar braced for the roof's collapse. She wondered if she'd see the fire, or if it would all be over before then.

SEVENTEEN

Pilar was young. The world constantly reminded her. But she was old enough to sense the passage of time. Late-teens Pilar existed in a different era than she had as a child. When she was living with her mom, she'd watched a lot of television. Kids' stuff, local news, infomercials, programs with people dating, surviving, singing. She loved getting up early to watch nature shows. Snakes hunting mice, spiders catching flies, gazelles getting eaten by just about everything.

She had a memory of a Saturday morning when she came across a program about marine life. In one segment, the camera followed a great white shark as it swam past a diver's cage and disappeared into the ocean's abyss. It looked more like a parade balloon than a living creature. The show's narrator said this species needed to keep moving in order to pass oxygen-rich water over its gills. If it stopped, it would die.

Pilar was injured. They didn't have the money to find out how badly. Dom was sitting on her futon, tearing his hair out. She wished she had the will to scream at him, to ask if she had his attention now. She was on Dom's bed, slow cooking in her ring gear. She couldn't remove it.

B had left, saying her mom had ordered her to run an errand. Even for her, it was a poor excuse. Pilar needed a friend to distract her from how much shit she was in, to tell her she hadn't lost everything. Was B too dense to see that? Was she too heartless to care?

Pilar had thought the Hangar was going to collapse. What was most upsetting was that she'd embraced it, indulged in its promise of release. In that lust for the end, she proved her weakness. A competitor would've found a way to walk from the ring. A survivor would've held a white-knuckle grip on life. Again, Pilar had been carried away in her brother's arms.

"Can you help me take my gear off?" she asked.

"Let me check your grip," Dom said.

"Why?"

He pressed his index fingers into her palms. She glared at him and squeezed.

"Good," he said. "Now wiggle your toes."

"We did this in the car," Pilar said.

"Just do it."

"I'm not paralyzed."

Dom filled his lungs with the apartment's damp air and forced it through his teeth. "If your spine is bruised, the swelling might start affecting things. We need to keep tabs on it."

"I'm glad you feel qualified to have a medical opinion."

"I'm not qualified for shit. I'm doing what I can. You got an alternative?"

"Sure. Stop pretending you care and leave me the fuck alone."

Dom threw up his arms. He packed some gear and pocketed his keys. He ignored Pilar's grunt of protest, retrieved her phone from her bag, and slipped it next to her.

"This isn't by choice," he said. "If you call and I don't answer, I'm in the ring."

"And what if I can't move my arms? Isn't that what you're worried about?"

"Call 911."

"How the fuck am I supposed to do that?"

"Where there's a will, there's a way."

"Tú eres tonto."

"Shut up!" Dom roared. He slogged into the bathroom and emerged with fistfuls of pill bottles.

"Let's solve things your way," he said, ripping off bottle caps and flinging pills at Pilar. "That's for the swelling! Here's some for the pain!"

"Stop, you fucking psycho!" Pilar shouted. The neighbor banged on the kitchen wall and yelled Spanish obscenities.

"There's your Plan B," Dom said. "Use your big fucking mouth to get your buddy over there to call the cops."

"I'm glad you waited until I was literally bedridden before you started throwing shit. You're a coward."

"A coward would've never come for you," Dom said.

Rage. Too much for tears. She wanted to hurt him, to cut him down however she could.

"I would've been better off with Mom."

Dom nodded. "Yeah, well, there's enough shit on that bed to take you back to her."

His tone was matter-of-fact—sharper than a scream. He shouldered his bag and took a breath.

"I'm going to try to get you a second chance. I think you should try too."

She swallowed hard and imagined her muscles ripping free from each vertebra.

"Your choice, I guess," her brother said. He slammed the door behind him.

Dom's steps faded down the hall, and though he was out of earshot when the thought came to her, Pilar yelled it anyway.

"Thanks for leaving me wrapped in this fucking gear!"

A dozen pills were on her chest. They looked unassuming— pale green, chalky white, different from the ones Sol gave her. She recognized them. Forcing down a couple would ease her, fade her into an old, familiar sleep.

She pressed her fingernails into her palms and stared at nothing. On her clammy skin, the pills started to dissolve.

Pilar mapped the ceiling's cracks and stains. A roach skittered from a kitchen cabinet. Her neighbor's television blared louder than usual, likely out of spite. She caught bits of the Spanish-language show. A wedding. A princess in a castle. Government workers trying to sort out some problem. She tried to put it together. When the show ended, the neighbor's apartment went quiet.

She fell asleep, and her phone buzzing woke her up. She found she could punch in her code and tilt the phone toward her without too much pain. The text was from a number she didn't recognize.

"U ded?"

She tried to type on the phone's tiny keyboard and pushed every button except the ones she wanted. She was ready to give up. Then she remembered the speech-to-text function. She was always activating it by mistake.

"Depends," she said. "Who's asking?"

"Depends who is asking?" Her phone transcribed. Good enough, Pilar thought.

A response quickly followed.

"Johnnie may. Ur bro gave me ur number. He wouldnt talk about u. in a big hurry."

"I need someone to help me out of my wrestling gear."

"Sounds like the worlds worst pick up line."

"I'm hurt bad please come," Pilar blurted out. Her phone mangled it into a sentence about badgers, so she had to record it again.

"Alone?" Johnnie May wrote.

"Yes," Pilar said. The three letters appeared in the message window. Pilar felt the danger pangs of having revealed too much, as if she were a squirrel chirping her location to a circling falcon.

"Where r u?" was the response.

Pilar's mom, in one of her more coherent refrains, had warned her—never, ever be alone. When her mom had no one, rather than confronting her fears, she dulled herself to them. Pilar had so much of what her mom hadn't. In the gym, she'd honed discipline. Dealing with Dom, she'd learned patience. She'd built an athlete's body from spinach and chalk. Johnnie May was no predator, and if she were, Pilar was kin a few limbs across the evolutionary tree, a cheetah to Johnnie May's lion or whatever. The intimacy shared in their match quieted Pilar's inclination to keep her distance.

Pilar dictated her address. Johnnie May sent a thumbs-up.

The cockroach appeared on the corner of the mattress, inches from Pilar's foot. Smashing roaches was a daily ritual in the apartment. They had a keen sense of the slightest threatening twitch. This one was brave.

"They're evolving," Pilar said to no one. She twisted more, enough to shoo the roach. Pain shot from her neck to her fingertips.

She focused on breathing. The pain cycled down until it got lost in the discomfort of her skin marinating inside her gear.

It wasn't only her injury, Pilar realized. The apartment's condition further tweaked her vulnerability. She'd joked when Johnnie May had asked if wrestling was her only game, but it was true. She'd passed through school doing nothing more than she was told. Everyone who'd pitched her on college had made it sound like a cult or a scam. She was a gym rat, not a trainer. Becoming an expert on her body hadn't transformed her into a student of the body. She lived in trash. She *was* trash.

Pilar thrust her jaw into an underbite and tried to click together her molars. To her surprise, her neck didn't complain, so she allowed herself the small pleasure of pushing it, stretching her tendons. The new force in her skull relaxed her and channeled out some of the anxiety. She tried to reset her train of thought.

The start of her match with Johnnie May had been rock fucking solid. There'd been a spark. They'd communicated without speech, and it was far more than body language. It was unique and a little scary. It was real.

She woke her phone up and instructed it to text B.

"What do you want to say to B?" her phone said in its robot voice.

"Whatever will take my mind off this," Pilar said. "I was a creepy weirdo and then she bailed on me and everything is screwed up and if I text her I'll make it worse."

Somehow her phone transcribed this exactly. "Ready to send it?" it asked.

"Fuck it. Yeah."

"I didn't get that," the phone said.

Pilar hit cancel and pushed out her jaw again. She tracked the roach's meandering ascent up the wall, hoping it might lull her to sleep. Her mind kept coiling her more tightly in place.

"Search 'Venus flytrap fairy people,' " she said to her phone.

The phone spit back a Botanical Society article on the "Mysterious Venus Flytrap" and a forum thread asking how long it would take a triggered flytrap to digest a human finger.

Pilar's scowl was cut short by a tickle on her leg. It was a second roach—bigger than the first.

She cried out and flailed. The pain jolt was tardy, as if her brain was losing faith in its power to keep her from further self-harm. The roach rode out her kick and darted away on its own. Her phone flopped to the edge of the mattress and toppled onto the floor.

EIGHTEEN

Sophomore year of high school, after she'd moved south with Dom, Pilar had this crusty English teacher who'd spout proclamations about his students' responsibility for the state of the world. There was a cliché he would milk over and over, especially when the class couldn't muster enthusiasm for some supposed classic work of literature: "Youth is wasted on the young."

The teacher must've forgotten his lesson on irony, because sitting through a scolding on how she was wasting her youth was in fact the biggest possible waste of her youth. If he really believed it, wasn't he, as a teacher, in a position to help? Midway through the semester, after the hundredth time hearing it, Pilar composed a countermaxim. If youth was wasted on the young, then being old was wasted on the olds.

Old people had a superpower. In all their lust for fresh bodies and good sex, they'd overlooked it. It was so much easier for them not to give a shit.

Even the most mundane adult life had catalogued so many experiences. Any new high or low was tempered by what came before. What's a breakup after you've done high school and your twenties and maybe a marriage or two? Pilar's English teacher had taught thousands of kids. He had children, a mortgage. He'd probably watched his parents die. Every day hammered another plate on his suit of armor.

Most olds wasted this power. They obsessed over their decay. When they could no longer trick themselves into seeing the person they used to be rather than the person they were becoming, they allowed fear to consume them, to drive a tide of resentment toward the young. Their chorus was loud and desperate. Kids have no taste, they said. Their music sucks. They're jerking off on our country's foundational moral principles.

How could a person who grew up steeping in pop culture despised by their parents not see themselves falling into the same trap? Why didn't they strap on their suits of armor and do all the things they couldn't do as young people because they were too embarrassed or naive or afraid? Pilar longed for the day when every good and bad experience felt less like the best or worst thing. She looked forward to being able to forget.

Pilar's most vivid childhood memory was the day her mom pulled her from school and drove to a dozen vista points around Cincinnati—Bellevue Park, Mt. Adams, Riverside Drive in

Covington. They got Coneys to go in Price Hill and ate them overlooking the Ohio River, its iron bridges and lazy curves. In Pilar's mind, the day stood out like one of the city's skyscrapers. The trouble was there were only so many Cincinnati skyscrapers. What would've been another happy day in a normal kid's life was her Great American Tower standing tall and crowned over the Queen City.

Pilar's phone received a call. Vibrating on the floor, haplessly rotating, it was a fish flopping on a beach, a fly buzzing between a screen and window glass.

Without falling off the bed herself, answering the phone was impossible. Pilar tried anyway, wrenching her body to its side and stretching until she could no longer endure the torture. Her fingertips grazed the floor. The phone was another two feet away.

There was a knock at the door, then Johnnie May's voice. "You dead?"

"Yeah," Pilar croaked. "Come in."

"Door's locked," Johnnie May said, jiggling the knob.

"It's janky. Lift when you turn."

"I can see the dead bolt."

"You can see the dead bolt," Pilar repeated, clenching a fist.

"Yes. I repeat—the door is locked."

"Sorry. My dumbass brother imprisoned me."

"You can't open it?"

In her nature shows, when a lion seized a gazelle in its jaws, the prey always seemed to give up. Pilar had willed the poor animals to bite back, kick at the eyes, anything. When she was young, she figured the fear of death had paralyzed the prey. As she got older, she better understood the animal's pain. A gazelle couldn't start kicking with a lion's teeth sinking into its throat. Now, as she considered what kind of lie she could tell Johnnie May to hide her vulnerability, she thought that maybe the gazelle was just too tired to care. Maybe after so many years of famine and drought and running for its life, it was simply done.

"I can't move," Pilar said. "I can't even take off my gear, remember?"

"Damn. You were serious?"

"Call Dom. Or you know what? Fuck him. Call a locksmith, maybe an exterminator while you're at it."

"Are your windows locked?"

"What?"

"Could I open one of your windows from outside?"

"Fuck that. Trying to shimmy up here will get you killed."

"So that's a no? The windows aren't locked?"

"Don't," Pilar said. "We can try to get someone from the office."

"You want out of your gear or not?"

Pilar groaned. The table was set. Johnnie May would climb up and, in her struggle to pry a window open, she'd slip off the building and break her neck. Pilar would fall out of bed attempting to get her phone. A bone under stress from her injury would shift, and she'd break her neck. Dom would return from being Captain Asshole, see the rotting corpses of his colleague and sister, lose his mind, and speed the Civic into oncoming traffic. He'd ram into a family driving home from vacation, kill half of them, and leave the survivors with debilitating trauma.

She was imagining the story blasting across the internet when Johnnie May jostled open the bathroom window and climbed inside.

"Easier than I thought," she said. She was in track shorts and a tank, so different than her ring attire it seemed she'd shed her skin. She saw Pilar and froze in place.

"Holy shit! What did you take?"

She rushed over like a nurse with a crash cart, her path leading directly over Pilar's phone. Her heel came down hard.

"You crushed it!" Pilar yelled.

"What are these? You need to tell me!"

Pilar remembered she was lying among dozens of pills. The arteries in her neck bulged.

"That stupid, fucking fuckhead!"

Johnnie May ripped her phone from her shorts' waistband. "I'm calling 911."

"Stop!" Pilar said. "I didn't take anything. Dom threw these at me."

"He did what?"

"We had a fight. He got pissed and chucked a bunch of pills around."

"Why?"

"Because he's an ass. Look, they're all over the floor and shit. If I was gonna wolf down a bunch of painkillers, I wouldn't be Cookie Monster and fling them everywhere."

Johnnie May came closer and scanned her body, pausing at her shoulders and the bruises seeping from underneath her kneepads.

"Did you go to the hospital?" Johnnie May asked.

"What do you think?"

"Can you move your arms?"

"Sorta."

"Then squeeze these," Johnnie May said, extending her index fingers.

"I already did this with Dom."

"And you're gonna do it again, or I'm calling an ambulance."

Pilar didn't try to pop Johnnie May's fingers as she had Dom's. The wrestler tested her range of motion and asked Pilar some basic awareness questions.

"You're fucked up but not in immediate danger," she said.

"You and my brother could open a practice."

"If you want to last in this business, it's best to learn some first aid."

"Sure. I'll pull up WebMD right now."

Johnnie May shook her head and collected loose pills from the bed and floor, plunking them into a dry coffee mug she found by the sink.

"My phone," Pilar said, mustering the strength to point. "Did you kill it?"

Johnnie May paused her search and followed Pilar's gesture to the device's corpse. It had bowed under her heel, the concavity reminiscent of how phones used to look. Its screen was obliterated.

"Sorry," Johnnie May said, picking it up so she wouldn't drop chips of glass. "She gone."

Pilar sighed. "It's my brother's fault. Don't worry about it."

"I can get you a burner. What else do you need?"

"I need to get out of this gear."

"Can do," Johnnie May said. She searched the drawers in the kitchen. "Scissors?"

"Buried somewhere, probably," Pilar said. "Why?"

"Never mind. This'll work."

She extracted a knife from underneath the mess of dishes. It was long and had a few patches of rust. The tip was bent. Pilar could see its curl from across the room.

"I was worried about this," Pilar said. "Now's your chance to take out your competition."

"You're talkative for someone in so much pain," Johnnie May said. She ran her thumb down the knife blade and inspected its ruined tip, then dropped to the bed and seized the orange hem of Pilar's ring top. "You ready?"

"Uh, no."

Pilar's best effort to evade scooted her a few inches up the bed. The price was another debilitating jolt.

Johnnie May let go. The top's elastic snapped onto Pilar's chest.

"You really want me to tug this off? I'd have to force your arms over your head."

"We're gonna have to try because this is the only ring gear I've got."

"I can sew it, good as new," Johnnie May said. "Or better yet, I can work on an original piece for you. You can watch and learn how to do it."

"I can't afford custom gear."

"Fuck me, Pilar. It's on the house, no charge. What's it in Spanish? El freebo."

Pilar's anxiety gave her skin a purple tinge. Johnnie May making her new gear, committing the time, having so much power over her appearance in the ring—she was too close.

Johnnie May took hold of the orange and blue top, lifting the bottom hem, and brought the knife near.

"Wait!" Pilar said.

"You're fine."

"Instead of cutting up the middle, why not whack off the straps and then cut down the stitch in the back. I can get on my side. I've already done it a few times."

Johnnie May agreed. She pinched a strap off Pilar's shoulder and held it thin and taught. The knife was surprisingly sharp, making quick work of the spandex. Once the two were loose, Johnnie May helped Pilar onto her side. She took her time with the back, where the fabric was tougher. The bottoms were easier. Johnnie May split the shorts at one hip, then the other.

"Done," Johnnie May said. "You okay?"

Pilar bit her lip and said yes. The musty apartment air felt incredible on her newly exposed skin.

"Whoops. Looks like you caught some strays," Johnnie May said.

A pair of pills was stuck to Pilar's sternum. They were disintegrating in the damp of her sweat. With a handful of spandex, Johnnie May whisked them away.

"I can do a quickie job on these in case you have a miraculous recovery."

"Ugh. No. They stink," Pilar said. "Leave them here."

"Doesn't bother me. You want a blanket?"

"It's too fucking hot."

"You sure? You want your brother to walk in and see you spread-eagle?"

"He'll deal."

Johnnie May peered around the tiny apartment and nodded. Her casualness struck Pilar. When people saw her naked, their eyes darted over her as if she were an alien, glittering thing. Everyone looked. Johnnie May didn't. She checked the fridge and brought her a glass of water.

"You should protect your privacy," Johnnie May said. "If you treat your home like a locker room, you'll never leave work."

She shook out the sheet at the foot of the futon and waved it like a bullfighter.

"Fine," Pilar said. As her sweat dried, her skin was starting to itch. It felt less obscene to indulge undercover, though the sheet itself, last washed an unknown number of months in the past, seemed to sharpen the demand for her nails.

Johnnie May pushed through the crap crammed inside the lower kitchen cabinets and removed a bucket filled with cleaning agents. There was crust on the rim, soap scum or mold growth or an unholy combo of the two. She removed the bottles and set to rinsing and scrubbing the bucket clean—no small task with the kitchen faucet locked in its tomb of dishes.

"Look at it this way," she said. "Sounds like you and Dom aren't having the best of it right now. What if the main cause is mixing business with family?"

"C'mon. We're wrestlers," Pilar said. "The McMahons. The Harts. The Anoa'is. The Von Erichs. Ric and Charlotte Flair. Nikki and Brie Bella. Everyone's related."

"And how'd they turn out? Ric Flair's son overdosed. Stu Hart ran a torture dungeon. Most of the Von Erichs jumped off the planet. Vince McMahon's stepdad beat him with a pipe wrench. His mother sexually abused him."

"A lot of wrestlers are fucked up. Who would've thought?"

"It's no joke. There are lines you cross at your own risk. I'd never work with family, let alone spar with my brother."

Johnnie May's elbow hit a pan in the middle of the dish tower, and it came precariously close to toppling. Pilar wondered how hard the neighbor would have to hit the wall before he punched through.

"What're you doing?" Pilar asked.

Johnnie May shut off the faucet and shook the excess moisture from the bucket. "Bedpan," she said.

Pilar shut her eyes. "Gross."

"You ever use one?"

"I'll figure it out."

Johnnie May spun the bucket underneath her and sat down next to the bed. She was at eye level, which Pilar appreciated. She was sick of looking up.

"I got some choice DMs this week," Johnnie May said. "Wanna hear?"

"Oh god. How bad?"

Johnnie May woke up her phone. "Put a pseudonym on your personal accounts while you can."

"Thanks, grandma."

"Hey, this wasn't a thing when I started."

"The good ole days," Pilar said in an old lady voice.

"@DarkStar6969 says, 'Am I in a twilight zone? You're a fake fuckin' fighter. This isn't wrestling. It's a fuckin' gymnastics exhibition.' "

"Smart guy," Pilar said.

"@88switchblade says, 'I'd take you to pound town, population you. Hashtag JohnnieBae.' "

"JohnnieBae! Steal it."

"Absolutely not. Here's a wrestling scholar. 'Johnnie Driver? It's like you took a steaming shit on Michinoku's grave.' "

"Michinoku died?"

"Nope."

Pilar laughed. "Maybe he has a site in his family plot, and you pooped on it before he got there."

"Maybe," Johnnie May said. "Let's see. 'Sit on my face.' 'Nice tits.' 'You're a fucking bitch.' Here we go. @BennySauce7: 'You are script.' "

"Jesus," Pilar said. "Maybe I can make it without social media."

"I could fill a book with these. But this bullshit is better than the alternative."

"Which is?"

"Radio silence."

Pilar considered this. A nerve in her foot decided to complain.

"Sounds peaceful," Pilar said.

"You want some peace?" Johnnie May asked. "I could go get you that burner. Bring it by in the morning."

"I don't mind you staying," Pilar said. "Could you text Dom? Tell him my phone died but not me?"

"You want to talk to him?"

"Definitely not."

Johnnie May's thumbs banged out a text that was longer than necessary.

"Why are you doing all this?" Pilar asked.

"It's the least I can do," Johnnie May said, leaning forward as if she wanted Pilar to press her on it.

"You climbed up here and literally prepped a shit bucket for me. We met this afternoon."

"I've been following you for a while. You're on everyone's radar. And I hope you've seen me in action before today."

"Of course. You're one of the best in the company."

"Thanks. You're young, but you know your shit."

The Y-word hung between them for a moment. Of course she had to say it, Pilar thought. Why did everyone have to say it?

"There was something to our match today, wasn't there?" Pilar said.

"Yeah," Johnnie May said. "It was good."

"We clicked. We were so close. So—"

"Intimate?"

"Yes! Exactly."

"There's nothing like it. Ask people why they do this silly thing we do. The nobodies will say the crowds or the glory or putting smiles on kids. The pros will tell you it's the closeness. I've experienced it before. Always with women I've worked with for years. Never with someone like you."

"I'm so glad," Pilar said. "I was scared to bring it up. I don't have much for comparison, and honestly I've been pretty screwed up in the intimacy department lately."

"You mean with Dom?" Johnnie May asked. "I'm trying to tell you. Is he your coach? Your brother? Your competition? If you're not sure, can you trust him?"

"It's not him."

The sheet was stifling the pleasantness of being free from her gear. Sweat dripped from her underarms, and droplets gathered on her chest.

"So who?"

"There's this friend of mine. I think I crossed a line with her."

"Her, huh? You have feelings for her?"

"Friend feelings. But feelings feelings? It's complicated."

Johnnie May held herself a little higher. "It's not complicated. It's just new."

"No," Pilar said. "It's pretty fucking complicated."

"You make a move, and she wasn't having it?"

"It wasn't a move—at least not what you're thinking."

"So what did you do?"

Pilar couldn't say. Johnnie May let out a sigh and shrugged her shoulders.

"Do you ever have intrusive thoughts?" Pilar asked.

"What do you mean?"

"You're minding your own business, then something completely fucked pops into your mind. Like this one time, I had a terrible day. I came home and guys from the city were trimming trees. They had this massive wood chipper, and I thought how easy it would be to walk to the machine, feed myself in, and become a billion pieces. I was with her, and I had one of those thoughts. Not violent. Just really weird. And I did it."

"Did she like it?"

"Not exactly."

Johnnie May rubbed her eyes and laughed.

"So you might be gay, or bi, or maybe this one particular friend gets you going. That happens a lot. You'll look back on this and see it was all pretty simple."

"Would you be saying that if we were the same age?"

"Yes! You're ahead of the curve. Plenty of people never figure this shit out. Everything has to be so convoluted. Look at what we had today! Was there anything complicated about it?"

"It was completely natural."

"Exactly. Don't sweat this chick. Experiment, stay friends, dump her ass. It doesn't matter. You've got a good thing going. Well, you will once you rehab outta here. So why make things tough? Why care so much?"

The room must've been getting warmer because the sheet was now sticking to Pilar's belly. She imagined it getting wetter, heavier, clinging to her skin, the exposure worse than lying naked.

"I'm straight, by the way," Johnnie May said, her eyes asking for acknowledgment.

Pilar stared, and Johnnie May said nothing. Finally, Pilar managed a blink.

"I should go," Johnnie May said. "You need rest. I could fix up something to help you sleep."

Pilar said no without telling her about Cincinnati or her mom or the drugs—not the ones from before and not the ones that had helped chain her to the bed.

Johnnie May shut off the apartment lights and promised to visit in the morning. "I'll take the stairs this time, and I'll leave this unlocked. Good plan?"

"Sure," Pilar said.

"No text from your brother."

"Must be busy."

Once the veteran was gone, Pilar bit the inside of her cheek until her molars began to sink in. In a single, painful maneuver, she tossed the sheet to the floor. Alone in the dark, she listened for skittering roaches.

"I want to eat her," she said, the words insisting on their escape. "I want to eat her."

She said it again, louder, and again, until the neighbor mimicked her cries and hammered on the wall.

NINETEEN

Before Pilar, Dom remembered a class trip to the museum in the heat of late spring, splashing in the old rail terminal's fountain. His mother had been a chaperone. Back then, she'd always had time. His lunches were packed. The house was clean. They lived comfortably, though his mother was never specific about where their money came from. A few times a month, Dom would arrive from school to his mother hosting her lady friends in the living room. They were always well dressed, and they drank from steamy mugs and laughed like Dom never heard adults laugh. His mother and these ladies called him Dom. His friends called him Dom. Teachers did the same. Dom Contreras? Here.

When his sister was born, Dom learned his real name.

He was eight years old, and he hadn't thought much about his family. There were kids at school who looked like him.

Other parents had accents like his mother's, though they didn't sound the same. The markers of his mother's origins were subtle. They ate dinner late. She never bought peanut butter. They once drove through Toledo, and its anemic skyline nearly brought her to tears. The real Toledo, she explained, was the most Spanish of all the cities in Spain. This place in Ohio was its evil stepsister, rusting near the shores of a poison lake, the most American place she knew.

His sister's name was weird. The spelling, the sound—so foreign. Dom had tried to convince his mother to change it. Branding her with that name was mean, he argued. It would speak for her before she learned her first words. He imagined the bullying. Pee-lar. Pee-lar peed her pants. Pee-pee-lar.

In response, his mother revealed his real name, his full name. Domingo.

It translated literally as "Sunday." At his school's library, he'd researched its roots. In Latin, it meant "Belonging to the Lord." He didn't understand. They weren't religious. He'd searched for his sister's name. It was short for "María del Pilar," the Virgin Mary, as she supposedly appeared on top of a pillar to St. James the Apostle.

"Pillar?" He remembered shouting it and getting shushed by the librarian.

Sunday and Pillar. He was mortified.

After he'd learned his real name, he couldn't escape it. In social studies, they learned the days of the week in multiple languages, and there it was. A group of blond-haired girls took to yelling "Plácido Domingo!" as they passed him in the halls, drawing out each "o" in operatic mockery. He was the first boy to hit his growth spurt, and his voracious eating earned him the nickname "Super Bowl Sunday."

Dom came to see all the ways he wasn't like his classmates, and he felt no closer to those who looked more like him—the Latino kids who had relatives, fathers, clear pictures of who they were.

He'd blamed Pilar. She was an easy target. Her birth had started it. As she got older, he was burdened with her care. Their mother would leave the house late at night, an open secret never discussed. She slept until afternoon, leaving Dom to feed Pilar and compel her to sleep. Dom carried her roughly. He refused to change her diapers. When she wailed, he ignored her cries.

The house got dirty. His mother's friends stopped coming. Dom had suspicions about how she earned a living, and every one disgusted him. Her health declined. For every year she aged three. Dom kept as distant as possible. When he was sixteen, their family a wreck, he left. He didn't look back for years.

At the Hangar, the night's card was underway before a decent draw that had no idea how close the structure had come to obliteration. MCCW's motto was the same as every scrappy entertainment company. The show—rain, shine, or forthcoming FAA investigation—must go on.

Had the flyby happened in less eventful times, Dom would've lost hours trolling for coverage. He would've read every post, every clickbait article, all the speculation about the event's causes and consequences. He would've watched every vertical cell-phone video no matter how shaky. Each iteration of the jet's precarious dip would've been another shot in a schedule of vaccinations. These short exposures would've dosed out the fear stirred by his glimpse into death's abyss.

Backstage, much earlier than his ritual prescribed, Dom partook in an alternative treatment. He shook three hefty pinches of Yucca Mountain grounds into his water bottle. The grit in the improperly brewed sludge collected between his teeth.

There was no room for experimentation tonight. He needed to show his best. He tossed the cursed black trunks aside and fastened his flannel shirt, buttons askew. He pulled up his jeans, wet his hair. He leered at himself through his phone. His beard was dry Spanish moss, his eyes sunken, his mouth black. He was Hack Barlow, as unhinged as ever. The sludge superdose centered him. He could play this character. There was gold yet to mine. He was confident.

Bonnie hadn't yet scratched Dom from the night's card. Pilar had flopped, and if he had any hope of convincing the boss to grant her a second chance, Dom had to demonstrate his resilience. Bonnie expected professionalism. She'd stood up to men with far more box-office clout. If he could put on a textbook show, he might persuade her to expect a similarly rigorous comeback from Pilar.

A text came in from B. She asked if Pilar was okay and apologized for leaving. Dom ignored her, cracked his knuckles and toes, and sped through his prematch exercises. The sludge sloshed in his stomach. He willed it to absorb, to help him find a notch between his guilt and his worry where he could carve out a fight.

The bout was a tag match at the top of the undercard against Duke Natterjack and an up-and-comer Bonnie wanted to shine up before trying him in singles. Dom was paired again with Gorilla Trotsky, who dragged at the start—still sour over Dom's shoot on Cee-Saw. When the newbie scored an early takedown on Dom and was flexing atop the turnbuckle, Dom crawled to his partner and directed him into a fire-up gimmick to get him back into the match. Gorilla slapped him, his palm cracking legit across Dom's cheek. The audience got into it, cheering "Woo!" with each smack. Dom slacked his tongue and shook his head eagerly, letting his spit, snot, and tears goo up his beard. Gorilla punctuated the bit with a tremendous backhand. Penance paid and adrenaline coursing, Dom rolled toward his showboating opponent. He ripped him down, lifted him clear above his head, and threw him over the ropes.

He and Gorilla gained the advantage. Dom showed his top stuff—his trademark *enzuigiri*, a sit-out Powerbomb, and a Coast-to-Coast, a leap from the top rope across the ring's twenty-foot width to spike his heels into the new guy's chest. The draw loved Dom's intensity. He fired them up, seeding a chant with a hatchet swing of his arm.

"Chop! Chop! Chop!" the audience cheered. Dom owned it, swinging his arm harder, more maniacally. The fans bought it. They'd buy anything, Dom thought, if he delivered with conviction.

Reaching deep into his bag of tricks, Dom pulled out a self-authored maneuver, Felling General Sherman. He stunned Duke into a wobble, rebounded off the ropes, dropped into a baseball slide, and took out Duke's legs with a double-axe handle. The crowd went wild. Dom teased further pageantry by producing a lighter and gas can from under the ring. The ref stalled him long enough for Duke to recover and make the tag.

Dom polished the new guy to a high gloss during his comeback. His takes were magnificent, with hair and beard accentuating each strike. As the match wrapped and Gorilla prepared to lie down for the faces, Dom noticed Duke selling the General Sherman. He hopped along the apron on one foot, and he climbed the turnbuckle for a frog splash with no help from his right leg. He crashed onto Gorilla but couldn't hold the pin. He rolled away, clutching his knee. His screams cut into the crowd, and their cheers for Duke's signature move became gasps.

The ref checked him—a true check, Dom noticed. Duke flashed the all clear. He chafed to his corner and tagged the kid. After some theatrics, the newbie got the count on Gorilla.

"Not bad," Gorilla said backstage. "You controlled your bloodlust."

"You forgive me?" Dom drained his remaining sludge, tapping the bottle to catch any stray drops.

"Almost," Gorilla said. "Say ten *Aves*, ten *Padre Nuestros*, call your mother, and buy your sister some good Russian vodka." Gorilla chuckled at himself and his cough caught up with him. He hacked into the crook of his arm. Dom heard the gunk loosening in his chest.

"You okay?" Dom asked.

"Don't get excited," Gorilla said. "You're stuck with me a long time."

Dom smiled and looked to the ring. The winning duo gave their final salutes. They hobbled up the ramp, Duke leaning heavily on his partner.

"Quit peeking," Gorilla said. "He's fine."

"You sure? Duke doesn't oversell."

"He's protecting your move. Take the rub."

Gorilla left for the locker area. Dom watched Duke labor up the ramp. Once out of the audience's view, he picked himself up and walked normally.

"Good effort out there, Contreras," he said. "Didn't expect to see ole Sherman."

"Sorry if I stung you with it."

"Only a pinch. How's your sister? Heard she took a spill."

Dom squeezed fists and cracked his knuckles again. "She'll be fine. Have you seen Bonnie?"

"Nope. You check control?"

"Headed there now," Dom said. "Solid match, Duke."

"You too, brother. Give me a shout if your sister wants me to swing by. My bedside manner does wonders for circulation."

Dom glimpsed his lewd smile and kept moving. He climbed the steel stairs bolted to the interior wall of the Hangar. The control platform was on a catwalk high above the action. They were shooting the evening's event to tape, so there was a smaller crew compared to broadcast nights—a few techs, dudes with headsets scared to look Dom in the eye. No Bonnie.

"This figures," Dom complained to Gorilla. "I needed her to see me, and it's the first night she's not breathing down our asses."

"Oh, she saw you," Gorilla said. "She's got cameras. Woman doesn't take days off."

"Where does she live?" Dom asked.

After fumbling with the map on his phone, Gorilla pointed out a block of apartments just up the road.

"You think Pilar has a chance with her after today?" Dom asked.

Gorilla tugged on a shirt the color and size of a putting green. He was a giant man, over six feet tall and wider than most doorframes. He had to crane his neck to look Dom in the eye.

"I think she's got a shot if you let her take it," Gorilla said.

"Well, she's stuck in bed. She's not taking much of anything right now."

"Can she talk?"

Dom laughed. "Oh yeah."

Gorilla poked him in the chest and squinted. "Then make sure you're listening."

*　*　*

Dom had started wrestling when he was sixteen. They'd never had cable TV, so he didn't grow up a fan. He got big early, which put a target on his back. The typical teenage aggression outlets didn't suit him. Any kid foolish enough to fight him got creamed. He tried football. He hated the team and its cult of jocks.

Running became his respite. He ran through downtown Cincinnati, into the suburbs, across the river on the Purple People Bridge. One weekend run took him as far north as Evendale, where he happened to pass the warehouse arena of the Queensland Wrestling Association, catching the eye of the boss, Les Stryker. The old man ran him down, bought him a sack of burgers, and sold him on giving the business a try.

Compared with his Queensland peers, Dom wasn't all that large. Most of them were looking to jump into a regional promotion en route to the big dance. They were serious, and Dom fit in. His first bumps knocked the wind out of him. With his breath, so went his anger. He loved getting stronger week by week. He gunned for the appreciation of the washed-up wrestlers who showed up to mooch off Les. He marveled that he could hurl an opponent to the thinly padded floor beside the ring and get a hearty clap on the back from the man after the match.

He had not taken to wrestling because he wanted to hurt people.

TWENTY

Dom had pictured his boss's residence in a McMansion suburb with overwatered lawns, four-car garages, and lawyer foyers. He should've guessed that wasn't Bonnie. There was an asphalt facility across the street from her apartment. The air smelled like fresh tar.

Bonnie opened her door wearing the same polo and slacks she always wore.

"Good evening, Domingo. To what do I owe the pleasure?"

Audible to both of them, new texts buzzed in Dom's pocket.

"We need to talk about what happened today," Dom said, flustered.

"Of course," Bonnie said, ushering him inside. "How is Pilar? I'm glad we paired her with a veteran. Her fall could've been much worse."

"She'll be fine," Dom said. "And once she shakes off this spill, I want to make sure she has a roster spot."

"Straight to the point," Bonnie said. She invited Dom to take a seat on her couch and asked if he wanted anything to drink. Dom refused.

An old video game, resolution so low it looked like abstract art, was playing on her TV. Two sprites clipped around each other atop a blue backdrop fenced in by a red line. At the bottom of the image, a timer and two names underscored by red bars. It was a wrestling game—the Bronx Buster versus, Dom had to blink and reread, King Solomon.

"BluTron 3000," Bonnie said, gesturing to a black box on a shelf under the television. "My father's company made these. This was our wrestling game."

"Solomon Lung was in it?"

"Not in the release edition. No one was thinking about licensing. We were at war with Atari. The strategy was to flood them from the market with as many titles as we could make—Winter Olympics, badminton, jai alai, you name it. This game was bare-bones at launch. Afterward, a developer programmed an enhanced version for me. It's got the entire 1979 Big Apple Wrestling roster, Solomon Lung included. Accurate heights and weights."

A rudimentary AI controlled the wrestlers. They bumped into one another and a counter appeared—one, two—and they separated. The wrestlers had been animated with the least number of pixels required to create vaguely human-shaped sprites. The Buster's pixels were white, Sol's brown. Dom cringed at the thought of a developer choosing the color to represent Hack Barlow.

"Could you shut it off?" Dom asked.

"I'd prefer not while it's simulating," Bonnie replied.

Chewing his bottom lip raw, Dom paced to the TV, ran a finger along its frame until he found the power button, and switched it off.

"You can let it run in the dark," he said. "You know who's going to win."

"I like to watch," Bonnie said, sitting on the couch.

"Pilar showed what she could do today," Dom said. "You could put her in the main event tomorrow. She's got three years on the youngest woman in the company. When she moves up, everyone will ask where she came from."

Bonnie crossed her legs. "Tomorrow? She could work Tanya Flex *tomorrow?*"

"That's not what I meant."

"Then what did you mean, Domingo? It's not wise to use inexact language in a contract negotiation."

"I'm leaving tonight with a verbal guarantee of a full-time roster spot for my sister, or she's packing. And you'll have to watch the woman who could've been your biggest star make someone else a shit ton of money."

Dom took a breath. Bonnie didn't immediately return fire, so he continued.

"And it's not only Pilar. I was cash in the ring today. I'm in the best shape of my life. I have the experience and the will to show you how this company has undervalued me. I'm going to break through."

"As who?" Bonnie asked. "Hack Barlow? You think he can rise to the main event?"

"Fuck yes, he can," Dom said. Too strong, he realized. He'd never intimidate Bonnie into agreement.

"It doesn't matter who I am," he said. "Give me Hack. Give me anything. I have the skill and confidence. I'm getting to the top."

Bonnie excused herself, stepped around Dom, and switched on the TV. The screen booted bright blue and the game reappeared, massive pillar boxes on either side of the image.

Dom clenched a fist. He saw the sprites flickering across the screen. Thirty-five years earlier, stomping around decaying New York theaters, the wrestlers couldn't have been more different—Sol the regal behemoth, Buster the pug-faced scrapper. On the TV, they moved identically. They were the same number of pixels.

"We played a lot of games when I was a kid," Dom said. "Someone always knew someone with the latest system. Whatever we played, it wasn't long before the entire neighborhood figured out the best character. And let me tell you, if you chose that character, everyone thought you were a little bitch. The best players could kick your ass with anyone. That's what mattered."

The sprites blipped together, and the counter flashed—one, two, three. The Bronx Buster put his arms over his square head. Bonnie watched the celebration and smiled.

"I've put much thought into you," she said. "I've discovered we share a peculiar kinship. We're both in the prime of our careers. We don't attract close friends. We are skilled and hungry. Yet we haven't taken steps beyond our current stations. Hack Barlow has stalled, and though there are roles you could take to make people love you, you can't bring yourself to do it. Throughout my life, I too have been expected to play various parts, and yet I've had the insatiable urge to resist."

"My old man didn't own a video game company," Dom said.

Bonnie stewed in his words and refastened her ponytail.

"You're right," she said. "I didn't mean to imply a shared privilege. I can only imagine the mountains you've had to climb."

"I've had a lot of luck I didn't deserve," Dom said.

"You've been a heel most of your career. You understand playing a bad guy in the ring is nothing like being a villain in the world. The masses confuse the two. Your life has been defined by situations in which strangers expect you to be unsavory."

"That's true."

"Good. I try to be receptive to what our profession tells us about people. Look at how TV wrestling is written today. The heel can often be the wrestler the audience is most encouraged to love."

"I've always had a hard face to warm to."

"We could cover it," Bonnie said.

"A mask? No way. Wrestling 101—cover your face, you'll get erased."

"Didn't you say your character didn't matter?"

"Looks matter. It's why people see me and cross the street."

Bonnie nodded. "You're not a dummy, Domingo. I like you."

"Gee, thanks."

"Hack Barlow was never your destiny. Frankly, it's shocking you took him this far. You're reaching a turning point, and you're starting to get nervous, to make mistakes."

"I'm not afraid of anything."

"Oh, Domingo. I just complimented your intelligence."

"It's Dom," the wrestler said, knuckles white.

"How much weight have you lost in the past year?"

"About fifty pounds."

"How have you lost it?"

"More cardio. Eating less trash."

"What's the last thing you had to eat?"

"Coffee," Dom said. Bonnie didn't need to hear about the sludge.

"And before?"

Dom had to think. "Protein shake."

"What's the last meal you've eaten?"

He could've lied, said chicken breast and steamed broccoli, lemon zest, some egg whites with hot horseradish. He feared Bonnie would catch him. He tried to remember the contents of his last meal. By then his silence had proved her point.

"You're crash dieting," Bonnie said. "Fine, as long as you can level out before you start losing muscle. My bet is you're not paying adequate attention."

"It's my body, my business."

"Wrong. As long as you're under MCCW contract, your body is very much *my* business."

The Bronx Buster beeped and booped in his next match with a BAW undercarder. The simulated draw's cheers sounded like static from an old radio.

"Tell me about Cee-Saw," Bonnie said.

Dom's blood simmered. "He got what he had coming."

"And you thought what? Nobody would mention it?"

"I thought you would've had bigger fish to fry than some pissant greenhorn from Sumter County."

"I take it there was no apology."

Anger pinged up Dom's spine and radiated into the room. Bonnie smacked her lips with it.

"You say that as if he deserved one," Dom said.

Bonnie asked Dom to follow her into the apartment's backyard. She was light on her feet, seemingly unperturbed by Dom confirming his violence. The tract of gravel and crabgrass was flat. A tall fence separated Bonnie's rectangle from those of her neighbors. The hum from the asphalt plant blanketed everything in white noise. The yard was private. Closed to the world. Open to the sky. Dom fantasized about a free afternoon, a lounge chair, a case of beer.

A barrel stamped with SeACOat Asphalt stood in the center of the plot. Bonnie pulled a knotted trash bag filled with something light from a can next to the back door and gestured Dom over.

"This is chic," Dom said, flicking the side of the barrel.

"Beautiful, isn't it? Firelight licking through the rust. The metal's warmth after the flames disappear."

"You rich have no taste."

"I lived in Mexico City for a decade. Quite a few late nights out of doors, I was thrilled to have one of these lovelies roaring. It's more temperate than you'd guess. The altitude."

Dom set his jaw and nodded. A lizard sought shelter through a hole in the bottom of the barrel.

"You ever been?" Bonnie asked.

Dom's denial came too quickly.

"Shame," Bonnie replied. "You're leaving a lot of money down there."

"Oh fucking well," Dom said.

Bonnie kicked some dirt, plugging the opening at the bottom of the barrel. "I understand your fear. You've spent your career trying to convince people you don't belong in a mask. Had you explored it, you would've found it's exactly what you've wanted. Americans get so wrapped up in identity. Everyone reads your face and writes your story before you say a word. Lucha is different. In a mask, it's not about who you are. It's what you do."

"If it's so good, why didn't you stay?"

"*Luchadores* are acrobats," Bonnie said. "I always joked that *lucha libre* is literally 'fight free.' They're consummate performers—showmen. My education came from the *barrios, luchadores callejeros*. They can take a punch. I wanted to run with them, but their ceiling is only so high."

"How high do you want to go?" Dom asked.

"A new promotion," Bonnie said. "I'm removing wrestling from the ring, stripping its pageantry. We bring the show to the people. No advertisements. No artifice."

"How do you get attention?"

"You've seen a bar fight, haven't you? We pick a crowded place and start a ruckus. People watch. It's human nature."

"No tickets?"

"Tickets are obsolete. Think about the future. The WWE isn't selling pay-per-views anymore. They're pushing subscriptions. What comes next?"

"Holograms," Dom said.

"You stop selling," Bonnie said. "Make people the product. You earn their eyeballs and milk them for advertising."

"How?"

"We create a platform and host videos of the fights."

"C'mon. You'd need half the country clicking ads to make any money."

"How many people watch the Super Bowl?"

Her words hit Dom's palate like a chunk of hard gristle—too much to chew.

"You're serious?"

"No. I'm Bonnie Blue, the notorious prankster."

Dom cut off his reply with the thought of Pilar. He had a couple of buddies from his Ohio Valley days who could land them some gigs. He could get his foot in the door while praying that whatever was wrong with his sister would fix itself.

"We need to talk about Pilar."

"Three-year deal," Bonnie said. "Full medical. She'll have an open road to the main event long before we shutter MCCW. Vince would be an idiot not to poach her. All you have to do is agree to become my new star."

"A hard sell," Dom said, running a finger along the lip of the barrel. "It's not like you."

Bonnie untied the knot atop the trash bag. "You've heard the rumors about me, right?"

"Everyone has."

"I don't hide it. The truth is always the best story."

Bonnie opened the bag and showed Dom its contents— shredded paper.

"These are lies," Bonnie said. "Forty years of exaggerations, fabrications, and self-aggrandizing—letters from my former partner. I've been told I was the closest Clout Crawczak ever came to having a friend. He was a twentieth-century P. T. Barnum. He conned rich men to invest in a show that conned poor men. The only reason I didn't take him down like I did my father was that I knew I could redeem this business. There's magic in what we do. It's why you risk your neck. It's why you sacrifice your free time teaching your sister. Wrestling is special. What if we could do better?"

Dom watched her dump the nest into the barrel. She shook the bag until the last shards fell free, pirouetting to rest atop the feathery mound.

"What makes it better?" Dom asked.

"I get what I want. You get what you want." Bonnie produced a lighter and flicked it to life. "Think about it. Ignore your excuses and justifications. Be honest. How did you like breaking Cee-Saw's arm?"

The paper, some of it decades old, embraced the flame.

"It felt fantastic," Dom said.

In seconds, the nest blazed orange and red, though Dom's attention dropped from the fire to the barrel's bottom rungs, the plugged hole.

"That's because it was real," Bonnie said.

TWENTY-ONE

Bonnie had revealed her proposal efficiently. She'd called it The Pit. Dom would be its star. He'd work matches like any Street Fight or Falls Count Anywhere bout until the climax. He'd defeat his opponents with devastating final moves, inflicting actual injury. Orchestrated drama, real consequences.

He'd caused harm. It was unavoidable. In Evendale he'd botched a piledriver and nearly paralyzed a guy—a dad, three kids. In Louisville he clipped a ref with the blunt side of his axe and screwed up his eye. Simply by wrestling, he'd put extra miles on each of his opponents' odometers, wear and tear leading to knee replacements, arthritis, addiction, CTE. The damage he'd wreaked was catastrophic, and he could no longer say he'd never intended it.

If Dom didn't play ball, Bonnie had cause to cut him loose. She would spread word of his violence. He wasn't a big enough draw for a promoter to risk paying him a living wage. Queensland had folded. His other Ohio Valley promotions were struggling to survive.

If he agreed, Bonnie would sign Pilar to a three-year contract with MCCW, health insurance included—a rarity. She'd add another zero to his pay, and if he remained champion for over a year, she'd double it. She guaranteed him 2 percent of the gross with a renegotiation clause after five years. She promised some creative control. The contract would've made WWE Superstars jealous. He could move out of his tenement. Pilar could get her own place.

The Pit was performance, so no need for sanctions like boxing or MMA. Intention to harm didn't matter if both parties agreed to participate. Hockey fights were legal. Performance art in which people hung up their friends by hooks through their skin was legal. Filming stunts with premeditated genital injury was practically its own genre. The Pit was not fundamentally different than professional wrestling. How often had Dom submitted to a beating from a blunt object that left disgusting welts? How many blading scars were hidden above his hairline?

Dom left Bonnie's and stopped at a convenience store. The coffee machine didn't have an option to fill a cup of hot water, so Dom paid the eighty-nine cents for a small brew. Outside, he poured some of the coffee on the pavement and shook in half of his remaining Yucca Mountain grounds.

A container would typically last him a week. After dumping a bunch while chasing the Omegle Girl, he was almost out.

Heat was building in the Civic, and his warm drink hastened the discomfort. He started the car and blasted the air-conditioning. Another text from B arrived.

"Shes not answering. Im sorry I left. Please tell me shes ok please."

He sipped sludge and pulled up the Omegle Girl's profile.

"Hey," he wrote. "Was that you at Yucca Mt. Coffee this morning? You walked up to me at the sugar table and asked what was in the bottle of raw. I checked with the barista. It's raw milk. Unpasteurized. Hope that clears things up!"

He cut the note from the message window and brought up Charlotte's Craigslist. On the Missed Connections board, above an entry seeking a "pizza delivery hottie," he pasted the note, and sleaze oozed from the screen. He couldn't believe the board was so active. There were a dozen recent posts—desperate, late-night gasps. Dom imagined himself huddled among those lecherous men, sweating and wheezing. He entered his email address. When the system asked him to verify it, he flicked to his email app. A sudden tap on his window stopped him.

"Good evening, sir." It was a cop.

He was short, with blond hair cropped close and a neck that told Dom he was stronger than he looked. He had a partner on the other side of the Civic. The angle and his flashlight prevented a read. Dom wedged the sludge into the cup holder, lowered the window, and gripped the bottom of the wheel.

Speaking to Dom's lap, the dashboard, the foot well, the back seat, the officer mumbled an introduction. He identified his partner and asked how Dom was doing.

"I'm okay," Dom said. There were risks to giving police bad news.

"We noticed you when we pulled into the lot. You've been idling a while and your rear windows are obscured. I can't see through them. Why are they like that?"

The curtains Dom had rigged were drawn so he couldn't see them across the doors in the dark but not so far as to block his view out the rear window. While not in use, they were usually stowed in the spaces between the front and rear doors. Someone had fiddled with them—maybe B when they'd driven together to the Hangar.

"Those are my blinds," Dom said. "I'm on the road a lot so I sleep back there—like a camper."

"You take this thing camping?"

"No. Rest stops and stuff."

"You planning on sleeping here tonight?"

"I wasn't. They're usually pinned back."

The partner bent over and peered directly through the driver's-side window. He held his flashlight right next to his head so Dom couldn't see his face.

"You mind if we take a quick look?" the first officer asked.

Dom did mind, but he consented. Any resistance would trigger a full search. Dom didn't need the headache of explaining his glove-box pharmacy.

The cops had Dom shut the car off and provide his identification. Their lights danced over the seats. The partner opened the trunk without asking. The first officer joined him behind the car, and they exchanged words Dom couldn't hear. After a few seconds, the partner returned to the squad car, parked behind the Civic in the outer ring of spots surrounding the convenience store.

"You sleep in here?" the officer asked, pressing the edge of the mattress.

"If I have to," Dom said.

"What do you do that requires you to sleep on the road?"

"I'm a professional wrestler."

The officer trained his light on Dom. "Like the WWF?"

"Maybe someday," Dom said with a wince. "I'm on the independent circuit."

"I watch with my son. He's big into wrestling. Streams crazy matches from Mexico and Japan. Honestly, you look like one of his favorites. He's a lumberjack."

"Hack Barlow?"

"Holy cow. Yeah."

"Well, that's me," Dom said. This recognition gave him an angle. Work the child, he thought. Distract from the stereotypes. Get a read on the partner.

"I'll be damned. It's nice to meet you," the officer said. "We watched you a few Sundays ago. You and the Russian."

"How old is your son? Kids aren't supposed to like me."

The officer pointed his light to the ground. "He's twelve. He gets bored with the good guys. Would you mind taking a picture? It'll blow his mind."

Dom laughed. "No problem, brother."

"Thank you so much. Hold tight one minute."

Dom watched him through the rearview talking with his partner in the squad car, pointing at his onboard computer. Dom sipped his sludge. A sinewy older guy trudged out of the convenience store and scowled at him against the police lights. The clerk nervously peered out his window around an advertising board for the national lotteries. One had reached a jackpot of $950 million. Dom couldn't help doing the math. Two percent was $19 million.

The cops were taking too long for a simple run of his information. A second squad car arrived, lights flashing. Two additional officers emerged. After a chat, they lingered behind as the original officers returned to Dom's window.

"Hack—I mean, Domingo, would you mind stepping out of the car, please?" the original officer asked.

"What's going on?" Dom asked.

"Do you have anything in your pockets or something that could stick us?"

Dom was wearing track pants and a T-shirt, his typical post-match gear. He left his wallet, phone, and keys in the Civic.

The officers failed to conceal their surprise when Dom stood to his full height. He got a look at the partner, who started patting him down. His eyes were iceberg blue, almost unnatural. He was sporting a thick moustache straight from a 1980s police serial.

"For everyone's safety," the officer explained. His voice had lost confidence. His partner found nothing, and the three looked at each other for a moment.

"What's in the cup?" the partner asked, reaching for the sludge.

"Coffee," Dom said.

"Doesn't smell like coffee," the partner said, his moustache a caterpillar on the foam rim.

"What's it smell like?" Dom asked. He cursed himself under his breath.

"Is everything all right out here?" the clerk shouted from the entrance to the store. His volume was triple what it needed to be, startling both Dom and the cops.

"We have it handled, sir. Thank you," the first officer said.

"It's handled. Good," the clerk yelled. "Please handle it quickly. No one will stop here with the police outside."

"We understand. Thank you for your patience," the officer said.

"I don't want a reputation. This is a safe area. I've worked here fifteen years."

The officer gestured to his backup, and the two newly arrived cops marched over to placate the clerk. As if he were checking the time, one officer removed his baton from its holster and held it against his hip.

Dom blinked his attention to the officer in front of him.

"I add espresso grounds to it," he said. "Gives an extra kick. Though I can't vouch for the taste."

The partner took another whiff of the sludge and shined his light into it. From inside the car, Dom's phone buzzed with three texts in quick succession.

"Who's blowing you up?" the partner asked.

"Probably some girl," Dom said.

"Do you mind if we do a more thorough search of your vehicle?" the first officer asked.

Yes, I fucking mind, Dom thought. At least he was asking permission. He could've been playing cordial, or he might've not yet had whatever he needed to stop asking questions.

"Look, what's this about?" Dom asked. "I worked late tonight and my sister's ill."

The partner took a small sip of the sludge and, curling his lips under his teeth, forced it down. The first officer sighed and squeezed his temples. "Here's it straight," he said. "Earlier today we got a call—attempted assault, street not too far from here. You fit the subject description. Tall, bearded, Latino—"

"I'm not Latino," Dom said.

The officer's response caught in his throat, and he stared at Dom as if he'd claimed he was Martian.

"So where you from?" the partner asked.

"Cincinnati."

"I mean, where is your family from?"

"My mother is Spanish, and she's been here my whole life."

"Spanish, Latino—the point is you fit the description," the first officer said.

Dom kept his poker face. Those catcalling assholes had reported him—of course they had. They'd called him Speedy and thought it was funny. They'd witnessed Dom's phenomenal restraint. They'd left unharmed when he could've spared the parking meter and bent their spines.

"What you been up to today, son?" the partner asked, thumb hooked on his belt.

"Excuse me?" Dom said.

Shouts from the clerk snapped the three's attention to the convenience store. The clerk slipped between the two officers and burst outside.

"This is gross misconduct! This is disturbing the peace. Who is behind this? Who is paying you to disrupt my business?"

The partner sprang to action, intercepting the clerk and threatening an obstruction charge. The clerk gave some ground, stopping at the store entrance.

"Sorry," the officer said. "My partner doesn't recognize you, and he's been itchy. I love wrestling. Watching people use violence to solve their problems is fun when you know it's all a show."

Dom took a breath and made sure his tone reflected the officer's.

"You'd be surprised how real it can get."

"I think we've made a lot out of nothing here," the cop said. "Do you have anyone who could confirm your whereabouts around four this afternoon? It'll help with the report."

"My sister," Dom said, and it was the truth. His encounter with the men had been earlier, before noon. He was in luck. Maybe they hadn't wanted to peg themselves at that place and time. Maybe they'd flubbed it, those dumbasses.

The officer asked if he could contact her. Dom retrieved his phone and pulled up Pilar's info. The officer tapped the call button and wandered a few steps away.

"Straight to voicemail," he said.

Pilar not answering should've alarmed Dom. The sludge was kicking in.

"There's someone else we were with—her friend B," Dom said.

"Bea? Like Bea Arthur?"

"Oh no, sorry. B's short for Bonnie, I guess."

"Last name?"

"I'm not sure. We met today."

The officer had the look of a man who expected all this would come back to bite him in the ass. Dom tapped her number and gave him the phone. At least he knew B would answer.

"No, miss. This is Officer Rick Evans with the Charlotte-Mecklenburg Police. I'm standing here with Domingo Contreras."

The officer stepped away, and the conversation was lost behind the shouting clerk. He was screaming about civil forfeiture and the unconstitutional use of state power. He claimed his store had never been robbed, yet the cops were always loitering in his parking lot.

The cop smiled as if he were shooting the shit with a buddy. Though it punched Dom's ticket to freedom, he wasn't thrilled to see it. The cop didn't deserve to smile—not today, not while talking with B. When the cop returned the phone, he was still wearing it—a grotesque, leering mask.

"It's Bonnie Hicks," the cop said. "She's a nice young lady. Sorry about your sister."

"Thanks."

"I think we're good here. Make sure you secure those curtains or whatever before you roll out. I hope you understand we have to take this kind of thing seriously, even if the woman who called in the description is a frequent flyer."

"Woman?" Dom said.

"Yeah. She sends out for us every few weeks. One time she reported a burglary, said someone took her antique plates. Meanwhile she has electronics and jewelry out in the open. None of it touched."

The three cops had coaxed the clerk inside. He was behind the register, ripping papers from drawers and flinging them onto the countertop. One of the backup officers picked up a document by a corner as if it were a sweaty gym sock.

"This woman reported that a bearded Latino guy tried to beat her up, and you thought it was me?" Dom asked.

"A big, bearded Latino," the officer answered. "So, you know. A hoss like you must be used to getting second looks."

Of all the gear on the officer's belt—baton, handcuffs, pepper spray, stun gun—his pistol was the only weapon Dom hadn't faced in the ring. He'd heard LEOs in training were subjected to their nonlethal ordnance. When the officer was frozen by Taser shock, perhaps it also reminded him the tongue was a muscle. When he showered, maybe he too had wept when the water reactivated the mace. They'd both voluntarily subjected themselves to this pain. They had that in common.

As Dom shook the officer's hand, he dared not stray from the thought. Right beneath it was the urge to put the man's head through the cruiser's windshield. Officer Rick hadn't earned his smile, his empathy, or even the right to move along. He deserved to be hurt.

"You mind if we take that picture real quick?" the officer asked. "My kid will love it."

TWENTY-TWO

Dom drove across the street to a strip mall's empty parking lot.
He let the last of his makeshift sludge drip onto his tongue.

The Civic did look suspicious. The curtains and mattress were
bizarre. The front-seat foot wells were covered with loose receipts
tracked with mud. Only one plastic hubcap remained on his
wheels. Layers of dirty clothes and forgotten shoes and unopened
bags of plush axes could've concealed a lot of contraband.

That was no fucking excuse.

Dom popped his glove compartment and swallowed a few
pills. He texted Bonnie two words: "I'm in."

Her response came swiftly. "Excellent choice. I'll have the
contract ready tomorrow."

He dialed B's number. Her hello was shaky, as if she were
expecting another cop.

"It's me this time," Dom said.

"They let you use cell phones in jail?"

"Cops are gone. I owe you one."

"I'll cash that in right now. The fuck is going on?"

She was bumming free cones from a twenty-four-hour McDonald's a few minutes away. Dom told her everything was fine and to hold tight. He drove to her with windows down, speakers crunching, curtains flapping like mad.

B was wearing Pilar's shirt. She sat in a booth opposite a greasy kid with a bad goatee and golden arches stitched into his polo. They were the only two in the dining room. Dom overstated his entry and smiled when the kid stopped gawking at B and cowered.

"You're quick," B said, taking a bite off the top of her soft serve.

"Hi. I'm Michael," the employee said with a wave. Dom ignored him.

"That looks like the best thing I've seen anyone eat in days," Dom said.

"You want one? Mikey will get it."

Dom licked the corner of his mouth. "Sure. Thanks, Mikey." He clapped the kid on the shoulder hard enough to leave a bruise and watched him scuttle away. When he got behind the counter, Dom yelled, "And five cheeseburgers. Add Mac sauce."

The kid gave a look as if he'd discovered his favorite indie rocker had offed himself in a hotel bathroom. He disappeared into the kitchen.

B lapped up the melt before it reached the bottom of the cone.

"I take it Pilar is okay?"

"She'll heal," Dom said. "Why'd you leave? She could've used you."

B took a bite from the edge of her cone and chucked the remainder across the restaurant. It careened off the trash can lid and came to rest at the foot of the entryway.

"Just tell me what happened with her."

And so Dom did. He told her about carrying Pilar away from the Hangar. How her hundred pounds and change had felt like a thousand.

"She was well enough to be pissed at me when I left," Dom said.

"I gave her the lamest excuse," B said. "Then she didn't answer her phone."

"Didn't for me either. She needs the space, I guess."

"How do you stomach it? I saw the way she bent. I thought I was going to be sick. Then the fucking plane. I had to get out."

"It's hard," Dom said. "If it weren't for me, she never would've stepped foot in a ring."

"If it weren't for you, she'd be five hundred miles away doing fuck all."

Dom wondered how much Pilar had told her, what she wanted her memory of those days to be. He had an impulse to spill the whole story. At least he could show he'd tried to do the right thing. After a decade of risk and idiot stunts, ripping her away from their mother was the scariest thing he'd ever done.

The employee arrived with Dom's food. B snatched the cone, topped with far less soft serve than her first one.

"You owe me," she said to Dom.

"You guys mind if I join you?" the kid said with a dry cough.

B stood and slipped a ten into the kid's pants pocket. "We're leaving. I'll catch you later, Mikey."

Her fingertips loitered against him as she started her exit. Dom followed and gave the kid a fist bump. On his way out, Dom stepped on B's misaimed cone, gooshing out a vanilla mess.

"Ooh, my bad, man," Dom said, hopping out the door.

In the Civic, Dom chowed. The burger toppings were off-center, leaving one side of the meat bone-dry and smearing cheesy gore onto the wrapper.

"Do you think he spit in this?" Dom asked.

"You were kind of an ass to him," B said.

Dom nodded and killed the burger in four bites.

"I need to thank you for talking that cop off his shit. He was playing it so easy, like he was doing me a favor. You'd think a cop would know there's no such thing as a casual stop for someone like me."

"I told the truth. It's bullshit that a guy with a gun can hassle you for some tiny thing wrong with your car."

"They didn't need a reason." Dom opened his pharmacy and removed a bottle, small and unassuming, though he'd slapped one of his forged labels on it. He opened his palm as a prompt for B and shook out a heavy dose.

"You are welcome," B said, eyes wide.

"Busy tonight?"

B tossed the pills into her mouth and washed them down with a bite of soft serve. "Not anymore."

Dom followed suit. She offered the cone. It tasted chemically sweet, nostalgic.

"There's someplace I want to take you," he said. "I think you'll get a kick out of it."

B buckled up, tilted her seat until the mattress stopped it, and propped her feet out the window. Once Dom accelerated onto the highway, the wind hastened the melting of her ice cream. She squinted hard and tried to chomp it down, but she couldn't stomach it. With far less fanfare than before, she threw the cone out the window.

"Brain freeze," she said.

TWENTY-THREE

The Yucca Mountain patrons gave no indication of the late hour when Dom and B arrived. The shop was busy, with the young, sludge-powered automatons working feverishly. As always, the guy with red shoes looked suspicious of Dom. The guy who'd threatened to throw his laptop was there. He held a cell phone and was scribbling on a notepad with alarming ferocity.

"What is this place?" B announced. She dipped a finger into the holy water font and looked disappointed when it came up dry. She knelt and traced the right angles of Rita's rose.

The barista was the same dude from earlier. His bubbly "Good evening, sir!" was an open-pit mine at the bottom of the uncanny valley.

"Hey," Dom said. "How're you doing?"

"Swell," the barista said. "Another spectacular day atop Yucca Mountain. How may I help you?"

"Listen!" B called from the sugar table. She shushed them, clearing the air for the clicking keyboards, scratching pencils, and quiet slurping. She soaked in the white noise and brought her fists to her head as if she were clutching a pair of antennae.

"It's so productive in here," she said.

The barista's grin somehow grew wider.

"It's her first time," Dom said.

"Splendid! Welcome, miss. We're so happy to have you."

"What is this place?" B asked again.

"It's Charlotte's best coffee joint," Dom said before the barista could respond. "And I'm its favorite regular."

"Do you work here, too?" B asked. "Do you write stories for your wrestling character? Oh my god. Do you have a screenplay?"

"Not yet," Dom said. "Do you want to help me with one?"

"Yes!"

"This is wonderful!" the barista said. "It's times like these I'm proud to be in this business. Imagine the thrill of seeing your names in the opening credits of a blockbuster. I could say I witnessed your partnership's inception. I helped fuel your creative process! So how about it, friends? What can I start for you?"

"You know Shamrock Shakes?" B said. "Could you do a coffee version of that?"

"What? No, no," Dom said, snapping to the barista. "You don't go to Paris and order meat loaf. We'll take my usual."

The barista's smile collapsed.

"The grounds?" Dom whispered.

"Sir, we distributed your allotment this morning."

"I goofed and spilled a bunch. I've had a rough day."

"He really has," B said. "His sister escaped paralysis. The police harassed him. He was almost crushed by an airplane. He—"

"He gets it," Dom said. He moved to eclipse B from the barista's view. "Maybe do me a solid and get the next batch a little early?"

"That would be most unorthodox," the barista said.

"Please?" B added, refusing to stick in Dom's shadow. "We'll give you a Special Thanks credit."

The barista scratched his nose, and in a lapse of concentration, slid his index finger up a nostril and picked it.

"Oh heavens!" he said. He shot to a wall-mounted sanitizer dispenser and pumped more foam than necessary. Scrubbing like mad and muttering apologies, he elbowed open the hot water tap of the sink and scalded his fingers beneath the stream.

Dom saw an edge. "It's okay, brother. Only—I think I see some nose gunk here on the countertop." He gave B a nudge.

"Uh, yeah," she said. "There's some gnarly booger action going down. Disgusting."

"I am terribly sorry!" the barista exclaimed. He doused the counter with disinfecting spray.

"You started here recently, right?" Dom asked. The answer was the same for every barista.

"Yes, sir. I assure you, this was not representative of my professionalism."

"Of course," Dom said. "We all slip up here and there."

"Give us the shit or we're reporting you to corporate," B said.

"I'll check the back!" the barista croaked. He fled into the kitchen's mysterious reaches.

"I'm asking a favor, not robbing the joint," Dom mumbled.

"You've clearly never worked in customer service," B said.

"This isn't Starbucks. I have a special relationship with this place."

"Then why are you letting yourself get treated like shit? At least ask for the manager."

"Do you see a manager? Have you noticed the time and how many people are here? Trust me. This is higher stakes than your run-of-the-mill latte order. Chill."

"Chill," B imitated. She withdrew to the sugar table, fiddled with a few of the bottles, and from there she spotted the beaded curtain separating the main floor from the restroom hallway. She parted the strands and slipped through.

Dom blew air out his nose and noted the freshly disinfected countertop. He hopped up to sit on it and surveyed the café. Before the house of worship had changed its allegiance, the counter might've been the lectern or altar. The patrons, their heads once bowed in prayer, were now consumed by devices, books, legal pads. Dom was the only one looking up—the only one except the guy in red shoes. He was staring right at him.

"What's it to you, buddy?" Dom said.

"You've lost weight since you first came here," the man said.

"Good eye."

"You a bodybuilder?"

"Something like that."

"Humans evolved for persistence hunting. Big muscles are inefficient. Today's culture overvalues strength, which is pushing us away from our natural frames."

"Jesus Christ," Dom muttered. He spun off the counter, and the barista returned.

"You're not carrying a small dairy container," Dom said.

"I'm sorry," the barista said. "There are strict rules."

"Yeah? Who makes them?"

"I don't know."

"So you blindly follow them? Why?"

"They're wrong to court you!" Red Shoes shouted. The barista looked to him over Dom's shoulder as if he could bail him from the confrontation. Dom seized the kid's chin and reminded him who had the rightful claim to his attention.

"I get it," Dom said. "Rules are rules. Secrets are secrets. I'm no bully. I hate bullies, actually. You know how often I got picked on in school?"

The barista offered a timid nod. Dom smiled, took out his debit card, and tapped it on the countertop. "As luck would have it, I don't need to be Yucca Mountain's charity case anymore. Give me a cup of the good stuff."

"Excuse me?" the barista said.

"The sludge," Dom said. "The seventy-five-dollar-a-cup rip-off that keeps all these jokers in the pews. I want one. To go."

"I can't."

Dom nearly put his tongue through his cheek. "Why not?"

"It's reserved for top-tier influencers."

"Influencers?"

"I can whip up a different drink. It'll strip the pink off your tongue."

"I don't want another drink. What do you mean, *influencers?*"

Red Shoes rose defiantly from his pew. "Stop tyrannizing the young man!"

Dom wheeled from the barista and charged him, stopping inches from collision. As if cued, the chorus of Yucca Mountain patrons snapped to attention. Pens fell from fingers, books closed, cursors silently blinked on screens.

Dom pointed to the man's shoes. "You want to find out how persistent you are in those?"

"Do you see me running?" the man asked. He was skinny. His thin hair made him look older. Dom could've lifted him with a tight grip on his ankle. The man scratched his nose. His voice remained steady. "It's time you quit pretending in here."

"Easy boys," B said, appearing beside the men. "Everyone's a badass. Everyone's a big, strong man."

She took the crook of Dom's arm and started to lead him away. "Let's go. Tactical withdrawal."

She mouthed a quick "trust me," and he acquiesced. Rather than be led out the café, Dom dashed ahead and opened the door. He had all the eyes in the building. It was almost a comfort. Dom knew what it was to be hated.

"After you," he said to B with a flourish. Before exiting, he bowed to the patrons. "Have a nice evening, fuckheads."

B backpedaled on the sidewalk. "Second time tonight I've bailed your ass out. I thought you were a fake fighter."

"I haven't been in a real fight in years," Dom said. He locked on a piece of asphalt from a pothole and readied to heave it through Yucca Mountain's front window.

"No, asshole," B said, grabbing the slab. "You're done with them. I got the shit."

She reached under her shirt and removed a full Yucca Mountain coffee bag secured by her shorts' waistband. Dom rolled the bag open. The black powder inside smelled like his grounds.

"How'd you get this?" he asked.

"There was a sack full of it in storage. It looked sketchy, so I filled a bag."

"This is like a two-month supply. We could start our own coffee shop. Sixty bucks a cup—undercut those fuckers."

"The hell are you talking about? What's in this?"

Dom insisted they try some. His moka pot brewed the best experience, but he wasn't about to take B to the apartment. All they needed was water.

"What's it do?" B asked.

"Roots you in the present. Throttles down your guilt to a tolerable level. Lets you see the world, and helps you appreciate your place in it."

"Sign me up."

They passed a few dark and unattended gas stations. Even the late-night joints shuttered for a few hours between Sunday and Monday. Dom had faced many close calls at this hour. His show had marked the end of the wrestling week. When he was touring, the empty roads tempted a sprint home for a day or two of rest. He tried to forget how often highway rumble strips kept him driving straight.

In the city, these long Sunday nights were Dom's favorite. With its residents hidden, Charlotte sparkled without distraction. The weekend had refreshed its neighborhoods. Lawns were cut, weeds pulled. New paint was splashed on railings and doorframes. Dom's body worked through a similar process— filling with promise, corroding, and then recharging. The two cycles were never synchronous. When Charlotte slept, Dom was working. When it geared up, he was winding down. When it was quiet, he was up to no good.

"Pull over," B said, putting her hair up with a tie from her wrist. "I've got an idea."

Dom stopped the Civic before a row of homes with short driveways and square patches of grass in front. B had Dom grab the bag of grounds and an empty soda bottle, and they hustled down the sidewalk.

"Someone's gonna take us for burglars," he said.

"Not if you stay quiet," B said. She halted them in front of a squat house flagged by a realtor sign. It was dark inside and no cars were on the curb. A vacant lot separated it from its neighbor. B took long, careful steps and tapped on her phone light.

"Yes!" she whispered. She held up the end of a garden hose coiled in a knot of weeds.

Dom shook some grounds into the bottle. They filled it halfway with hose water.

"Should've let it run for a bit," B said, inspecting mold spots on the hose's covering.

"Couple of spores won't kill you," Dom said. He shook the bottle. B held her phone to it. The mixture inside swallowed the light.

Dom offered B the first sip. She held her nose and gulped.

"Ugh. The fuck?"

Dom smiled and slurped. He swished the liquid like mouthwash, grit collecting between his teeth.

"It's good, right?"

B grimaced and took another sip. "It tastes like burnt espresso."

"Its beauty is in the subtlety."

"Fuck subtlety. You sure there's something in this? I wanna go to Mars."

"You'll see. Let's go."

"Wait. Let's explore. Maybe they left a key somewhere."

Dom drained the bottle. "Must be nice to consider casually breaking and entering."

"I'm not breaking anything," B said, testing a first-floor window.

"Of course not—especially when getting caught means the cops giving you a free ride to your parents' house."

"Boo hoo. You want to switch places? I'd love to see how unfair life is for a dude built like the Hulk."

B climbed the porch and tried the door before checking the mailbox, the welcome mat, under the plastic deck chairs. Dom waited as she hopped the railing and disappeared around the corner of the house.

The heavy summer air kept their voices from carrying. Dom was less anxious than he expected. Though he could step across the front yard in a couple strides, the property's boundaries offered protection—the chain-link fence around the backyard, the strip of grass between sidewalk and street, the tall oaks in the lot next door. He wanted to live in such a place. He was sick of sharing space. Even when he was alone in his apartment, he'd hear his floor mates fighting or fucking or watching TV.

It was no longer a fantasy, Dom realized. With his new deal, he could afford it.

"C'mere," B said, leaning over the fence. "You're gonna freak!"

Dom paused to listen for anyone who'd heard her. The neighborhood remained quiet, and they had an hour or two before the earliest would be rising for work. He hopped the fence, and B's phone light threw its cone over a trampoline behind the house. The circle of its mat was squared by four turnbuckles, ropes strung between.

"You need to make these people an offer," she said. "They're selling this place with a backyard wrestling ring."

Dom appreciated the love put into it. Each post was two poles welded together with metal attachment points for the ropes affixed in the groove between them. Padded inserts covered the gaps between the trampoline's curve and the turnbuckles' right angles. Dom strummed a rope—thick bungee cord. They were nowhere near the strength required to support a wrestler his size.

The trampoline sagged beneath Dom. After a few test jumps he saw he was clear from bottoming out. The springs were well greased and discreet. The pain in his tailbone and spine from his Freedom Fest match was gone. Maybe his new frame had expedited his healing. Maybe he'd taken enough to trick his body into feeling good.

"Watch this," Dom said. He leapt high and bounced hard, flipped, landed on his ass, and rode the momentum to his feet.

"Whoa. You're graceful," B said.

"Your turn," he said, floating into the corner.

"I don't have any fancy moves."

"Lemme show you one. Put your right hand at the base of my neck. Don't actually squeeze. It's fake, remember? Then I'll sell it like this." He grabbed her forearm and feigned a struggle to tear her away. Next, he had her seize his right arm and toss it over her right shoulder.

"Now grab my trunks with the same hand."

"Trunks are your shorts?"

"You got it. Take them on my right hip."

"It's like learning a dance step."

"When you have the physics down, tempo's the next thing to practice."

B laughed. "What's next?"

"You're gonna slam me."

"Yeah, okay. You're three times my size."

"Look where you've got me. You could be Hulk Hogan, you wouldn't be able to lift someone like me with one arm by the neck. We'll both crouch. You keep your feet on the mat, I'm going to jump. If you stay sturdy I might even push on your shoulder to boost myself higher."

"So my arm's along for the ride?"

"Yep. Sell it like you want to break my spine."

"Unjustified aggression—check."

Dom gave her a count of three. They bent their knees and rocked together. Dom coiled his muscles and took off. The trampoline's spring launched him high. He kicked out his legs and fell, striking the trampoline square across his back.

"Boom!" he shouted. He went stiff in the air on the rebound as if knocked unconscious. He hit face down and came to rest.

"Chokeslam," he said. "Ten outta ten."

B took a bounce, spinning and pumping her arms in victory.

"Is every move that easy? The victim does it all?"

"Not every move, but there's always teamwork."

"Then let's switch it up. I want to play a bigger role."

"Okay. How good are you at sit-ups?"

"You kidding? Check these out." B exposed her midriff and yanked Dom's wrist. When she let go, he kept pressing against her, feeling her waist.

"Damn," he said. "Not bad."

"Fucking right," she exclaimed. "They said I couldn't eat McDonald's and keep a tight core. You gotta stoke a fire to get it this hot."

"Let's try a Powerbomb," he said.

Its machinations were more complicated. B would start bent over, head between Dom's thighs. Again, they'd jump together, this time B leaving the trampoline with Dom wrenching her skyward by her waist. She'd help the process with a push off his knees and a sit-up in midair. At the move's apex, she'd sit on his shoulders. Finally, he'd heave her to earth.

"Keep your chin tucked," he said. "This one could snap your neck."

"Like Pilar," she said.

"Yeah, actually," he said, recalling where they were—the darkness, the fake ring, its unfamiliar bounce. "Maybe we shouldn't do this."

"Fuck it. I'm doing most of the work, right? If I get hurt, it's on me."

B cut off Dom's reply by ducking between his legs. She left much less clearance over her head than a pro would've granted him.

He gave another count. She didn't get a solid push, but she was so light. He was plenty strong to pull her through. Her stomach tightened under his locked fingers. At the top, he held her there. She yelped as he spun, broke into the slam, and left his feet to complete the fall with her. They landed and bounced together, howling with laughter.

"She's down, ladies and gentlemen!" Dom said. "This may be over!"

He stood and dropped an elbow, bending over her torso so his hip and triceps took the impact. He shot to his feet and brought down a leg. His massive limbs came within millimeters of striking her. She sold the blows with gut-busting cries.

Dom arched his back across her chest, hooked her leg, and counted, "One, two, three! Barlow takes it!"

"Terrible," B said. "Who writes this trash?"

Dom rolled up and straddled B across her hips, keeping her pinned. The low clouds reflected the city's yellow glow. It was plenty bright to see her. B was tiny compared to most MCCW women. Dom could imagine a time when he wouldn't have noticed her simply because there wasn't enough of her. Now, he could see why the McDonald's kid looked ready to lick dirt off her toes.

"What's it like to have the Timber Terror put you down for the three-second tan?"

B snickered and sat up, taking it slow as if to show Dom once more she was serious about her core strength. She held there, biting her tongue through a smirk.

"That was the lamest thing I've heard in my life," she said.

He leaned down and kissed her, and she kissed back.

She pressed against him, tangled limbs, meshed fingers—a closeness so intense it stymied movement. Feeling her muscles completely engaged in consuming him spurred a painful want for more. Keeping tight to his body, she reached under his waistband. He worked beneath her shirt—his sister's shirt, he couldn't help remembering—sternum, bra, ribs, breasts. He flexed his thigh and she clamped it between her legs.

"We can't do this here," he said, with barely enough breath for the sentence.

"Your car," she said. She slipped even lower and squeezed harder than he would've asked.

At the Civic, she pinned him against the door before he could open it. She lifted his shirt as high as she could and he took it the rest of the way. His exposed chest brought her nails, and he shuddered at the terrific friction as she scraped south. "Harder," he said, loving the sting, needing more of it. Women could be tentative to hurt him. B didn't need further persuasion.

It was a clunky scramble onto the mattress. Dom remembered the Alabama girl, how claustrophobic the Civic had been. Though the cabin was stuffy and getting stickier with their breathing, the discomfort only heightened the urgency to tear off clothes.

This is happening, Dom thought. Had it really been that simple? Find a girl, get fucked up, bounce on a trampoline. He only needed to believe it could happen, to see proof someone like B could find him so voraciously enticing.

A streetlight bathed the Civic in its jaundiced cone, but it was darker in the cabin than in the backyard. B moved by touch, finding him again. She licked his length and laughed, coming up to kiss him.

"You're very tidy down there," she said.

"Never know when they might put me in spandex," he said.

"Yeah. But like, there's a shape to it?"

"Oh, right. It's the letter 'H.' I lost a bet."

B laughed and bit his lip. She scratched him again on her way down.

He had her full, enthusiastic attention. She was thrilled to have him. She moved as if she were batting down idea after idea on how to please him, working to stay focused. Dom labored to center himself on the sensations she was so eager to provide. It wasn't easy. There was so much he wanted to do, so much of her to process. He wished he'd switched on the dome light to see her better. He wondered if it would ruin the mood if he excused himself to fire up the air-conditioning. He could slow the sweat dripping from his brow, the irritation building in his eyes.

As much as she may have enjoyed giving, it felt unfair to simply wait his turn. There wasn't much to do from his position, and the Civic's confines limited the possibilities for rearrangement. He tried to voice his appreciation—moans and yeses, contractions and shivers. His words sounded more silly than sexy. Something was digging into his shoulder.

He was watching, not participating. He fixated on the noises, which on their own were kind of gross. He brought B up, kissed her, helped her onto her back, a jumble of elbows and knees. He kissed her neck, her collarbone, mirrored the route she'd taken. He reached her hip, and she stopped him.

"That's not my favorite thing," she said.

"Oh," he said. "Sorry. I thought—"

"It's okay. Here." She directed his hand between her legs.

There was nothing else in the world. Her absorption was complete. Its gravity should've drawn Dom into the moment. Instead, he grew jealous. How was she comfortable? They were both slick with sweat. Her hair had come undone. Damp strands fell into her face. Why was she having it so easy? This was his car, his home for countless nights.

"I'm close," she said. "I want you."

And he wanted her. He was sure of it, but his certainty was no help. It added weight to the truck driving over his chest. He'd been a fool to think this would proceed differently. He was fucking broken, and he'd exposed a beautiful, well-meaning person to his ugliness.

"I can't," he said. He struck the side panel, denting it, and triggered a rockslide of obscenity. B was frightened at first, then confused. Soon she discerned the problem. She forced his arms to his sides and held him.

"Hey," she said. "It's okay. This doesn't have to happen right now. I'm cool with it."

She could only reach around half of his torso. Dom tried to shrug her away, but her grip was steady.

"These are not ideal conditions," she continued. "So much happened today."

She paused as if awakened from the dream in which her romp with Dom was a frolic without consequence. Never mind the unwritten rules keeping people from doing stupid shit like sleeping with their best friend's brother. Their sin struck deeper.

Rather than respecting her relationship with B, a bond forged with so few of the privileges other women her age were afforded, Dom had robbed Pilar of one of her few claims to privacy. He'd done it wantonly, to no one's benefit. Whatever blame B was due tripled for him. He was older. He'd supplied the pills.

"I'm fucking useless," Dom said. He stared at the glow-in-the-dark plastic toggle one could pull if locked in the trunk. Though it dangled into his sleeping space and served no purpose with his seats removed, he'd never cut it off.

"You're not," B said. "You're a good guy, and we all have shit. I've screwed up so many times. I've always had someone to listen."

"There's nothing to talk about," Dom said.

"We don't have to talk," B said. She found the dome light and put on her clothes. Dom buried his face in his hands.

"Seriously. I'm here for you," she said.

Dom managed a thank you and said he'd take her home. Behind the wheel, he cranked the defoggers and waited for the windshield to clear. The street faded in—the proud homes, the clean yards. He'd never live in a place like this. After the new promotion began, would he even stay in Charlotte? If he made the money Bonnie had promised, buying in this part of town would be a poor investment. He had to think long term—equity, resale value, retirement. The neighborhood was a goal he'd outgrown but hadn't achieved.

TWENTY-FOUR

The night of his debut in The Pit, Dom poured his drink into a toilet bowl in the men's bathroom at Bar Pavón, a hole-in-the-wall on Charlotte's east side. The stalls were covered with graffiti scrawled with the desperation of those squeezing their markers much harder than necessary. Music crackled through a disk speaker hanging by wires. A man and a woman sang to each other and played guitar. Their voices were almost whispers.

At the bar, Duke Natterjack had ordered Dom a glass of Manzanilla. The bar was filling with patrons unaware of the spectacle the two giants had planned. Dom left for the restroom fifteen minutes before showtime.

They'd rehearsed on the Skyport grounds in a general aviation garage. This was new work for each of them. No mat, no ropes, no barrier separating the onlookers. The cameras would roam, and Bonnie promised they wouldn't notice them amid those catching the action with their phones. Since the performances at the Hangar were streamed, the wrestlers worked to the hard camera, even during satellite shows. Bonnie practiced Duke and Dom until they broke the habit. "It has to look new," she'd said.

They had to find the right mix of excitement and authenticity. Dom could bump once or twice on concrete, maybe a few more times on a wood floor. Without the spring of a wrestling mat, many preferred maneuvers were impossible. Broken bottles, spilled drinks, low lighting—they anticipated solutions. What to do if not enough people were paying attention, if there was a child in the bar, if a hero tried to intervene, if someone pulled a gun.

Dom had never liked Duke. He was a wrestler from an era when a big frame and a bigger attitude could compensate for a lack of technical skill. He brownnosed to Bonnie behind closed doors. He'd also wipe salamander slime onto MCCW recruits. True to form, he wasn't the easiest practice partner. Duke refused to protect himself, taking gruesome bumps on his chest and face. He demanded Dom work his punches strongstyle. When Dom kept pulling his strikes, Duke walloped him and told him to sack up.

Dom almost quit right there. The veteran called a truce.

"You ever have to get rid of a ride you really, really liked?" Duke asked.

"Sounds like a rich man's problem," Dom replied.

"How about women, then? Did you ever have to dump a chick even though she made your eyeballs pop out in bed? You can't just let her go. Before you cut ties with what you love, you have to run it into the ground. If you don't, you'll miss it."

Weeks later, inside the men's room stall at Bar Pavón, Dom removed a mask from his duffel. Teardrop eyes stamped into its skull-white skin leered at him. He'd been forced into one years before, when he was wrestling backyards. It restricted his breathing and vision. It collected sweat and chafed his nose and chin. When he botched, spectators laughed at him, told him to get his ass back over the border.

Dom usually lied when asked where he got the idea for a gimmick like Hack Barlow. The truth was that after months of catcalls he burned the mask and decided to run—from high flyer to lumbering monster, from luchador to northern woods-man. He grew the beard. He put on weight. He thrifted flannel and trapper hats.

The slurs stopped, but it wasn't only that. The marks still jeered him. He always played the heel. But their voices changed tune. It reminded him of when he'd started hearing the difference between his colleagues' cries of pain and the bite of an actual injury.

His old mask was Velcro. This one had laces crossing finely stitched eyelets. Dom loosely strung them paratrooper-style like his wrestling boots, though he wasn't wearing those. He had on jeans and sneakers. A simple, white T-shirt was taut on his chest.

Dom painted on a coat of eye black, a mask behind the mask. He cut his beard as short as his pair of scissors would allow. The pile of trimmings collected in the sink, and he left them there. He saw his true jaw line for the first time in years and hated it. He'd lost all prominence in his chin. It looked atrophied, forgotten like the calves of the college meatheads infesting the gyms before spring break.

He wasn't worried about the fight. He was worried about the period after the fight had started, before the patrons understood the two men weren't drunk idiots disrupting their evening. In those moments of surprise, when everyone would see the gigantic man who'd spent an inordinate amount of time in the shitter fly through the restroom door wearing a luchador mask, Dom would have to bear the weight of their confusion. So many faces asking, "Who does this motherfucker think he is?" He knew the words they'd use to insult him.

The inside of the mask was impossibly dark. Dom checked the eyeholes and mouth slits for obstructions. They were clear. He felt how hot the mask would be, how stifling.

Duke gave a quick warning knock and slipped inside, moving with the flair of a man who'd been drinking too confidently.

"You look spooky," he said.

"What's that supposed to mean?" Dom asked.

Duke dropped his bag and squared up at the urinal. "You're a big-ass dude with tar-covered eyes. You're scary. What else would it mean?"

"How's it looking out there?" Dom asked.

"It's dim, dirty, and cheap. Choice spot for my final bow."

"You could put retirement on hiatus. Pop up out West somewhere. If you're wrestling small-time under a new name, I doubt Bonnie would give a shit."

Duke flushed and took out his mask. It was red and leathery, something asylum staff would strap to an inmate with a bite risk.

"Nah," Duke said. "This is my exit. Hardest thing for a lifer is to know when to hang it up. Huge payday, pension, and a chance the rub I give you will actually have meaning? I might be a fool, but I'm not a damn fool."

"Retirement," Dom said. "What a concept."

"I'm going to start my own business," Duke said. "You been to the Serpentarium in Wilmington? You pay to walk around this guy's collection of deadly snakes. It's like a zoo if they let a real entertainer run things. I'm gonna do that, only with poison frogs. I'm calling it Ghosts of the Amazon."

"I'd invest, but I think life insurance would be the better bet."

"You laugh now. A good tourist trap is a mint. Here, help me with this."

Duke gestured to the web of buckles and straps hanging loose behind his head. There were a dozen or so stitched at bizarre angles. All were aesthetic, of course. The mask fit snugly with elastic straps hidden beneath the showcase leather.

"Need a tie?" Duke asked.

"No," Dom replied.

"Then let's go. Time's a-wastin'."

Dom looked into the black hole of the mask, nearly choking on the urge to fight against its gravity. He'd felt its pull the first day he stepped into the ring. Now he'd crossed the event horizon. It would stretch him into oblivion.

"I don't think I can wear this," he said.

"Why not?" Duke said.

"It feels like giving up."

Duke grabbed the sides of his mask, wrenching it left a quarter inch to center his eyes in their slits. He nodded and spoke without irony.

"Brother, if that's the case, you quit a long time ago."

"You don't understand," Dom said. "I swore on my life I'd never wear one of these things again."

"So fuck your life. If everything goes to plan, that mask is going to give you a better one."

"It's not my life I'm trying to improve."

Dom cracked his knuckles and slipped the hood over his head. He pointed Duke to the laces. The wrestler tightened them one rung at a time.

"Nobody hates something without being curious about it," Duke said.

Framed by the mirror, the mask granted a shock of menace. Thin, black strips of Lycra hashed across his lips like stitching. The figure was foreign, yet familiar.

"How's that?" Duke asked, finishing the knot.

"I need a drink," Dom said. He reached into his duffel and removed a bottle of sludge.

"Oh, fuck me," Dom said, touching the Lycra over his mouth.

"Smooth," Duke said. "You should've kept pace at the bar."

"It's not booze."

"Oh yeah? What is it?" Duke asked.

"Forget about it."

Duke seized the bottle and brought it where his nose would presumably be. "Smells like paint thinner. I want me some."

"Well, you missed your chance."

"Bullshit." Duke stuck the tip of his tongue through a narrow hole between the straps crossing his face and poked at his phone.

"We're minutes to curtain."

"Let 'em sweat," Duke said. "Hola. We're in the bathroom and have an emergency order for a straw."

Duke repeated himself, holding the phone where his ear should've been. "Yep—a straw. The thing you sip through. Sí, señor. The men's restroom."

Duke continued and Dom bent over the sink and stared at the figure in the mirror. When Bonnie had told them there would be no speaking, no pageantry, Dom had approved. In the ring, he was never much of a talker.

"That was difficult," Duke said, hanging up. "How do you say 'straw' in Spanish?"

"Fuck you," Dom said. He pulled the lid from a plastic trash bin and, as planned, stashed his bag inside.

"No need for a tantrum. Daddy's getting your bottle."

"I see why Bonnie's putting your sorry ass out to pasture."

"Bonnie would have me as long as I'm slinging tees and filling seats with ass. This was my choice, brother."

Duke gathered his loose gear, shoved it in his bag, and stuffed it in the trash can. Dom couldn't see his expression beneath his mask. His movements bore no signs of nervousness.

"Not sure how the boss sold this to you. To me, it's a big fucking favor," Duke said. "I'll be straight. It's not Bonnie I'm worried about following through."

There weren't many people on the planet who could stare Dom in the eye without looking up. Duke was one of them. Dom stepped to him, and the veteran held his ground, crimson-leather nose to white-Lycra nose.

The bathroom door opened, and the clamor from the bar washed in over the lovers' crackling voices singing through the speaker. A man followed. He was wearing an apron and holding a straw sheathed in its paper wrapper. The wresters turned their heads in tandem, and the man jumped.

"¡Coño!" the man said.

"How you doing, boss?" Duke said. He took the straw, thumped the man on the chest, and ushered him out the door.

Duke's shoulders bounced as if he were laughing. He tore away the end of the wrapper and brought the straw's naked end to the hole in his mask.

"Heads up," he said, blowing into the straw and shooting off the wrapper. It struck Dom in the forehead.

"Bull's-eye," Duke said.

"I hate you," Dom said.

Duke gestured for the bottle of sludge, the straw in his mouth a plastic proboscis. Dom gave it to him, and Duke sipped.

"Hmm. That's a whole lotta nothing," Duke said.

"What do you mean?" Dom said.

"Ain't a substance on God's Earth that hasn't passed over these lips," Duke said. "That's strong coffee at best." He returned the sludge with the straw in the bottle.

"It's subtle," Dom said. "You have to wait for it."

"That's what they tell you," Duke replied. "Who'd you get this from? He's got some balls. Most snake-oil guys respect you enough to put *something* in it."

Dom sipped the sludge. Its familiar bitterness took him back to his pew among the Yucca Mountain faithful. They were always there, always looking so intently at their screens, their notebooks, whatever was right in front of them. Behind the patrons and the baristas, someone had decided to give Dom his allotment of grounds. Whether this was a gift horse or a free lunch, Dom had been avoiding the obvious questions.

Though he'd received the sludge without exchange, he could imagine it as reimbursement for the years he'd toiled with few favors. It wasn't a sports car or a fancy watch or complimentary bottle service, but it was a taste. He'd earned at least a taste.

Dom took another sip—bitter as always. He wasn't so naive as to deny his arrangement had been transactional. Nor was he too proud to believe he was immune to marketing schemes and brand psychology. It was almost comical to think that he, with few fans and fewer friends, had any real *influence*. The barista wouldn't even let him purchase the shop's signature product.

Then what was Yucca Mountain buying with all those containers of spent grounds? His presence? He was a bruiser stuffed in sweats, heaving in the back pew. His loyalty? The hope that his craving for the sludge could grow into a more expensive dependence? Or was it his future? Dom might've been a no-name the first time he'd trod upon the old church's headless patron, but if Bonnie was right, he was moments away from catching a rocket to stardom.

Dom poured the remaining sludge into the sink.

An alarm sounded on his phone. It was buried in the trash can, but its cheery ping straightened both wrestlers to attention.

"Sixty seconds."

Duke eyed the door. "Have you ever thought about what you would do if you stopped wrestling?"

"I could open up a deadly lizard zoo right next to your deadly frog zoo and put your ass out of business," Dom said.

Duke didn't return the volley. He chomped the straw until it crinkled into his mouth. The tinny singers harmonized the final notes of their song.

"If I could do something else," Dom said, "I don't think I would've gotten this far."

Duke fished out the plastic and flicked it away. His hand was shaking. It was slight, subtle enough to be mistaken for a flicker of the lights.

"I've got a real, honest-to-god chance to get out, and I believe you're going to do right by me. But it's a lot less scary imagining you fucking it up, and me returning to the ring next week."

"I'm not botching this," Dom said.

"Then do me a favor," Duke said. "Make it hurt."

The crowd at Bar Pavón was not a draw. There'd been no advertisements, no tickets. When Dom and Duke tumbled through the restroom door, there were no announcers, no entrance themes. There wasn't a show until they built one.

The surprise of the fight swung all heads to attention. A man clutched his chest in fright, his longneck tumbling from his hand and drenching his lap. Another patron darted behind an arcade cabinet. He had a bulge on his hip—a radio, a weapon? An old woman at the bar ignored the calamity. She sipped her drink neat, her twiggy claw clasping the tumbler.

Wasting no time, Dom charged Duke, who ducked and carried his momentum into a Death Valley Driver. Dom tucked his head, his ear against his opponent's thigh. He heard the crack from Duke's pelvis as it absorbed the impact with the wood floor. There were shouts of surprise, moans of fear. Among them, Dom heard what he'd been hoping for. The guttural hoot of someone who'd recognized the spectacle unfolding before him—the sound of a man entertained.

Bonnie was right. Earning that validation in an environment where no one had expected them was transcendent. It was a higher high than any drug could provide. The sludge in comparison was instant decaf. His neck stung. Dust ground from his clavicles scraped inside his shoulders. That damage was nothing. He'd take whatever punishment necessary to win over every person in the bar.

Improvisational maneuvers blended with their planned steps. Duke flowed with him, slick as wet glass. Dom felt as if he were on God's puppet strings. A precise strike won him more cheers. A devastating Powerbomb through one of the bar rounds made the patrons erupt.

They pushed the fight outdoors where their twenty-foot center stage had appeared under the yellow parking lot lights. Their steps cracked on broken glass, decades of discarded bottles pulverized into sand. The crowd ringed the wrestlers, some on their knees to give those behind a clear view. They were gritting their teeth, clenching their fists, even wilder than the mob at the Freedom Fest. Dom was giving them exactly what they wanted.

"Time to go home, buddy," Duke whispered as he clutched Dom in a headlock.

Not yet, Dom thought. The drama blazing the faces of those circling could burn hotter. With an elbow to Duke's gut, he broke the hold, reversed it, and whispered to Duke to counter.

" 'Go' and 'home' are two simple words," Duke said into the crook of Dom's arm.

"Drop me," Dom said. "Figure Four."

"Fuck that. You can't puss out now."

Dom planted a hard foot to his left, positioning Duke's thigh behind him as a fulcrum. He coiled and sprang back, forcing Duke to play along. With Dom's leap and Duke's begrudging lift, Dom vaulted into the air and stuck the asphalt across his back and shoulders, collapsing the hold—a devastating counterreverse.

Duke rolled to his feet, clasped Dom's ankle, and spun it over his knee. Legs tangled, Duke fell and locked in the hold.

"How's that?" Duke shouted. He pressurized the lock far more than aesthetics demanded, hyperextending Dom's knee, testing the flex in his shin.

"More," Dom said without disguise. Duke snarled. The veteran's body went taut as he leveraged everything into the lock.

Dom slapped the pavement. Bits of gravel stuck to his palm. His ligaments stretched. The marrow in his tibia crackled like rice cereal. The crowd reared, anticipating the snap.

"Is that all?" Dom cried.

Duke released the pressure but contorted his body as if his life depended on breaking Dom's leg.

"Give up!" Duke screamed. Half the circled faces cheered it. The others barked them down, willing Dom to escape.

Dom writhed in faux agony, reached for the ropes that weren't there. He clutched his head and shrieked his larynx into failure. His arms flailed. He brushed a shard of glass cut like an arrowhead.

The crowd drew a long breath as Dom stretched for it. The feigned effort fell from Duke's face. Dom's fingertips coaxed the glass into his grasp. He held it high for all to see.

Duke grimaced and shot Dom a nod, ready to take a slash and release the hold, but Dom brought the shard to his scalp. Without breaking eye contact with Duke, he pressed its point above his hairline. He'd never bladed though a mask. Nor had he ever made such a show of it. The Lycra resisted puncture. He drew the glass across until the friction split the material.

Blood welled in the cut and dripped down his forehead. Some collected underneath the mask and drained from the eyeholes. Dom roared and drew his neck taut, forcing more blood through the wound. Whether Duke was truly stunned didn't matter. He did nothing to deflect Dom's right from cracking across his jaw, dissolving the hold.

Dom stood, blinking through the red seeping over his brow. He threw the glass to the ground and smeared blood across the front of the mask. The crowd was raving. Several who'd been filming with cell phones were shaking, too caught in the moment to hold steady frame. Amid the excitement a chant rose up—three syllables, strong consonants. This time, Dom didn't listen.

Duke got his feet under him and lunged at Dom. His haymaker was meant to throw himself off-balance. Dom sensed this and dodged low, striking Duke's knees. The axe-handle swing rag dolled Duke to the pavement. Dom pounced, seizing Duke's left arm. Anticipating the end, the veteran locked his fingers against his chest. Dom took his time finding the proper grip.

"You ready?" Dom whispered.

" 'Bout time," Duke said, allowing a smirk to curl under his mask. "Thanks, kid."

"Thank you," Dom said. He anchored his legs across Duke's torso.

Instinct told Dom to draw it out, make it last. His conscious begged him to stop. He could fake it. Would the onlookers notice? Were the cameras sharp enough to catch the deception? Duke thrashed against him, selling the danger, his fear. It seemed so real.

"He's meat," Dom whispered. "Man is meat."

"Quit bleeding on me and do it," Duke said.

Dom listened. He wrenched the arm free and finished his work.

After the match, once Dom was confident he wouldn't require the services of Bonnie's emergency medical team, he parked the Civic beside an army-navy store a few blocks from his apartment. The radio was on, an ad with a Geiger counter crackling in the background. Dom switched it off. He closed his eyes and touched the tacky scab above his hairline.

The finale had stunned the crowd and put him over. He'd been efficiently whisked to his getaway vehicle seconds after he'd raised his arms in victory. The circled onlookers had parted for him, a school of scavengers ceding a predator his berth. He'd sustained no serious injury. He'd done well.

It was late. He needed to wash the blood out of his hair. As it dried, it snowed onto his lap with the dandruff from his chin, now free from the tangles of his beard. He peered down the empty street and switched on the dome light. In his phone's camera, he looked as if he'd endured a month of trench warfare. He snapped a photo and replaced the fat ass on his lock screen.

A head above The Pit's crowd, Dom had seen them all. The rapturous majority had buzzed, confused and elated. They'd spread what they'd witnessed, eager to boast being there first.

Not everyone had been cheering him. Dom had seen two men on the pack's outskirts gape into their wallets and count out cash for their buddy. He'd caught the bartender bracing himself in his establishment's doorway, drawing down his cigarette as if it were his only source of oxygen. Near the street, a group had gathered around a pair of younger patrons on their phones. They peered expectantly down the block and allowed themselves only a few guilty peeks toward the spectacle. Among them was the old woman, fists buried deep in the pockets of a coat far too thick for the heat of the night.

He wasn't the lumberjack anymore. The violence of the arm's snap had obliterated him. Whoever he was now wanted to win these people, to force their attention. He wanted to make the old woman shatter her hands in applause.

Dom was hungry. What had he eaten over the past few days? He checked his phone to find what was open, and his screen flashed to his messenger.

The keyboard below, a field of white above, and between, a blinking cursor and a blank canvas. Atop the window was her name—Catie.

"Hey," Dom wrote. He paused, thinking about those three letters, and he hit send.

TWENTY-FIVE

Bonnie's wrestlers were superstitious. They'd immersed her in their rituals. Sacred foods, priestly gestures, incantations and hymns—she didn't hold it against them. Fortune steered their lives. It was only natural to seek patterns in the chaos, to feel one could influence the tides of luck. Belief was seductive, hard baked into humanity's cultural genetics. Even the most pragmatic couldn't deny its allure. Bonnie was no exception.

When the jet had buzzed the Hangar during the Contreras girl's tryout, Bonnie indexed the logical explanations—radar problems, computer glitches, pilot error. Once, a Cessna hobbyist had mistaken the airstrip for one of the nearby municipals and attempted landing on the overgrown runway. This was different. There'd never been a plane so large and powerful. The jet's apocalyptic roar begged to be read as an omen.

She never could shake its memory. Decades later, wrestling would be a star in the constellations of her past. The Pit, having burst into the Charlotte underground and grown into an international sensation, burned its fuel and became one of a million curiosities in the evolution of entertainment. She'd spot a contrail streaking across the stratosphere and revel in superstition. All those years ago, the world had been watching and had chosen to speak.

The Cutman, as he came to be known, performed brilliantly in his first encounter with the anonymous Duke Natterjack. Word of mouth spread the fight across the country. It had been vicious, and yet, like poetry, what was raw and dirty had been transformed. Grainy cell-phone videos were posted and shared and upvoted. Eventually, a clear video emerged, author unknown, with multiple cameras, crisp editing, crunching sound.

The match's climax was grisly. A car had rushed Duke from the site, the parking lot of a dive bar on Charlotte's east side, and rolled him onto the stoop of a nearby ER. After a successful surgery, and after she was sure Duke had given officials the cover story, Bonnie found him alone in an observation room. He was awake, propped in his bed next to the window. An oak limb with bright green leaves blocked his view. The lights were dim, the TV off.

"You paid me," Duke said, waving his phone with his good arm. "I got the deposit notice."

"Feels good, doesn't it?" Bonnie said.

"I feel like a sack of shit, but I've done worse for less."

Duke's face was black-and-blue, a dozen stitches on his chin. His left arm was disaster. Calico bruising. Tubes draining fluid. An Erector Set of pins and screws held everything together.

"Don't spend it all in one place," Bonnie said. "Be a year until you get the next one."

"A wrestling pension. That's gotta be a first."

"You're not so special." Bonnie pulled a chair next to Duke and noted the lunch tray on the bedside table. The food had been pushed around, not consumed.

Bonnie pointed to the sandwich. "May I?"

"Really? Knock yourself out."

Bonnie removed its contents—iceberg lettuce, unripe tomato, questionable cold cuts—leaving only mayo smeared across the bread.

As Bonnie chewed, Duke held his painkiller button in front of her face and pressed it repeatedly.

"How long you in here?" she asked.

"They won't tell me. Doc kept saying she'd never seen a break this bad. Said it would've been better if it didn't have so much muscle to tear through."

"Sorry to hear."

"Sure you are."

As Duke watched, Bonnie tore the crust from the bread slices, rolled it into a tight ball between her palms, and set the ball next to the carton of milk on the tray.

"You going to ask me?" Duke said.

"Ask you what?"

"Have some respect for the infirmed. Even Clout couldn't get you to his bedside, so I know you're here with a motive. There was a hiccup in your script."

"Maybe I love hospital food," Bonnie said.

Duke inflated his cheeks and pressed his button again. "Keep stalling. I'm starting to get sleepy."

"They never get it right, do they?"

"Of course they don't. They had the fucking C-team anesthesia crew in there, too. Woke up right in the middle of it with my face in the surgeon's crotch."

"Nightmares for years, no doubt."

"Ask me already."

"Okay. What happened with the finish, Duke?"

"It was me, not the kid. He was all lined up to crack the elbow. Then I thought, fuck it. If I'm going out, I'm going out with a bang."

"Well, mission accomplished."

"How did it look?"

"Not the way we'd planned it to look."

"Good," Duke said. "No match is complete without the element of surprise."

"We rehearsed for a reason," Bonnie said. "The story we're building is essential to our success. A shard of your ulna could've nicked an artery. You might not have an issue with wagering your life, but I've invested too much to tolerate an unauthorized escalation of force. Forget the lake of blood I had to mop up, imagine the difficulty of dealing with a manslaughter charge—"

Bonnie cut herself off when she saw Duke had rolled his head away and was staring out the window.

"Keep going," he said. "I'm listening."

"I'd appreciate your full attention," Bonnie said.

Duke laughed. "Don't worry. I can chew gum and pat my tummy at the same time."

Bonnie took a breath and watched Duke's eyes. His lids were drooping. She peered out the window. Nothing but leaves rustling in the wind.

"What do you see?" she asked.

"Do me a favor," Duke said. "Take a picture of the window. Horizontally, please."

Bonnie took his phone. Duke pointed as if concerned for its safety.

"Hit the button on the top, then you gotta flick up the menu and—"

"I've got it," she said.

She took the picture, making sure it was in focus.

"Thank you," Duke said, reaching for the phone. "You were saying?"

"I need to know whether you're covering for him."

"Nah. He nearly puked when I leaned into it."

"You did more than lean into it."

Duke met her eyes. "I was talking to a nurse. Smart guy. Familiar with the biz. Said he'd watched wrestling as a kid. Said some friends convinced him to give it another shot. They told him there was stuff they hadn't noticed—storytelling, improv, maybe even some smart shit once in a while.

"He said he gave it a go, but didn't like it. He said he has a philosophy. And I said, philosophy? Sounds like you're in the wrong profession, brother. And he's like, man, you wouldn't believe the assholes around here who root for shit to get wheeled in. A lot of docs want the twenty-car pileup. They want the botched suicide. They want the old wrestler who says he took a bad bump. Why? Because they want to be heroes. The surgeons who sculpt mashed potatoes into a face? They're celebrities here. They're artists.

"The nurse said once he got wise to those kinds of people, he swore he would never take pleasure in someone else's pain. He knows wrestling's work. He also knows there are dopes like me who take big risks. He's read the news. Even the safest wrestlers are dying at sixty because their brains get scrambled. He says he can't convince himself to be entertained by people hurting themselves, especially when their audience thinks it's fake."

"And what do you think?" Bonnie asked.

Duke winced and pressed his button again. The machine beeped a warning and dispensed the drug.

"Kid's a nurse," Duke said. "Says a lot."

Bonnie finished the sandwich and took a sip of syrup from the fruit cup on Duke's tray.

Phone in his lap, Duke pinched into the image Bonnie had taken.

"Take a look," he insisted.

It was blurry and small, but Bonnie could make out the shape of a frog clinging to one of the twigs close to the window. "*Hyla cinerea*," Duke said. "Tree frog. Pretty far off the coast for that little guy."

Some critics doubted the authenticity of The Pit's violence. Though matches were held outdoors before unsuspecting audiences with no announcers, no entrances, none of the fanfare one would expect to precede a fight between two masked men, it was unmistakably professional wrestling. Skeptics claimed the gruesome finishes were fake—computer-generated imagery, state-of-the-art practical effects. Sportswriters analyzed matches frame by frame and purported to expose cracks in the veneer of violence. In the first match, the Cutman's debut, a slow-motion GIF ripped from cell-phone footage of his opponent's arm breaking was said to show the bone tearing through a prosthetic. Then the HD video dropped and ignited a new round of debate.

A reporter from a national magazine retrieved a blood sample from a match. Testing confirmed it was human. The internet fell over itself to scream back. The blood in professional wrestling had always been legit. As one commenter put it, using blood to support a theory on The Pit's authenticity was like closing the case on the Kennedy assassination after discovering real bullets.

Before The Pit, professional wrestling had an audience of millions. That number was dwarfed by those who preferred entertainment with unmitigated violence. Broadcast and cable offered mixed martial arts, boxing, and football. On the web, streamers watched videos depicting extreme sport accidents, backyard disasters, drunk bros flipping off toolsheds. The Pit mixed the drama of a scripted narrative with the addictive pop of real bodily harm. It was a new way to package what audiences had always craved.

Others thought The Pit's secret sauce was its guerrilla operation. There were no tickets, no metal detectors, no pat downs. Matches were over in minutes, competitors spirited away before police could get a sniff of them. Holes-in-the-wall up and down the East Coast spray-painted rings in their parking lots, hoping to convince patrons they had been or could be a venue. The more cash she earned, the more independence Bonnie could buy. By the third match, she patched up her jobbers without involving local hospitals.

The masses pined for answers. Who was the Cutman? Who was pulling his strings? The Cutman never spoke. He wore only his mask, a regular pair of jeans, a white T-shirt. Fans gobbled up his ruthlessness, his stoicism. Opponents tried to intimidate him. The Cutman took a pipe to their knees. One fighter attempted to remove the mask, and the Cutman broke his fingers one by one.

A faction within The Pit's fandom militantly defended its anonymity. When a match began, always at a new and unannounced location, they fought into the first ring of spectators and prevented those bent on disrupting the bout from gaining entry. After the matches, they distracted the authorities as the fighters slipped into the night.

Establishment owners welcomed the increase in business, especially when it became clear any one location had nothing to do with The Pit. Rings appeared minutes before a match as if by magic. The police couldn't publicly voice support, but disturbance calls plummeted as would-be rabble-rousers waited to watch a fight instead of starting their own. Pit loyalists were quick to identify copycats and merciless in expressing their offense. No one tried it twice.

Bonnie was pleased. Her vision had come to pass, and it was as beautiful as she'd imagined. The honesty of The Pit was surpassed only by the purity of its fans' reactions. There was no better way to exhibit the promise of the human body, to show the stakes of combat and the art of orchestration. As the Cutman's opponents lay down, they contributed to the biggest push in history. Bonnie offered them a fitting climax to their careers: hope for life after wrestling.

The public speculated over the identity of The Pit's creator. They hounded the suspects—wrestling promoters, famous libertarian podcasters, eccentric billionaires. Vince McMahon was forced to denounce The Pit and affirm his noninvolvement under oath before a Congressional panel. When he lurched into the chamber, limbs stiff with muscle, seven networks broadcast it live. No stranger to the microphone or the icy stares of elected officials, the chairman of history's biggest pro-wrestling company made his words ring strong and true down Capitol Hill.

"This isn't entertainment," McMahon said. "This isn't professional wrestling. It's pornography. I believe the responsible party will be brought to justice. He will be held accountable for this sick disregard for human life before the people of our beloved country and before Almighty God."

Bonnie replayed clips of McMahon's testimony over and over. She couldn't stop smiling.

Every match Bonnie produced for The Pit was a bank heist. They commanded her full attention. She installed a manager to run shop at MCCW. She participated enough so that, after the initial shock of her withdrawal, no one asked questions. But without a hold on the wheel, the promotion stagnated and fell into the red. The straying of her business gnawed at Bonnie. Her sleep pattern collapsed. She'd stay awake for three days until her body would break down, forcing her to sleep through the night.

The first personal day Bonnie ever took came on the first morning she woke up with the sun. The air was cool and clear, a rare break in the late Carolina summer. She awoke dehydrated and nauseous, pulling her eyelids free of the crust sealing their corners. She dumped a tablespoon of instant coffee and two packets of powdered ascorbic acid into her morning shake. Her stomach, usually ironclad, churned on itself, and she couldn't stand from the bathroom floor without dry heaving.

She thought of the slugs clocking in and out at their

replicable jobs. Her father had built her privilege from their labor. She was squandering it.

Bonnie could not suffer MCCW's insolvency. She doubled her efforts overseeing its operation, scouring the Southeast for poachable talent. She attended two-bit events in vacant lots and school gymnasiums. She organized a Northeast tour, meeting in secret with wrestlers employed by MCCW competitors and even a few minor players in the WWE. She lost weight, and it was most noticeable in her skin. It thinned and wrinkled, drooped from her triceps. Her gray hair was no longer such an anachronism.

In the past, upticks in professional wrestling's popularity had spelled doom for many promotions. As a whole, the industry had benefited. Vince McMahon's wrestling empire crushed dozens of local players. By the time the WWF's Superstars were flexing on cereal boxes and starring alongside Hollywood action heroes, more people were watching wrestling than ever before. Ted Turner's World Championship Wrestling went supernova in the early 2000s, squandering its chance to unseat McMahon and elevate wrestling to the level of the major American sports. Still, the crucible of the WCW and WWF's Monday Night Wars forged a legion of die-hard fans. Fifteen years later, their nostalgia and discretionary income fueled sellouts of NFL stadiums.

The Pit's rise produced no such expansion. The promotion brought in viewers new to scripted combat while leeching fans from conventional pro wrestling. WWE's ratings and Network subscriptions dipped. The Pit hurt indie wrestling the most. There was little MCCW and its ilk could do to keep up with their audience's evolving demands. McMahon's deep pockets offered him star power and spectacle. His cultural capital helped him manufacture controversy, keeping some viewers engaged. MCCW had none of this. It could find talent, it would write brilliant matches, but the shine of those draws had dulled. Audiences wanted surprise. They needed to hear their champion break bones.

Six months after The Pit's launch, Bonnie leaned over the mezzanine railing in Charleston's Caroliniana Theatre. Below, two hundred people were blinking through a midcard spat from Old South Championship Wrestling, the last promotion in the state Bonnie had yet to evaluate. Though she thirsted for sleep and the wrestler she'd traveled to scout was at the top of the card, Bonnie was glad she'd arrived early, because the theater was an even more curious place than the Hangar.

The Caroliniana was built in the late 1920s, when the boom in vehicle tourism invited the construction of a motion-picture palace similar to those in the North's industrial centers. Its Italian Renaissance architecture was an outlier from the city's Colonial public buildings and Georgian single houses. Concentric archways soared over the proscenium. Rose petals molded in plaster bordered classical frescoes. Thousand-pound crystal chandeliers shimmered in the lobby. Twelve office stories were stacked above, making its modest tower one of the highest commercial buildings in the Holy City. It was a true jewel, though ambivalence from locals dampened profitability. In a gambit to capture the public consciousness after losing money throughout the Depression, investors enticed MGM to hold its South Carolina premiere of *Gone with the Wind* at the theater. The gala featured a caravan of limousines carrying the film's stars. Clark Gable chose not to attend, much to the disappointment of the press and the event's high-paying attendees. Thelma McQueen, Hattie McDaniel, and Everett Brown weren't given a choice.

The Caroliniana closed soon after and was sold to the US Army Air Corps. It was gutted for a parking structure serving the offices above. In the haste to get the facility operational, dismantling the theater's architecture was considered a needless expense. The auditorium floor was flattened and paved. The mezzanine was reinforced with giant concrete pillars and stacked with another layer of parking. Anything removable was sold or scrapped. The ceiling's fascia, adornments beyond vandals' reach, remained.

Bonnie leaned on the rail of the old mezzanine. The OSCW ring stood in what would have been main floor's middle rows. It hugged one of the building's long walls. On three sides, behind a few rows of folding chairs, there was ample space for parking. Some guests, rather than sitting close to the ring, were loitering beside open tailgates. Above them hung the theater's old shell—murals faded, cracks spidering from gaps in the plaster. It was the discarded carapace of a beautiful insect.

Down the rail from Bonnie was a man smoking beside an old pickup. He leaned over to watch the bout, his gut pressed against the rail. The match ended with a count-out. As the fans booed, the man crushed his cigarette and replaced it with a stick of gum.

"Can you believe that?" he asked.

"I've seen worse," Bonnie said.

"You've seen some shit," the man said. He removed a tissue from his jeans' pocket and grunted down to retrieve his discarded cigarette. Once he'd folded it into the tissue, he spat on it and wiped up the loose tobacco and ash from the concrete.

"I mean, who books this shit?" the man said.

"Phil Heyman," Bonnie replied. "He's owned OSCW since the mid-nineties."

"Maybe it's time for him to hang it up. Everyone is watching that Mexican murder people on the internet, and he punches back with a fifteen-minute count-out? It's pitiful."

"Phil answers every email sent to OSCW's account. You could send him your suggestions."

"I'm gonna send him an offer. Five hundred dollars for the whole operation. I'll part it out for scrap."

"I doubt you're prepared for the difficulties of owning a professional wrestling company."

"I've run a business," the man said. "If you're going to roll over, cut the rope and give your boys a chance. Don't put their necks on the line for this bullshit."

"That we can agree on," Bonnie said.

"Smoke?" the man asked, offering his pack.

"No," Bonnie said.

"Gum?"

"What kind is it?"

"Blazing hellfire cinnamon. I buy it off eBay."

Bonnie took a stick and thanked the man. The gum was chalky, barely any spice.

"I'll take the wrapper," the man said. Bonnie obliged, and he crammed it into his pocket.

The winner of the match was stuttering through a promo against his competitor, who was hobbling to curtain. Halfway there the limp switched to his opposite leg.

"Shameful," the man said. "Why do we subject ourselves to this?"

"I'm here for work," Bonnie said.

"I hope you're not a critic. You should've seen enough by now."

"I'm scouting talent."

"Talent? Sister, if you think you're gonna see any talent tonight, let me give you my number, because I'll bet I've got a better move set than half of these turkeys."

"There's one individual, Casper Strongweight, who has promise. He's booked next, if they stick to the advertised card."

"The Friendly Ghost? Jesus, lady. If you think Strongweight is any kind of competitor, you must be hurting for warm bodies. Who do you work with?"

"Mid-Coast Championship Wrestling."

"Never heard of it. You guys new?"

Bonnie cleared her throat. "We've been operating out of Greater Charlotte for a decade."

"That long, huh?" The man fished his phone from his pocket.

Bonnie watched him struggle to type. She'd assumed her perch on the mezzanine would be the ideal vantage point to evaluate Strongweight. Now an empty row on the floor caught her eye. Closer to the action, she could get a better read on the wrestler's expressions. They had to be camera ready.

"Karl Crawczak!" the man exclaimed.

"Excuse me?"

"You work for Clout! I didn't know he had a promotion down here. I lived in Queens when he was running Big Apple. That was wrestling, let me tell you—when men were men. None of the flippy shit you see nowadays. Some will say Jimmy Hart, others will say Rhodes or Flair, but Clout was the best talker. I remember going to a show, must've been three thousand people. Old bastard didn't use a microphone. Crystal clear from the top row. How's he doing these days?"

"He's dead."

"Oh. The Mid-Coast wiki page says he's the owner-operator."

"That page is outdated."

"Well," the man said, scratching his chin. "That's a damn shame. Who took over the reins?"

"Me."

"You?"

"Correct."

"Are you his daughter or something?"

"We were partners."

"You're a rare bird, then. Not many ladies running pro-wrestling shows."

"There are a few," Bonnie replied.

The man asked for her name, and she gave it. He introduced himself as Fred. His last name got lost in a squeal of speaker feedback. The crowd groaned and held their ears. An announcer in the ring tapped his microphone, and no sound came out. A man in a headset emerged from behind the curtain and pointed angrily at a pair of techs sweating and cursing over a soundboard.

"How're y'all weathering the storm?" Fred traced a circle in the air.

"We've seen a dip, but it's above industry average."

"That's optimistic from an owner who can't pay someone to visit this pit."

"I find it rather pretty," Bonnie said.

"Wait a couple years. The way this town is going, some tech guru will buy it and restore it to its former glory. They'll charge ten bucks for a beer and play artsy-fartsy shit. It'll be hailed as a service to the community."

The thought of workmen tearing up the pavement inside the Caroliniana cast Bonnie's imagination to the Hangar and a future she'd never considered. Its runway leveled. Fresh concrete poured. New model Gulfstreams sharing space with sport flyers and refurbished World War II fighters. A new radar tower with its hypnotically rotating dish.

"The problem with progress is no one considers what's left behind," Fred said. "Hell, pro wrestling's survived home video, cable, even the goddamned internet. I don't think it resurrects this time. Whoever's behind The Pit doesn't give a shit. Wouldn't surprise me a bit if it was another one of those Silicon Valley brats. They shouldn't let kids that young have money."

"I give a shit," Bonnie said.

"You're not following me," Fred said.

"I'm following you perfectly. Your assessment is inaccurate."

A loud pop came from below. The announcer quit hitting his microphone and flashed an okay to the sound guys. He joked through an apology and announced the next competitor, Casper Strongweight, who burst through the curtain with too much pep. He skipped around, pointed in random directions, and whipped his hair to the music.

"The Pit is forever entwined with traditional wrestling because it was created to help the very people wrestling was hurting most," Bonnie said, ignoring Strongweight's prance to the ring.

"How the hell do you figure that?" Fred said.

"I created The Pit," Bonnie said.

Strongweight took his corner to limp cheers. The lights dimmed. The announcer's voice was low and serious.

"And his opponent, fighting out of the darkest reaches of the Okefenokee Swamp. Weighing in at two hundred eighty-three pounds. El Sapo!"

Fred sputtered at Bonnie's revelation. She paid him little mind. Her attention locked on the wrestler making his entrance. He stood like the Matterhorn, imposing and angular. He wore a long cape of shimmering scales. His walk to the ring bore none of his opponent's compensatory cockiness. He was a man going to work. His face was masked, but pangs of recognition struck Bonnie.

"Lady, I think you need a strong drink and a good night's rest," Fred said.

Bonnie said nothing. Instead, she smacked her gum, removed it from her mouth, and stuck it to the railing.

Bonnie marched to the stairwell and descended to the main floor. She passed a group of men loitering near a muscle car. Their taunts did nothing to impede her. She moved directly to the barrier separating the ring from the seats.

"Duke!" she shouted.

The masked competitor who had wrestled a final match for the ages, who would never again want for money, who'd been given a way out, heard the call. He looked at Bonnie and waved.

TWENTY-SIX

Pilar's eighteenth birthday arrived with little fanfare. The day was like most in her convalescence—willing her body to heal, wincing to her feet for an unlicensed physical therapy session with Johnnie May, pained shuffling to the bathroom. She'd ditched the bedpan as soon as she could.

With her phone in Valhalla, she'd lost her contacts. She programmed the brick Johnnie May had bought her with Dom and Johnnie's numbers. It also had a calculator, a notepad, a dozen ringtones, and Snake. She played every day but never got any good.

Even if she'd been healthy, she wouldn't have liked celebrating. Sixteen had felt much more important. She'd been settling into a new city, life with her brother. She'd gotten her driver's permit. She borrowed the Civic whenever Dom allowed and sometimes when he didn't. She'd taken part-time jobs at the dairy bar and the chicken shack. She was older.

At eighteen, she could get out of Dodge whenever she wanted, free from the worry of her mother appearing and demanding her back. She'd survived a childhood worse than far more fucked-up people had endured. Eighteen should've been a big deal.

There were some signs of growth. She imagined a younger Pilar going absolutely bonkers with so little to do. No one had visited her. This would've crushed Baby Pilar. Adult Pilar understood the summer after senior year was an easy time to lose touch. When she could get online—Dom was being incredibly stingy with his phone—all the familiar chatter was there. People wishing her well. Girlfriends inviting her to grad parties. Midnight confessions. Guys who needed to quit their church and jerk off more. B was the friend close enough to know where she lived. Her number was one of the few Pilar knew by heart. She hadn't called it.

Her seclusion was important. She could focus her mind, reflect on mistakes. If she could find serenity in her apartment prison, maybe she could avoid the self-sabotage that had put her there. A call from Bonnie had steeled her resolve. Despite her injury, she'd been signed.

"Not a second chance," Bonnie had said. "You earned it."

"Trust her," Johnnie May said after hearing the news. "She smells money on you."

Pilar couldn't shake the feeling she'd duped them all. She tried to project confidence. Her contract guaranteed the stability needed to heal. The doctor visits—paid from Bonnie's pocket—confirmed there was nothing rest wouldn't fix.

After admiring the work Johnnie May had done with her cut-up ring wear, Pilar had her new friend teach her the basics of costume design. Johnnie May got her a rummage-sale sewing machine and some leftover fabric. Once Pilar rigged a mound of pillows and dirty clothes to help her sit up, she was learning her first real hobby, stitching together hideous quilts and vinyl underwear fit for Frankenstein's monster.

Weeks after her injury, healed enough to crawl out of the apartment, Pilar drove with Dom to a gig outside Columbia. A local promotion had landed an appearance from a pair of WWE gray hairs fresh off their Legends' Contracts and had rented a few bodies from MCCW to fill their card. Pilar volunteered to staff Dom's merch table. Even though she'd refused to wear a neck brace in public, Dom agreed, and the two saddled up the Civic and headed south.

The ride was stuffy. The Civic's AC failed to strain the soup from the late summer air. Dom was lost in thought. The pines flanking I-77 whizzed past, blurring into a drab wall. Pilar wanted to look upon the countryside, to see the world was open and full of possibility. The trees narrowed her view to the road ahead.

The heat, the proximity to her brother, the unresolved animosity from the pill-chucking fight—these were Petri-dish conditions for conflict. Yet one change Pilar had made, maybe one that could define her entry into legal adulthood, was patience. The worst of her recovery had forced it upon her. This was an opportunity to own it, to put it into practice.

She cleared her throat. "You look good with your beard trimmed. I'd forgotten what your chin looked like."

Dom broke his trance. "Thanks."

"Weird being back on the road, eh?"

"It is. It feels so different."

"You want an update on anything? News? Texts? Booty calls?" She pointed to his phone nestled in the driver door's junk pocket.

"We need to get you a new phone," Dom said. "You're having withdrawals."

"Not at all. This is why it's good we're out here. You can meet the new me."

"The new you."

"If I say it enough, it might come true. I've been off the grid. It's healthy. We've created too many distractions for ourselves. Life would be better if we simplified things."

Dom looked over and shrugged. "Well then, let's abstain. At least until we get to Spring Valley."

"Have I been there before?"

"Once, I think, when we first started."

"You excited to be on a card with Hall of Famers?"

"Not really. If you were anybody and Vince thinks he can squeeze out few nostalgia bucks, he puts you in."

"Did I ever tell you about the clown in Fayetteville who tried to impress me by talking up some battle royal he was in with Ric Flair? I was like, dude. This is North Carolina. Ric's probably my dad."

"In order to be the man, you have to brag about that one time you in were in the same building with the man."

"Imagine how many girls will cheer when they tear old Space Mountain down. Fucking slimeball."

"Woo," Dom said, cracking a smile.

"Ah," Pilar said. "There it is. They said it was a myth."

"Things have been good, if you can believe it."

"I wouldn't have known."

The Civic's wheel could've been a toy under Dom's grip. When he tightened at ten and two, he looked as if he could crumple it.

"I never said I'd be good at taking care of you," Dom said.

"You didn't," Pilar replied.

"I have to remind myself. The same woman raised us."

"Technically."

Dom paused as if charging up a comeback. He let out a sigh instead. "In a fucked-up way, I understand her. It's terrifying to think about what could happen to you. You're tough as hell. I know better than anyone. I wish she could see you now, or I wish she could've seen then who you'd grow to be."

Pilar laughed. "Yeah. What a resume. Zero for zero and a broken neck."

"Anyone else's would've actually broken."

"Anyone else wouldn't have let it get that far."

"I don't blame you," Dom said.

"Breaking news."

"I'm sorry. I shouldn't have been so pissed."

"You're fine. I scare me too."

Dom smiled again and offered Pilar a fist. "Communication," he said. "Like old times."

"Sure thing, coach," she said, popping his knuckles with more pep than necessary. "And what better way to start than giving me your phone? My thumbs are itchy."

"What do you want to know? I'm an open book."

"Ugh. Why would I want that swill when the good stuff is right there?"

"Off the grid. You're full of it, sis."

"C'mon. As far as fixes go, this one won't kill me."

"We'll get you a new phone on the ride home. You have an income now. You can buy shit."

"You've done something stupid, haven't you? Who're you falling for?"

"No one. See for yourself." Dom tossed the phone into her lap.

There was a different photo of Dom on his lock screen—a recent one, judging by the length of his beard. Pilar opened his texts. Dom's inbox was wiped clean. Same for his email and photos. He'd removed his dating apps.

"The fuck? There's nothing here."

"I simplified things. Fresh start."

"I'm serious. What is this? Do you not trust me?"

"Of course I do."

"Then what the hell are you doing? I thought you liked this. I thought we could share."

"We can. Ask me anything."

Pilar scoffed and tried to read his face. Dom never got close enough to anyone to worry about what was and wasn't on his phone—unless there was finally someone. Much easier to nuke the thing than pick through all the correspondence he wouldn't want a partner to see.

"You know how guilty this makes you look?" Pilar said.

"Aren't I entitled to a little privacy?"

Pilar opened his contacts and scrolled through. "Has Johnnie May been in your ear? You two conspiring to trick me into developing healthy work-home boundaries? Imagine the luxury of keeping a part of my life away from your busy fingers."

"Listen to yourself. 'Stay out of my life but let me snoop on you.' No, I haven't talked to Johnnie May. You've seen the look she gives me when I have the audacity to walk into my own apartment. Maybe trust me and consider you're not the only person who's been thinking about shit for the past two months."

Dom caught himself before the edge in his voice cut too deep.

"You're a professional now. You'll be in the ring soon. For once we have some money. We've been on top of each other for so long, we forgot what it could be like to have separate lives."

"You gonna kick me out?"

"No, Pilar, but it's not crazy to dream about getting our own places. It's a sensible, adult goal."

Pilar fished a lock of hair free from her ponytail and wrapped it around her finger, pulling hard enough to rip a few strands from her scalp.

"Do you agree?" Dom asked.

"Yeah," Pilar said, giving him the phone. "Whatever."

Among the merchandise tables ringing the basketball court at Spring Valley High School, center stage for Valley of Pain II, Hack Barlow's was the outlier. There was no poorly photoshopped banner with Dom's scowling face. No T-shirts screen printed with lewd slogans. No DVDs of his matches with C-list stars. Dom had his plush axes, a few signed posters, and whether he liked it or not, a variety of items Pilar had made with Johnnie May during her recovery—scarves, ear warmers, and fabric coasters stitched from scraps.

"These are cute," a fan said, sipping a can of Sprite and poking one of the axes. "My son would get a kick out of 'em."

Pilar forced a smile. The show wasn't well attended. A few marks had trickled in, hit up the concession stand, stepped down to the floor to peruse the merch. Some wrestlers had wives or children run their tables. Most were manned by the wrestlers themselves. The most approachable was Big Country, the five-hundred-pound weekender set up to Pilar's right. Children liked to take a run at him and mash into his tremendous gut. Men measured him from a distance, holding their chins high. Pilar watched dude after dude put on this little show before loitering uncomfortably long in front of her table. Nobody bought her stuff.

"Where's Hack?" the fan asked. He was lanky with bad facial hair and an "Austin 3:16" hoodie.

"Locker room," Pilar said. "He's jerking curtain."

"What?"

"He's in the first match."

"Oh. You his girlfriend?"

"No," Pilar said, sensing what was coming.

"Huh. Well, I can tell you what you are, and that's drop-dead gorgeous."

"Aw, thanks, hun. What an original thing to say."

"I'm going to buy this axe, because a fine young lady like you deserves honest business. And—what the hell—something else for me. What's this thing?"

"A dish towel."

"It's pretty."

"Thanks," Pilar said. She was already tired of her pitch, which couldn't conceal her rookie sewing skills.

"This looks like the stuff that golfer sells. I could sink a grommet into it and hang it on my bag. You know the one, right? Polka-dot pants. Smacks drives offa cans of Mic ULTRA?"

"Can't say. Tell you what, I'll knock a buck off the sticker price and get you on your way."

"No need. I've been a Hack supporter for years. We're lucky when we get him in Columbia."

The man fished a twenty from his pocket.

"You wouldn't happen to be the sister, would you?" the man asked.

"The sister?" Pilar repeated.

"There've been rumors in the dirt sheets that Hack's grooming a protégé. I think I see a family resemblance."

No one had ever claimed she and Dom looked alike. Truth be told, she'd wondered whether they shared the same father. Dom's silence on the matter gave some weight to the theory. He would've been old enough to remember their dad had he hung around until Pilar popped into the world.

After weeks of sequestration, she wasn't prepared to taste life as a public figure. Her imagination had always skipped to the good parts—fame, money, cutting promos on cable. She'd envisioned the adoring masses, never a single person recognizing her.

"What're they saying about me?" Pilar asked.

"Knew it!" the man said, thumping the table. "It's a pleasure to meet you. Don't mind what they print in those rags. Bunch of wannabe Dave Meltzers with even worse grammar. Keep working and remember we're pulling for you."

"Thank you."

"Name's Jim," the man said, offering his hand.

Pilar took it, and her name got caught in her throat. Did he know it? He hadn't said it. In fact, he'd called her the sister, which was unsettling. She needed to tell him who she was— Pilar Contreras, independent person. Or maybe just Pilar. Her name was the one thing she'd never shared with Dom.

But he'd called her brother Hack. Here, Dom was Hack Barlow, villainous lumberjack. If this guy was any kind of fan, he'd know you called a wrestler their ring name until told otherwise. Crossing that line was disrespectful. It was creepy.

Pilar was officially a wrestler now. Dom had brought her the paperwork. Her ring name sure as hell wasn't going to be Pilar Contreras. Not in the Carolinas. Not in the world of Johnnie May, Sarah Jade, and Tanya Flex. Not with the legions of internet assholes waiting to dox any woman brazen enough to step into the public eye.

"This jabroni giving you trouble, little lady?" The gravel-road voice of one of the headliners broke up the handshake. It was Bobby Stetson, half of the tag team Midnight Train, a pair of Mid-South journeymen who peaked in the early eighties, parlaying their train-whistle catchphrase into a respectable stint on WWF's main roster. Stetson gripped the fan's shoulder, pinching the tendons at the base of his neck.

"Let's go, buddy. We wanna make sure everyone has a chance to purchase this girl's adorable weapons."

Whether the fan was starstruck or losing blood flow to his brain, he let the wrestler steer him to Big Country's table.

"I didn't need saving," Pilar said.

"Course not," Stetson replied. "You're a smart doe. You weren't lost in the headlights."

The wrestler winked, his lazy left eye making the wink more lurid. He was stooped at the hips. His long, dyed hair ringed his bald crown like a grass skirt.

"Let me tell you something," Stetson said. "When you've been in this business as long as me, you'll see that we all need saving."

A shriek from next table snatched the smile from the wrestler's face. A kid had ramped up too much speed taking his leap at Big Country. He ricocheted off his gut, and his head thunked the hardwood.

Stetson doubled over, covering his ears. Big Country tried to quiet the boy with a piece of candy. The attention encouraged another scream. This brought Stetson to a knee. Hunched and shuddering, he clenched his teeth and removed a device from his ear.

Hearing aids, Pilar saw, and not the discreet kind. His hair had been covering them. As he staggered to the locker room, Pilar heard a chorus of tinny whistles, reminiscent of the eerie sounds that would float up from the rail yard near her childhood home.

TWENTY-SEVEN

Before Dom and Big Country burst through the venue's curtain to the tune of Big Country's self-produced rap-rock entrance music, Pilar had moved only two of her creations. Dom's axes, on the other hand, were bestsellers. When Dom entered the ring, the kids swung them maniacally, landing felling swoops onto siblings, strangers, moms and dads. One little girl chopped a nacho bowl from her father's grasp. Liquid cheese dripped from the blade like the blood of a promiscuous camp counselor. When the dad bent over to salvage his chips, she hacked the goop into his hair.

Dom and Country squared off against a charismatic local team called the Nasties. They wore pink headbands and singlets plucked from the most colorful part of the eighties. Marks stood and cheered, and Pilar spotted the fan from earlier. He was by himself in the bleachers, sitting on his hands and staring right at her.

"I'm just sitting here, dude," Pilar said to herself. She took out her phone and remembered she had no internet.

Pilar wished she could watch anonymously as she had before. She wished she could've replaced Dom and drawn the eyes of all in attendance. Anything but this—her state of in-between, ogled not for what she'd done but for who she was. And who was she? Hack Barlow's sister, of course.

She tried to concentrate on the match. She hadn't watched any wrestling since her tryout with Johnnie May. When the bell sounded, Nasty Number One leapt to action, working Dom into a choke hold. Her brother clawed at his attacker's arm. He gasped for air. Veins on his forehead bulged even though the hold was loose.

Dom could always sell. He looked in precisely the right amount of distress. It was why he'd been a heel his whole career. Even in a throwaway opener for a partner promotion, he could shine up a babyface and make his attacks look devastating. Caught in a submission, he projected such crisp pain.

Though Pilar had watched Dom feign suffering many times, this was unusual. He set his jaw, struggled to free himself. Pilar could feel his teeth grinding, smell the intermingling sweat from Dom's chin and the crook of his opponent's arm. Two heaving, stinking sacks of meat smashing together. It was grotesque.

She blinked away from the ring and saw the fan drinking her in. She let her focus blur on a different part of the audience.

The figures jeered when Dom reversed the hold and flipped the Nasty to the mat.

She tried to find blame—low blood sugar, fatigue. She knew it was the match.

The farce unfolding before her made a mockery of her bout with Johnnie May. The throws were so clearly a collaborative effort. Punches deflected harmlessly off the men's beefy shoulders. Heads spun in the breeze of fists flying past. They stomped their feet so their blows became booms. It sounded like the movies. Acted. Produced. Fake.

Her stomach churned. The fan gave her a smile and a shy wave. Pilar flipped him off and left the table.

Wrestlers in various stages of undress jawed at Pilar as she walked through the locker room. She ignored them, concentrating on her mission—Dom's gym bag. There were lockers all around, but Dom had never paid much mind to security. Men his size often didn't.

Dom's bag was under a bench. Pilar dug through, found his phone, went out to the Civic, and shut herself inside.

She woke the phone up and saw Dom's new photo on his lock screen. He'd taken a selfie in the Civic after a match. Between the cuts on his face and his patchy beard, he looked as if he'd been attacked with a Weedwacker.

She checked his search history. Empty. Dom always browsed incognito. He'd trashed his photos. She moved to his contacts. To her surprise, he hadn't wiped them. Right there, no scrolling required, was a name she recognized.

She didn't remember B offering Dom her number, and Pilar certainly hadn't told him. She hadn't talked to B in weeks. Her single letter was right above the entry for Bonnie Blue.

Why did he have B's number? Had he stolen it when he was playing secretary? She clicked on the name hoping for answers and saw the ten digits, confirming it wasn't some other B.

She was locked in the Civic, nestled among two pickups and a minivan, and she felt as if she were naked before a packed house. She had no place to put her secrets. She had only herself, her neck and its lingering soreness, and a deepening pit in her stomach. The void's vacuum was strengthening. What a horror it would be—her body folding into itself, the pressure crumpling her into a dense, pitiable speck.

"i wanna eat you," she typed to her friend.

The words frightened her. The more she read them, the more she wanted it. After a minute, a response arrived.

"Congrats. Youve made the list. Top 5 creepiest texts."

Pilar imagined her receiving the message, thinking it from her brother. Of course her reply came quickly. B had lots of practice with disgusting men.

Another text buzzed in. "Sry. I shouldnt joke."

Pilar gaped at the apology, unable to decipher it before the next message came.

"If you think it could help I might be willing to try... could be fun. ;)"

Pilar scrutinized each word. Sarcasm? An inside joke? No. Even the wink was sincere. Pilar's fingers trembled. She was tempted to crack the phone over her knee. Adult goals. Privacy. ¡Ese cabrón hijo de puta!

She typed the ugliest words she could conjure, drawing power from the bile boiling in her gut. Her thumb stalled over the send button. She read what she'd written—obscenities, insults. She deleted the tirade and sent a question.

"what are you talking about?"

"... uh... whatre YOU talking about?" was the response.

"this is pilar," she wrote, striking the keys as if she were typing the launch code to a warhead.

The reply took longer this time. "...Why are you on your brother's phone?"

"cause im always on his phone. and hes always on mine. we live in a box and we have no privacy and its mindfucked the both of us."

Dots appeared showing B was typing. The car was getting hot in the sun. Pilar didn't want to crack the window and break the seal between her and the world.

"I tried with yall," B wrote. "This is too much. Maybe hit me up when you and Dom get your shit figured out. Im sorry I cant be a better friend. Tell that to dom too. Or dont. Whatever. Good luck."

Pilar fought the impulse to put the Civic into drive and see how far it could take her. She cooked for spell, then returned to the Spring Valley High School gymnasium. Dom was staggering into the locals' sloppy finishers. Nasty Number One was new, Pilar recognized, a rough draft of the wrestler he'd never become. His throws were reckless. Instead of cracking square across his back, Dom's bumps struck his hips and shoulders. A pop of air burst from his mouth. Real pain.

Pilar promised herself she wouldn't run. The crunch of Dom's joints, the torque stressing his sockets—it was punishment, and that was the trap. His pain looked like penance. How difficult would it be to withhold the urge to dress his wounds? What grudge could survive his agony? Dom hadn't lived a pain-free day in years. Pilar could split. Guilt would drag her back.

Dom kicked out at two and a half. His opponent hooked a leg and applied a loose facelock. Dom sold hard and whispered to Nasty Number One, who cocked an ear then shook his head. Dom kept talking, and the ref dropped down.

"Whaddaya say, Hack? You wanna give up?"

"No!" Dom bellowed.

The ref signaled to the crowd and, playing up the drama, shuffled around the wrestlers to get a second angle on the submission.

"Tap!" Dom's opponent yelled. He spit the words through his teeth and didn't tighten his grip.

"Make me, you pussy!" Dom shouted. The crowd yelled and inched forward in their seats.

The ref shot a look to Big Country, who was busy outside the ring with Nasty Number Two. Sensing trouble, Country seized his foe by his headband, tossed him into the barricade guarding the first row, and lumbered into the ring to break the hold. Dom and the Nasty rolled apart, and Country allowed the ref to press him into his corner.

"What's your problem, bro?" Dom's challenger said, staggering to his feet.

"I've gotten tighter hugs from my mom," Dom said. He hurled himself at the Nasty, who slid underneath, caught Dom's leg, and reapplied the facelock. The wrestler flexed his forearms under Dom's chin. Dom's torso arched off the mat, his spine cracking.

"Weak!" Dom grunted.

The crowd flinched at the violence of the hold. The ref's head swiveled as if he'd lost track of the narrative. He begged Dom to give up.

"Pull," was all Dom said. The Nasty obliged. Pilar saw his fear. He was pissed, and he wanted to shut this asshole up, but he didn't know how far he could stretch Dom before he broke.

Dom's face was purple. Breaths gurgled from his throat. The timekeeper raised his hammer. Dom refused to slap the mat. The crowd mumbled their concern. A man Dom's size shouldn't have been able to bend that far. It was horrifying. They couldn't look away.

What had been a forgery now had Pilar's full attention. She flashed to her tryout with Johnnie May, how powerful she'd felt twisting her opponent across the uncanny valley. Every ligament in Dom's body was taut. His opponent squeezed the sweat from his pores. Like Johnnie May, with true pain in the mix, it looked real. It was real.

Country folded a chair from the front row and cracked it across Nasty Number One's back. The ref called the disqualification.

Dom got up and cursed Country, who screamed at the ref. Nasty Number One, selling the chair shot, yelled something. Dom kicked his gut. The Nasty immediately popped up and stuck his nose in Dom's craw.

It unraveled from there. Country tried to restrain Dom. The timekeeper's area cleared to assist the ref in coaxing the Nasties backstage. Someone in the scrum threw a punch, which flipped a switch in the crowd. Soda cans and trash started flying. The MC fumbled for his microphone and yelled for peace.

Alone on the highway, Pilar flipped radio stations until she landed on an NPR affiliate in the middle of a pledge drive. The host's banter was polite and upbeat. She cast the station's phone number like a spell. She impressed Pilar with how well she could shame her for not donating to a station she'd never listened to.

I-77 was lonely and featureless. The sun set behind the overcast, and Pilar became another pair of headlights floating above the highway lines. She'd gotten so much of what she'd wanted. The contract, a shot at the top, a budding apprenticeship with Johnnie May. Yet she didn't feel any older or wiser. If anything, she was less prepared than ever. However she spun it, she was running. She'd said she wouldn't, and here she was.

Something was happening to Dom. First the broken arm at the Freedom Fest, now this.

.

They had no privacy. Their secrets only hid how they were hopelessly tangled. Whatever was pushing Dom to violence had rooted in her too. When Dom was in pain, she'd leaned in with the audience. She wanted another taste. She wanted to hurt and be hurt.

The phone buzzed in the stained cup holder. Dom's phone, Pilar remembered.

It was a Columbia area code. She answered.

"Pilar?" It was Dom.

"Yeah," she said.

"I figured. Where are you?"

She ended the call and pulled to the shoulder. A truck rumbled past blaring its horn, close enough to rock the Civic in its airstream. Pilar drove farther onto the grass and clicked on the hazard lights.

She stared ahead and waited for Dom to call back. A minute passed. Five minutes. Then the phone lit up. A message.

"Hey. Sorry I don't check this very often. Do I know u from somewhere?"

It was from a girl she didn't recognize. Her name was Catie. In her profile she looked about Pilar's age. She was beaming a big, fake grin beneath the sign for that tourist trap, South of the Border.

What Pilar first typed was incoherent filth. She was thinking revenge. What her thumbs clicked out was so ridiculous it made her laugh. The girl had sent a friend request, so Pilar accepted and scrolled through her photos. Catie wearing a pair of expensive headphones. Catie giving the biggest hug in the world to a shiny blue convertible. Catie in a graduation cap and gown. The fabric was a deep maroon and far more substantial than the scratchy gown Pilar had borrowed from her school.

She could've been a dating-app girl. Dom had messaged her weeks ago—a simple "hey." It was a pathetic opener, even for him.

Pilar logged out of Dom's account and into hers. She typed her password, and a dart of loneliness pierced her and released its venom. She eyed an SUV as it passed. Its taillights never glowed any brighter.

There was no good way to open the conversation, but if there was one thing Pilar knew they'd have in common, it was dealing with skeevy dudes like her brother.

"heads up," she wrote. "dom is an asshole. dont waste your time."

A reply came quickly, as if Catie had been waiting for a response.

"Hm. And what if I'm looking for assholes?"

"then you hooked a fat one," Pilar wrote. "have fun reeling him in."

Catie replied. "They usually find me. And they always pay well."

Pilar read the line. Bent over the phone, her blood pressure spiked. Her neck throbbed. Dom had probably been throwing money at dozens of girls. Bookers often paid cash. He had probably squirreled thousands into his perv fund while Pilar ate frozen spinach and lived in squalor. Trust and privacy. Bullshit.

"pay well for what?" she asked.

"Look and see," Catie wrote. A link popped up, and Pilar followed it.

TWENTY-EIGHT

Most people familiar with Bonnie Blue found her exceptional. She was a mutation, an alien, a glitch in the system. People resented and feared her.

In its moment, The Pit seemed exceptional. After all the blood sport and brain injury—gladiators, the gridiron, the octagon, foxy boxing, basketball with trampolines—The Pit topped them all.

The Pit's claims to the extraordinary were proven false. Alternatives sprang up, copycats, fresh pursuits that scratched the same itch. They were more violent, more mysterious, more artistic, more titillating. Like everything once new, The Pit lost its favor. Audiences yawned as soon as they detected the rust.

The end came quickly. In a vacant lot outside a highway bar near Raleigh, a woman who claimed membership in one of the national organizations protesting The Pit pierced the ring of onlookers and unmasked the Cutman. A hundred pictures from every angle shot around the world. The Cutman had a name—Domingo Contreras, a twentysomething from Charlotte, a middling heel from the indie scene, some guy. Without the mystery, who was he?

A wrestler embodies the stories of old. Good and evil. David and Goliath. The People versus The Man. When an aging champion lies down so the next in succession can rise, the occasion can be regal. It can be heartbreaking or wrought with controversy. As Bonnie Blue watched her freshly conquered empire crumble, she knew Domingo's final match would be The Pit's best hope to survive.

Bonnie braced for a fight. She schemed and postulated. She called her champion to her side. In one of the true surprises of her life, Domingo volunteered to step off his throne.

"They've seen my face," the wrestler said. "From now on, it's all they'll ever see."

Bonnie booked the match. An exhaustive search produced a challenger and a venue. Every beat was rehearsed. She tracked the lighting and camera moves like a Hollywood director.

The conquering blow would be The Pit's most gruesome yet. Given the devastation the Cutman had inflicted, his felling had to balance the scale. The maneuver was intricate, its results hideous. Ensuring Domingo's survival was a true feat. The challenger, green to The Pit as all challengers were, would require a surgeon's precision.

The match never happened.

The end of The Pit is a story not often told. In most fans' memories, it faded away as so many fads and gimmicks had before. The postmortem commentators speculated. Contreras had gone into hiding. The money had dried up. A backdoor deal had been struck with the feds to remove the shows from the public eye. A venture like The Pit, blazing into the cultural atmosphere like a meteor, was expected to crash and burn. Under different circumstances, a behemoth like the WWE might have purchased it. It could've become an entertainment mainstay or evolved into something new. The truth, however, was far simpler. It ended. Bonnie Blue quit.

After Bonnie doomed her father to burn his prime retirement years in federal prison, a video game journalist wrote a poor-selling book on the rise and fall of BluCon Industries. During her exile in Mexico City, Bonnie read the book, its final chapter detailing the interview its author had negotiated with her father.

The book's characterization of Bruce Blue was a hit on the corporatization of the industry and capitalism in general. Still, the real Bruce could be found between the lines. As much as a CEO of a major American corporation could be, Bruce had been a good dad. He'd made time for Bonnie, encouraged her studies, introduced her to his favorite parts of the business. He loved the warehouses, the efficiency of the factory floor. The hum of headquarters' cubical farm was like music to him—phones ringing, printers churning out reports, keys clacking, muffled conversations.

Bruce was a numbers man. He saw the world in black and red. Bonnie expected him to be serving his time working puzzles, playing bridge or dominos. Instead, he'd come to lead his block's tabletop role-playing group. The book read like the journalist couldn't get the old man to shut up about his characters and their quests, his joy improvising fantasy worlds.

"We need to stop telling kids that anything is possible," Bruce said. "It's a lie. I was a millionaire. I would know."

The journalist described his stroll with Bruce across the grounds, more retreat center than prison. A fundamental divide between the inmates fascinated the journalist. For some, their time served had been the freest they'd ever been. After enduring day-to-days tangled with lies, extortion, and alpha-male posturing, their lives had been simplified. They had three squares. Time to watch daytime television. Blissful, basic routine.

For others, prison was hell. These were men with legal rosters bursting with Harvard grads, politicians spilling from their pockets. They'd been caught, and they weren't banished to Alcatraz or Rikers or Florence. They were sent to this place, a goddamned kindergarten with no fences, no guard towers. The rules holding them were no stronger than the ones they'd broken to get in. Each day was a reminder of their true selves, a testament to their cowardice. It drove them mad.

"The world is full of disappointment," Bruce said. "The more you achieve, the more you see how powerless you are to get what you truly want. When I got here, I realized I could ignore that world and build my own."

Bonnie read and grew angry. Her father would likely survive his sentence. His retreat into fantasy was a waste of imagination.

The world could be changed—of this Bonnie was sure. Look at what one woman had accomplished. Wildly successful investments. The dismantling of a Fortune 500 company. Her donations had funded hundreds of nonprofits. While her father played in his head and cried about getting caught plagiarizing the success of smarter men, she had tried to build something original and true.

In quitting, Bonnie saw she could be different. She'd thought The Pit would successfully blur the line between entertainment and reality. She'd thought it would give people trapped in the maw of a predatory industry a way out. Bonnie did not indulge in the think pieces and obituaries that trickled out once it was clear there would be no more matches. She had failed. She could take it and move on.

Bonnie's failure might've been the most mundane, unexceptional part of her life. She learned loss and frustration had a silver lining. Unlike her father, she could fail and still believe the world could be moved. She'd read the library of pro-wrestling biographies wall to wall. Nobody ever told readers that quitting was sometimes the best thing to do.

Duke Natterjack, born Charles Gruden, died at the age of fifty-five. Until the end, he kept wrestling, knees creaking through a few bookings a month. Bonnie attended his funeral in Fort Lauderdale. His casket descended with a healthy group of family, friends, and wrestlers in vigil. It was February, with an insistent Florida dampness in the air. The funeral home director, with his slicked hair and slicker suit, said some final words. A jet trailing a streak of condensation cut the sky in two.

Bonnie lingered after other attendees had left. She watched the cemetery's backhoe. The groundskeepers slapped sod into place, tested for soft spots. They hosed down the grave site and washed away all evidence of the ritual.

Duke's headstone was simple—bronze on granite, flush with the ground. One major flood from the creek at the cemetery's boundary would cover it forever. The marker said nothing about wrestling or who Charles Gruden actually was. Bonnie placed a small, ceramic frog on its corner. Its glaze reflected the sunlight like wet amphibian skin.

"Adorable," a voice said behind her.

It was Gorilla Trotsky. He looked even more a human barrel than he did in MCCW. The ring of hair on his scalp was shaved close. His forehead bore the telltale scarring from a lifetime of blade jobs. He was an old man, aged more by his labor than his years.

Bonnie readied her knees and rose to her feet. She was almost as tall as the wrestler. His shoulders hunched and legs bowed.

"You hear how it happened?" Gorilla asked.

Bonnie shook her head. There'd been a time when she would've known. Those days had long passed.

"Heart attack," he said. His voice caught on the end of the word, and he coughed into a black handkerchief. Once his throat relaxed, he folded the fabric and stuffed it into a pocket.

"They said he could've survived it," he continued. "He was driving to a gig. Veered off, took a cypress to the driver's side. Real shame. I would've liked to drink with the stubborn bastard one last time."

"I didn't think you were close."

"We weren't," Gorilla said, scowling at the six feet of earth between him and the deceased. "But he whipped me enough in the ring. I didn't think he'd beat me into the ground."

Bonnie had grown tired standing through the service. Her hands were swelling painfully in the heat. She smiled at the old vet. "That makes two of us, Trotsky."

As if by magic, he appeared a plastic bottle with a slosh of dark liquid inside.

"To Duke!" he toasted. Bonnie glugged a mouthful of the sour brew. Gorilla poured the dregs in front of the marker.

"Drink up, ya bastard." He shook the bottle dry and, creaking to a knee, placed it on the grave next to Bonnie's frog.

"That was really tasty," she said.

Gorilla craved chicken, so they ordered a car, which had a hard time finding them in the labyrinth of cemetery roads. Gorilla produced a second bottle while they waited. When they got moving, Bonnie didn't care about where they went. She and

Gorilla were losing themselves in old stories. Gorilla dished like a stand-up comedian. Bonnie sweetened his punch lines with details from her encyclopedic knowledge of her former employees' lives. Duke's passing had erased one of her failures from the earth. No more would his name mock her from the bottom of the Southeast's trash-tier cards. He was gone.

The chicken restaurant was wedged into a touristy strip mall. Parents in flip-flops left a beach store with armfuls of pastel wares. Couples Bonnie's age gazed through the foggy windows of a soft-serve joint and licked their cones.

The blinking lights of the VRcade next to the restaurant distracted Gorilla, who limped to the door and peeked inside.

"They have one!" he shouted, frightening a boy arriving for a birthday party. "Come look!"

"I don't care for places with this many children," Bonnie said, drawing a stare from the boy's mother.

Gorilla held the door. The noise pouring out sounded like warfare waged on the galaxy's most annoying planet.

"You said you wanted chicken," Bonnie said, pointing next door.

"I've been reading about these," Gorilla said. "We have to try it."

Her body, unmoored from her will by Gorilla's brew, allowed itself to be ushered in. There was likely no place on earth more the cemetery's opposite. The cacophony of light and sound enveloped Bonnie like a straitjacket. Children ruckused though the electronic maze. A rocket ship blasted off with two screaming boys inside. Its hydraulic arm raised the cab to the ceiling. Two teenagers held powder-blue pistols sideways and fired. Along the wall beyond a holographic Ping-Pong table was a row of 1980s-style arcade machines. Bonnie recognized a few of her father's games—a Missile Command clone and a game called Pamplona! in which a vaguely person-shaped sprite fled from vaguely bull-shaped sprites.

Bonnie didn't see where Gorilla was leading her until it was impossible to overlook. Looming over the corner of the arcade was a life-size projection of André Roussimoff, the seven-foot-four, five-hundred-twenty-pound wrestling colossus known to the world as André the Giant.

André was snarling. His arms were extended, creating two entrance portals to a virtual-reality experience called Wrestle with André. The line snaked through switchbacks leading to a row of lime-green cubbyholes fifteen feet across. Inside, guests stepped into plastic suits of armor and tugged on virtual-reality helmets. What they saw streamed on displays above each box. Bonnie recognized the time and the place. March 29, 1987. WrestleMania III. André the Giant versus Hulk Hogan. The biggest match in wrestling history. The Pontiac Silverdome packed with ninety thousand fans.

"We bury and raise the dead on the same day!" Gorilla said.

"This is ridiculous," Bonnie said. "I'm not waiting for this."

"You are," Gorilla said. "This is exactly what we need!"

Gorilla blocked several children from entering the turnstile until Bonnie finally agreed. The line had photos of André's most famous moments and blurbs recounting *Larger Than Life* facts. André once drank over one hundred beers in a sitting. Samuel Beckett drove André to school. At twelve years old, André stood six feet tall and weighed two hundred pounds.

"He was the best of us," Gorilla said. "He's been dead how long? Forty years? These tykes' parents were toddlers, and he still draws!"

"You think these kids actually recognize him?" Bonnie asked.

"Of course they do!" Gorilla said. "He's King Kong. Even if you've never seen the movie, you know the story."

By coincidence or not, the attraction's portrayal of Roussimoff was decidedly Kong-like. The avatar's brow was exaggerated. His nostrils flared wide. His toothy grin flashed suggestively, a monster eyeing his prey.

"Here's a booking question for the great Bonnie Blue," Gorilla said. "It's 1973. Somehow Vince and his daddy missed the boat. André walks into your locker room at his physical peak. What do you do?"

Bonnie watched a child who'd just met the attraction's height requirement shake as the safety restraints cinched around him. The practiced bravery on his face was that of a paratrooper about to take his first jump behind enemy lines.

"I'd try to save him," Bonnie replied.

"C'mon, woman!" Gorilla said, shaking Bonnie's shoulder. "Have you learned nothing? There's no saving this lot. You either end up like Duke or like us."

"I gave it my best," Bonnie said, surprised she could utter such a thing out loud. "You wouldn't believe what I offered Duke to hang it up."

"A wrestler's a wrestler, no matter how big the carrot you dangle in front of him," Gorilla said. "For instance, Dommy Contreras. Remember we were tag partners when he was outed as that sicko. After he got unmasked, I was able to sneak through the cameras and get him alone. I says to him, 'Dommy, ya goddamned torino, this ain't you. You're no sadist. You have a career. People respect you.' And you know what he said? He said he felt like a fake until he put on a hood and started breaking bones. If he's breathing, he's probably doing that shit off the grid somewhere. Down south maybe—Juárez, Chihuahua."

"I doubt he's in Mexico," Bonnie said.

When they reached the end of the queue, a host directed them to their immersion suits. The padded interior resized itself to fit Bonnie's frame. She smelled the funk of the sporadically bathed preteens who had faced Roussimoff before her.

The suit's mechanics impressed Bonnie. Its limbs were fully articulated and self-powered so that raising an arm or leg required no extra effort. A tech helped her put on the helmet. Through its display, she saw the alcove she was standing in, glowing red lines containing her experience. The remainder of the arcade was screened out, replaced by fog. The tech's digital avatar copied the real kid's movements. Same height. Same hair and eye color. His uniform was corporate crisp, his acne cleared, his chin free from stubble. A voice in the helmet instructed Bonnie through a tutorial. In under a minute, it taught Bonnie how to walk, duck, dive, and punch.

A beautiful vase appeared on a wooden stool in front of her. The voice between her ears explained that this, like everything she'd see during her experience, was a creation of state-of-the-art virtual reality and the suit's patented physical feedback system.

The voice instructed her to pick up the vase. She listened, amazed by the fidelity. It had heft and resistance. If she imagined she was wearing work gloves, the immersion was nearly complete.

A bull's-eye appeared on the wall with neon arrows pointing to it. Instructions flashed bright red.

"Smash it!" the voice demanded. "Throw the vase!"

Bonnie heaved it, and the vase shattered. Two more appeared. Bonnie threw those. The game dropped four around her, then eight. Bonnie picked up a stool and gleefully swung it, splinters and porcelain shards flying everywhere. The suit's feedback mimicked the weight of the stool, the centrifugal force of the swipes.

The vases morphed into expensive electronics. Bonnie smashed them. Then, they became famous works of art— framed paintings from van Gogh and Jackson Pollock. She put a boot through a portrait of Henry VIII. Velázquez peered at her behind his canvas in *Las Meninas*. She punched him in the face.

The objects were replaced by a man. He was a wrestler of modest build, wearing basic trunks and sporting a ridiculous handlebar moustache.

"Well! You've wrecked history's priceless heirlooms," the man said. "Let's see what kind of punch you pack against a real fighter. Take your best shot!"

The man bent his knees, set his jaw, and pointed at his chin. Bonnie didn't hesitate. Following the instincts of a thousand thirteen-year-olds before her, she squared him up and swung the hardest kick she could swing directly into his groin.

"Egads! My precious jewels!" the man cried, crumpling to his knees. "You may have bested me, but you'll never defeat André!"

The man disappeared and congratulatory music played. Bonnie was transported to the ring under the Silverdome lights. The attraction host's avatar was there, now skinned as a ref. He flashed a thumbs-up and asked Bonnie if she was ready. She said yes and, with a gesture toward the entrance aisle, he triggered the simulation.

Spotlights trained on the tunnel at the corner of the stadium floor.

"And now, the champion," the announcer said. "He hails from Grenoble in the French Alps. He weighs five hundred and twenty pounds. André, the Giant!"

And he was a giant—all seven feet, four inches of his billed height. Cameras sparkled around the dome. *Also sprach Zarathustra* swelled behind him, Strauss's timpani drums accenting his march. The artistic license amused Bonnie. At WrestleMania III, André had no entrance music. He was the challenger, not the champion. He traveled the fifty-yard entry aisle riding a cart topped with a platform styled as a miniature wrestling ring.

The crowd had rebuked him, hurling jeers, insults, and trash. By then, Roussimoff was well into his decline. His shoulders had curled. His head craned up like a tortoise's. His enormous gut strained his singlet. The André stalking Bonnie wasn't the André of WrestleMania III. It was the André of myth, far more muscular and menacing than the man ever was. He stood proud, eyes focused on the ring. Fireworks scraped the Silverdome's roof, the fiberglass checkerboard held aloft on a pillow of air.

Roussimoff took his time climbing the ring steps. He dragged his feet on the apron and stepped over the top rope. He waved to the audience, holding his tree limb of an arm ten feet high. Unbuckling his championship belt, he flashed Bonnie a smile—close-lipped, confident, hungry.

If only her father had lived to see this, Bonnie thought. In his day, games were simple shapes, primary colors, beeps and boops. Bonnie couldn't fathom the processing power required to set this stage in such vivid detail.

The Giant looked at Bonnie as if she were an inconvenience, a messy kitchen he was too lazy to clean. He saw everything. Her failures. Her body's decline. The principles she'd so stubbornly followed into the labyrinth of old age. Roussimoff did not judge. It didn't matter who she was or what she'd done. He would fight her.

Bonnie threw a punch, and Roussimoff caught it in his enormous right hand. Her gauntlet constricted. The suit locked her arm in place. He kept staring, his eyes reflecting the stadium lights. Some corporation had bought the rights to resurrect a dead man. They'd digitized him, painted over his blemishes. He was a caricature—layered and complicated and true. The distortion told a hundred different stories. After everything she'd poured into The Pit, Bonnie had never imagined its opposite. Remove the blood, the danger, the humanity. Lessen the impact. Lower the stakes. Roussimoff's look was one of condescension, but also one of love. "Let me show you," it said.

The Giant seized Bonnie's other wrist and lifted her. Her toes left the mat. She couldn't tell whether some mechanism in the virtual-reality box had raised her up, or whether the immersion was tricking her mind. Roussimoff swung her into the turnbuckle and was on her in a flash, squeezing her into the corner. She didn't notice the suit. It was the wrestler's girth, his chest and arms wrapping her tightly.

There was one opening for escape. The game appeared to remember Bonnie's strike against the training dummy. Her right leg was free. Roussimoff's stance was open. Completely absurd, yet her artistic brain lost out. She wound up and kicked the world's biggest, most famous wrestler squarely in the balls.

Roussimoff staggered away. Bonnie landed rights and lefts. The Giant lunged for her. Bonnie ducked and seized him, transferring his momentum, sweeping him off his feet.

The physics were impossible, but that didn't matter in this world. Bonnie lifted the quarter-ton behemoth. She held him aloft, his tree-trunk legs kicking. A roar of surprise preceded a million flashbulbs. The Silverdome had hosted the Super Bowl, the Who, even the Pope. It had never seen anything like this.

Genetics, culture, the laws of gravity—all her life they'd pinned Bonnie to the mat. Men had laughed at her, dared her to prove her reputation. Her own father had underestimated her. Now, in this digital daydream, she was as powerful as she knew she'd always been.

Clout, the bastard, had tried to warn her. A body can't take infinite punishment. There are only so many ways it can break. Danger enticed, violence could titillate, but what kept audiences coming? As a child, when Bonnie's love for wrestling was its purest, she believed anything could happen inside the ring. Vicious beatings left no marks. Men soared on invisible wings. A peculiar boy from rural France became a legend.

The problem with wrestling wasn't the artifice. Bonnie simply hadn't seen it. She'd been wrong to start The Pit, wrong to quit the business she'd loved so much, and she could make it right. There was time.

"Slam!" the Giant yelled. He'd shouted the same to Hogan— the most famous call in wrestling. Hulk would later recount how frightened he'd been. Could he lift the monster? Would his spine shatter? Would he drop the ailing superstar on his face? Hogan was a man of countless faults. That night, he shined brighter than ever. When Bonnie hurled the Giant back to earth, she had no fear. She was perfect.

TWENTY-NINE

"You know. Don't you?" Dom asked

"Of course I do," Pilar said.

Dom squeezed his eyelids shut and leaned against the countertop. His elbow dislodged a bowl from the tower of dirty dishes. Through the wall, the neighbor's groan sounded like a dying animal.

It was morning. Dom had caught a bus home from the Columbia show. Pilar was awake when her brother came in.

"I swear I was going to tell you," Dom said.

"Sure," Pilar said. She was sitting cross-legged on her futon, still wearing her clothes from the previous day. "Separate lives, right?"

"If it makes any difference, it's a secret. That's kind of the point."

"Stop. I don't want details."

Dom opened the fridge and saw nothing edible. The cabinets were empty except for the jug of protein powder. He scooped some into his mouth and lapped faucet water to wash it down. His chin dipped into the liquid stagnating in the pile of dishes.

"Where'd you see it?" he asked.

Pilar paused. "See it?"

"Yeah. Clips are all over YouTube. Even cracked national news. Can you believe it?"

No, Pilar thought. She couldn't. There wasn't a viral sex tape starring the two people she knew best in the world. Dom wasn't confessing—at least, not to the secret she'd discovered.

"I'm famous," Dom said. "People love the character. They love what he does. They see the mask, and they don't care who's underneath."

"Famous?" Pilar said.

Dom asked for his phone. She worried he would see her messages with Catie. Though her transgression was nothing compared to Dom's actions, she felt ashamed. Whatever she was about to see was a far bigger deal to her brother than his romp with B. That betrayal, the worst Pilar could imagine, hadn't even crossed his mind.

He played a video. The audio crackled, the noise of a crowd blowing out the camera's microphone. The frame wobbled until steadying on two masked figures circling each other inside a white ring painted on the ground. Pilar could make out the brick walls of an alley. At least a hundred people were gathered close.

One by one, phone lights switched on. The tiny spotlights danced behind the figures. The glare made the action even harder to see.

Dom was one of the fighters. She recognized his movement, the lumber of a man whose body had not yet forgotten how big it once was. They were wrestling. She could name the maneuvers. Dom's opponent threw an elbow. He didn't spread the strike across his forearm. He connected with the joint. He didn't sound off with a stomp or slap to his hip. The thump of elbow on Dom's chest cracked solid. The recorder's cheap microphone was twenty feet away, but it was still a decadent sound.

"What is this?" Pilar asked.

Dom told her. The Pit. Bonnie Blue. The internet. His first match. The second. The fans' thirst for him. The secrecy. He'd made it. Soon, they could move out of this shithole. Separate, together—they'd figure it out. Pilar could ascend the company ladder confident she had a soft landing if needed. They could now afford to take risks. She could negotiate with the big leagues. She'd rise to heights never seen by a female wrestler.

The match's violence escalated. Real strikes. Anguished cries. Near the end, Dom peered over his opponent. The man's leg was injured. He couldn't get up. He could only scoot to the edge of the circle, his guard up in hopes Dom would make a mistake. A chant rose from the crowd, and Dom drew a chip of loose concrete across his forehead, splitting Lycra and skin. Blood trickled onto his opponent.

Pilar guessed what was coming. She couldn't look away. This was the mangled wreck at the end of a traffic jam. The lion tearing a gazelle's throat. It was, she realized, the final image of all the comics and videos and GIFs buried deep in those websites she'd visited in the dark. The eaten, having screamed and struggled, resigned to its fate.

Dom seized his opponent's leg and stomped. The knee cracked, and the joint bent the wrong way. The crowd roared, and their frenzy coalesced into a chant. Spanish, Pilar realized.

"Cortador! Cortador! Cortador!"

Horror gripped Pilar—at what she saw, at how easy it had been to watch. She let the clip end, and the app started the next video—even worse footage of the same fight from a different angle.

"Do you hear what they were chanting?" she said.

"What do you mean?" Dom asked.

"Cortador. You understand it?"

"I know what you're thinking," Dom said.

"You don't," Pilar said, a pained smile fracturing her face.

Dom took his phone, punched in some text, and showed her the screen. He'd searched for "the pit wrestling" and scrolled through endless videos, articles, and forum posts.

"They're writing about me. Not just the dirt sheets. Reporters, newspapers. Look. 'Underground wrestling puts nation in choke hold.' 'Masked luchador is new viral sensation.' 'Who is the Cutman?' "

"I saw the view count," Pilar said.

"The official uploads have triple the hits."

"Wow. Triple."

Dom tensed, then took a breath and dropped his shoulders.

"I'm sorry, okay? I should've told you. I had to do this. I was getting old. You were hurt. I wanted you to focus on getting better."

"Oh, swell. You had no choice. You had to star in a snuff film."

Dom let his mouth hang. The words that tumbled loose were quiet and pulped. "That's not what this is."

"Then tell me what it is, Dom! Tell me it's theatrics. Tell me that guy's leg was a prop."

"It's not theater. It's real."

Pilar took the phone. She didn't have to scroll far. "See? Right here. 'Viral street wrestling inspires deadly copycats.' 'Charlotte mayor says illegal fighting ring is scourge, not sport.' And oh, here we go. 'The Pit: latest sacrament in the cult of American violence.' They're writing about you, all right."

"Those are critics," Dom said. "They're paid to get pissed off."

The siblings jumped at a terrific bang against the wall. It wasn't a fist this time. The neighbor was wielding something—a skillet, a sheet pan.

Pilar didn't lower her voice. "Are you really so deep into this shit you can't imagine why a person would think it's disgusting?"

"Wrestlers get hurt, Pilar," Dom said. "No one escapes this business without injury. Hell, you almost broke your neck in your first match."

"That was a mistake."

"And that makes it better? It's a mistake when a football player gets blindsided and paralyzed. When a boxer with CTE can't remember his kids' names. When some stock-car idiot splats into a wall. But what is everyone hoping to see? Why can they sell all those beer ads? It's not for the thousands of mistake-free laps. It's not for two men having a pillow fight. We understand the world we live in and what people want. We make a plan. We execute as safely as possible."

"Nice speech," Pilar said. "But this is a gimmick. People are going to get bored. So, what next? You gonna cut off someone's ear? Kill someone?"

"Maybe you can trust that after ten years I've learned how to tell a story."

"Fuck you and your trust."

Pilar had put no thought to leaving. She allowed her body to follow its impulse. She jammed all that was hers into a bag—clothes, shoes, papers, junk she should've thrown away months earlier.

"Remember when we could talk about shit?" Dom asked, stepping in front of the door. "Hours on the road, we'd talk and talk and never get tired. What happened, Pilar? We're closer than this."

"Too close," Pilar said. "I'm starting to think you were right."

"I didn't want us to be at each other's throats. I thought it would be better to claim our own space."

"Then you shouldn't have fucked B," Pilar said. She made sure her words were clear so she wouldn't have to say them again.

A dozen responses tangled in Dom's mouth. What came through the mess was muted and resigned. "Is that what she told you?"

"You know, she didn't," Pilar said, struggling to zip her over-stuffed bag. "And that's the worst part. You can't allow me the one person who told me her secrets."

"We didn't have sex," Dom said, almost whispering.

"No?" Pilar said. "Too bad. She's really hot."

Pilar shouldered the bag and strode toward the door. Dom stopped her.

"You don't have anywhere to go."

"I talked with Catie," Pilar said.

This caught Dom on the chin. Had she wanted to, Pilar could have toppled him with a strong shove.

"She's nice. I would've thought a little young for you. I guess not. She's got a neat enterprise going. It's an expensive kink. You'd think once someone gets some money, he wouldn't imme-diately throw it away."

Dom looked ready to vomit. "What did you tell her?"

"Get out of the way," Pilar demanded.

"What did you tell her?" he shouted.

"I told her exactly who you are. And now that you've told me this new detail, she's going to hear about that, too."

If it hadn't happened right in front of her, Pilar might've laughed. The tower of dishes, stacked so high for so long she couldn't remember when it had become a fixture in the apart-ment, came crashing down. Dom pushed them toward her. Plates cracked, shards scooting past her feet. A wave of sink water broke over her toes.

"You will not say one thing!" Dom shouted.

A pot with an inch of liquid left inside had come to rest next to Pilar. She dropped Dom's phone into it.

"I'm leaving," she said.

Dom's eyes raced around the apartment, searching for a possession of hers to destroy. Her bag carried most of her stuff. He hulked between her and her exit. She wasn't afraid. Whatever secrets he'd managed to keep from her, she knew precisely what his body could do.

"Would you open your eyes?" he said. "Do you think it's a coincidence I started this at the same time you signed MCCW's best rookie contract from a sickbed?"

"Oh? Well, it was nice to think for a minute the world had quit shitting on me."

"Welcome to reality. Trust me. It gets worse if you spite Bonnie Blue. Even if you land somewhere, you're always going to be looking over your shoulder."

There was a hard knock at the door. Dom made a guttural noise that would've sent most mortals running.

Pilar stepped around Dom and opened the door to a middle-aged man in a work shirt. He had silvering hair, and though he wasn't tall and his chin was sunken into an overbite, he held himself straight and solid, a judge at the bench.

"¿Qué está pasando aquí?" he asked.

It was the neighbor, Pilar realized. His door was cracked and his voice, which she'd heard only through the wall, was rich and deep.

"Mi hermano es un pendejo," Pilar said. "Pero no pasa nada. Disculpe la molestia."

Pilar's Spanish sliced through the nerve the man had built before confronting them.

"¿Voy a tener que llamar a la policía?" the man asked. "El ruido es insoportable."

"No," Pilar said. "Solo discutimos. Lo siento mucho. Hablaremos más bajo."

The man let Pilar's words simmer, as if the silence would cook out the truth. He glanced at Dom. The tiny apartment made him look even more enormous.

"Hablas español muy bien, y eso que siempre discutes en inglés."

"Mi mamá era de España," Pilar said.

"¿Y tú qué, grandullón?" the man said to Dom. "¿Todo bien?"

The man didn't shy as Dom took a deep, intimidating breath. The wrestler spoke before his sister could.

"Es solo una discusión," Dom said. "No pasa nada."

"What?" Pilar said.

"No pasa nada," Dom repeated. "Ya nos lo hemos dicho todo, y ahora podemos limpiar todo esto."

His accent was Castilian, like their mother's. It was so familiar, yet nothing like Pilar's. Her Latina schoolmates and Hollywood had made her Spanish a mutt, and her Midwestern English had neutered it. Her *t*'s had lost their edge. *R*s limped from her mouth. She heard Dom speak that tongue for the first time, crisp with sounds from a childhood that had just ended but seemed a lifetime in the past. She'd never felt such pain.

THIRTY

Pilar didn't take the Civic. She rode the bus, catching a line that would drop her within walking distance of the Hangar. Johnnie May would be there, and unlike Sol, she didn't care about Dom. She'd understand Pilar's need to get out. She'd help her find someplace to go.

Pilar had nothing to distract her from the gray city blocks and her reflection in the window. Her face had kept a record of everything. If she relaxed, one of the men seated nearby would pounce. What's wrong, honey? You need some help? Why's a girl so pretty got a face so sour?

The longer she stared, the more she wished she could peel off her face and store it in her bag.

The thought kept cycling—she had nowhere to run. She should've built an escape pod. She should've made more connections, tended more relationships. She'd been complacent with her dreams and her one close friend and had failed to see how Dom could crush them.

In the future, she'd miss him. She missed her mother, after all. She thought about how much of a real-life heel he was—quick to anger, eager to bully, pathologically selfish. She loved that Catie had snared him. As delightful as his anger had been when she revealed their contact, it might've been sweeter keeping it hidden, letting their relationship develop, letting her drain him dry.

Her conversation with Catie the previous night had continued into morning. At first, curiosity had driven her. What did her brother see in this woman? How had he stumbled into her trap? Why was he pursuing yet another eighteen-year-old? Who was she?

Perhaps more than most teenagers, Pilar understood the desires that could drive a man to a dominatrix. MCCW's most popular women—Tanya Flex, Blair Jackson, even Johnnie May—were big, take-no-shit competitors. One could guess what fetishes were popular among their fans. As Pilar had cultivated her personal fascinations online, she'd explored what BDSM and its subcultures had to offer. The whips and handcuffs and other mainstream elements didn't do much for her, though she supposed her interests were perched on a branch of the community's tree.

She'd never heard of the niche Catie occupied. Apparently she wasn't alone. Catie's website, stylish and minimal, featured explainers describing her services and their appeal.

She was a findom—a specialist in financial domination. Clients provided her access to bank accounts, credit cards, even heavy-duty shit like stock portfolios and retirement savings. Then, she put a boot to their necks, withdrawing greater and greater amounts of cash, consolidating diversified investments into tanking startups. The tease, the site explained, was the loss of control, the titillating exposure of inviting a thief into your most private, protected space. "Money Is Power," read the website's banner. "Pledge to Mistress Mary."

In the site's photos, Catie looked like a CEO on the cover of *Time* magazine. Business suit. Arms folded. Confident eyes to camera. Perhaps a touch more skin than those corporate women revealed, though nothing explicit.

The heavy overcast weighed on the Hangar's arching roof. Pilar had no idea whether the jet wash from the lost airliner had weakened it. The last time she'd seen the building, she was sprawled beneath it, waiting to be crushed.

Dom breaking his opponent's leg looped in her mind—the knee cracking open like the joint of a buffalo wing. It was horrible, and yet, she couldn't dismiss Dom's argument. How different was it? She wanted to draw a line. He'd hurt someone. She hadn't. His intent was malicious. Hers wasn't. He wanted fame, cash, the respect he'd never gotten. Her goals were far more complex and artistic.

The thought couldn't support its own weight. This was fucking wrestling. She did it because she liked beating people up, and wrestling was as close as she could get without going to jail.

Pretending wouldn't be enough. She'd hurt others too. She'd snap a wing and suck the marrow. She'd dig for a fix until she got too deep to climb out. She was an addict. Always had been.

Pilar was surprised Johnnie May was awake. The veteran was stitching a hem in a pair of trunks. Even in the low light from the desk lamp on Johnnie May's sewing table, the trunks were vibrantly green with a bold cut of black trim at the waist. Pilar watched for a moment. Johnnie May's fingers worked precisely around the plunging needle.

"It's pretty," Pilar said.

"Good to see you up and around," Johnnie May said. "These are for you, funnily enough."

"Really? You don't have to do that."

"You deserve an upgrade."

Johnnie May offered Pilar a seat on a milk crate. Close up, she watched the machine pulse and the trunks advance. The thread was almost invisible. Johnnie May took care planning each pass, hiding the stitches in the garment's creases.

"How stretchy will it be?" Pilar asked. "You never took my measurements."

Johnnie May laughed. "Can you imagine? Me with a tailor's tape? Pins in my mouth?"

"Is there another way?"

"We wrestled, right? That's how they should do it in the bridal shops. Come in for a fitting and work a ten-minute submission. Seamstress would know way more than your waist and hips."

"You ever think about opening your own shop? You're really good."

"Less competition in wrestling," Johnnie May said.

"More broken bones," Pilar offered.

"Yeah, if you suck."

Johnnie May had several outfits hanging on a clothesline. Ornate tops and trunks—some sleek, some sequined. One pair of trunks had "JMY" stitched with a flourish across the ass.

"Could you sew 'I suck' into mine?" Pilar asked.

Johnnie May sighed. "You don't suck. You're green as turtle shit, but you've got it."

"Got what?"

"What it takes."

"What does it take?"

"Looks, talent, cutthroat instincts."

"See? That's my point. I don't want to cut any throats. Intact throats only."

"Where will playing nice get you?"

"Is there anywhere to go?" Pilar surveyed Johnnie May's modest comforts—her hammock and tarp, her trinkets, the stained Rhode Island flag with its laughable Hope motto.

"Okay," Johnnie May said. She stood more than a head taller than Pilar. Even without a warm-up, her biceps bulged. Her shoulders were broad and rock solid. "Why you here so early looking for a coach?"

"I'm done with coaches," Pilar said. "I need a friend."

"This isn't high school," Johnnie May said.

"Yeah. People can the get the hell out of high school. This is a swamp. Everyone's stuck. Everyone's sinking. Why are we killing ourselves to distract a bunch of idiots?"

"You're the dog that caught the car," Johnnie May said. "I heard about your contract."

"Did you hear about my brother?"

"What about him?"

"Have you seen The Pit?"

"Not really."

"Dom is the star."

Johnnie May paused. The Carolinas were abuzz with speculation. Both matches had taken place within Greater Charlotte. If he was local, there were only so many men it could be.

"Your brother is El Cortador?"

Pilar winced, then nodded. It was such a piss-poor name, and the media's translations of it were even worse.

"Are you sure?"

"Watch a clip. It's him."

"Honey, do you really think your brother's got enough upstairs to cook that up?"

"He didn't. It was Bonnie Blue."

Johnnie May peered over her shoulder as if her boss were listening.

"She sold the spot to him and gave me a contract," Pilar said. "He loves it. He's famous without the celebrity."

Johnnie May pried a juice box from her pallet. She had a

precise, efficient move to unsheathe the tiny straw from its plastic. "He could be lying," she said.

"He's not," Pilar said.

"Think about it. He's jealous of your success, so he concocts this conspiracy to make it all about him. What's more likely—he duped you? Or your brother, our boss's puppet, is drawing millions on the internet, and no one's talked?"

"The odds don't matter. It's him."

Johnnie May's juice was from a national brand Pilar always saw advertised during the nature shows she'd watched on Saturday mornings. She remembered the commercials—catchy jingle, sunny days, smiling children, straws poking through the gaps in their teeth. Johnnie May had gallons and gallons of it. The boxes were packed and wrapped—a layer of plastic protecting each straw, another layer wrapping each brick of eight boxes, yet another wrapping blocks of four bricks. Healthy, wholesome juice—a product as fake as professional wrestling.

"I'm never going to know him," Pilar said.

Johnnie May's face soured.

"You told me to stop making my life so complicated," Pilar continued. "I can't do that here."

"You're quitting," Johnnie May said.

"I have to," Pilar said. Her conviction's frailty was obvious.

"Sounds a lot thornier than working your contract and not sweating the drama," Johnnie May said.

"You could come with me," Pilar said. She hadn't practiced this pitch. She hadn't even convinced herself it made sense.

"You can leave, but no one ever quits," Johnnie May said. "This job eats you, or it spits you out."

"It can be different," Pilar said. "Don't you wish you had a choice?"

Johnnie May was quiet. Pilar had to listen carefully.

"You know, I am tired of doing this alone," Johnnie May said.

Like all good wrestlers, Johnnie May could hide what actually hurt. She looked no less powerful or striking than she had a moment before. Pilar wrapped her arms around her and felt anew the intimacy they'd shared in their match. It made sense to her now. Their closeness wasn't one of love or friendship or even teacher and student. They were patients in an infusion suite, an anonymous pair sharing their darkest moments in a church basement. There was comfort in surviving with someone, in suffering the same pain. Pilar had to walk before the sickness that brought them together took her for good.

Pilar left without waiting for Johnnie May to finish sewing her gear. She had no idea where she'd go. She picked through the bleacher supports and emerged in the entrance aisle. The empty ring loomed in the dark. As she took it in, Bonnie Blue appeared beside her.

"I'm done," Pilar said. "But thanks for the opportunity."

Bonnie no-sold the line and grasped Pilar's shoulder. She slid her words into Pilar like a knife. "No one will ever love you as much as you want them to."

"Jesus," Pilar said, knocking her arm away. "Get fucked, lady."

A smirk curling her lip, Bonnie said no more as Pilar stepped over the track guiding the Hangar's enormous sliding doors. Outside, the overcast squeezed out raindrops. It was just a sprinkle, but the plants growing through the fissures in the tarmac welcomed whatever they could get.

Pilar surveyed the gardens outside the public library a few miles from the Hangar. The breeze had picked up, clearing some of the humidity and clouds, shaping the morning into the first bearable day in weeks. She'd bought a pear from the grocery nearby. Sitting on the curb, she ate it, core and all. Velvet skin and sweet flesh.

Inside, she scrolled through her messenger as more and more men joined her in the row of well-used desktops. Nobody bothered her. The public privacy was wonderful. She soaked it in before getting to work.

Pilar's exchange with Catie the previous evening had stretched into morning. To Catie, Pilar had the interesting job. She asked the typical things about what was and wasn't real. She wanted to learn about Pilar's character, about who she was on and off the clock.

"I like to visit chat rooms," Catie had written. "I can practice being on camera, and I can be myself. Do u ever feel that? Do u ever wish u could wrestle without worrying about being someone else?"

Yes, she'd told Catie. She wished she could find solace in the ring. It was far easier to agree than to compress the truth into text. Pilar had never developed a real character. When she wrestled Johnnie May, she wondered if it was a fleeting high, a phony authenticity she'd kill herself chasing.

Pilar sensed Catie was lonely. She was, after all, a performer. To dominate was to set oneself above, to be distant, untouchable. Maybe that's why Catie was so interested in her. Maybe she wanted a friend.

Pilar couldn't be sure. She messaged her anyway. She needed someplace to go. Sitting at the library computer, she was as unattached as she'd ever been. The freedom was exhilarating. She thought about setting out, hopping a Greyhound to any-where and seeing if she could make it.

She convinced herself her attraction to Catie wasn't the want of another coach. It wasn't revenge against her brother. It wasn't the allure of ordering men to fork over their cash. She could be Catie's equal. They could be friends. Pilar chose to focus there. She could fly her middle finger and take whatever came.

The man at the computer next to her squeaked in surprise. He was older, signs of a thousand bad breaks on his face. He was streaming a video. Questionable banner ads framed the pixilated image. The figures holding frame were unmistakable. Two women, WWE Superstars, wrestling for the title in the main event of *Monday Night Raw*.

For decades, women had been a sideshow in wrestling's biggest company. They'd been valets, eye candy, damsels to be saved and won and held high on the champion's shoulder. Fans used their matches for bathroom breaks. The brass looped this feedback by ensuring there wasn't much to miss. The company elevated the wives and daughters of its men. It buried those who tried to earn a spot. Female characters were lustful. They were basket cases. They were airheaded and silicon chested. Stars of catfights, mud pits, lingerie matches, sex tapes.

This was changing. Pilar had the evidence right in front of her. Two women in a gimmick-free main event. Twenty minutes to show they could do more than slap and pull hair. The man beside her was enraptured, rooting for the babyface, sliding to the edge of his seat for every high spot. The world was opening to women's wrestling. Pilar had a clear path to the top.

If she walked, she'd close the door on an unprecedented opportunity. She was young and skilled and on the edge of the spotlight. She only needed to follow through. Wasn't she strong enough? Couldn't she survive in a business that was more hospitable than it had ever been? How many women had sacrificed everything to earn a fraction of the chance she was about to throw away?

The feed glitched, then focused. This match had transcended its corporate packaging. It was the Miracle on Ice passed around on a bootleg VHS tape. It was Ali vs. Frazier beamed to some kid's radio half a world away. The entrances were spectacles. The wrestling pristine. The new champion scaled the turnbuckle and raised the belt. Pilar only needed to reach out and take it.

Before the man closed the stream, he watched the new champion, tears streaming down her cheeks, thank the audience. She looked at her belt as if it were her newborn child. The arena sensed the history. The peak of a career, the evolution of an industry fans could be a little less ashamed to love. Fifteen thousand were on their feet. They'd come for sport. They'd come for theater. They'd paid for the story twists, the display of tempting bodies in combat. What united them in this moment was love.

The champion took her bow and hopped off the turnbuckle. Her right foot hit the mat a degree or two off-center. The force shot up her leg—her calf a lever, her ankle the fulcrum.

"Oh!" Pilar cried.

Startled, the man pulled his headphones from his ears.

"Did you see that?" Pilar asked, pointing at his screen.

"Amazing match," the man said. Following a thousand men before him, his eyes sank from Pilar's face.

"No. At the end," she said. "She tweaked her knee. Look. She's limping."

The champion walked up the ramp. She let her arm brush against the fans stretching to her from beyond the barricade.

"Don't worry," the man said. "It's scripted."

"She's hurt. She took a bad landing off the ropes."

"She's fine. It's fake. Trust me. She's an actress."

Before her final bow, the champion raised her title. The belts were heavy, even the second-rate MCCW ones, but the champion should've been strong enough to lift hers with ease. Instead, she struggled. Pilar watched her grit her teeth and swing the title over her head.

"Actors get hurt," Pilar said. "People have died in the ring, literally."

"Only because they're so juiced up," the man said. "I'm surprised we don't see more drop dead. I've taken steroids before. Prescriptions for my skin. Lemme tell ya, it's like signing a deal with the devil."

The champion left the stage. For a couple of steps her limp seemed to switch to her other leg. It was subtle, so much so that Pilar doubted she'd seen it at all.

Thank you to Justin Brouckaert, my brilliant friend and agent. Thank you to John McMurtrie, who edited this book, and Adi Gandi, for copyedits. Thank you to Raj Tawney, Sunra Thompson, Amanda Uhle, and the team at McSweeney's. Thank you to Lily Stephens for your help with the audiobook.

I've been very lucky to have learned and grown as a writer among some of the smartest, kindest people. Thank you to all these folks, and especially those who read and contributed to early drafts of this book, including Tracie Dawson, Jonathan Dunn, Cayla Fralick, Sarah Jane Huskey, Kurt Hoberg, Laura Irei, Rebecca Landau, Matt Mossman, Christina Phillips, Chris Schumerth, B.P. Scovil, Sam Slaughter, and Jon Timmons.

Thank you to Sarah Benal and Hannah Ford Warner for your friendship and for reading drafts of this book.

Thank you to the writers I met in Cincinnati, a city I miss dearly, including Becky Adnot-Haynes, Chelsie Bryant, Ben Dudley, Mark Manibusan, Nick Story, and Kathy Zlabek. Without you, I'd still be writing talking dog stories.

Thank you to Steve Bedford, Lisa Chau, Katelyn Dougherty, and James Milne—the Scrub Club.

Thank you to my teachers, especially David Bajo, Elise Blackwell, Jim Burnstein, Michael Griffith, Tish O'Dowd, Patrick O'Keefe, and Leah Stewart.

Thank you to my book club friends, who keep me loving books—Ryan DeWane, Tyler McDonald, Kellia Moore, and Lauren Schuldt Wilson.

Thank you to Matt Gassan for the title. Spring Break forever.

Thank you to all my friends and family. Thank you to my parents and sister for their love and support.

Thank you to the growing literary community in Columbia, South Carolina. It's an honor to be a small part of this lovely group.

Thank you to Julia Velasco, with all my love.

And finally, thank you to all the professional wrestlers who've worked so hard to entertain so many. Stay safe and take care.

ABOUT THE AUTHOR

A University of Michigan graduate, CHRIS KOSLOWSKI holds an MA in Creative Writing and Literature from the University of Cincinnati and an MFA in Fiction from the University of South Carolina. His fiction has been published in *Blue Mesa Review*, *Front Porch Journal*, and *Day One*. He lives with his family in Columbia, South Carolina.